LOG HORIZON
THE WEST WIND BRIGADE

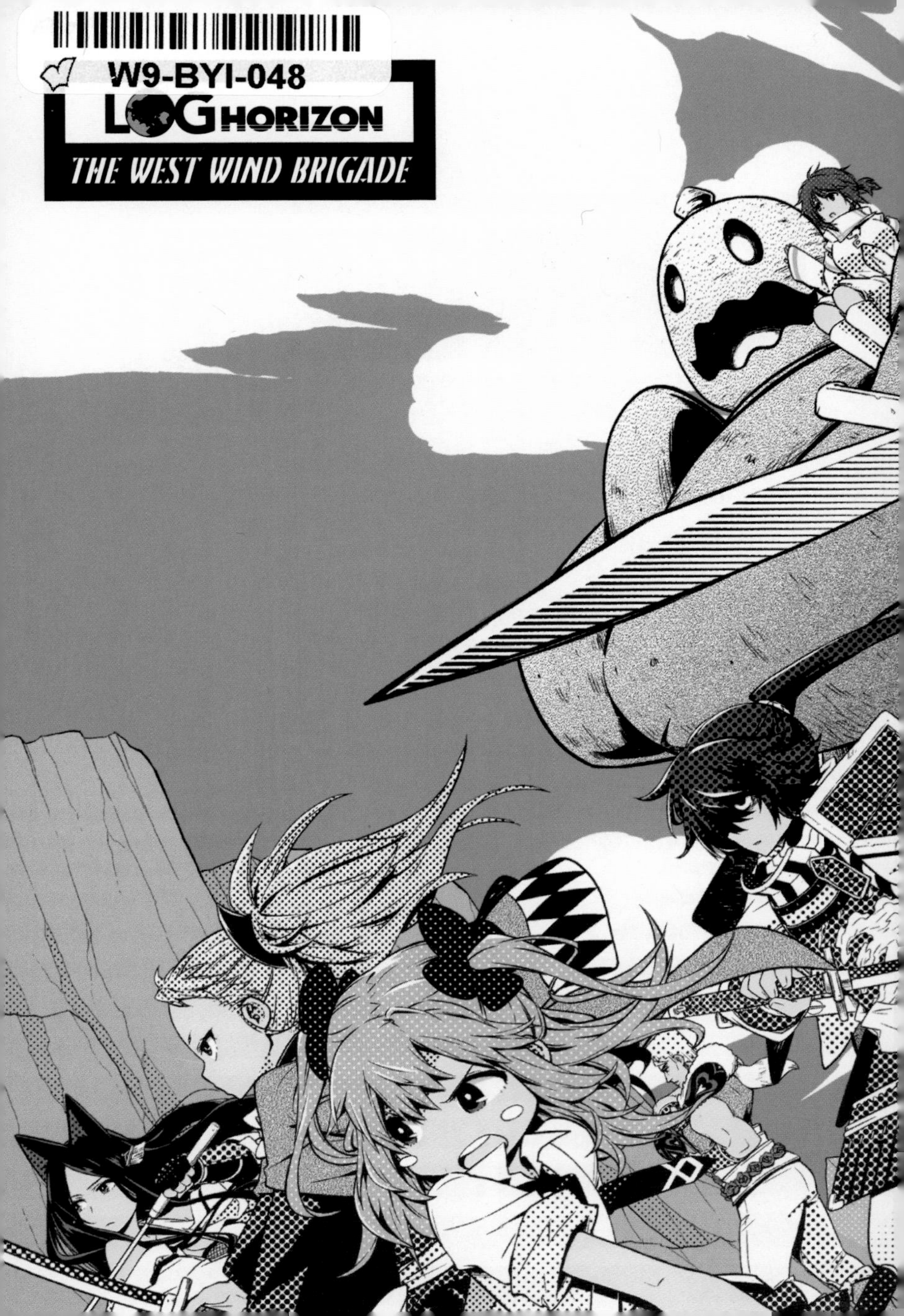

[CONTENTS]

LOG HORIZON **THE WEST WIND BRIGADE** ❸

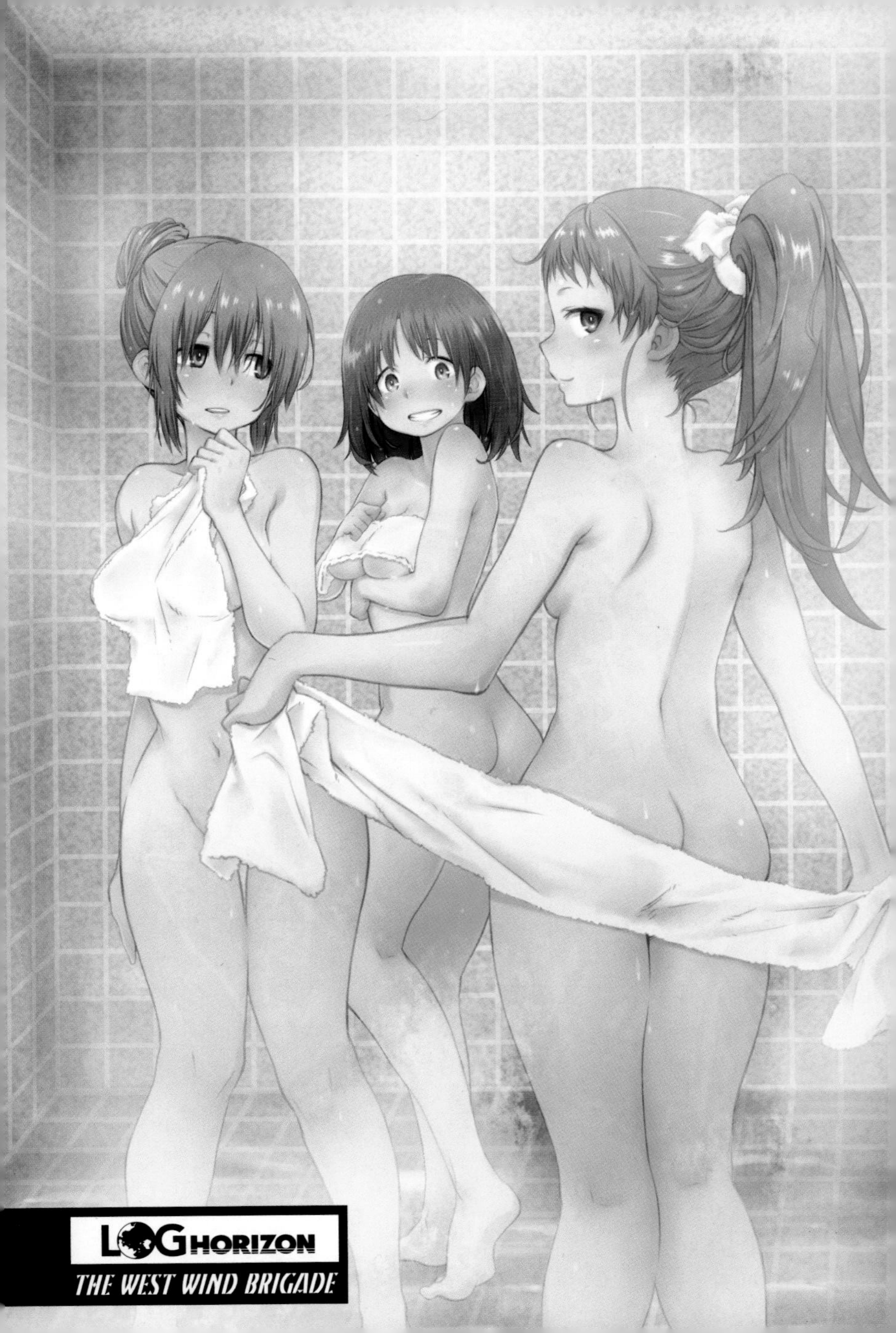
LOG HORIZON
THE WEST WIND BRIGADE

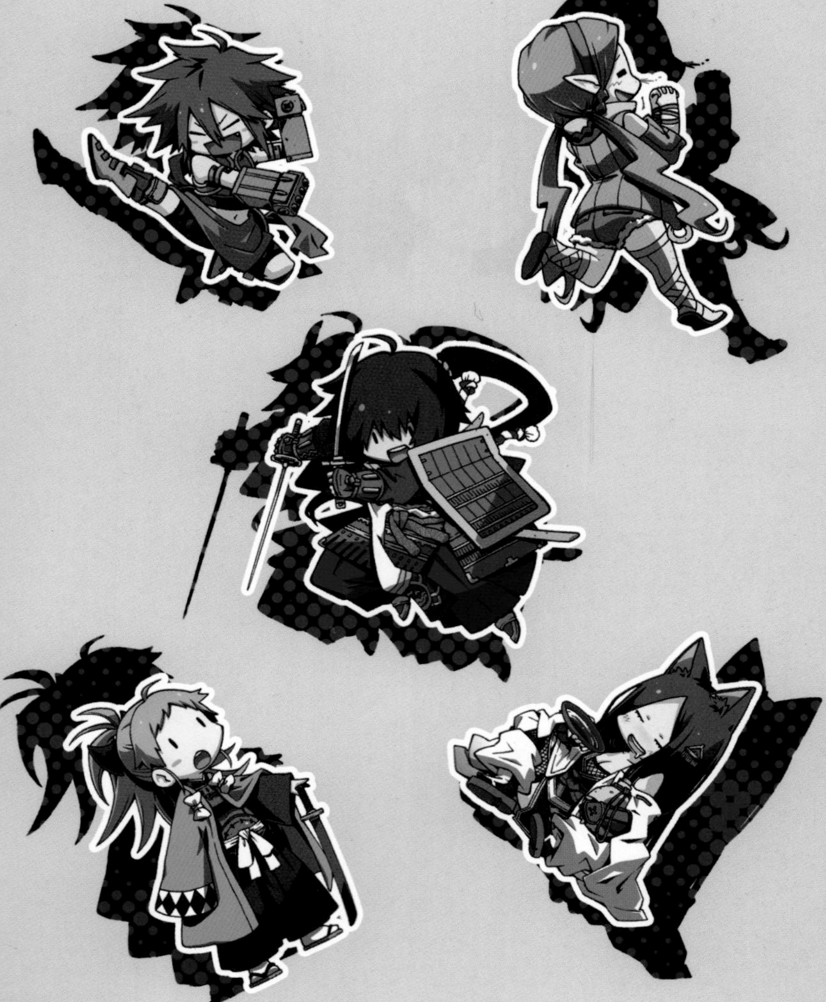

LOG HORIZON

THE WEST WIND BRIGADE

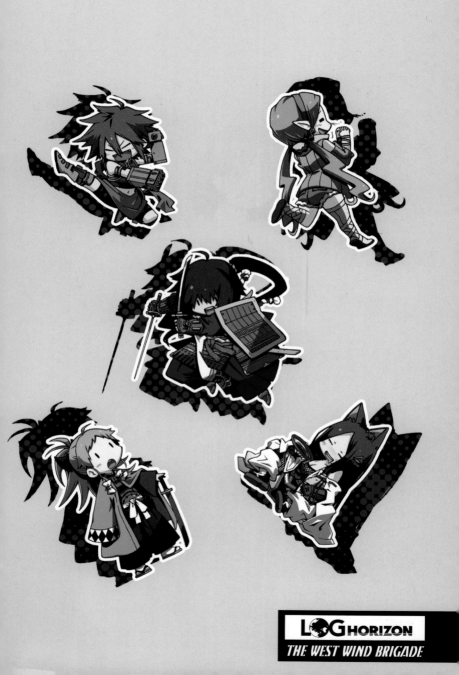

CHAPTER: 13 VS. HAMELIN

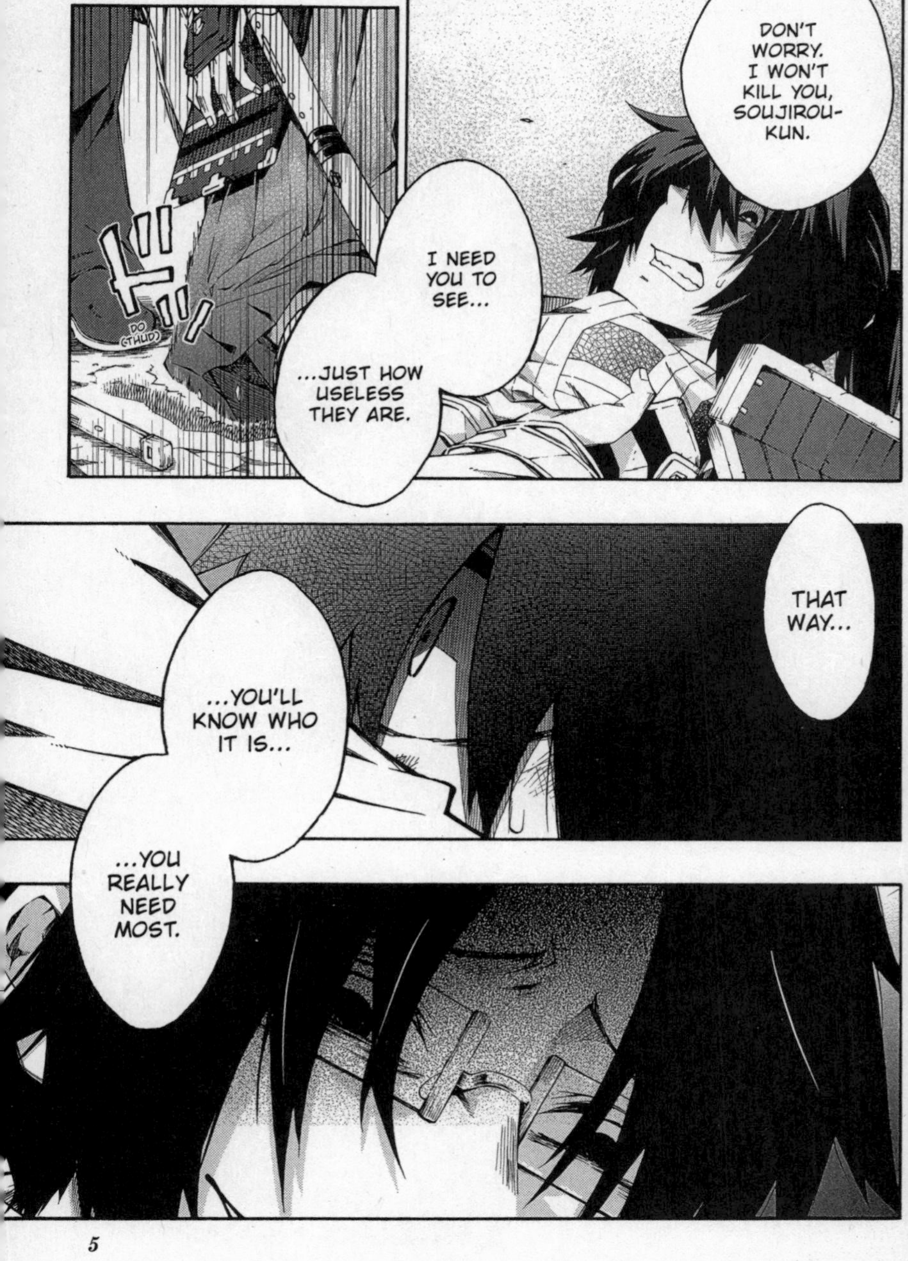
DON'T WORRY. I WON'T KILL YOU, SOUJIROU-KUN.
I NEED YOU TO SEE...
...JUST HOW USELESS THEY ARE.
DO (THUD)
THAT WAY...
...YOU'LL KNOW WHO IT IS...
...YOU REALLY NEED MOST.

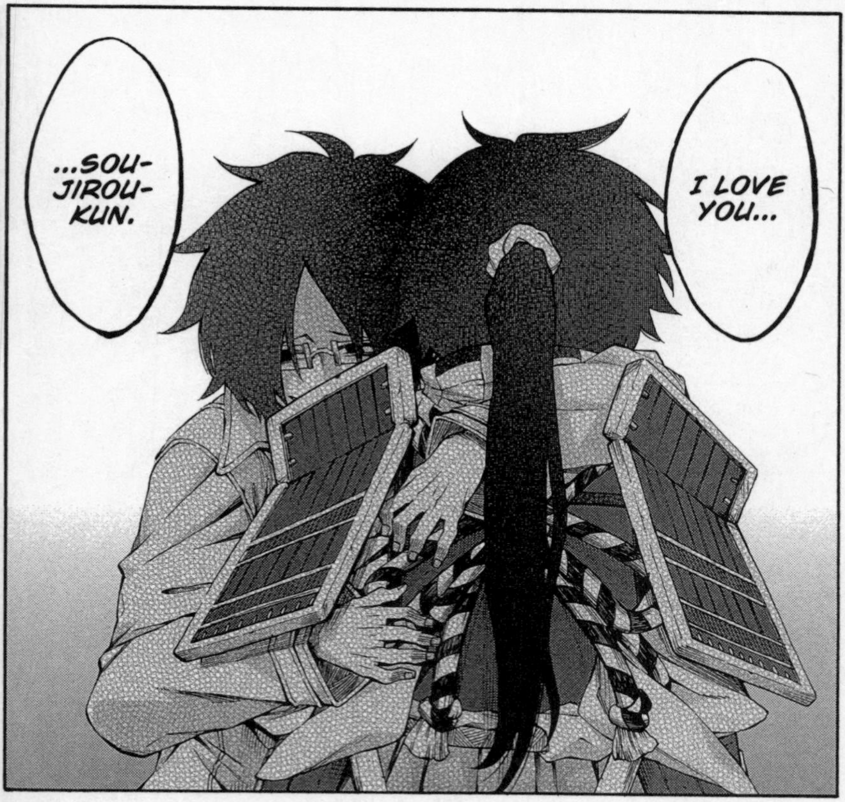
I LOVE YOU...
...SOU-JIROU-KUN.

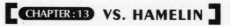

CHAPTER : 13 VS. HAMELIN

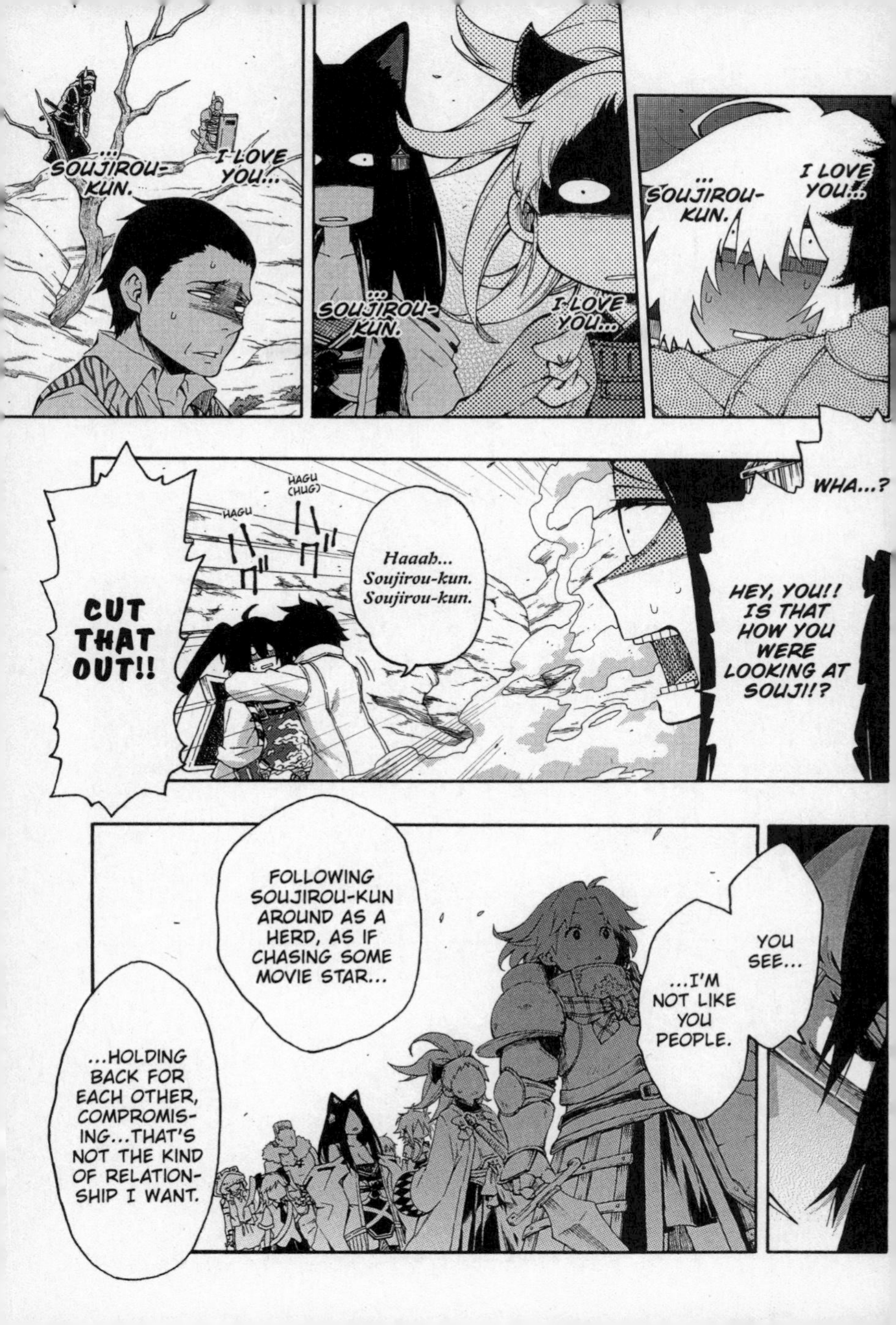

... SOUJIROU-KUN.
I LOVE YOU...
... SOUJIROU-KUN.
I LOVE YOU...
... SOUJIROU-KUN.
I LOVE YOU...
WHA...?
HEY, YOU!! IS THAT HOW YOU WERE LOOKING AT SOUJI!?
Haaah... Soujirou-kun. Soujirou-kun.
HAGU (HUG)
HAGU
CUT THAT OUT!!
YOU SEE...
...I'M NOT LIKE YOU PEOPLE.
FOLLOWING SOUJIROU-KUN AROUND AS A HERD, AS IF CHASING SOME MOVIE STAR...
...HOLDING BACK FOR EACH OTHER, COMPROMISING...THAT'S NOT THE KIND OF RELATIONSHIP I WANT.

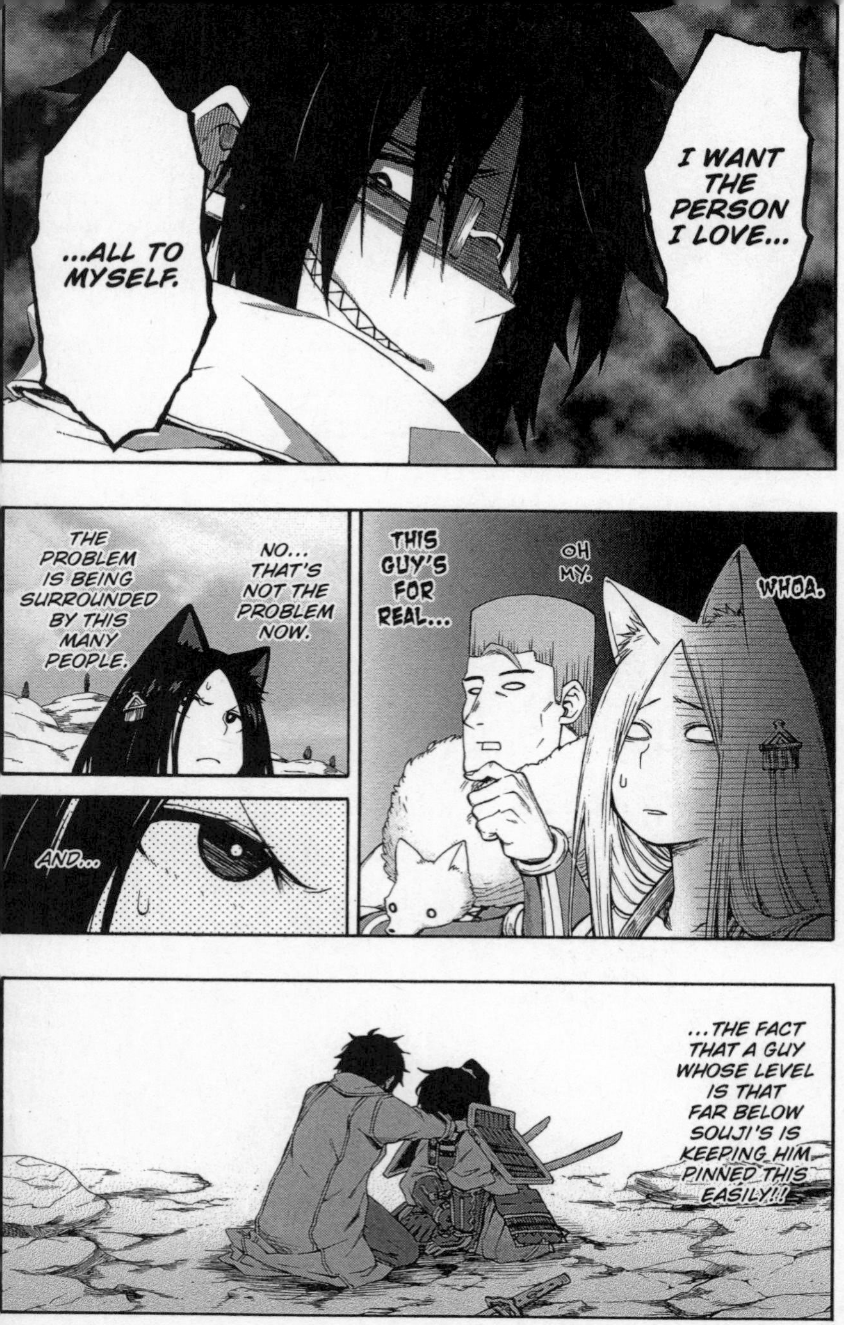
I WANT THE PERSON I LOVE...
...ALL TO MYSELF.
WHOA.
OH MY.
THIS GUY'S FOR REAL...
NO... THAT'S NOT THE PROBLEM NOW.
THE PROBLEM IS BEING SURROUNDED BY THIS MANY PEOPLE.
AND...
...THE FACT THAT A GUY WHOSE LEVEL IS THAT FAR BELOW SOUJI'S IS KEEPING HIM PINNED THIS EASILY!!

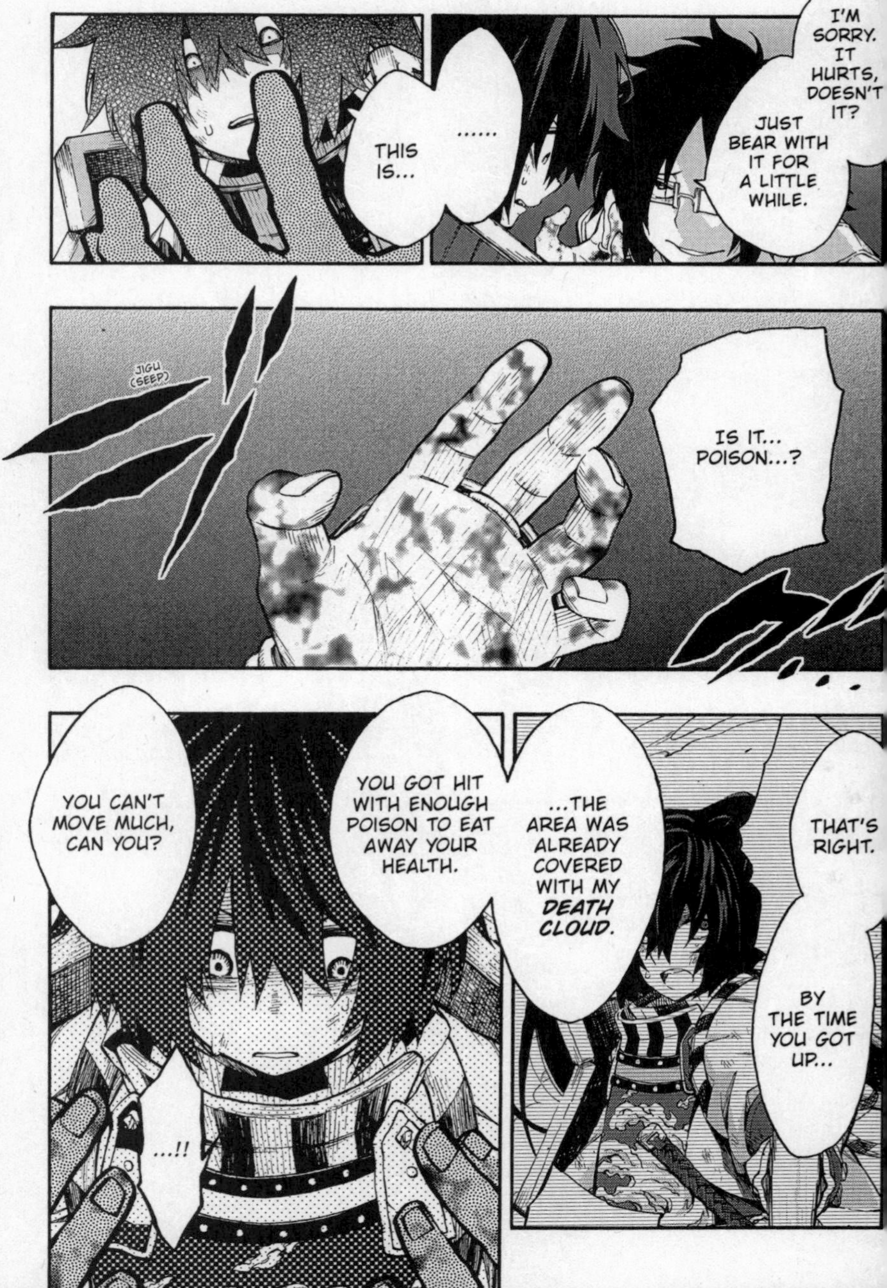
I'M SORRY. IT HURTS, DOESN'T IT?
JUST BEAR WITH IT FOR A LITTLE WHILE.
...... THIS IS...
IS IT... POISON...?
JIGU (SEEP)
THAT'S RIGHT.
BY THE TIME YOU GOT UP...
...THE AREA WAS ALREADY COVERED WITH MY *DEATH CLOUD*.
YOU GOT HIT WITH ENOUGH POISON TO EAT AWAY YOUR HEALTH.
YOU CAN'T MOVE MUCH, CAN YOU?
...!!

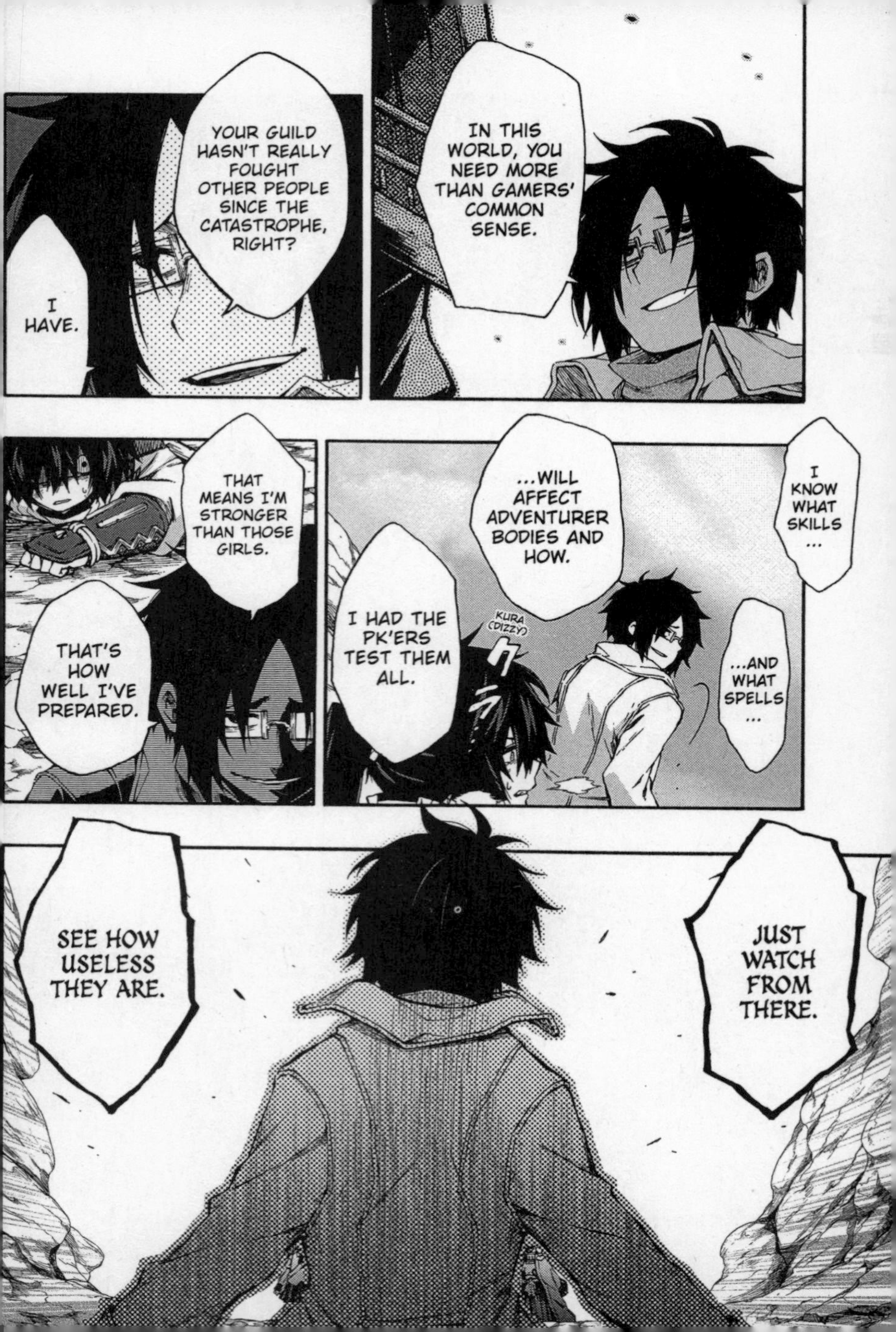
IN THIS WORLD, YOU NEED MORE THAN GAMERS' COMMON SENSE.
YOUR GUILD HASN'T REALLY FOUGHT OTHER PEOPLE SINCE THE CATASTROPHE, RIGHT?
I HAVE.
I KNOW WHAT SKILLS...
...WILL AFFECT ADVENTURER BODIES AND HOW.
...AND WHAT SPELLS...
I HAD THE PK'ERS TEST THEM ALL.
KURA (DIZZY)
THAT MEANS I'M STRONGER THAN THOSE GIRLS.
THAT'S HOW WELL I'VE PREPARED.
JUST WATCH FROM THERE.
SEE HOW USELESS THEY ARE.

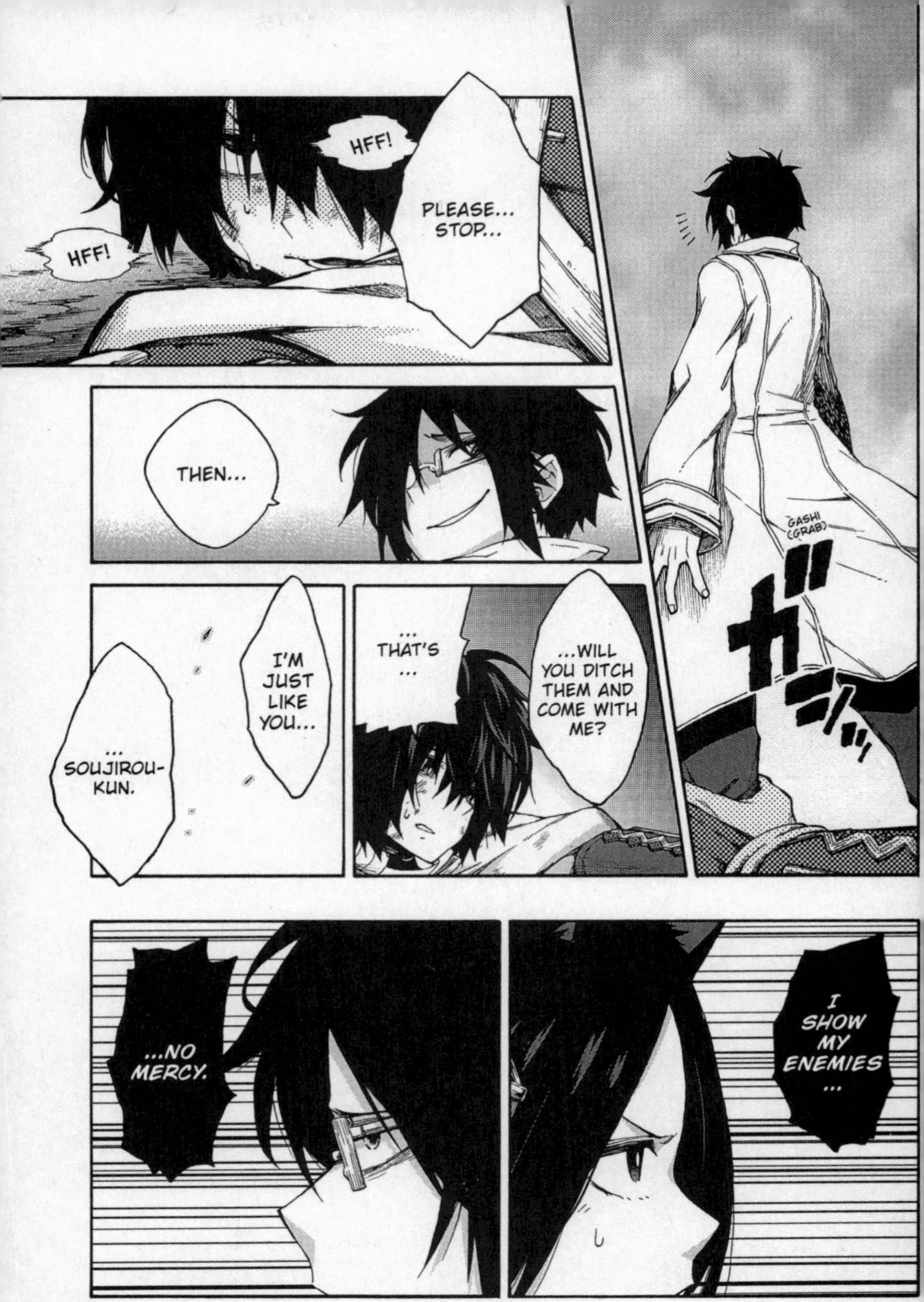
GASHI (GRAB)
ガシッ
PLEASE... STOP...
HFF!
HFF!
THEN...
...WILL YOU DITCH THEM AND COME WITH ME?
... THAT'S ...
I'M JUST LIKE YOU...
... SOUJIROU-KUN.
I SHOW MY ENEMIES ...
...NO MERCY.

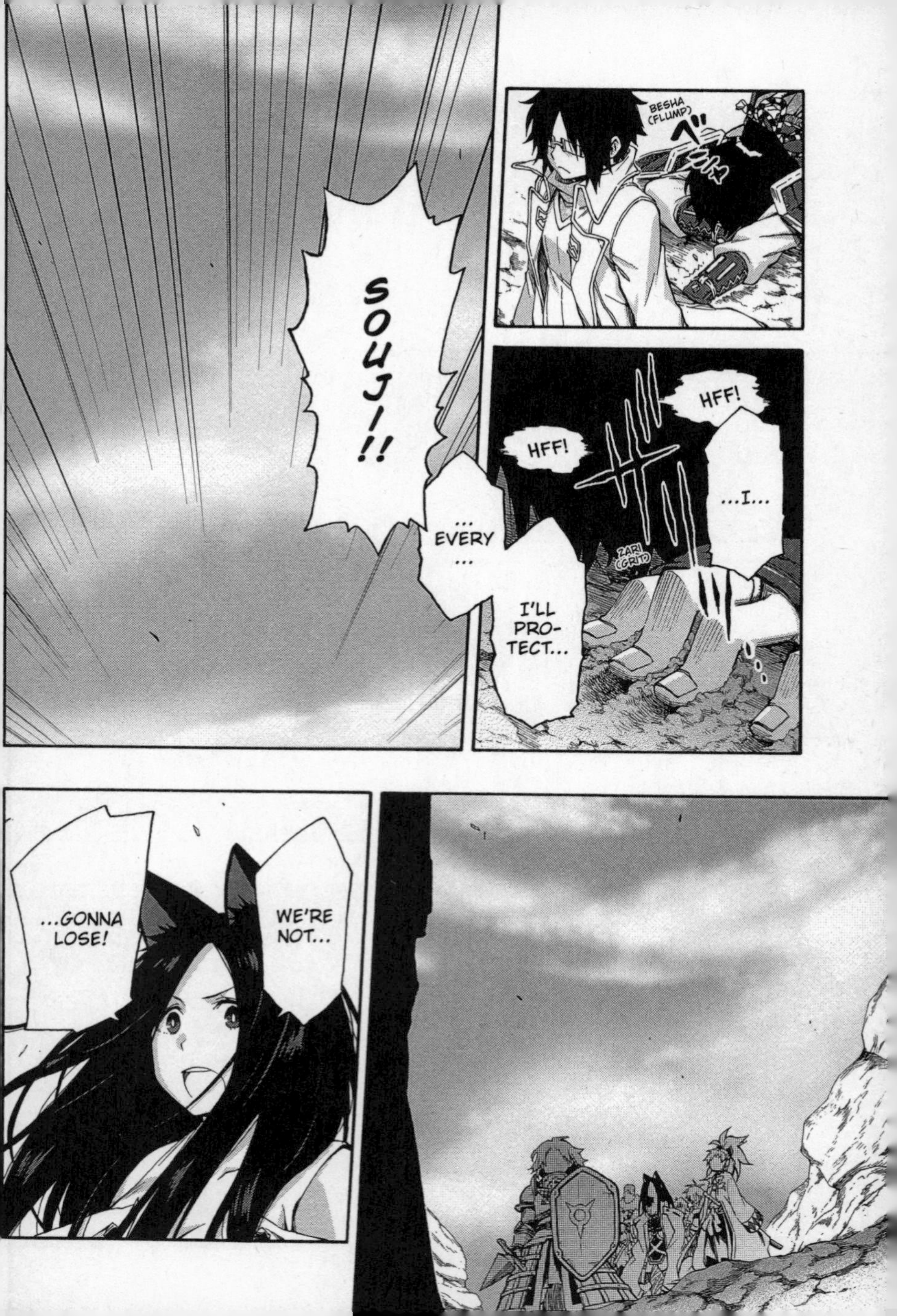
BESHA (FLUMP)
HFF!
HFF!
...I...
ZARI (GRIT)
I'LL PROTECT...
...EVERY...
SOUJI!!
WE'RE NOT...
...GONNA LOSE!

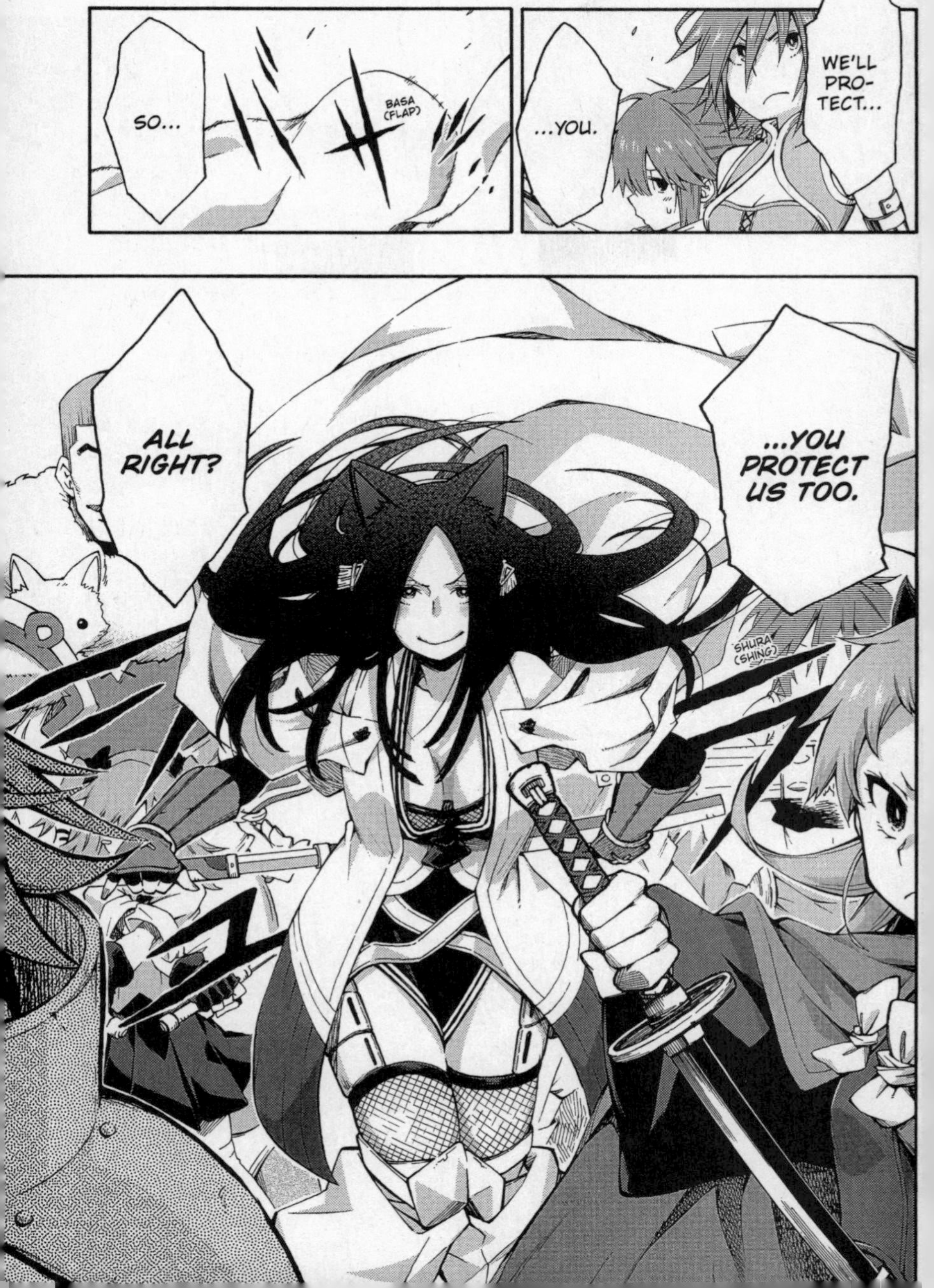
WE'LL PRO-TECT...
...YOU.
BASA (FLAP)
SO...
...YOU PROTECT US TOO.
ALL RIGHT?
SHURA (SHING)

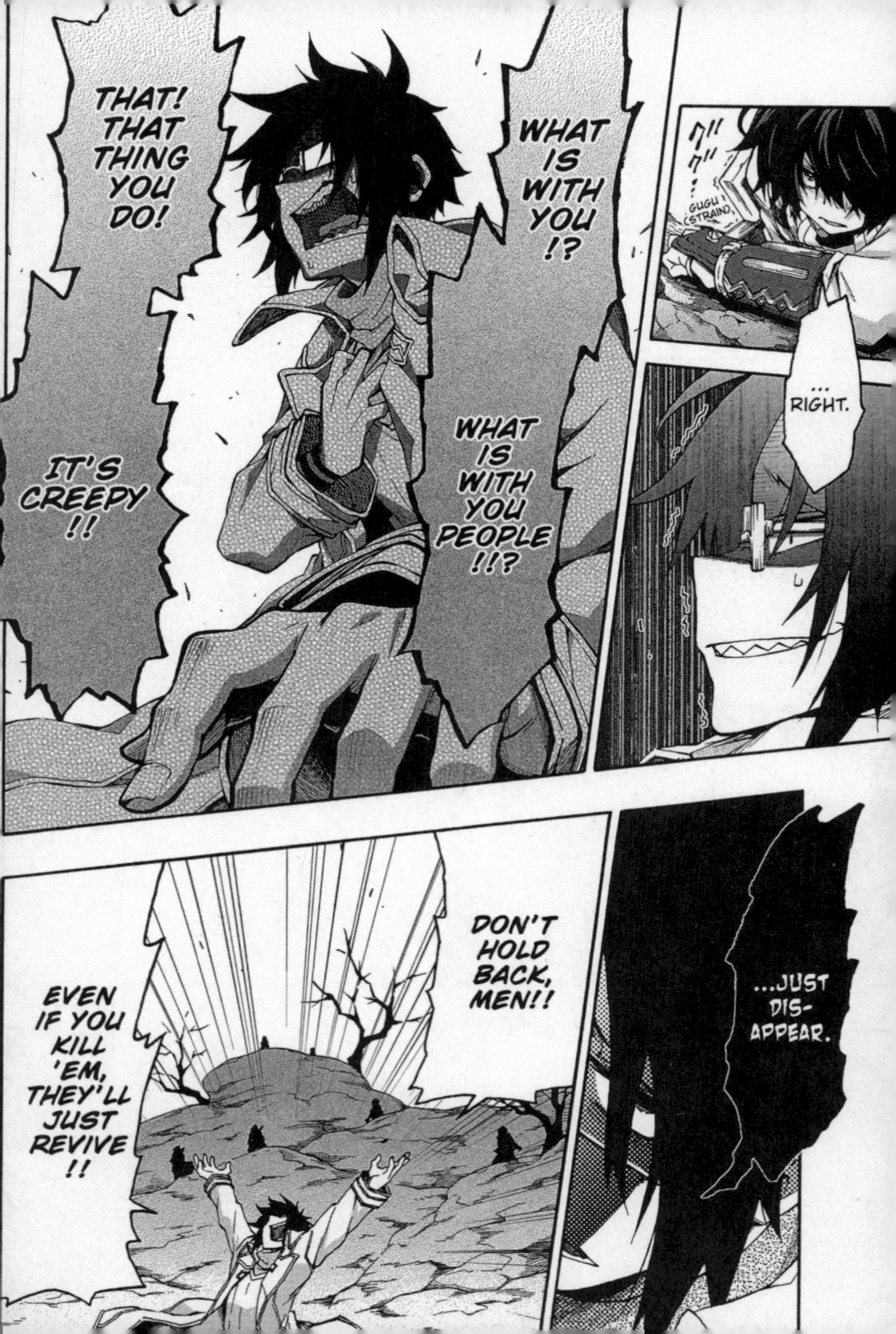
GUGU (STRAIN)
...RIGHT.
WHAT IS WITH YOU!?
THAT! THAT THING YOU DO!
WHAT IS WITH YOU PEOPLE!!?
IT'S CREEPY!!
...JUST DIS-APPEAR.
DON'T HOLD BACK, MEN!!
EVEN IF YOU KILL 'EM, THEY'LL JUST REVIVE!!

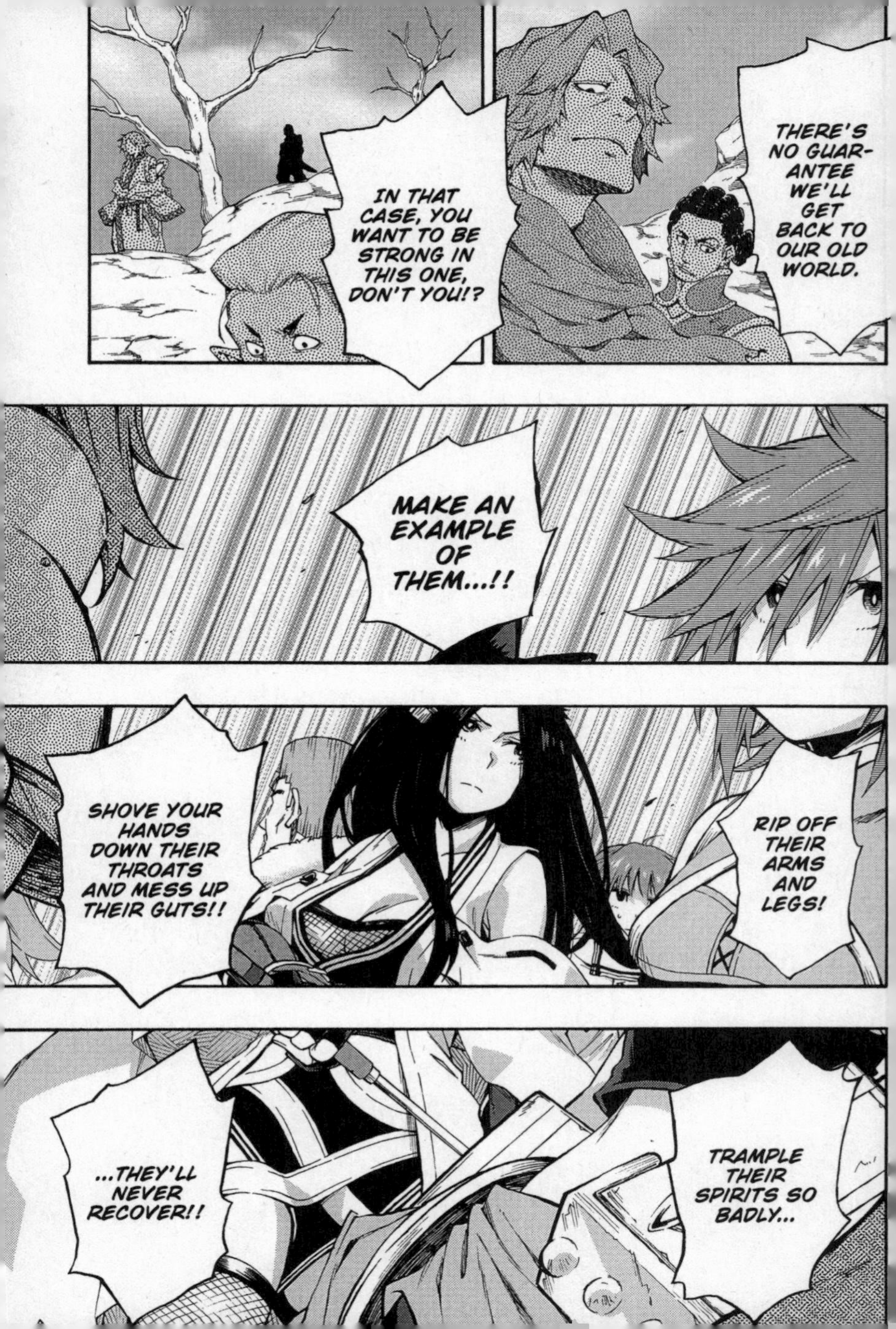
THERE'S NO GUARANTEE WE'LL GET BACK TO OUR OLD WORLD.
IN THAT CASE, YOU WANT TO BE STRONG IN THIS ONE, DON'T YOU!?
MAKE AN EXAMPLE OF THEM...!!
RIP OFF THEIR ARMS AND LEGS!
SHOVE YOUR HANDS DOWN THEIR THROATS AND MESS UP THEIR GUTS!!
TRAMPLE THEIR SPIRITS SO BADLY...
...THEY'LL NEVER RECOVER!!

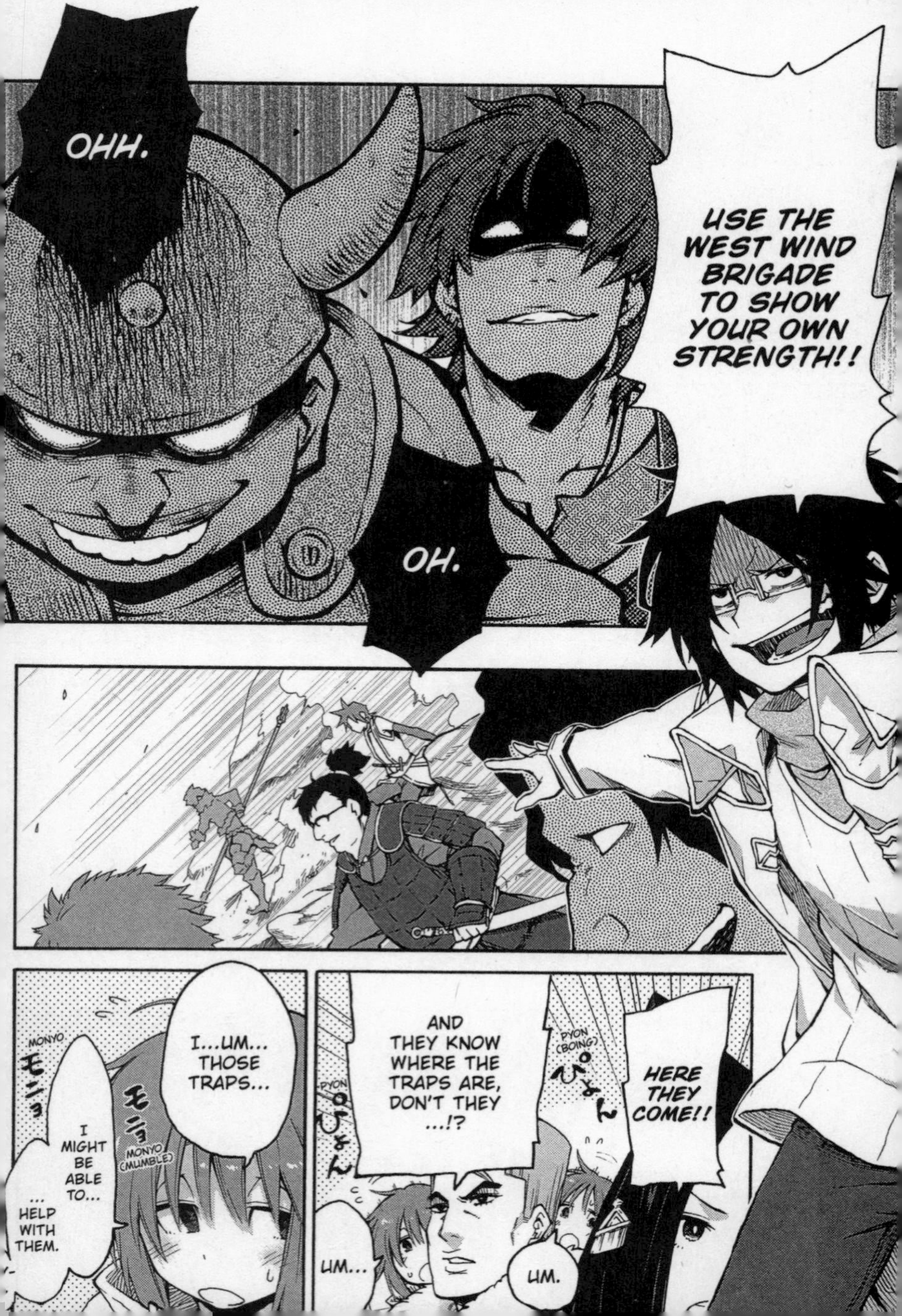
USE THE WEST WIND BRIGADE TO SHOW YOUR OWN STRENGTH!!
OHH.
OH.
HERE THEY COME!!
ぴょん
PYON (BOING)
AND THEY KNOW WHERE THE TRAPS ARE, DON'T THEY ...!?
ぴょん
PYON
UM.
UM...
I...UM... THOSE TRAPS...
モニョ
MONYO (MUMBLE)
モニョ
MONYO
I MIGHT BE ABLE TO...
... HELP WITH THEM.

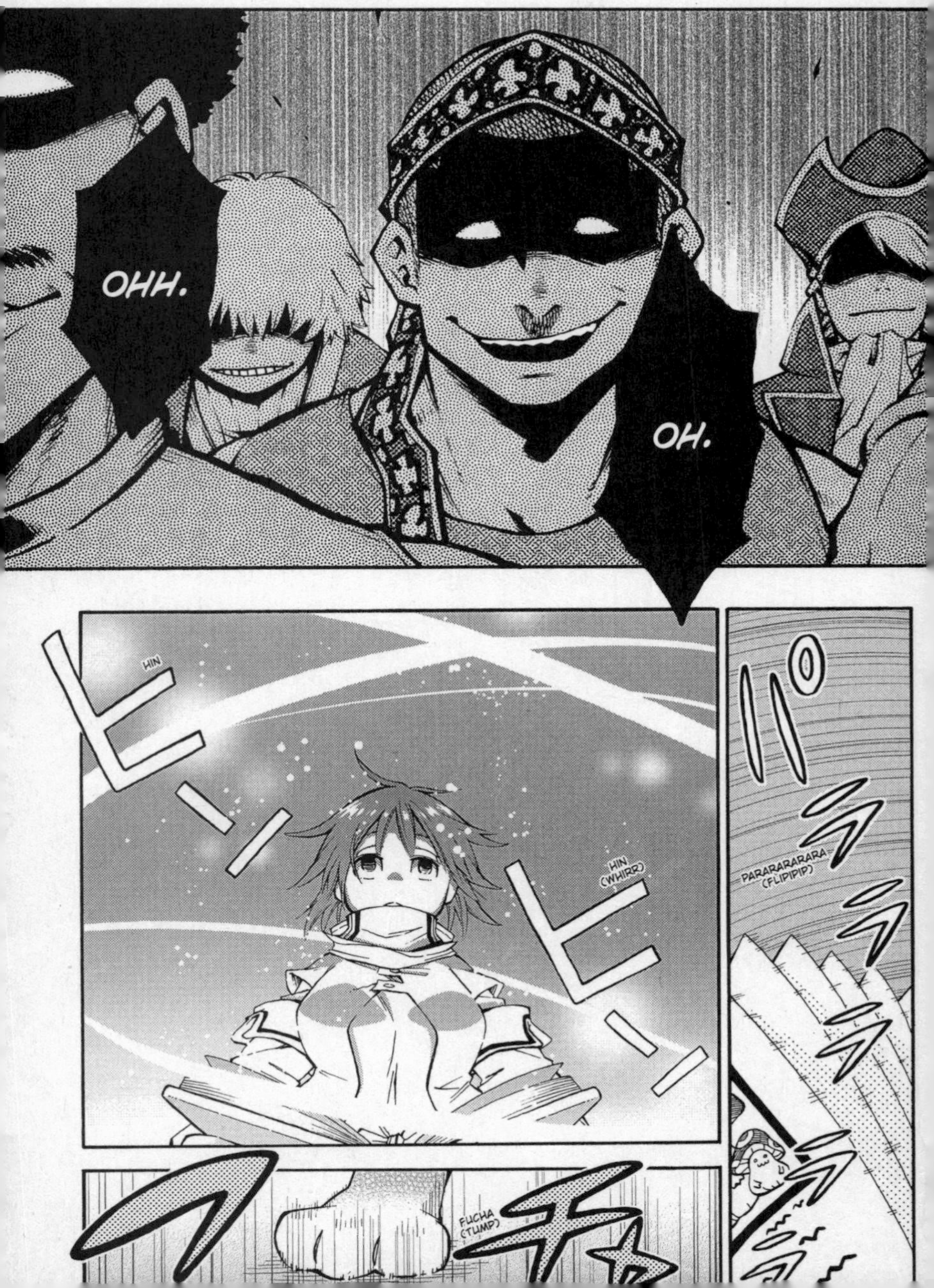
OH.
OHH.
PARARARARARA (FLIPIPIP)
HIN
HIN (WHIRR)
FUCHA (TUMP)

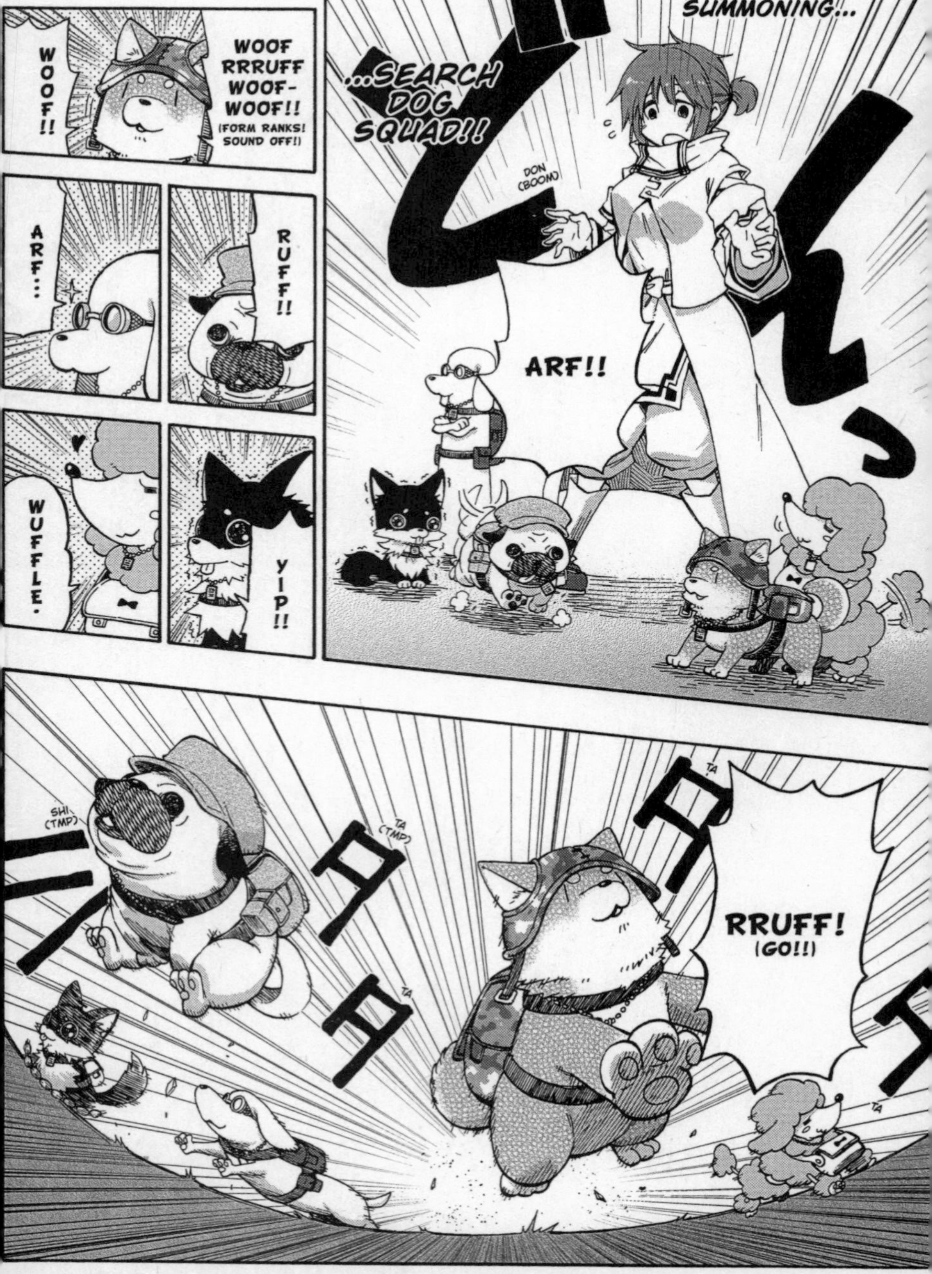
SUMMONING...
...SEARCH DOG SQUAD!!
DON (BOOM)
ARF!!
WOOF RRRUFF WOOF-WOOF!!
(FORM RANKS! SOUND OFF!)
WOOF!!
RUFF!!
ARF...
YIP!!
WUFFLE.
TA
RRUFF!
(GO!!)
TA
TA
TA (TMP)
SHI (TMP)

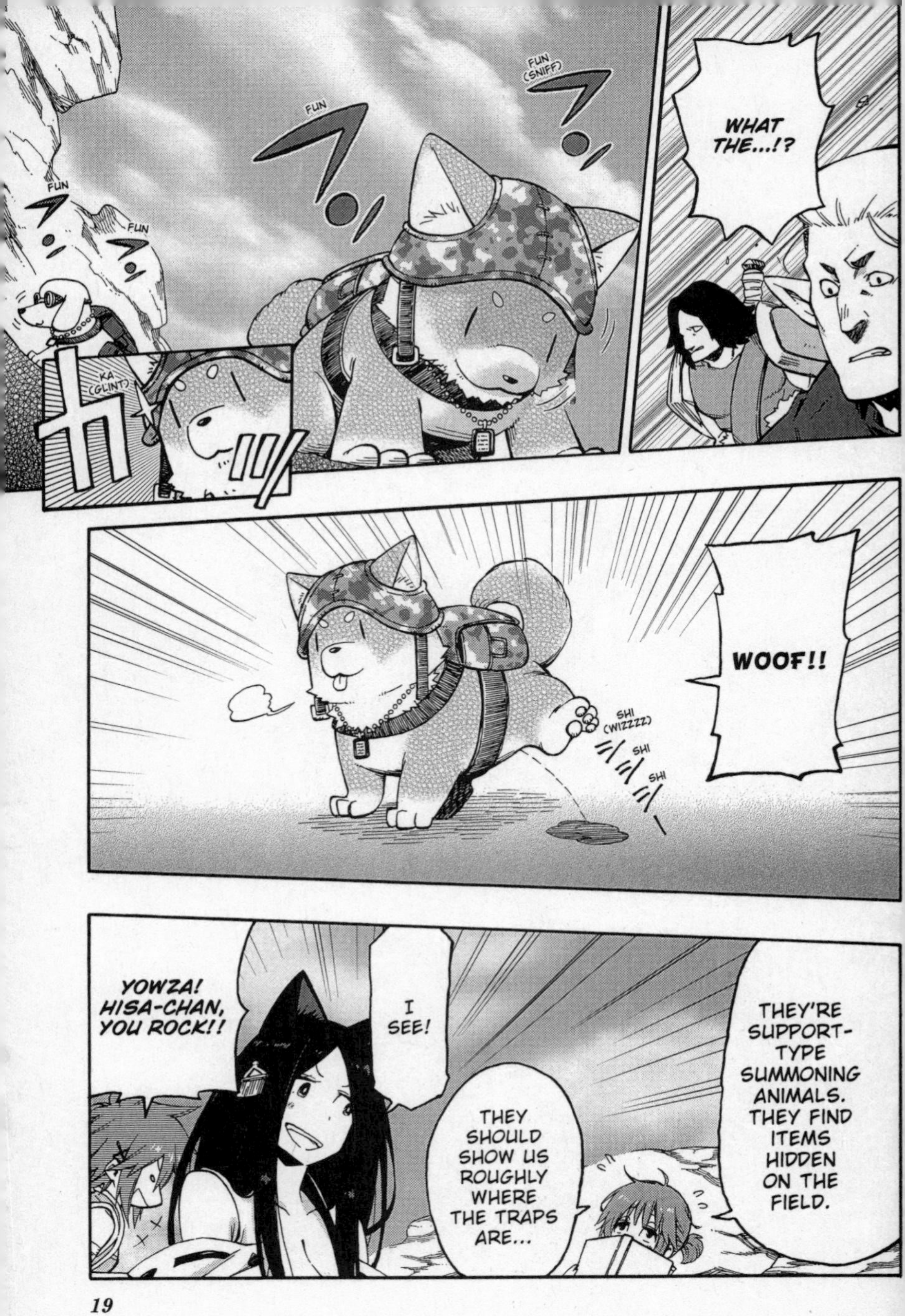
WHAT THE...!?
FUN (SNIFF)
FUN
FUN
FUN
KA (GLINT)
WOOF!!
SHI (WIZZZZ)
SHI
SHI
THEY'RE SUPPORT-TYPE SUMMONING ANIMALS. THEY FIND ITEMS HIDDEN ON THE FIELD.
THEY SHOULD SHOW US ROUGHLY WHERE THE TRAPS ARE...
I SEE!
YOWZA! HISA-CHAN, YOU ROCK!!

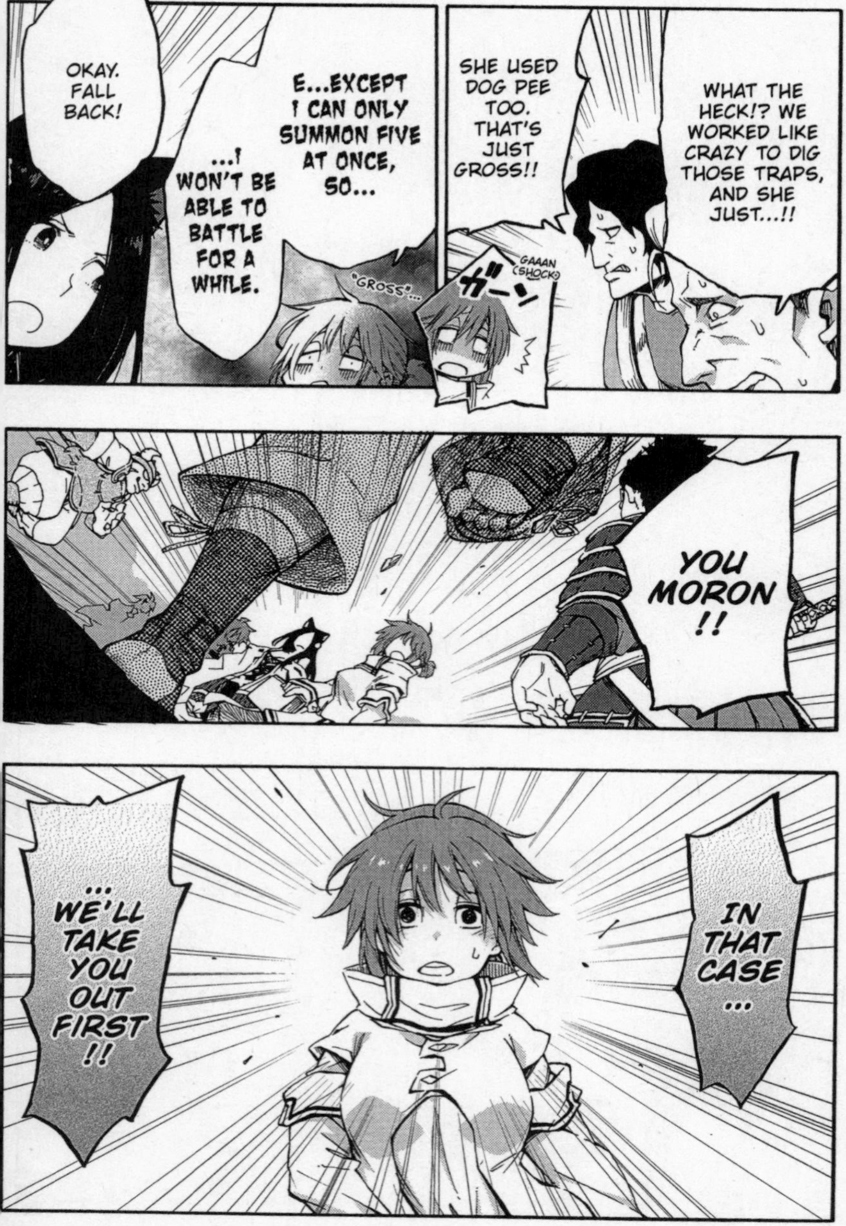
WHAT THE HECK!? WE WORKED LIKE CRAZY TO DIG THOSE TRAPS, AND SHE JUST...!!
SHE USED DOG PEE TOO. THAT'S JUST GROSS!!
GAAAN (SHOCK)
E...EXCEPT I CAN ONLY SUMMON FIVE AT ONCE, SO...
...I WON'T BE ABLE TO BATTLE FOR A WHILE.
GROSS...
OKAY. FALL BACK!
YOU MORON!!
IN THAT CASE...
...WE'LL TAKE YOU OUT FIRST!!

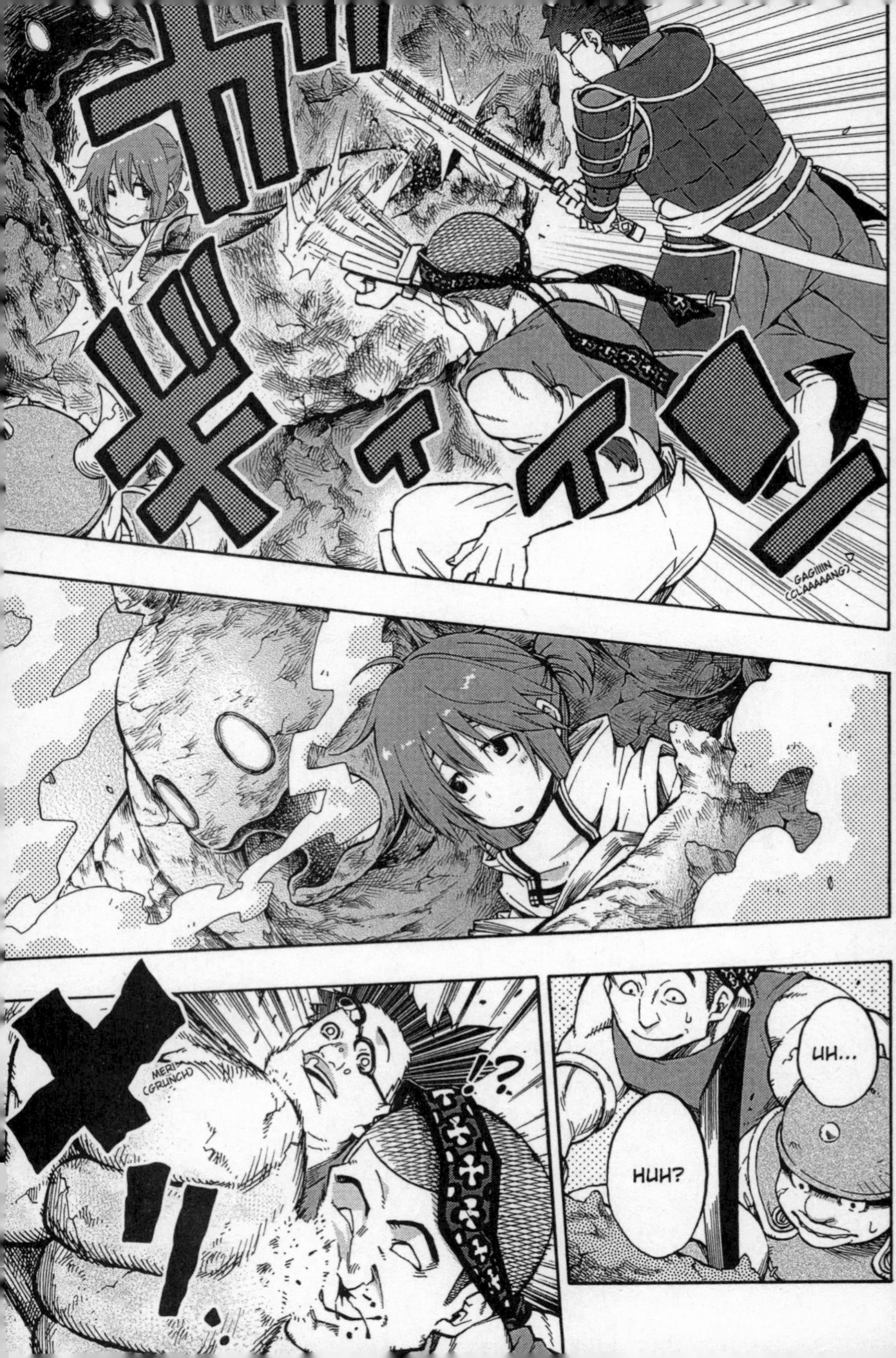
GAGIIIIN
(CLAAAAANG)
UH...
HUH?
!?
MERI
(GRUNCH)

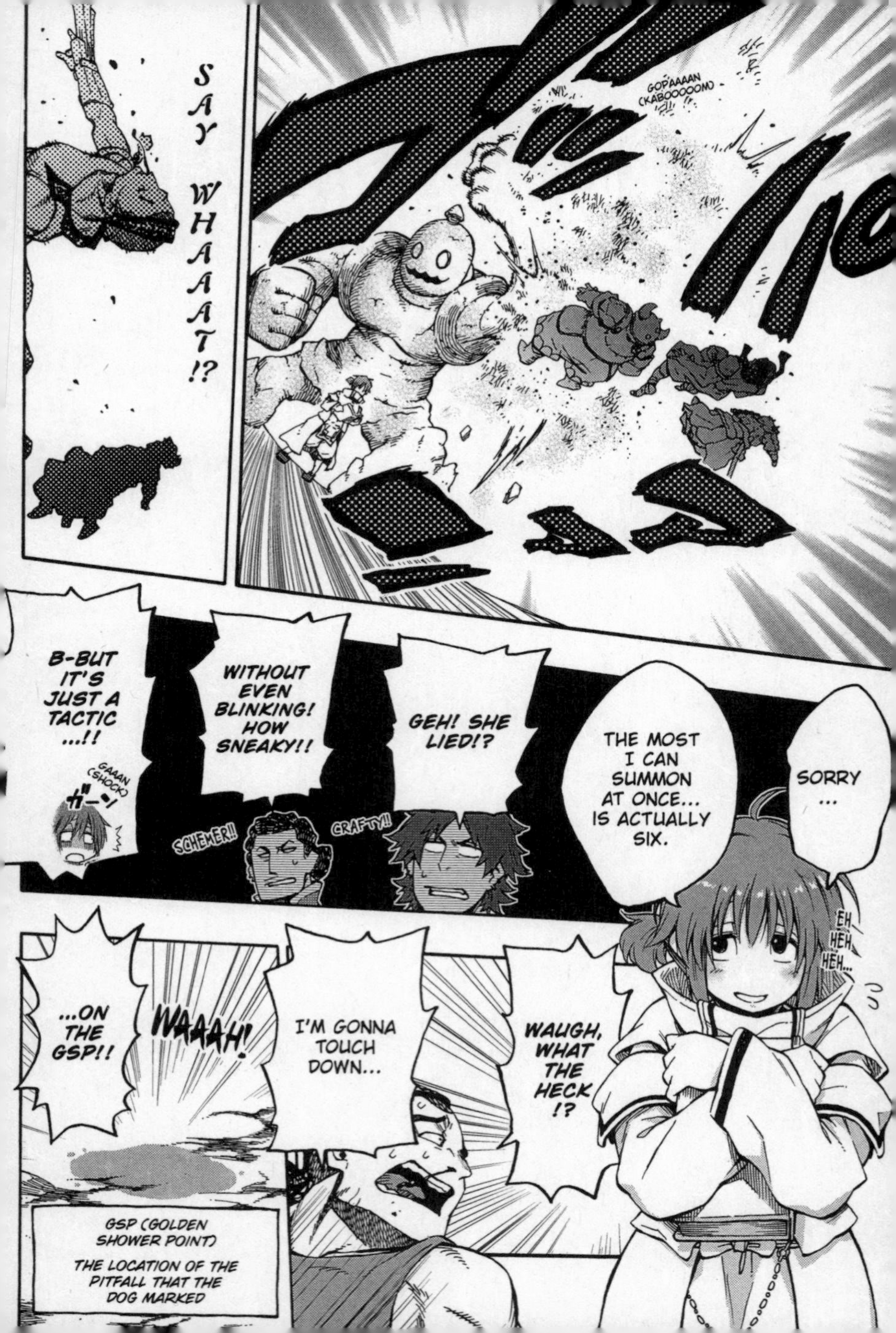
GOP'AAAAN (KABOOOOOM)
SAY WHAAAAT!?
SORRY...
THE MOST I CAN SUMMON AT ONCE... IS ACTUALLY SIX.
EH HEH HEH...
GEH! SHE LIED!?
CRAFTY!!
WITHOUT EVEN BLINKING! HOW SNEAKY!!
SCHEMER!!
B-BUT IT'S JUST A TACTIC...!!
GAAAN (SHOCK)
ガーン
WAUGH, WHAT THE HECK!?
I'M GONNA TOUCH DOWN...
WAAAH!
...ON THE GSP!!
GSP (GOLDEN SHOWER POINT)
THE LOCATION OF THE PITFALL THAT THE DOG MARKED

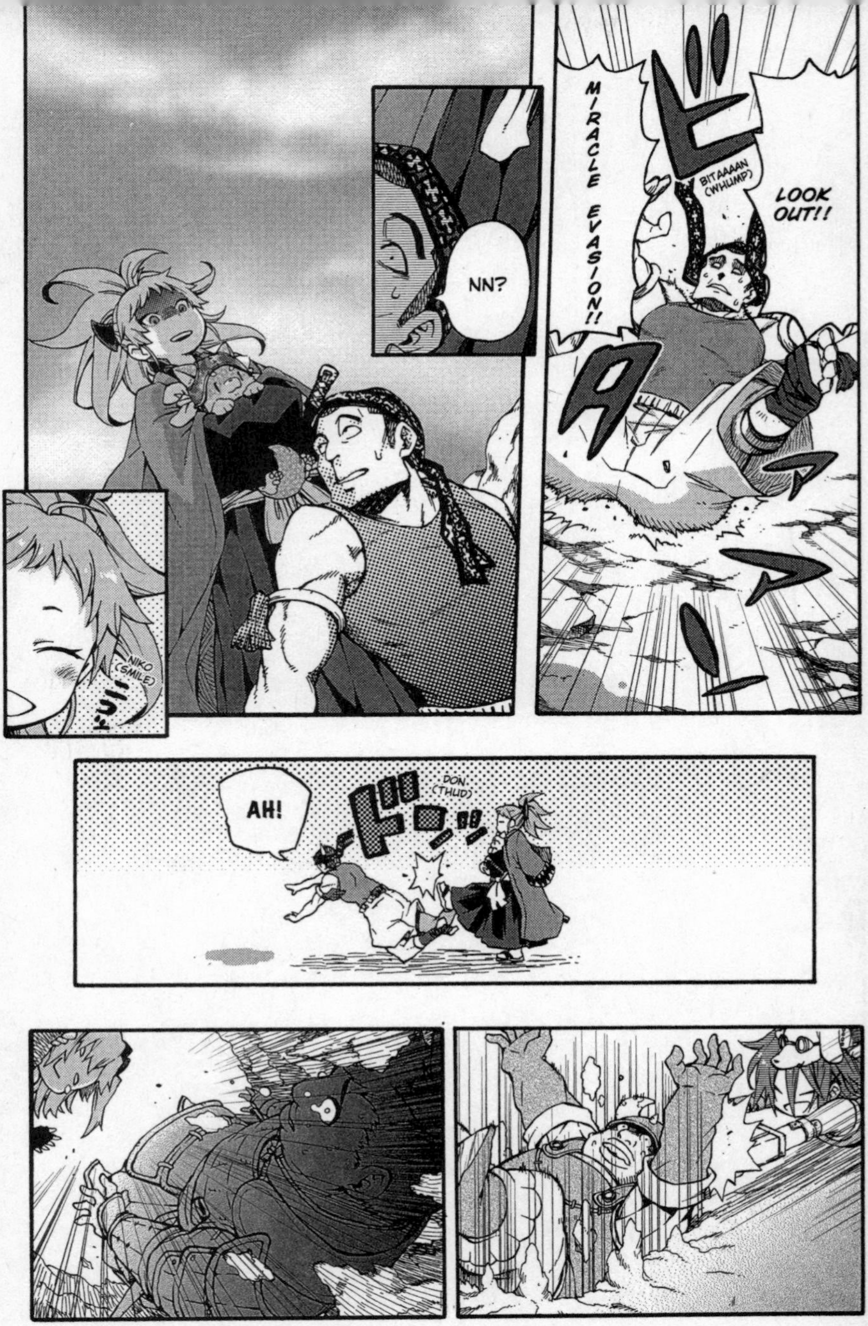
LOOK OUT!!
BITAAAAN (WHUMP)
MIRACLE EVASION!!
NN?
NIKO (SMILE)
AH!
DON (THUD)

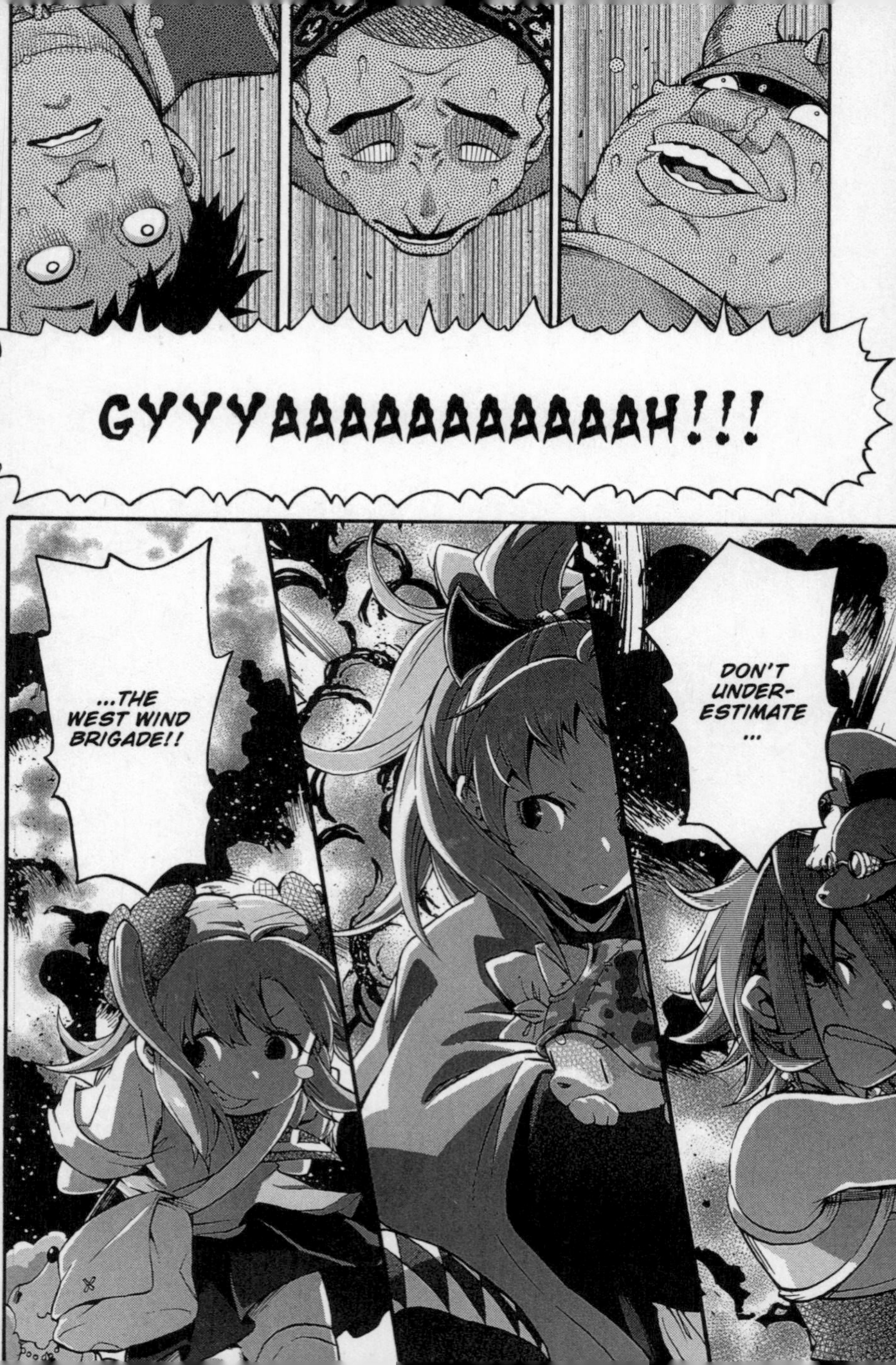
GYYYAAAAAAAAAAAAH!!!
DON'T UNDER-ESTIMATE ...
...THE WEST WIND BRIGADE!!

LOG HORIZON
THE WEST WIND BRIGADE

LOG HORIZON
THE WEST WIND BRIGADE

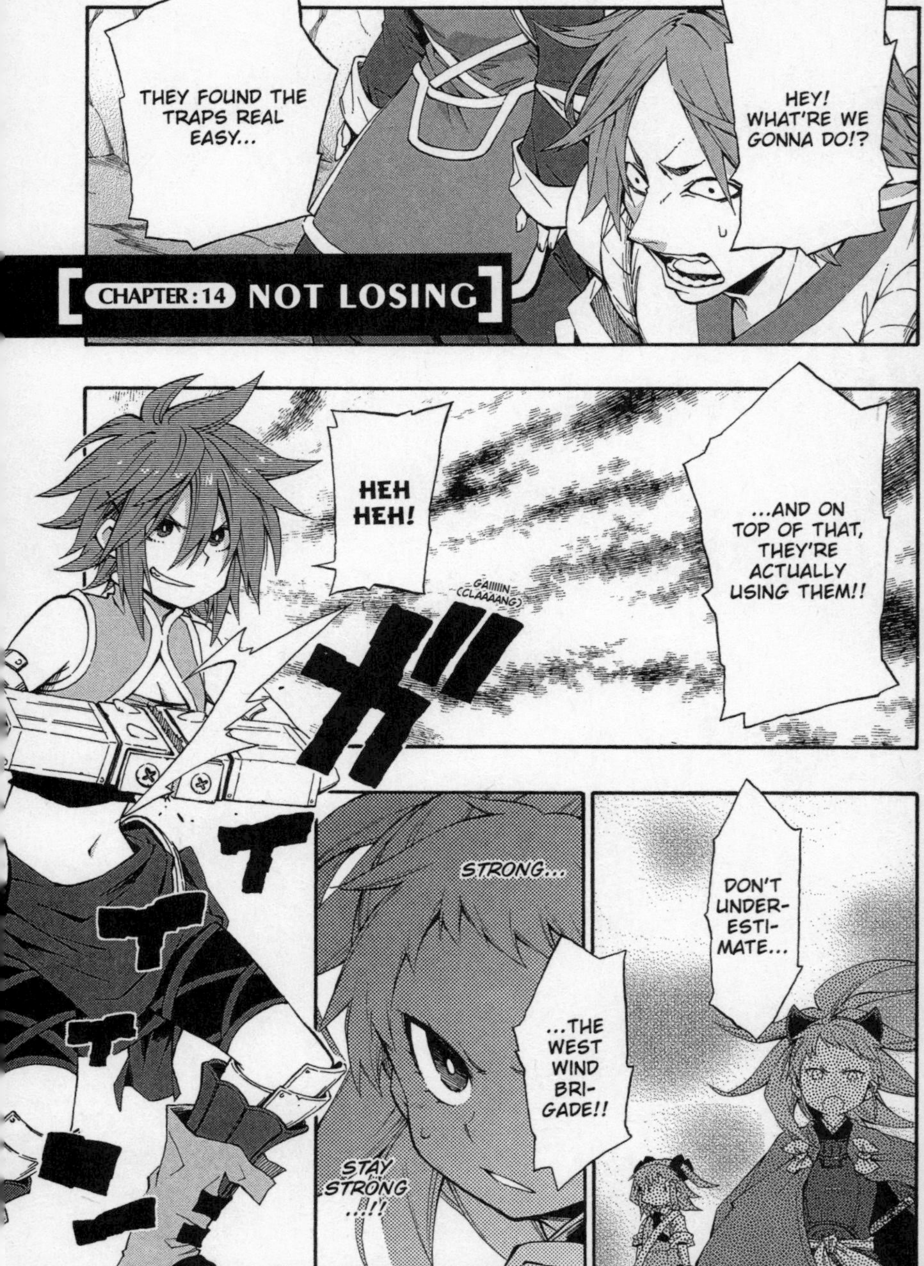
HEY! WHAT'RE WE GONNA DO!?
THEY FOUND THE TRAPS REAL EASY...
[CHAPTER : 14 NOT LOSING]
...AND ON TOP OF THAT, THEY'RE ACTUALLY USING THEM!!
HEH HEH!
GAIIIIN (CLAAAANG)
DON'T UNDER-ESTI-MATE...
...THE WEST WIND BRI-GADE!!
STRONG...
STAY STRONG ...!!

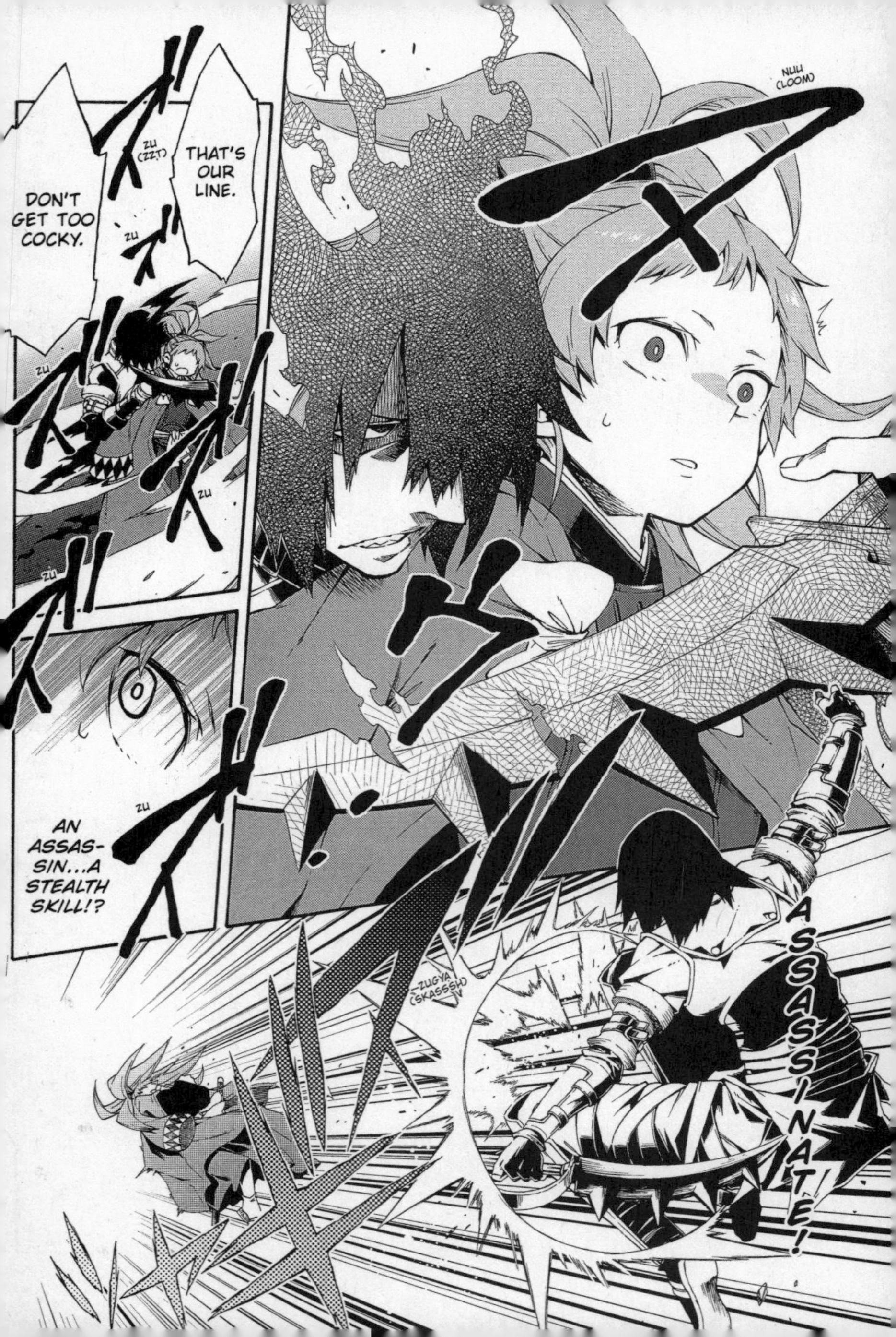

NUU (LOOM)
ZU (ZZZT)
THAT'S OUR LINE.
DON'T GET TOO COCKY.
ZU
ZU
ZU
ZU
ZU
AN ASSAS-SIN...A STEALTH SKILL!?
ZUGYA (SKASSSH)
ASSASSINATE!

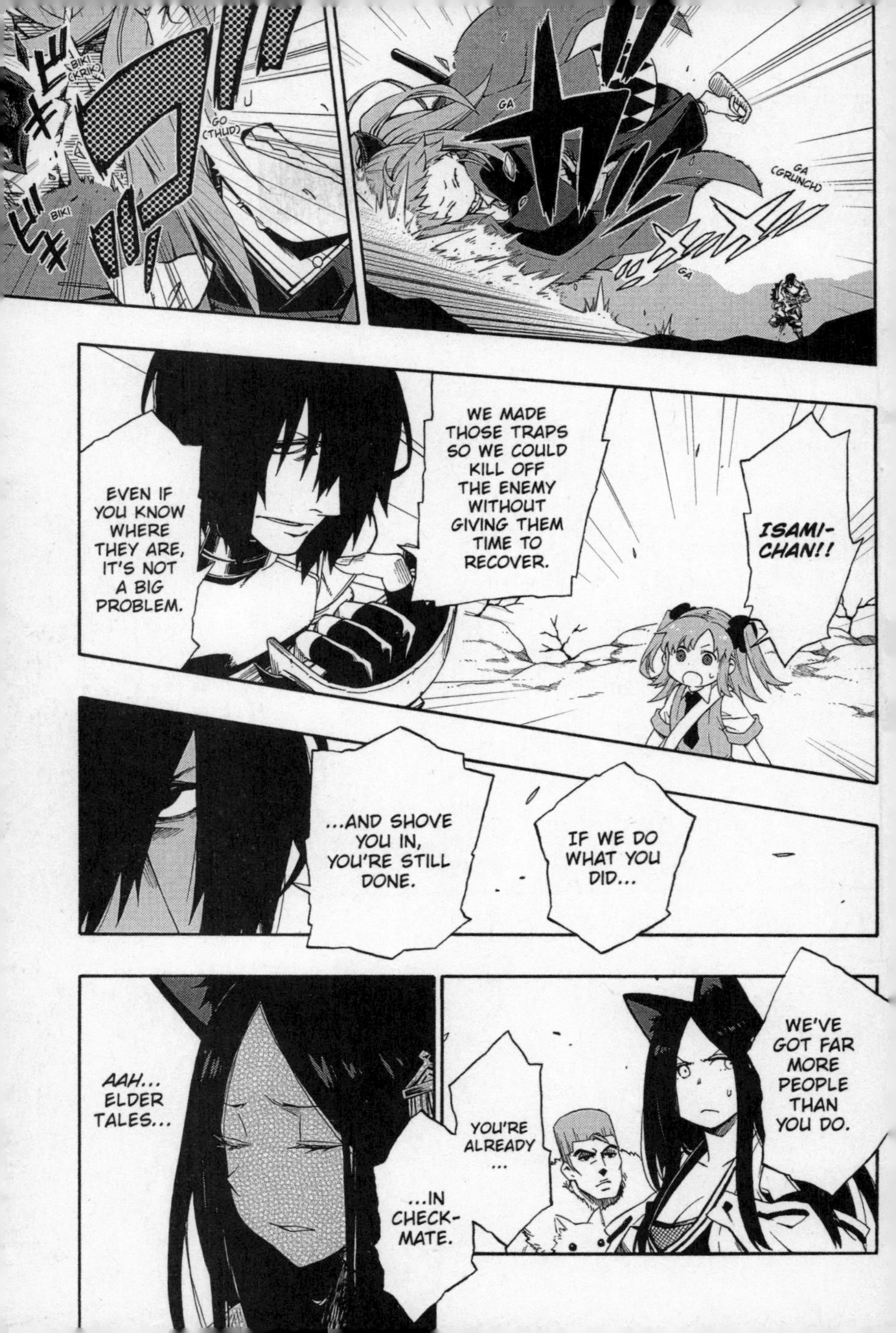
GA
GA (GRUNCH)
GA
BIKI (KRIK)
GO (THUD)
BIKI
ISAMI-CHAN!!
WE MADE THOSE TRAPS SO WE COULD KILL OFF THE ENEMY WITHOUT GIVING THEM TIME TO RECOVER.
EVEN IF YOU KNOW WHERE THEY ARE, IT'S NOT A BIG PROBLEM.
IF WE DO WHAT YOU DID...
...AND SHOVE YOU IN, YOU'RE STILL DONE.
WE'VE GOT FAR MORE PEOPLE THAN YOU DO.
YOU'RE ALREADY ...
...IN CHECKMATE.
AAH... ELDER TALES...

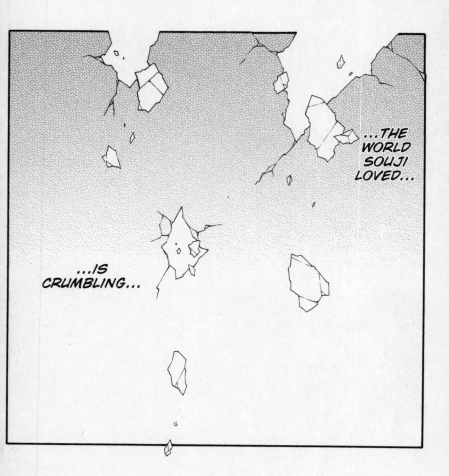

...THE
WORLD
SOUJI
LOVED...

...IS
CRUMBLING...

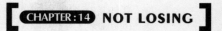

[**CHAPTER:14** NOT LOSING]

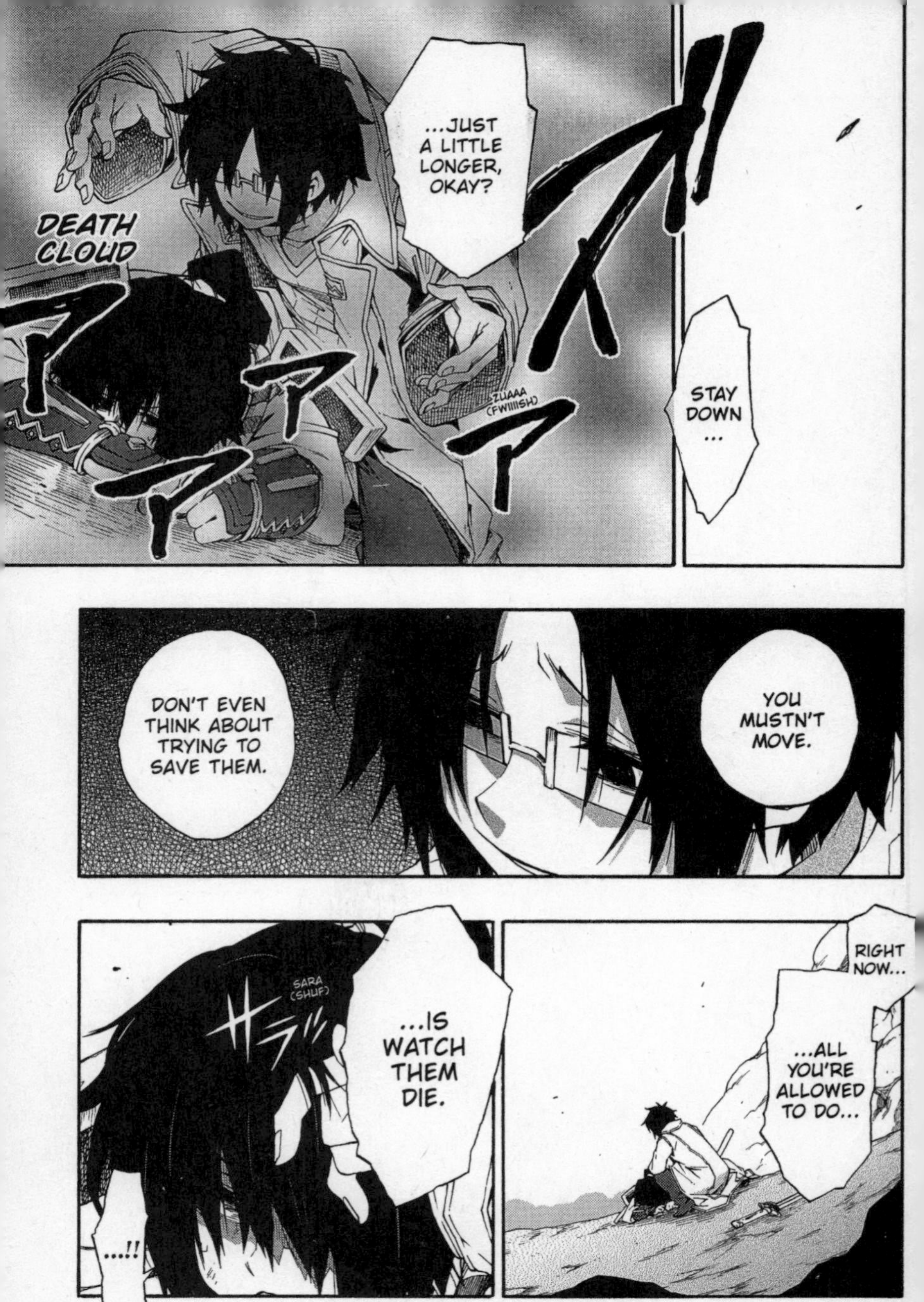
STAY DOWN ...
...JUST A LITTLE LONGER, OKAY?
ZUAAA (FWIIIISH)
DEATH CLOUD
YOU MUSTN'T MOVE.
DON'T EVEN THINK ABOUT TRYING TO SAVE THEM.
RIGHT NOW...
...ALL YOU'RE ALLOWED TO DO...
...IS WATCH THEM DIE.
SARA (SHUF)
...!!

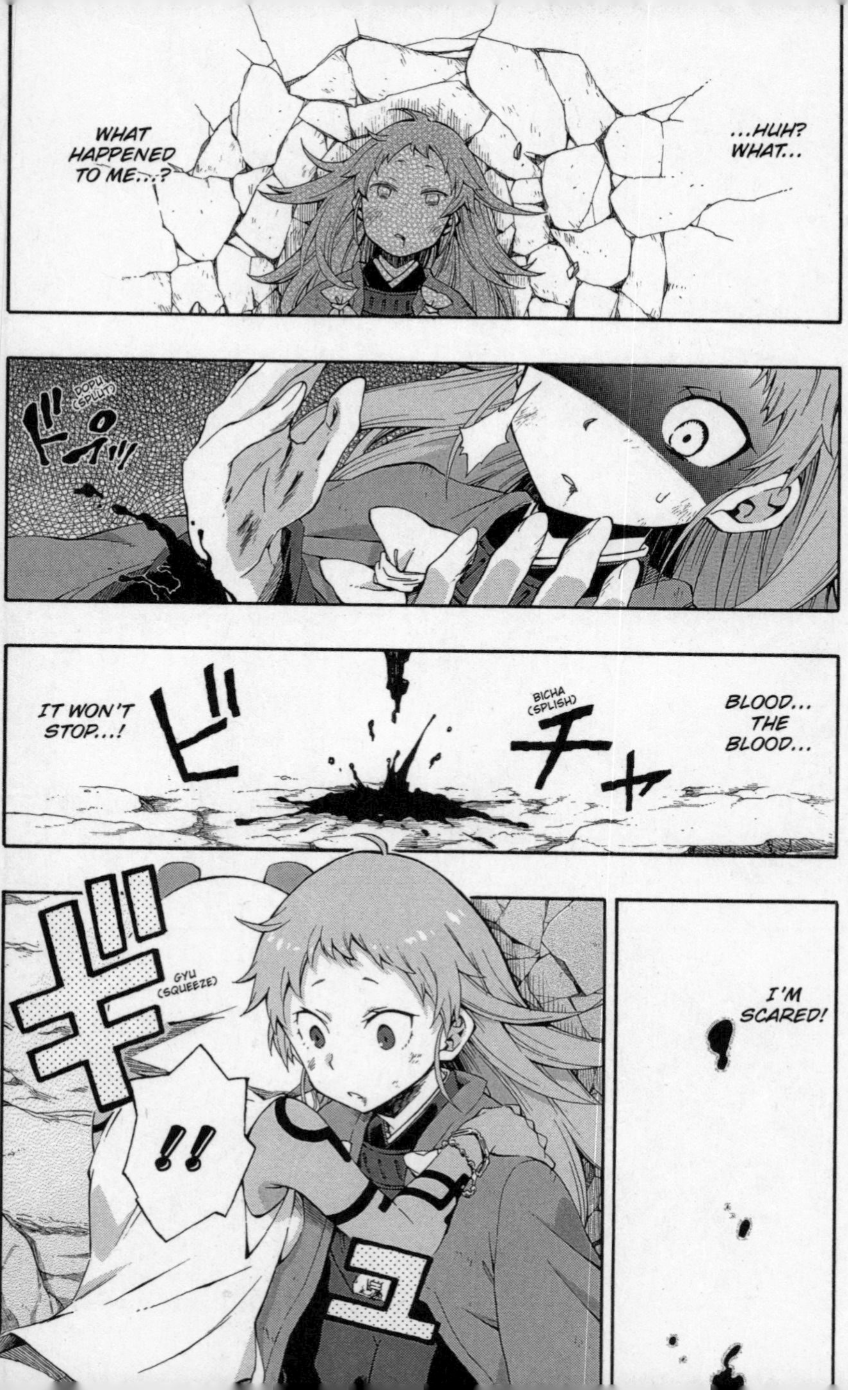
...HUH? WHAT...
WHAT HAPPENED TO ME...?
DOPU (SPLUT)
BLOOD... THE BLOOD...
BICHA (SPLISH)
IT WON'T STOP...!
I'M SCARED!
GYU (SQUEEZE)
!!

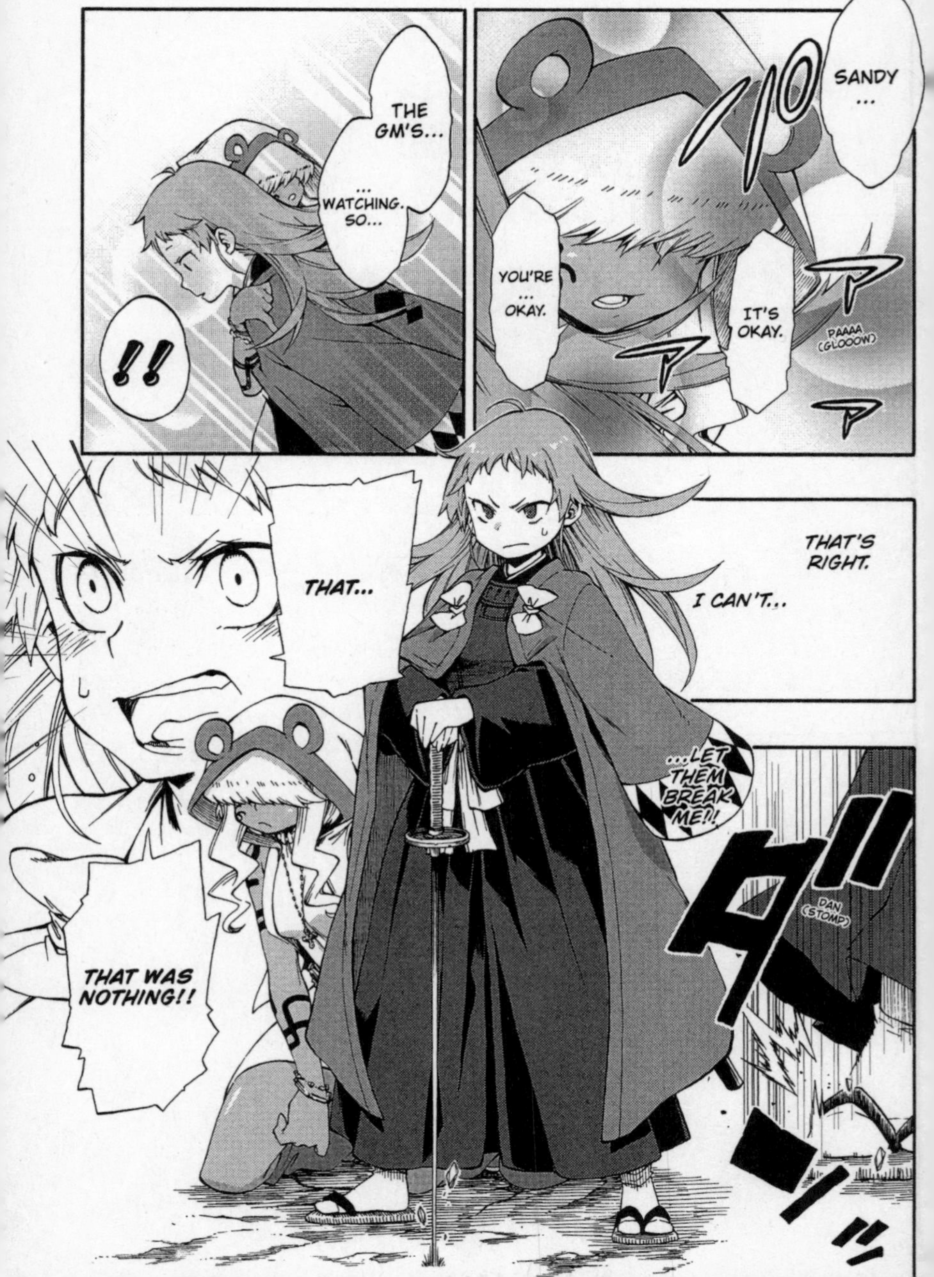
SANDY ...
IT'S OKAY.
YOU'RE ... OKAY.
PAAAA (GLOOOW)
THE GM'S...
... WATCHING. SO...
!!
THAT'S RIGHT.
I CAN'T...
...LET THEM BREAK ME!!
DAN (STOMP)
THAT...
THAT WAS NOTHING!!

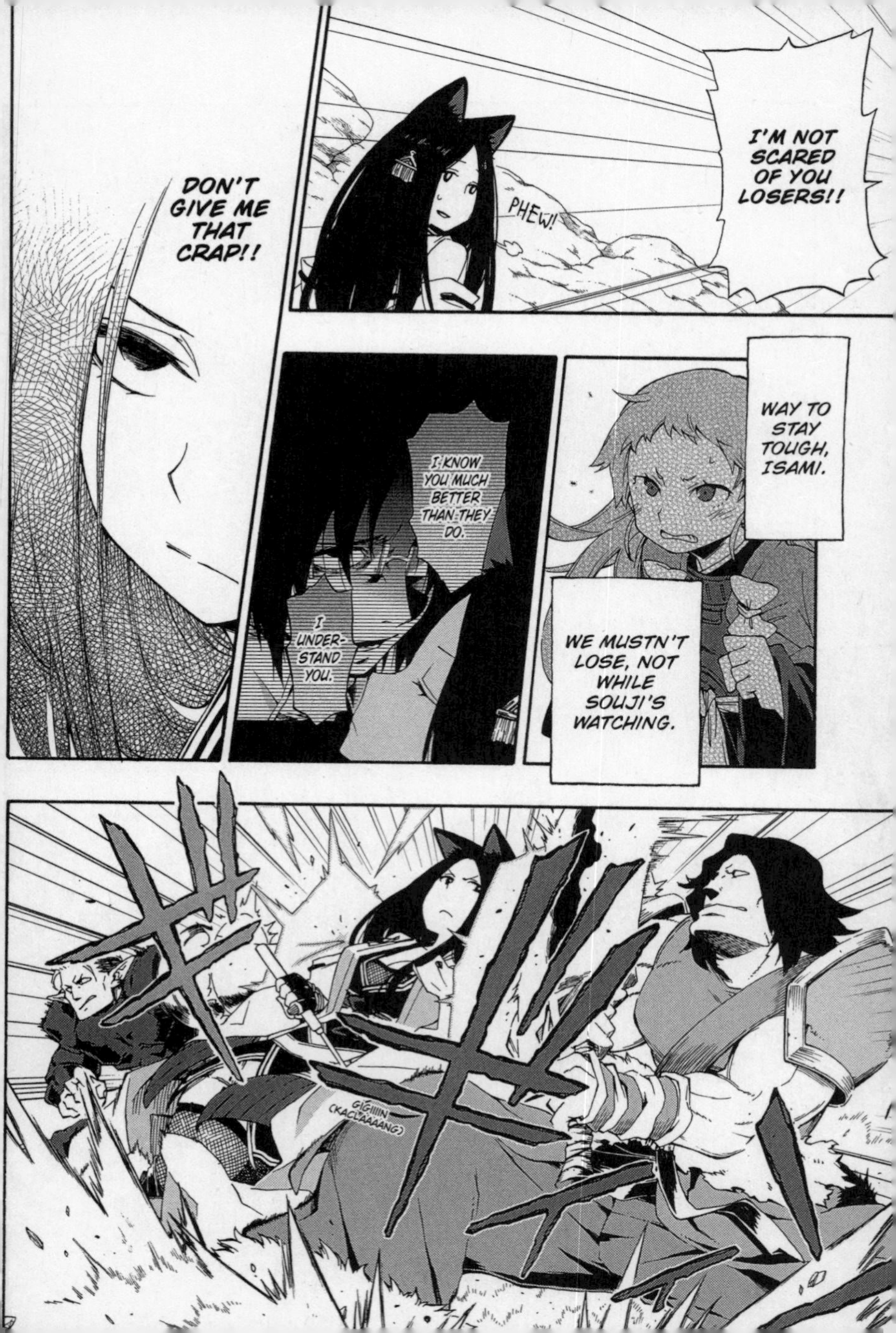
I'M NOT SCARED OF YOU LOSERS!!
PHEW!
WAY TO STAY TOUGH, ISAMI.
WE MUSTN'T LOSE, NOT WHILE SOUJI'S WATCHING.
I KNOW YOU MUCH BETTER THAN THEY DO.
I UNDERSTAND YOU.
DON'T GIVE ME THAT CRAP!!
GIGIIIIN (KACLAAAAANG)

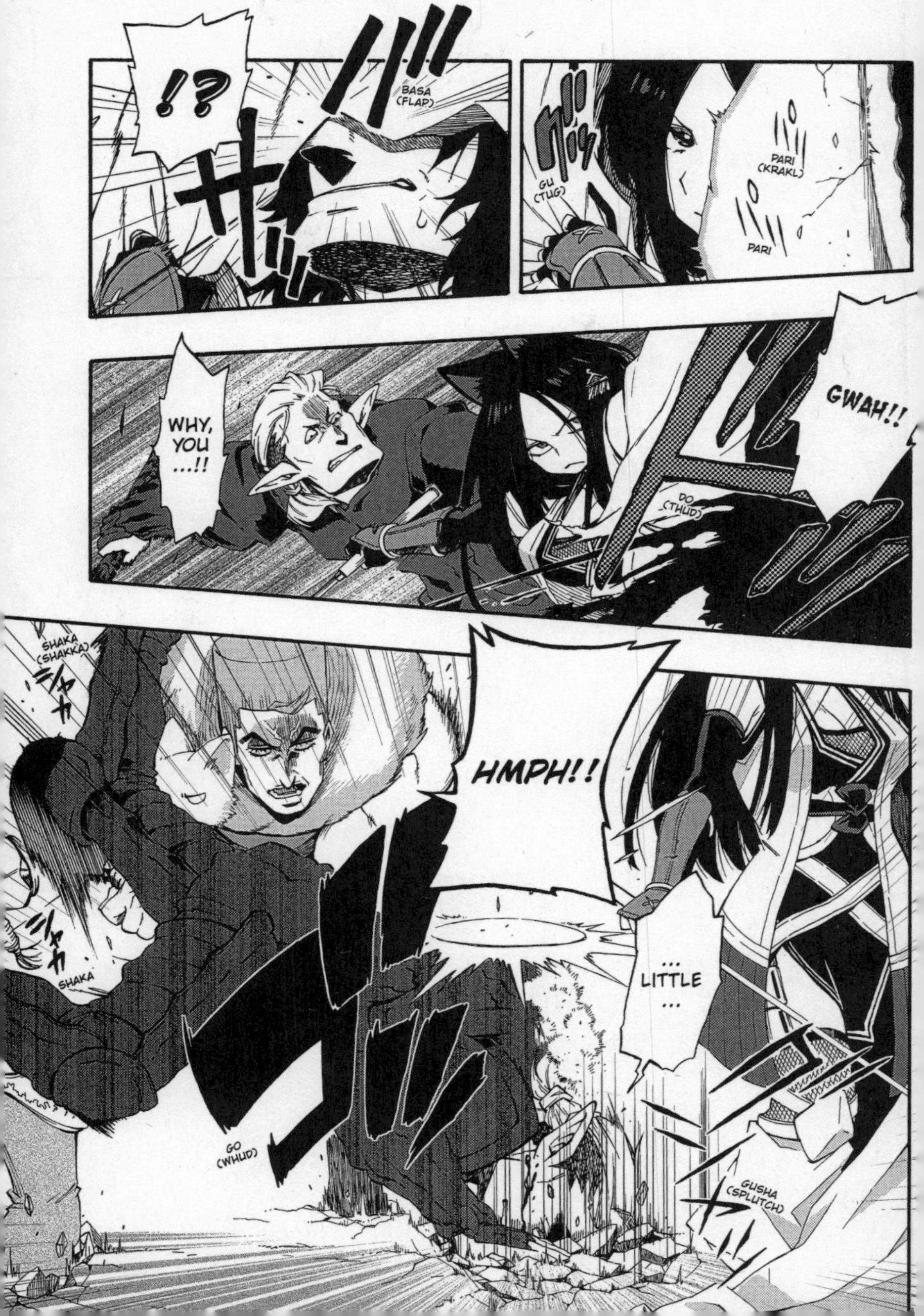
GU (TUG)
PARI (KRAKL)
PARI
!?
BASA (FLAP)
GWAH!!
DO (THUD)
WHY, YOU ...!!
HMPH!!
... LITTLE ...
GUSHA (SPLUTCH)
GO (WHUD)
SHAKA (SHAKKA)
SHAKA

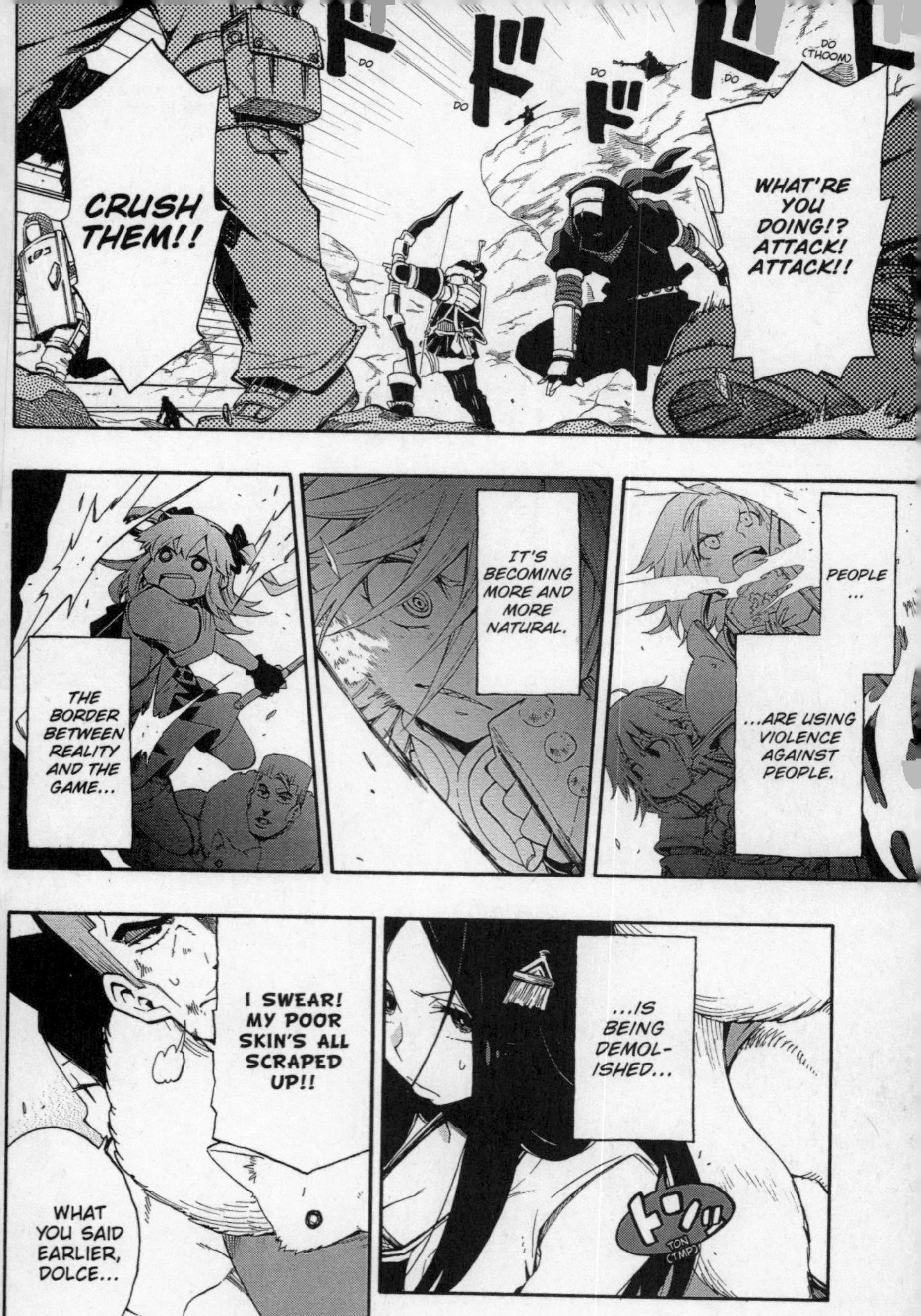
DO (THOOM)
DO
DO
DO
DO
WHAT'RE YOU DOING!? ATTACK! ATTACK!!
CRUSH THEM!!
PEOPLE ...
...ARE USING VIOLENCE AGAINST PEOPLE.
IT'S BECOMING MORE AND MORE NATURAL.
THE BORDER BETWEEN REALITY AND THE GAME...
...IS BEING DEMOL-ISHED...
TON (TMP)
I SWEAR! MY POOR SKIN'S ALL SCRAPED UP!!
WHAT YOU SAID EARLIER, DOLCE...

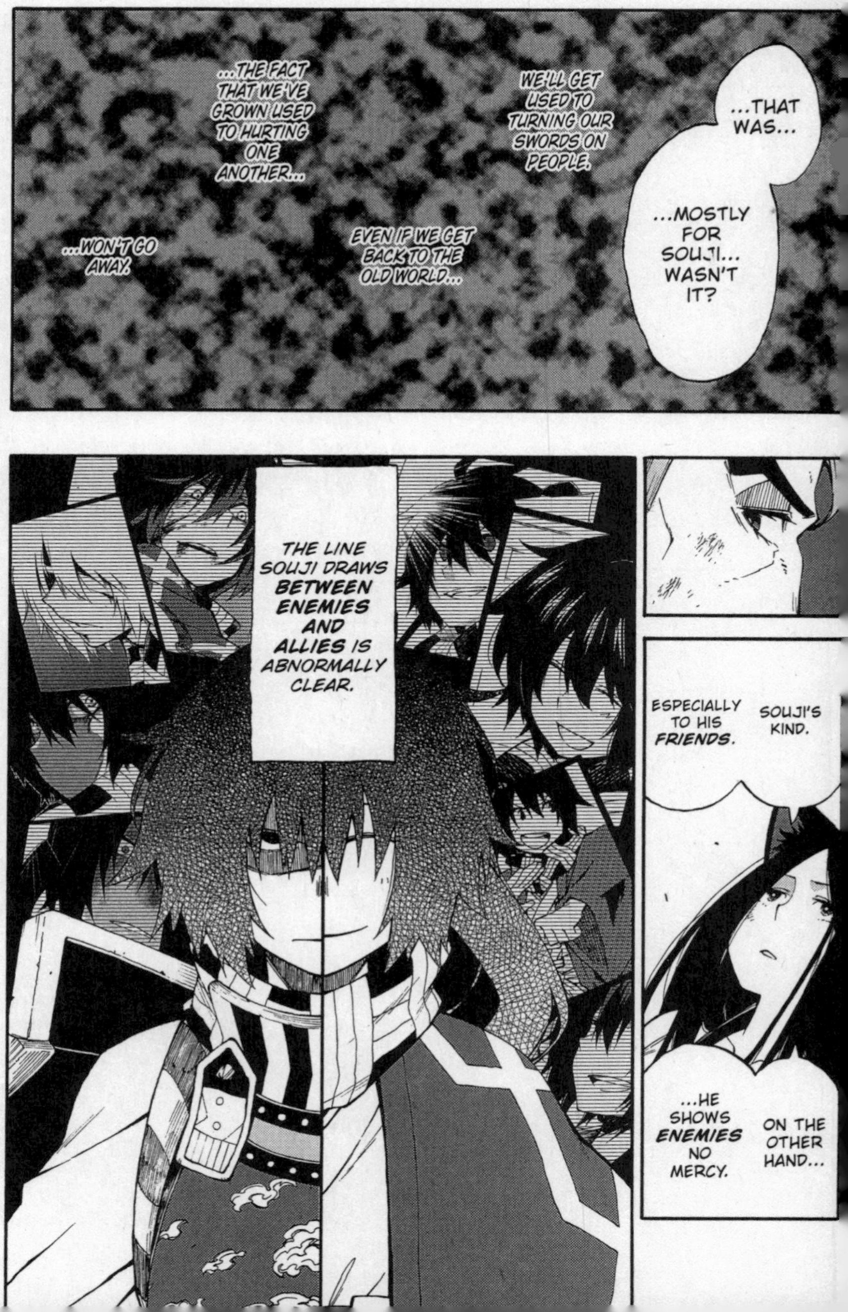
...THAT WAS...
...MOSTLY FOR SOUJI... WASN'T IT?
WE'LL GET USED TO TURNING OUR SWORDS ON PEOPLE.
EVEN IF WE GET BACK TO THE OLD WORLD...
...THE FACT THAT WE'VE GROWN USED TO HURTING ONE ANOTHER...
...WON'T GO AWAY.
SOUJI'S KIND.
ESPECIALLY TO HIS FRIENDS.
ON THE OTHER HAND...
...HE SHOWS ENEMIES NO MERCY.
THE LINE SOUJI DRAWS BETWEEN ENEMIES AND ALLIES IS ABNORMALLY CLEAR.

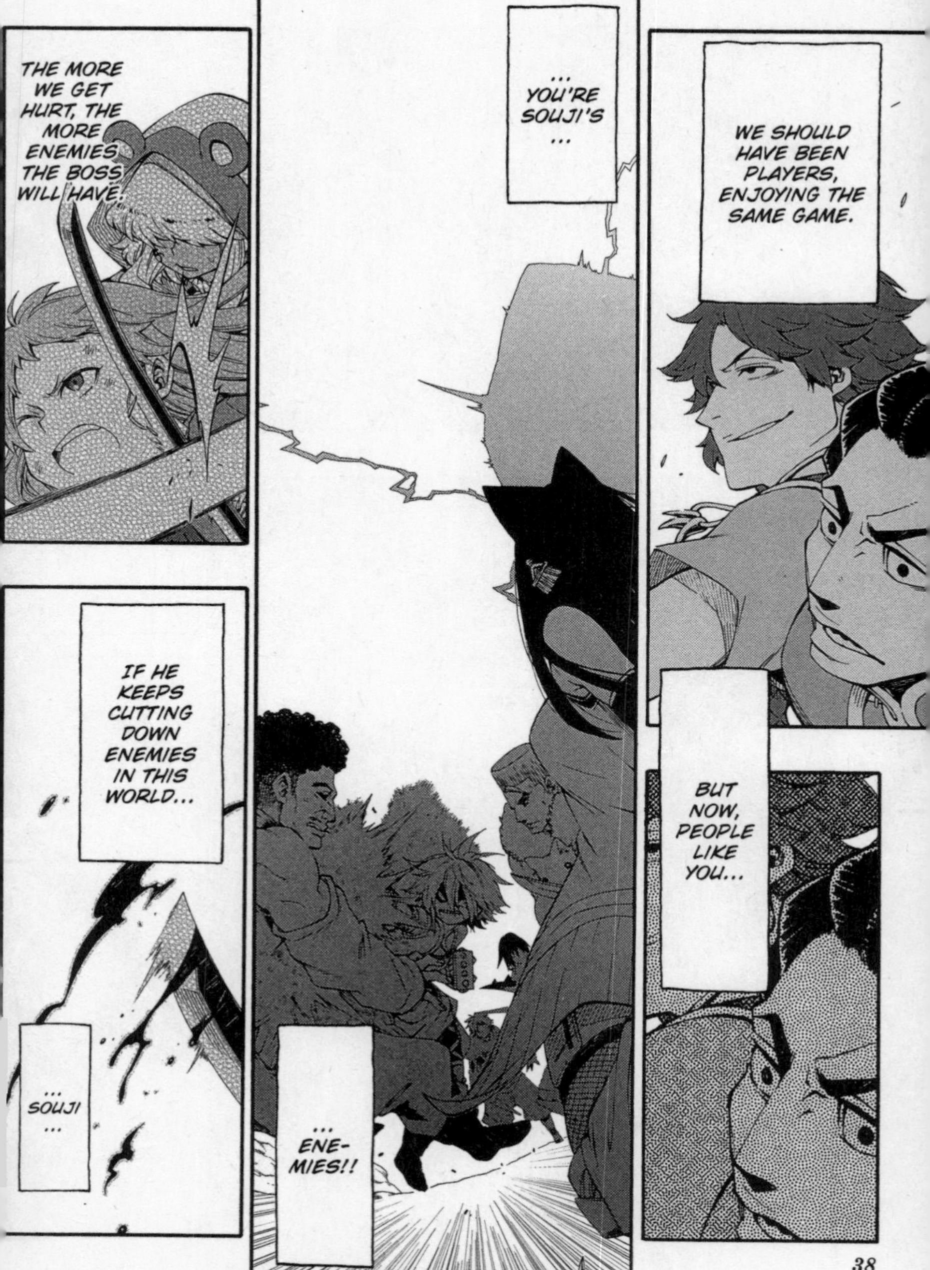
WE SHOULD HAVE BEEN PLAYERS, ENJOYING THE SAME GAME.
BUT NOW, PEOPLE LIKE YOU...
... YOU'RE SOUJI'S ...
... ENE-MIES!!
THE MORE WE GET HURT, THE MORE ENEMIES THE BOSS WILL HAVE.
IF HE KEEPS CUTTING DOWN ENEMIES IN THIS WORLD...
... SOUJI ...

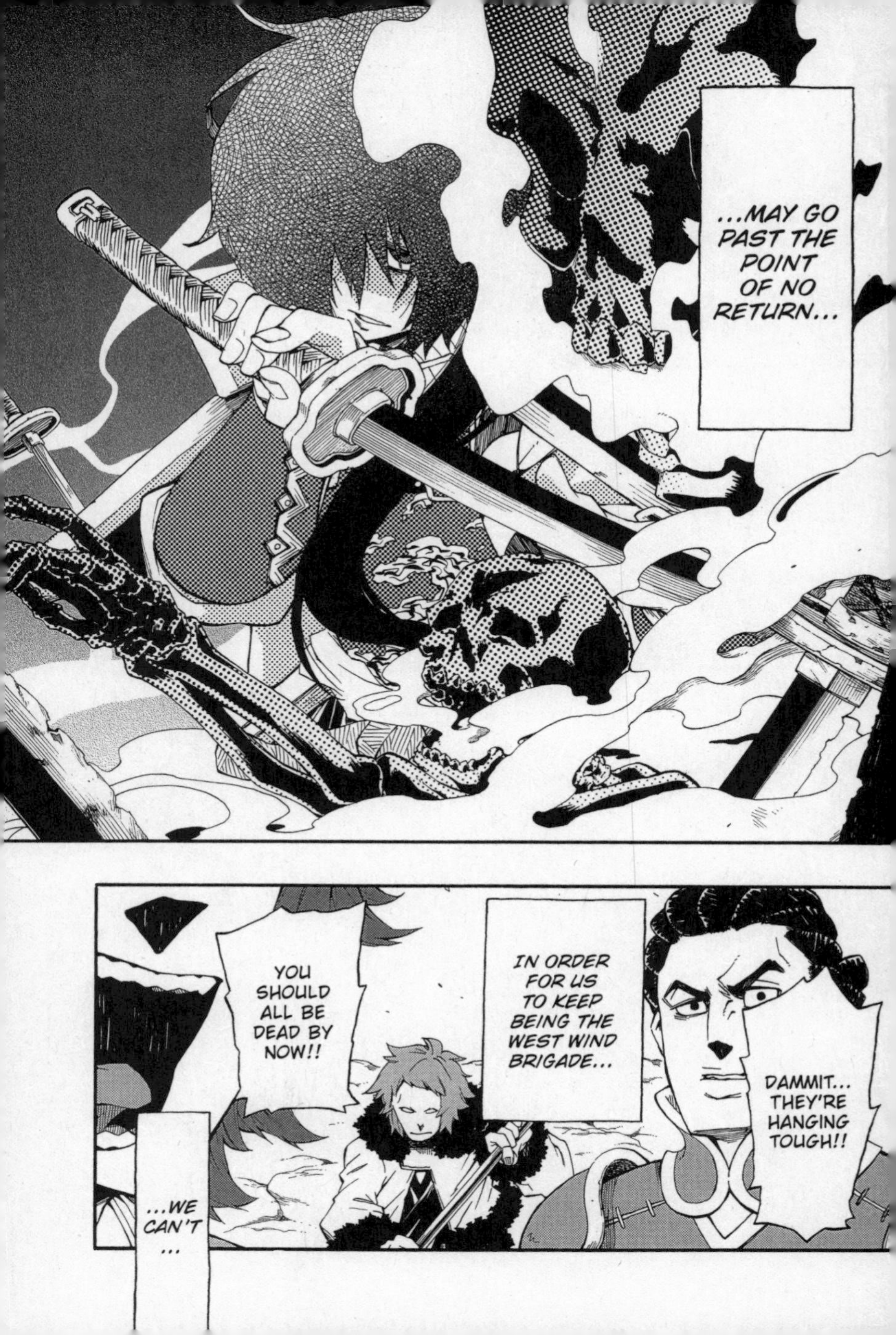
...MAY GO PAST THE POINT OF NO RETURN...
DAMMIT... THEY'RE HANGING TOUGH!!
IN ORDER FOR US TO KEEP BEING THE WEST WIND BRIGADE...
YOU SHOULD ALL BE DEAD BY NOW!!
...WE CAN'T ...

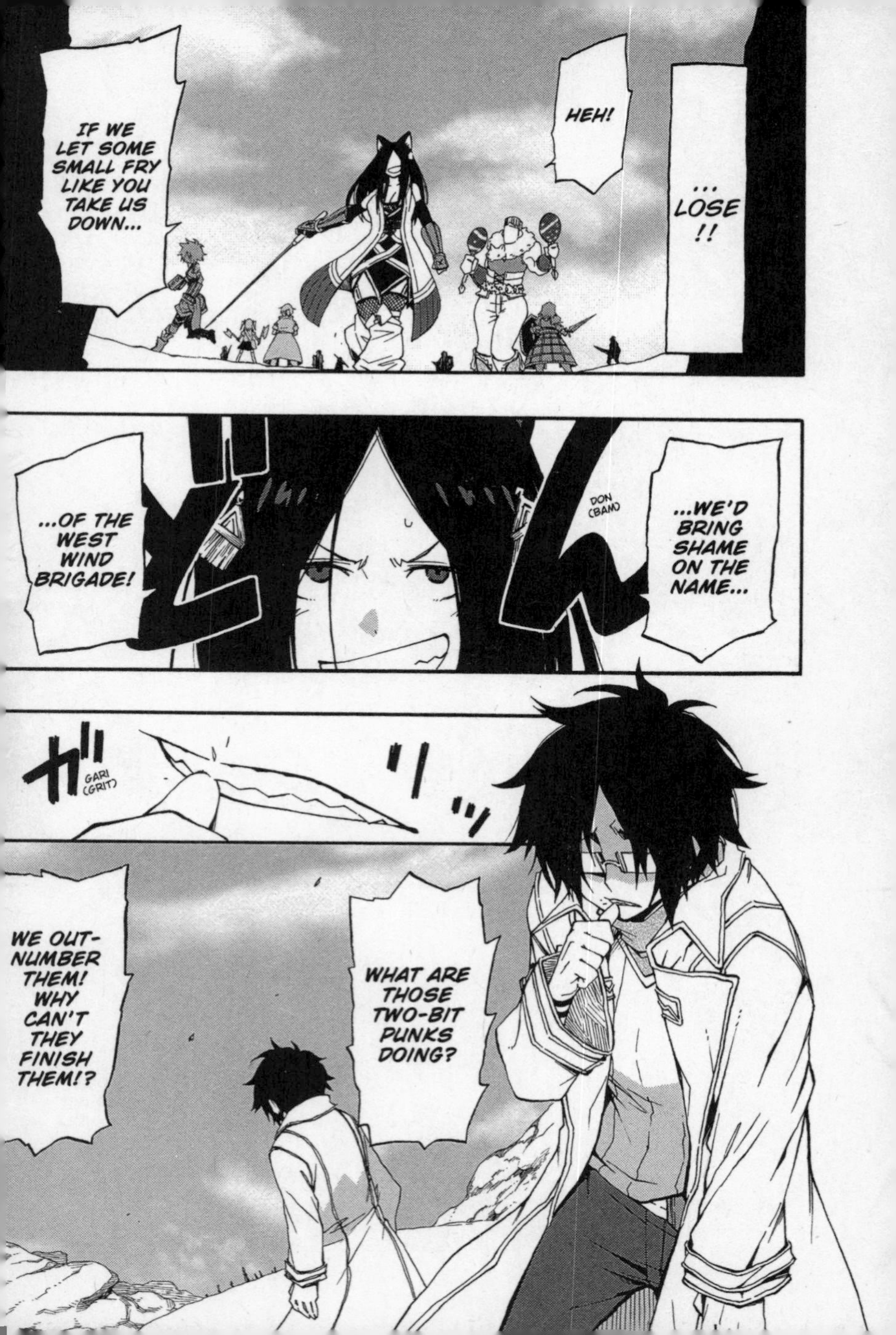
…LOSE !!
HEH!
IF WE LET SOME SMALL FRY LIKE YOU TAKE US DOWN…
…WE'D BRING SHAME ON THE NAME…
DON (BAM)
…OF THE WEST WIND BRIGADE!
GARI (GRIT)
WHAT ARE THOSE TWO-BIT PUNKS DOING?
WE OUT-NUMBER THEM! WHY CAN'T THEY FINISH THEM!?

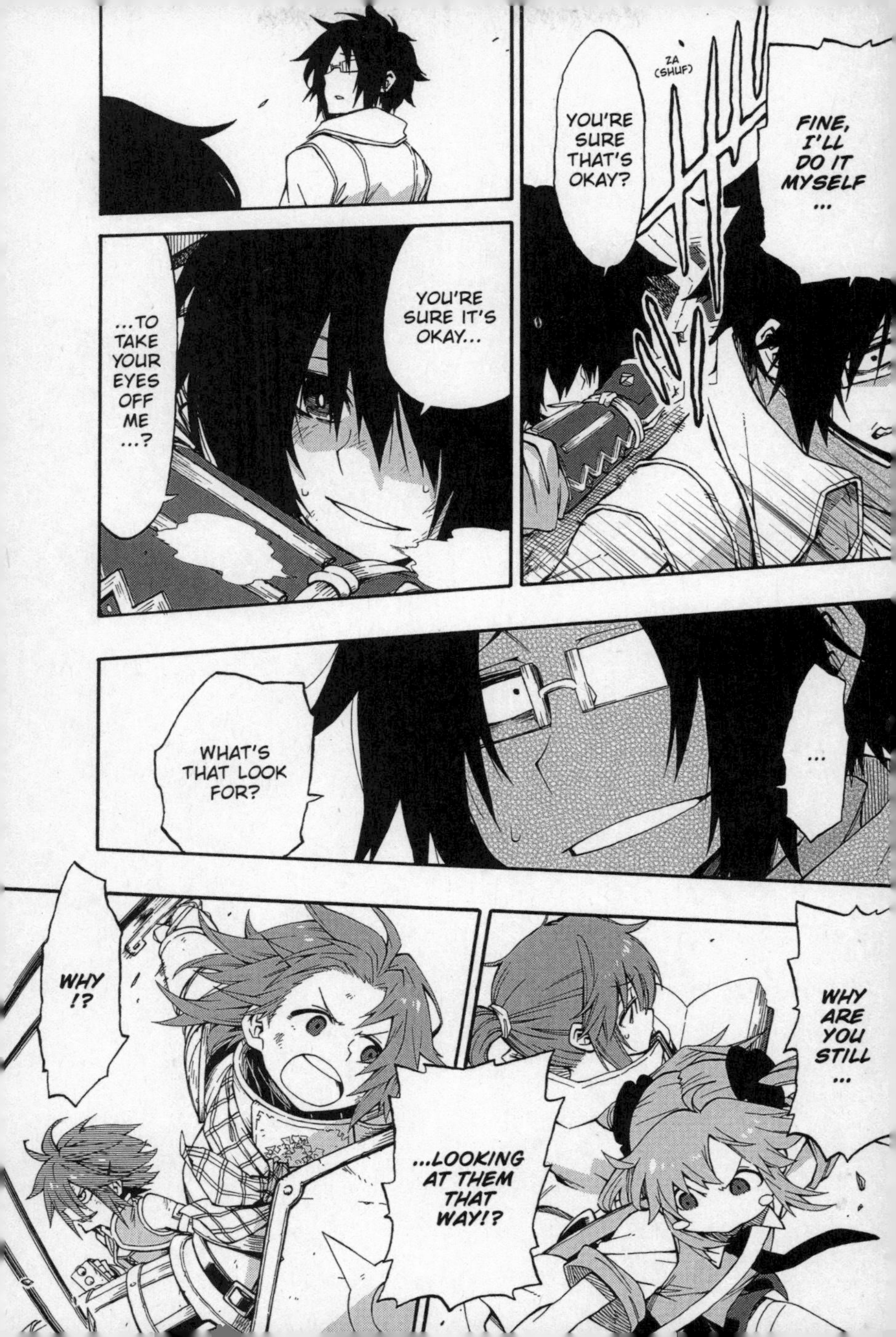
FINE, I'LL DO IT MYSELF...
ZA (SHUF)
YOU'RE SURE THAT'S OKAY?
YOU'RE SURE IT'S OKAY...
...TO TAKE YOUR EYES OFF ME...?
...
WHAT'S THAT LOOK FOR?
WHY ARE YOU STILL...
...LOOKING AT THEM THAT WAY!?
WHY !?

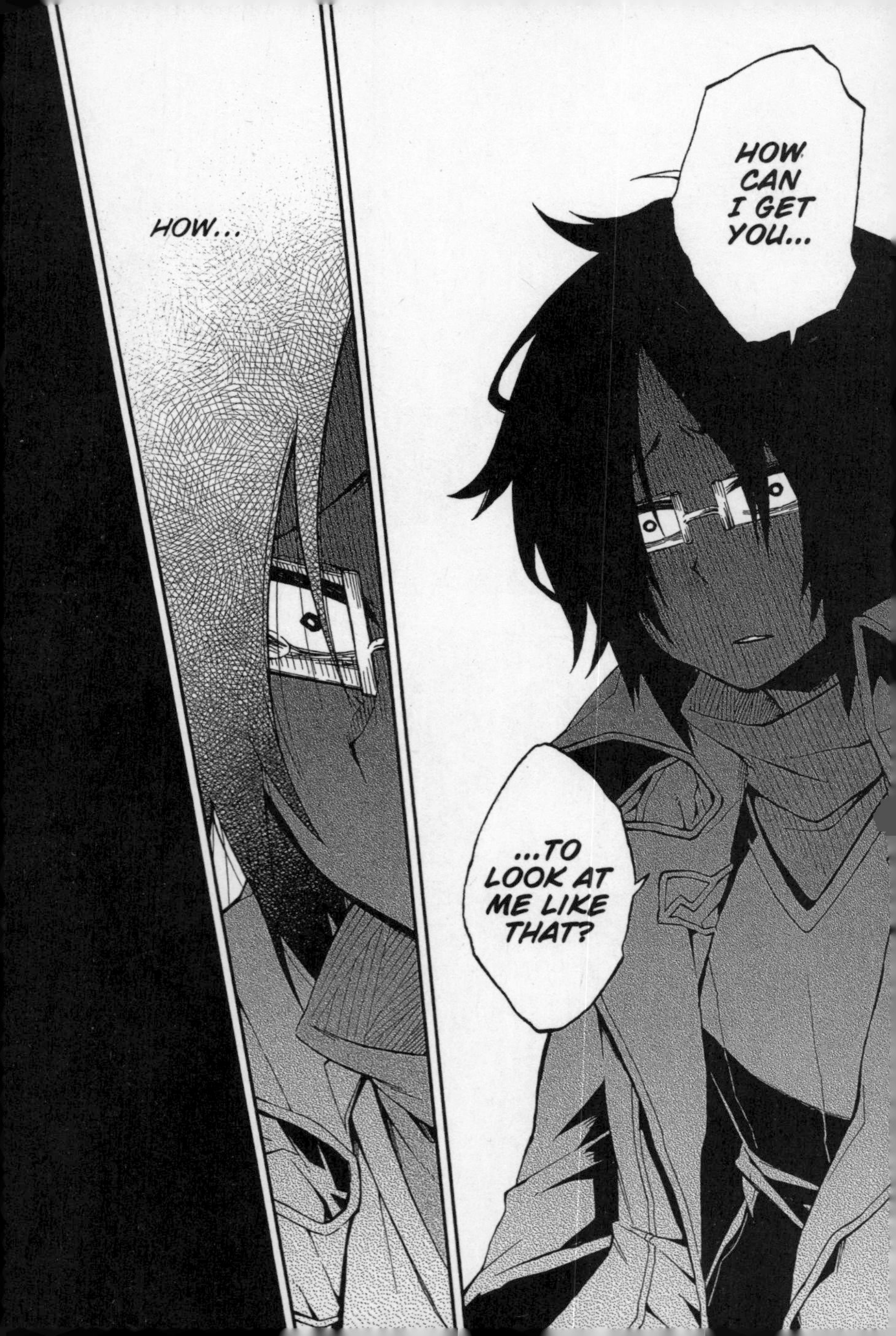
HOW CAN I GET YOU...
...TO LOOK AT ME LIKE THAT?
HOW...

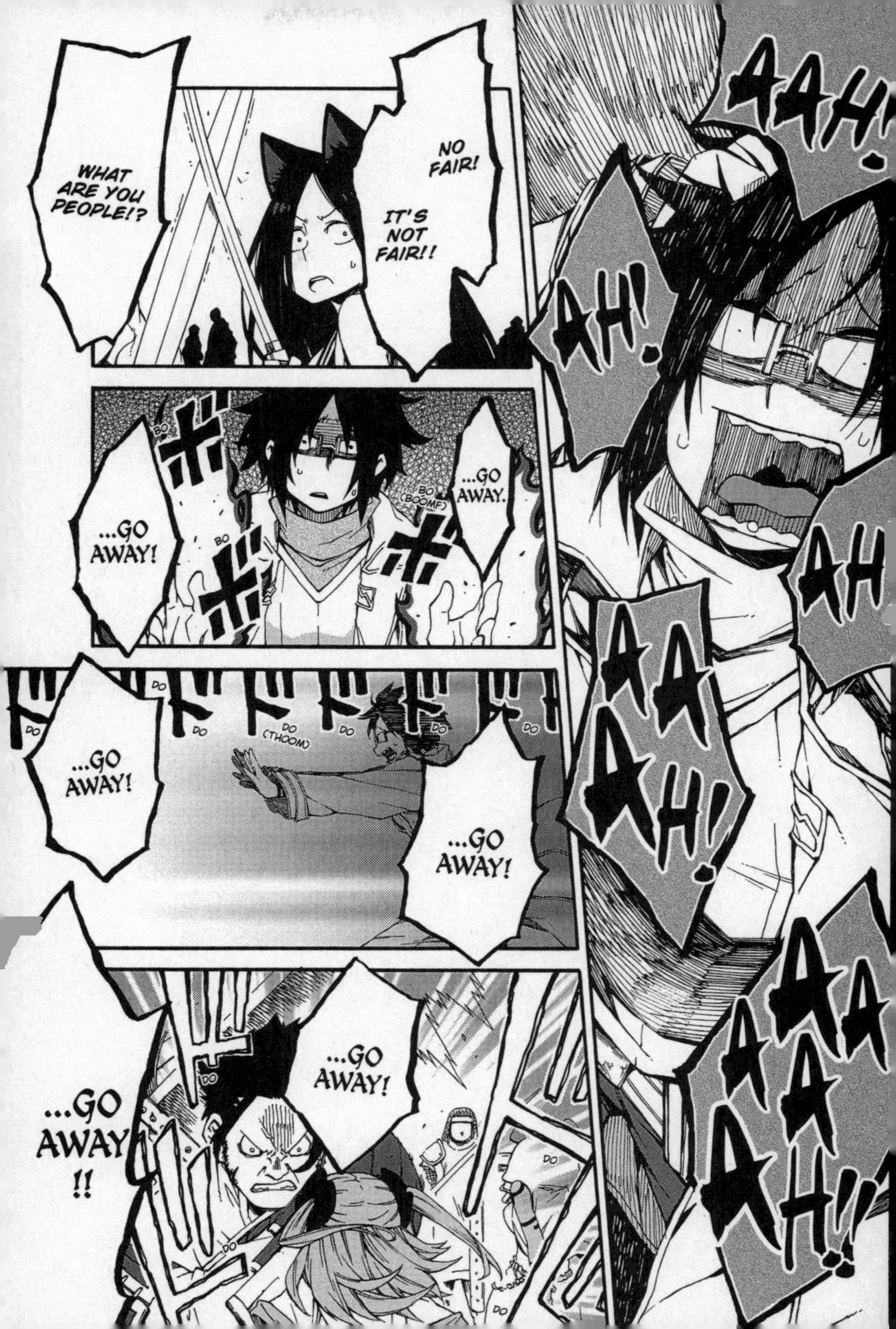
AAH!
AH!
AH
AAAAH!
AAAAAAAH!!
NO FAIR!
IT'S NOT FAIR!!
WHAT ARE YOU PEOPLE!?
...GO AWAY.
BO (BOOMF)
BO
BO
...GO AWAY!
DO (THOOM)
DO
...GO AWAY!
...GO AWAY!
...GO AWAY!
...GO AWAY !!

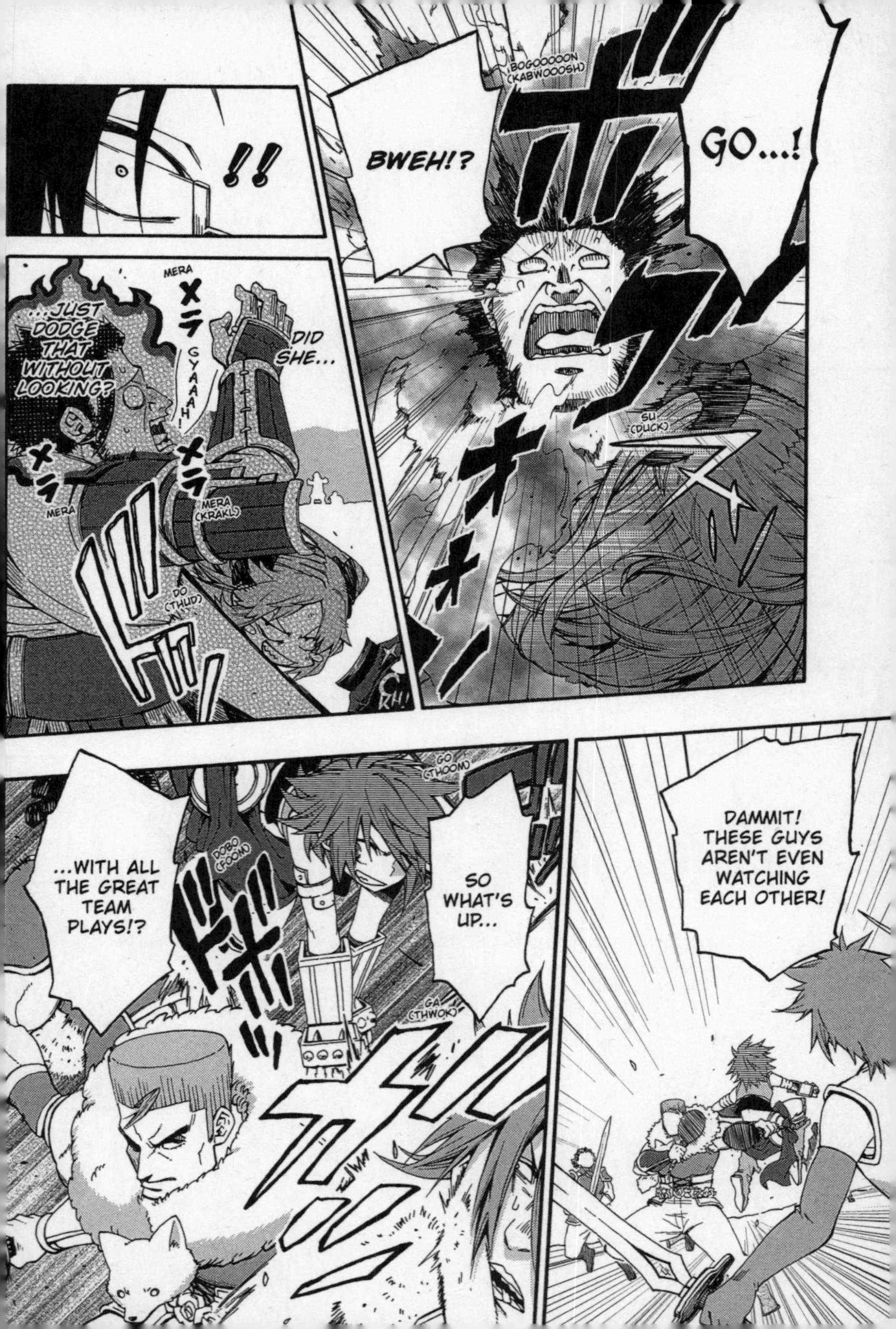
BOGOOOOON (KABWOOOSH)
GO...!
BWEH!?
SU (DUCK)
!!
DID SHE...
...JUST DODGE THAT WITHOUT LOOKING?
MERA
GYAAAH!
MERA (KRAKL)
MERA
DO (THUD)
DAMMIT! THESE GUYS AREN'T EVEN WATCHING EACH OTHER!
GO (THOOM)
SO WHAT'S UP...
...WITH ALL THE GREAT TEAM PLAYS!?
DOBO (FOOM)
GA (THWOK)

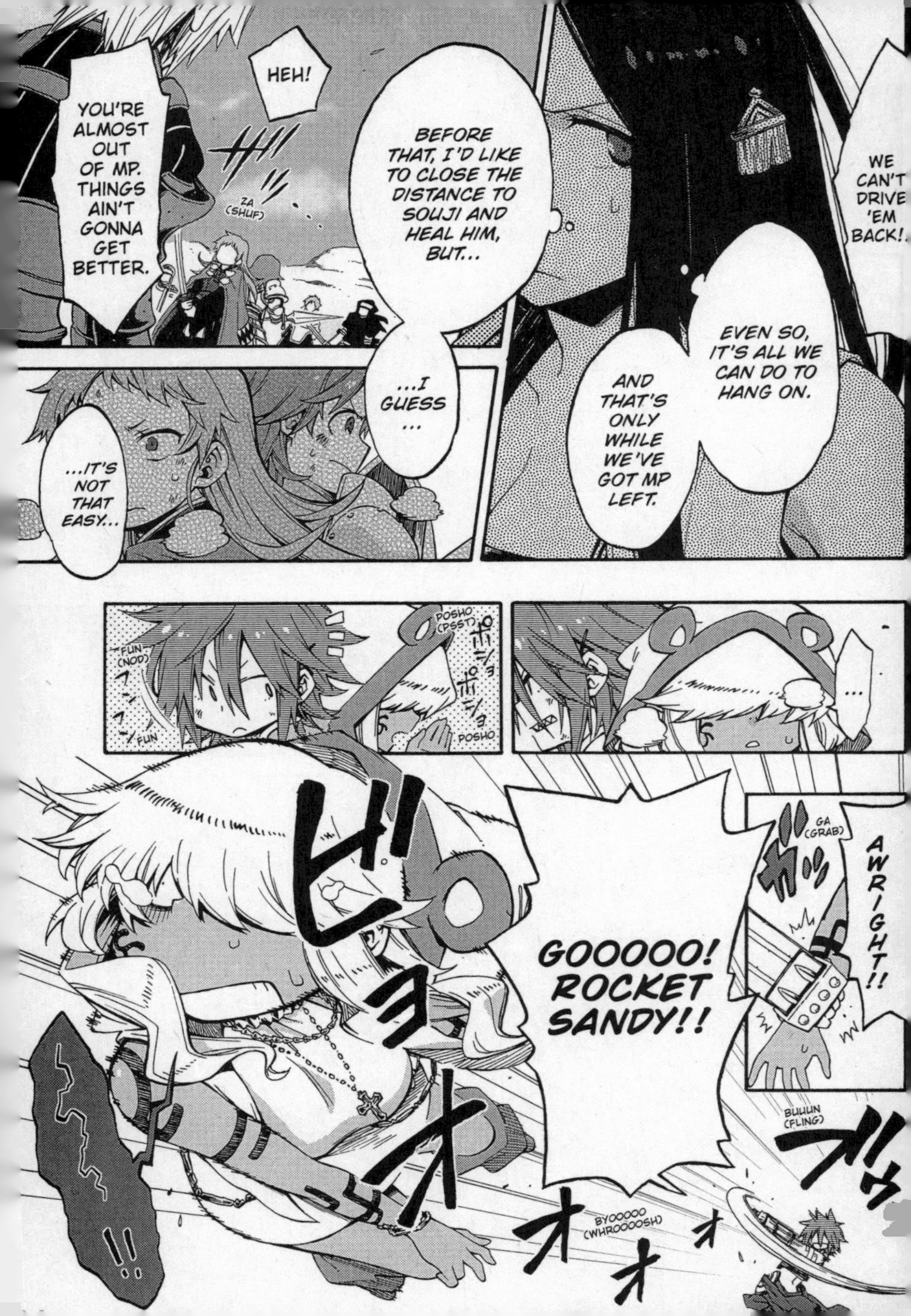
WE CAN'T DRIVE 'EM BACK!
EVEN SO, IT'S ALL WE CAN DO TO HANG ON.
AND THAT'S ONLY WHILE WE'VE GOT MP LEFT.
HEH!
YOU'RE ALMOST OUT OF MP. THINGS AIN'T GONNA GET BETTER.
ZA (SHUF)
BEFORE THAT, I'D LIKE TO CLOSE THE DISTANCE TO SOUJI AND HEAL HIM, BUT...
...I GUESS ...
...IT'S NOT THAT EASY...
...
POSHO (PSSST)
POSHO
FUN (NOD)
FUN
GA (GRAB)
AWRIGHT!!
GOOOOO! ROCKET SANDY!!
BUUUN (FLING)
BYOOOOO (WHROOOOSH)
!!

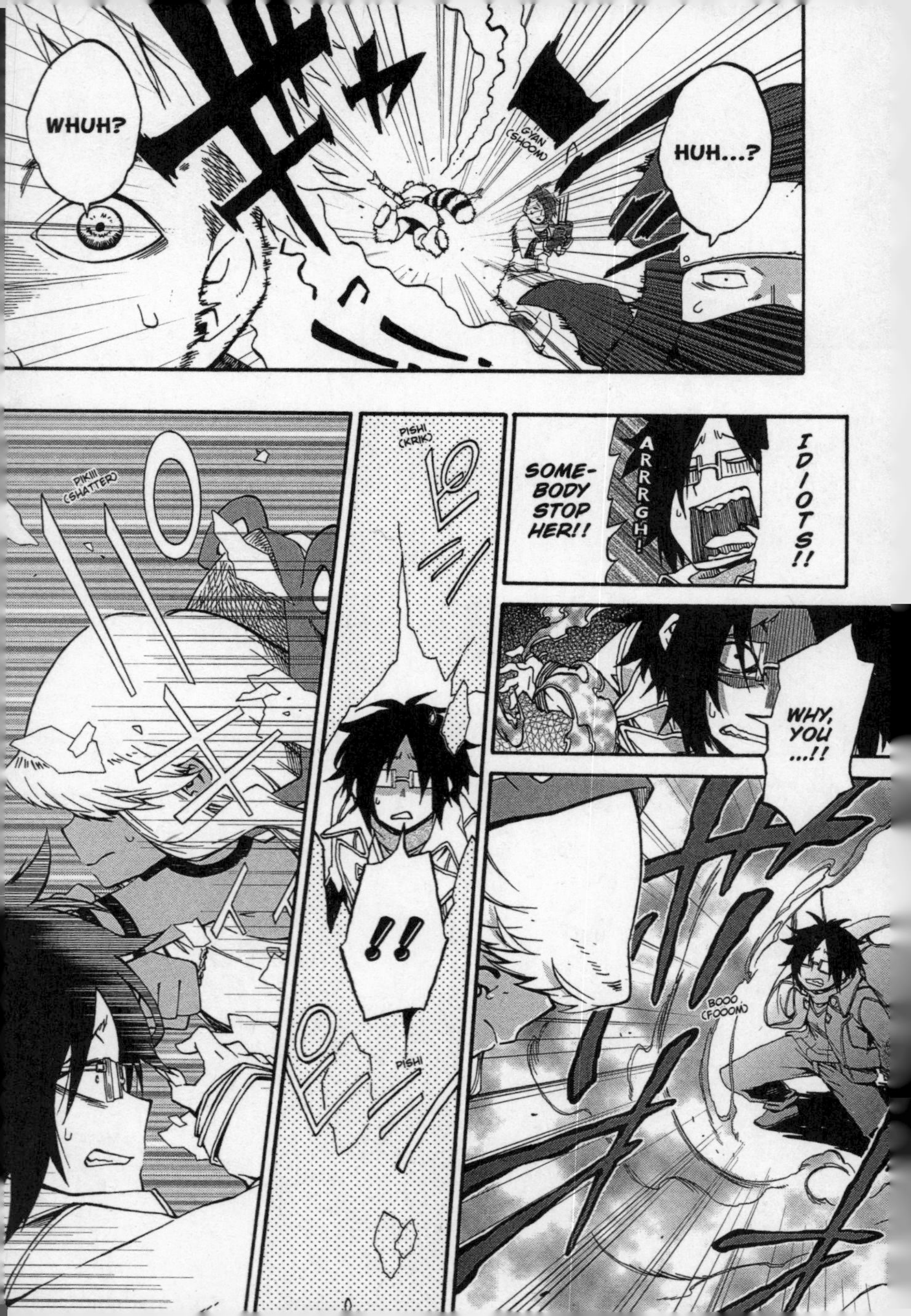
HUH...?
GYAN (SHOOM)
WHUH?
IDIOTS!!
ARRRGH!
SOMEBODY STOP HER!!
WHY, YOU ...!!
BOOO (FOOOM)
PISHI (KRIK)
!!
PISHI
PIKIII (SHATTER)

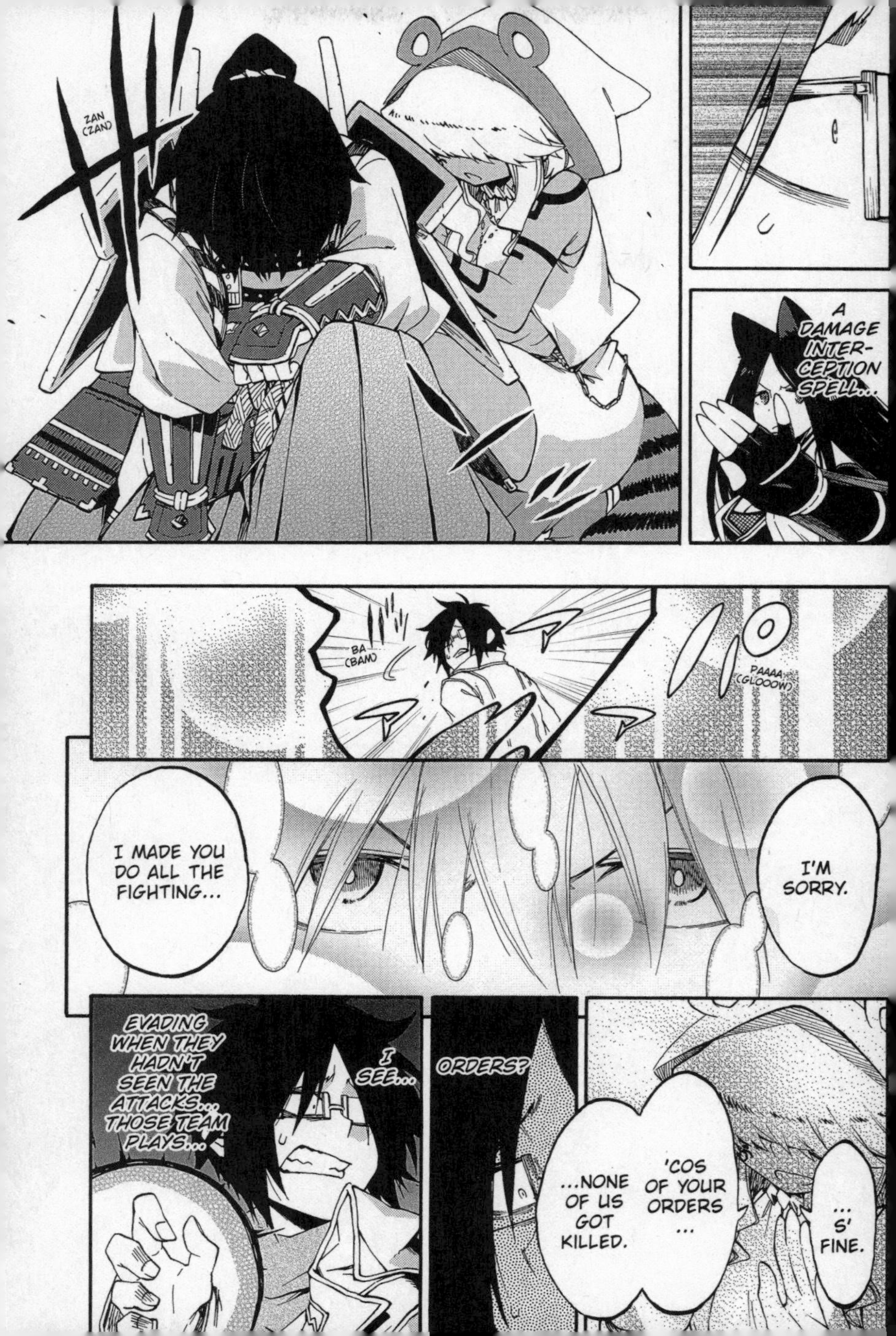
A DAMAGE INTER-CEPTION SPELL...
ZAN (ZAND)
PAAAA (GLOOOW)
BA (BAM)
I'M SORRY.
I MADE YOU DO ALL THE FIGHTING...
... S' FINE.
'COS OF YOUR ORDERS ...
...NONE OF US GOT KILLED.
ORDERS?
I SEE...
EVADING WHEN THEY HADN'T SEEN THE ATTACKS... THOSE TEAM PLAYS...

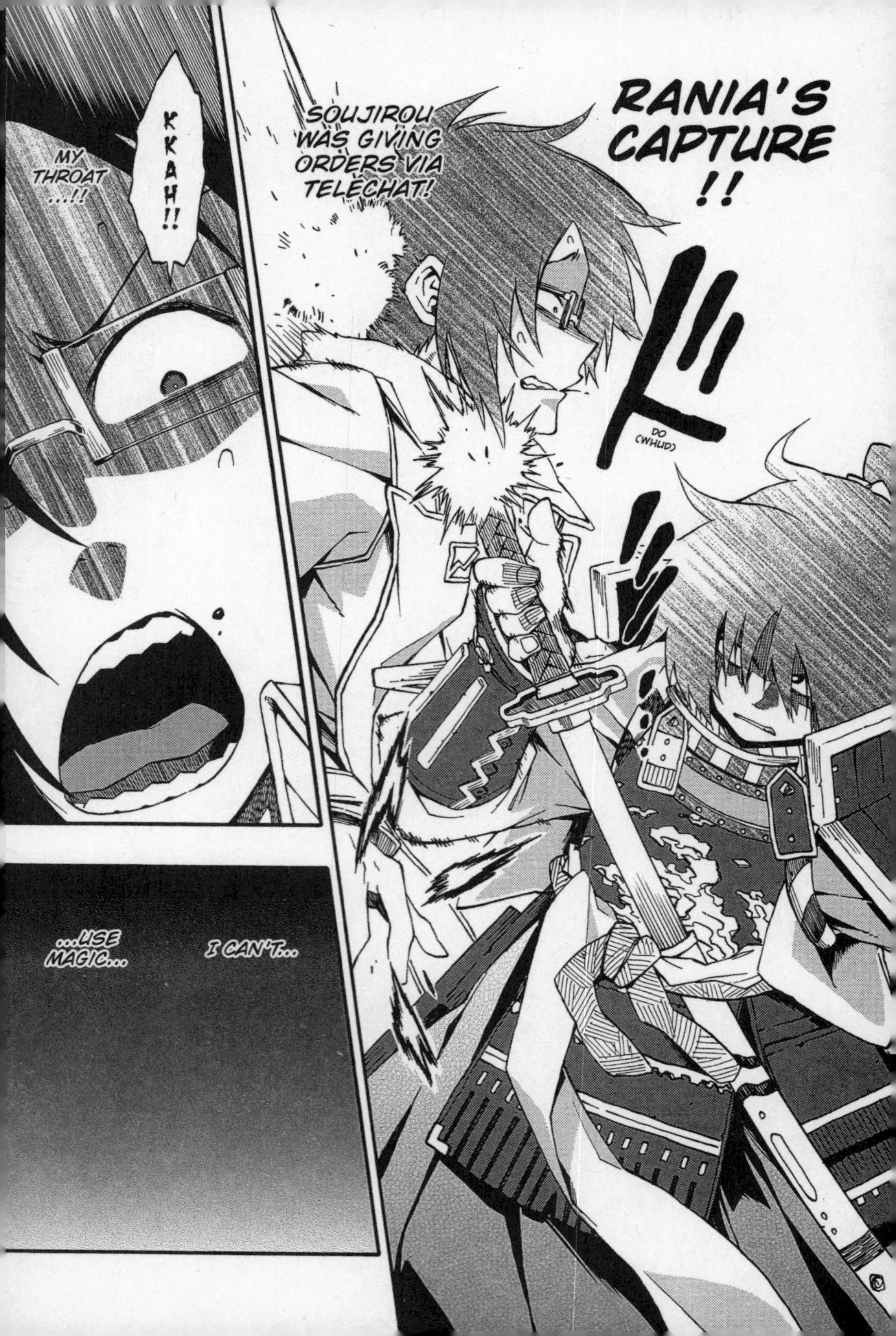
RANIA'S CAPTURE!!
SOUJIROU WAS GIVING ORDERS VIA TELECHAT!
DO (WHUD)
KKAH!!
MY THROAT ...!!
I CAN'T...
...USE MAGIC...

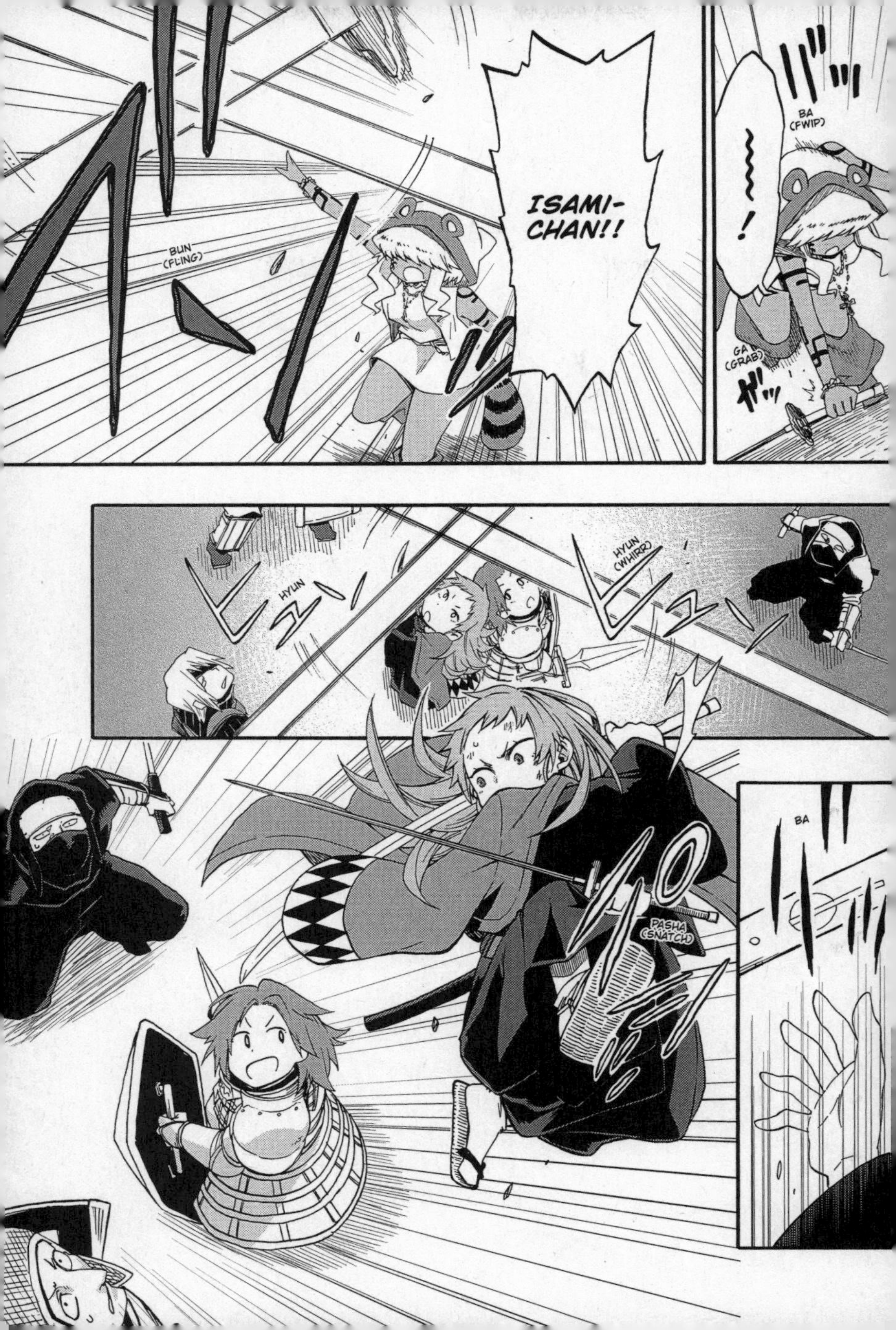
BA
(FWIP)
~~~!
GA
(GRAB)
ISAMI-
CHAN!!
BUN
(FLING)
HYUN
(WHIRR)
HYUN
BA
PASHA
(SNATCH)
~~~

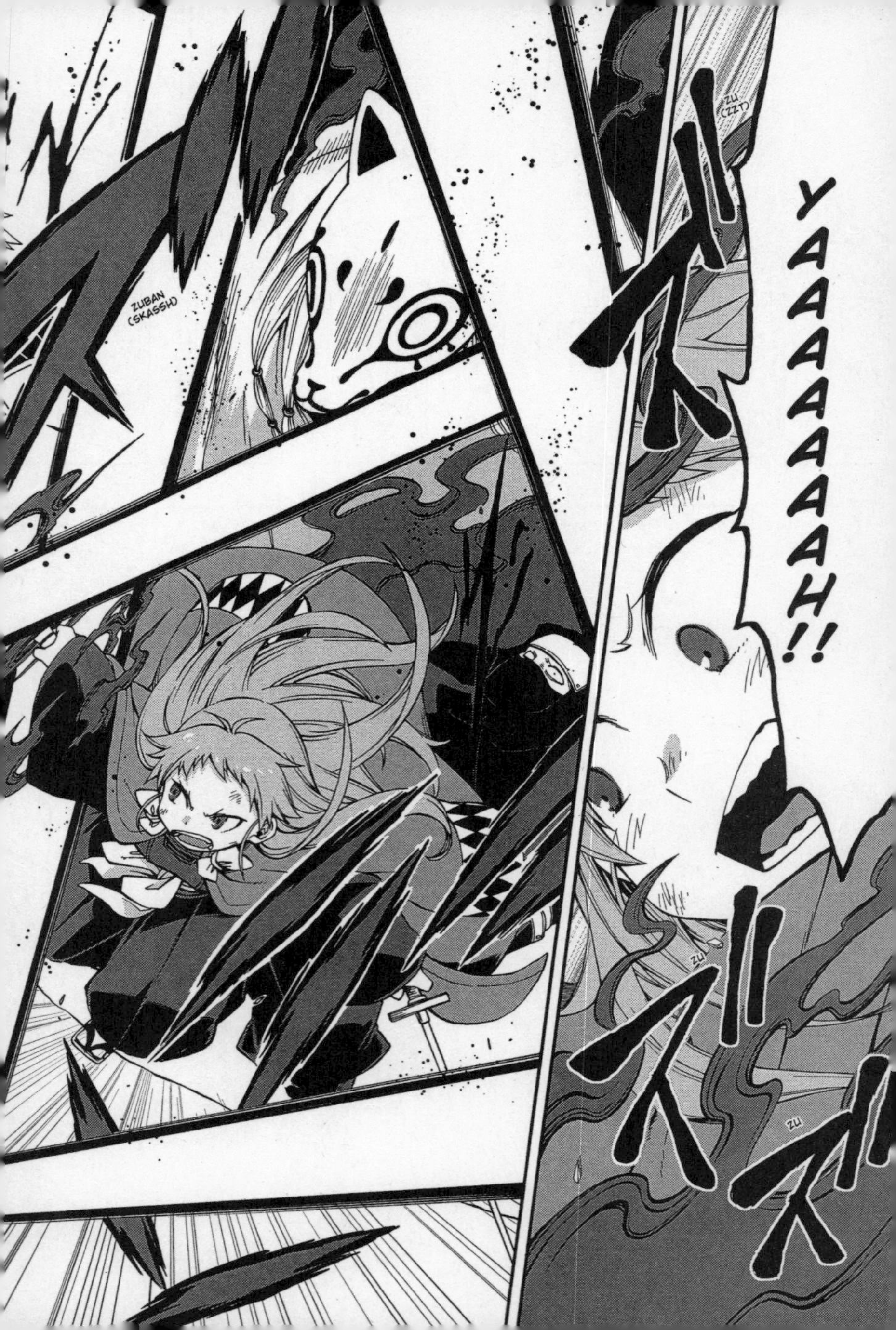
ZU (ZZZT)
YAAAAAAAH!!
ZU
ZU
ZUBAN (SKASSH)

LOG HORIZON
THE WEST WIND BRIGADE

LOG HORIZON
THE WEST WIND BRIGADE

CHAPTER : 15 FRIENDS

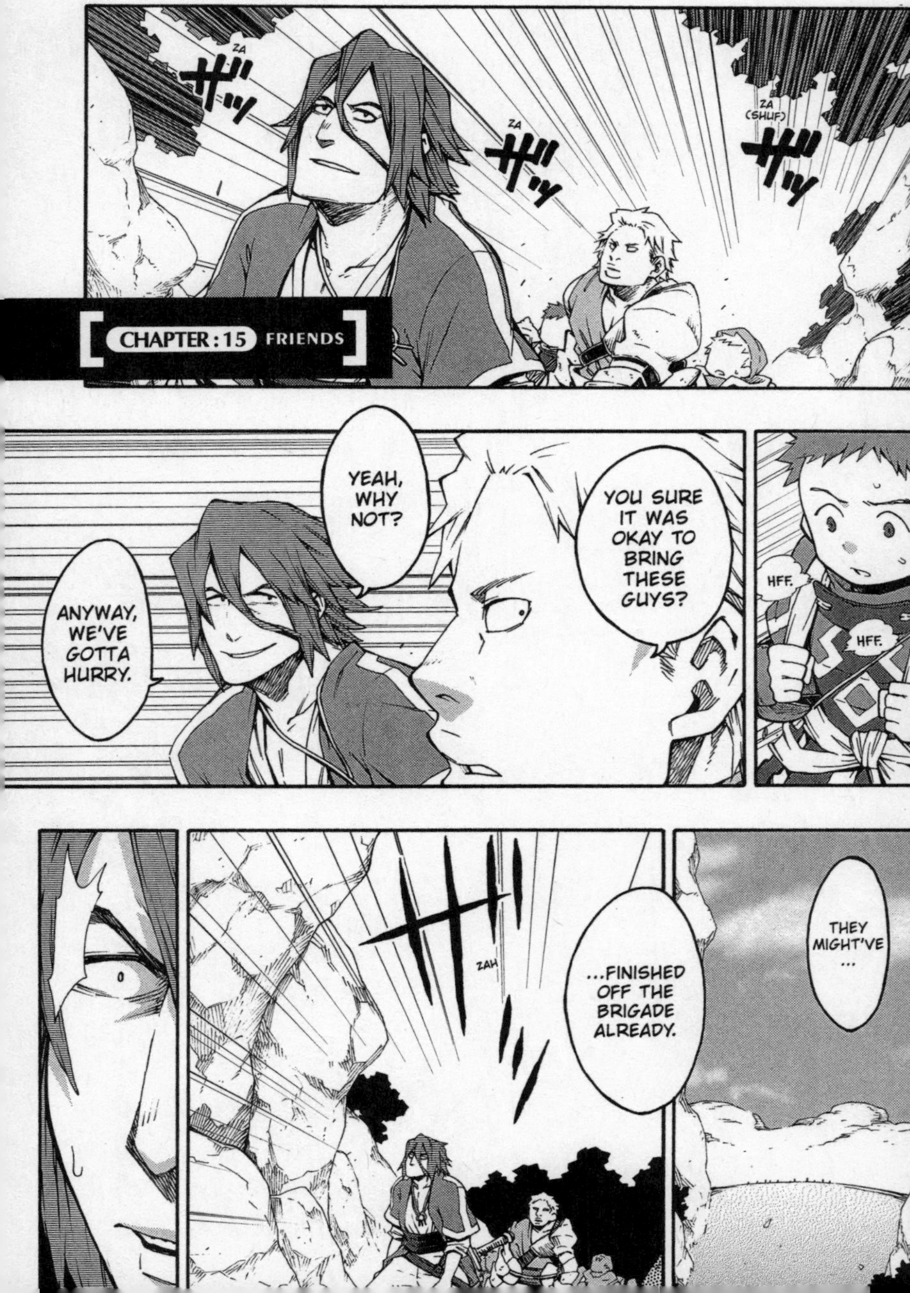
ZA (SHUF)
ZA
ZA
HFF.
HFF.
YOU SURE IT WAS OKAY TO BRING THESE GUYS?
YEAH, WHY NOT?
ANYWAY, WE'VE GOTTA HURRY.
THEY MIGHT'VE ...
...FINISHED OFF THE BRIGADE ALREADY.
ZAH

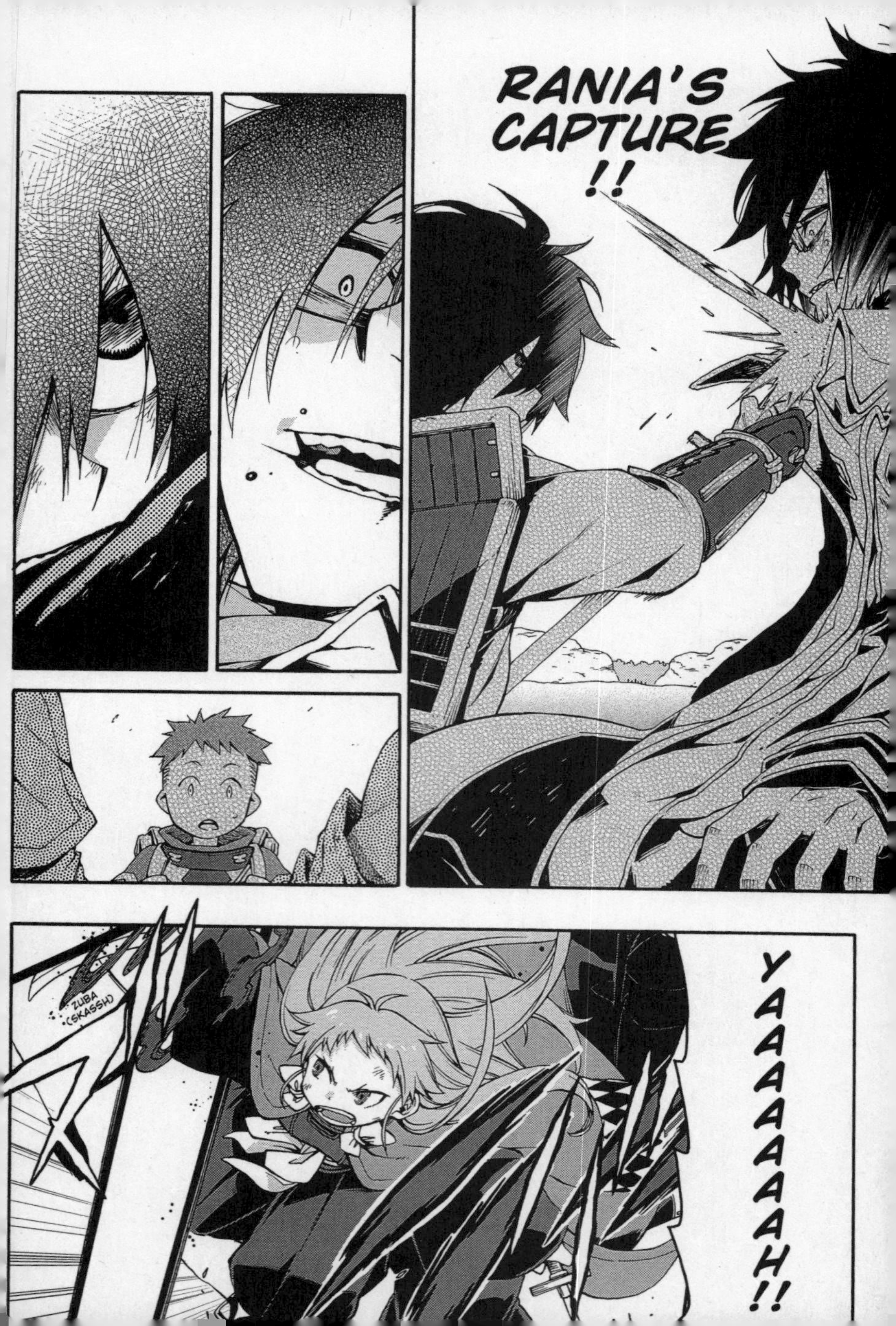
RANIA'S CAPTURE !!
YAAAAAAAAAH!!
ZUBA (SKASSH)

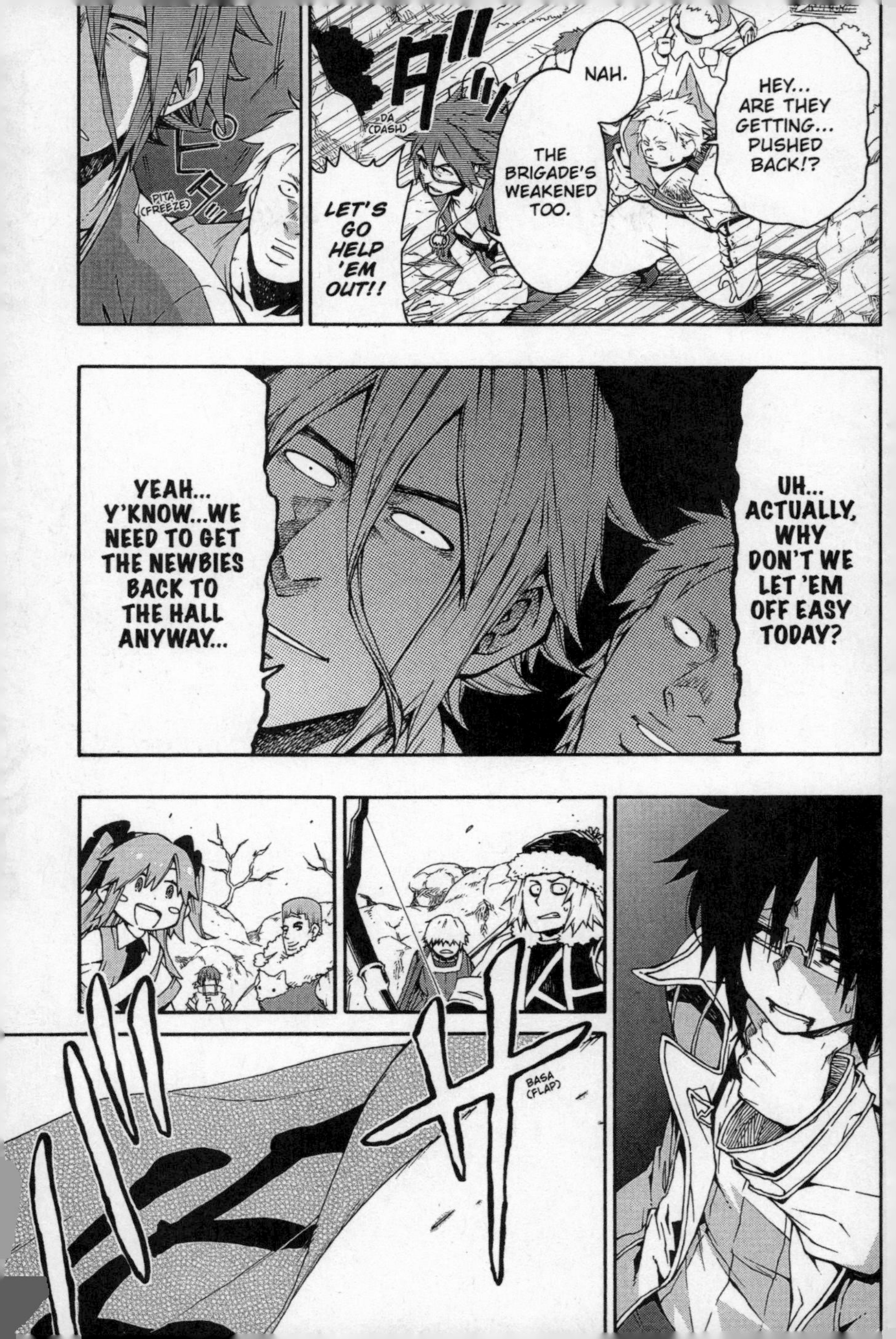
HEY... ARE THEY GETTING... PUSHED BACK!?
NAH.
THE BRIGADE'S WEAKENED TOO.
DA (DASH)
LET'S GO HELP 'EM OUT!!
PITA (FREEZE)
UH... ACTUALLY, WHY DON'T WE LET 'EM OFF EASY TODAY?
YEAH... Y'KNOW...WE NEED TO GET THE NEWBIES BACK TO THE HALL ANYWAY...
BASA (FLAP)

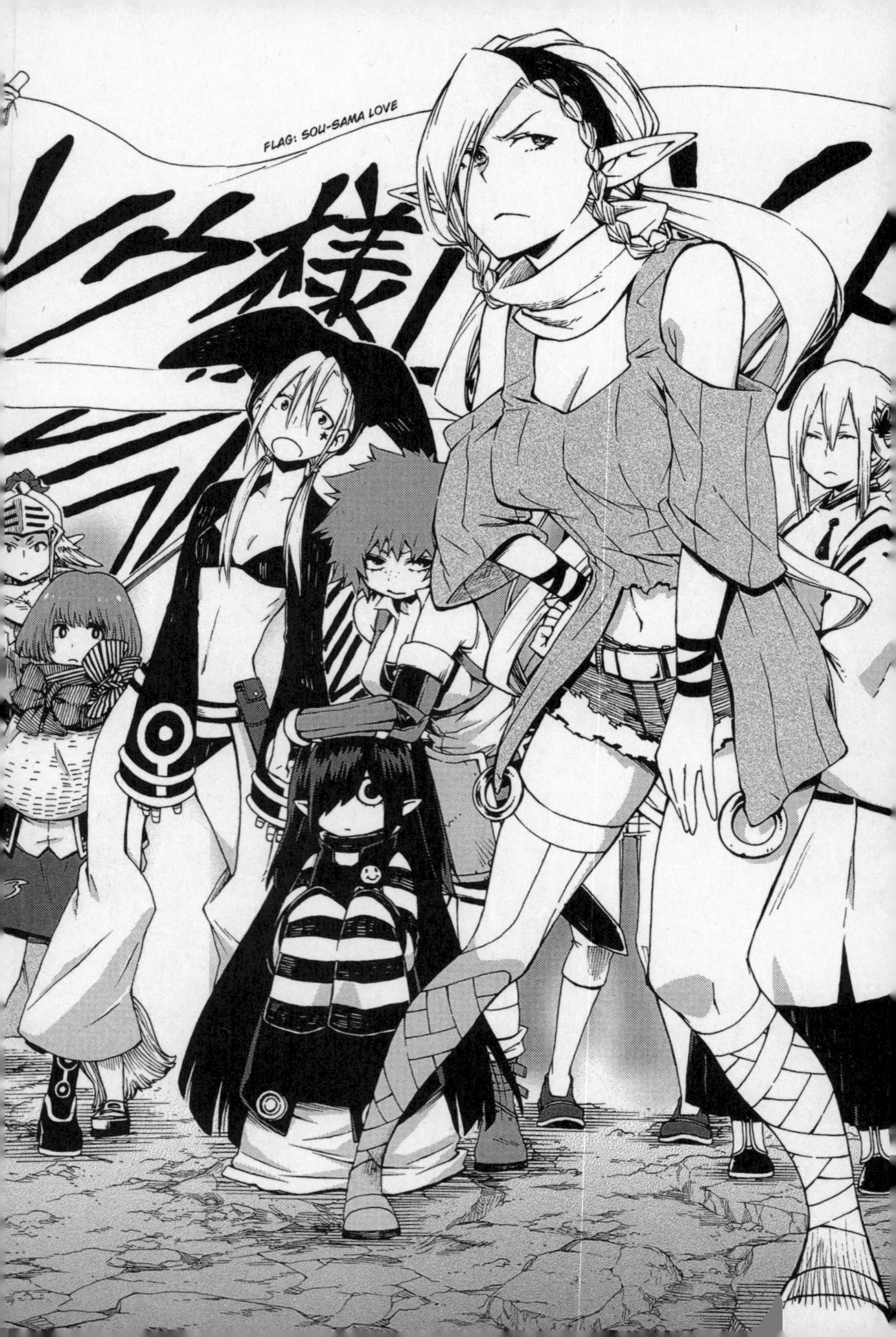
FLAG: SOU-SAMA LOVE
様

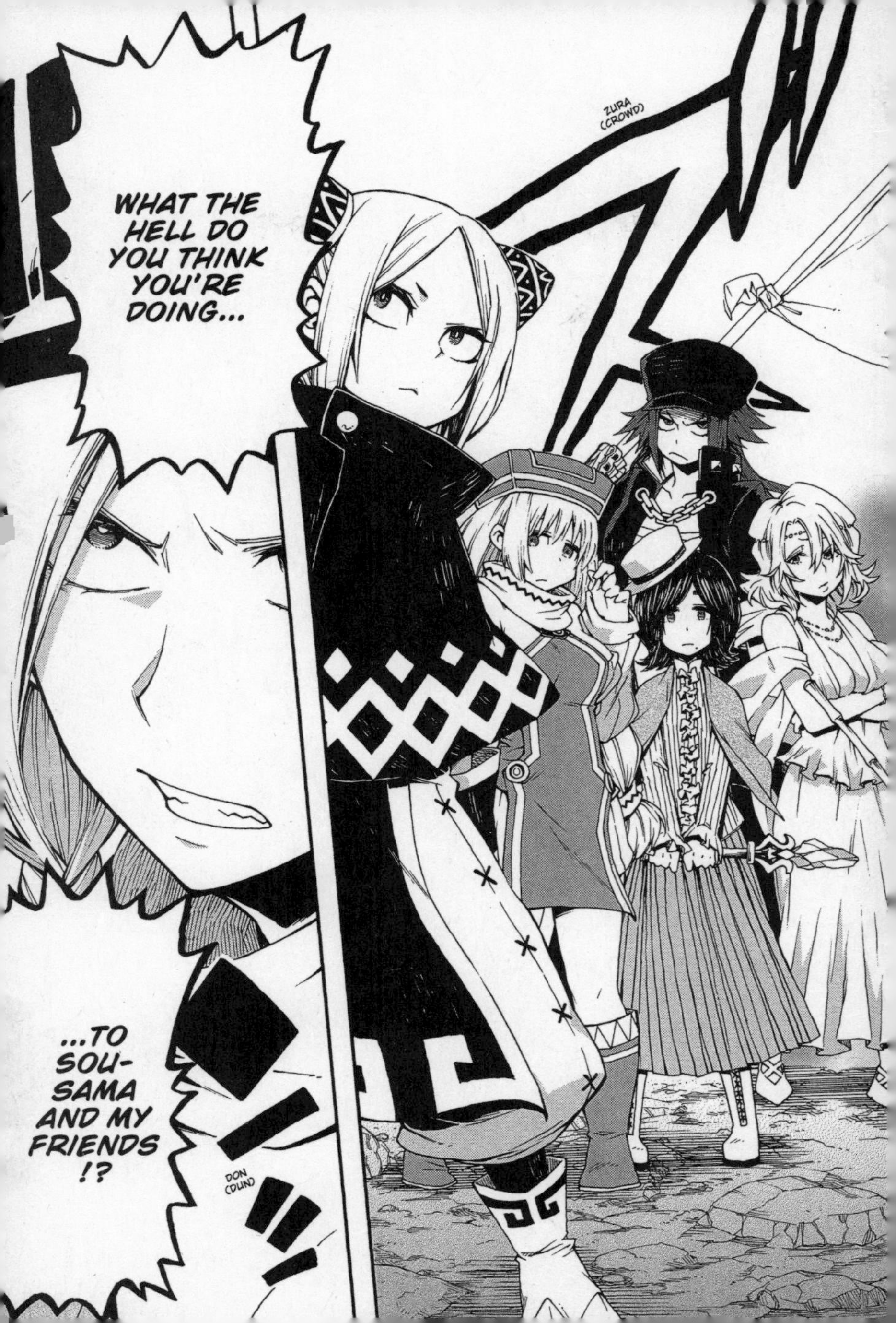
ZURA (CROWD)
WHAT THE HELL DO YOU THINK YOU'RE DOING...
...TO SOU-SAMA AND MY FRIENDS !?
DON (DUN)

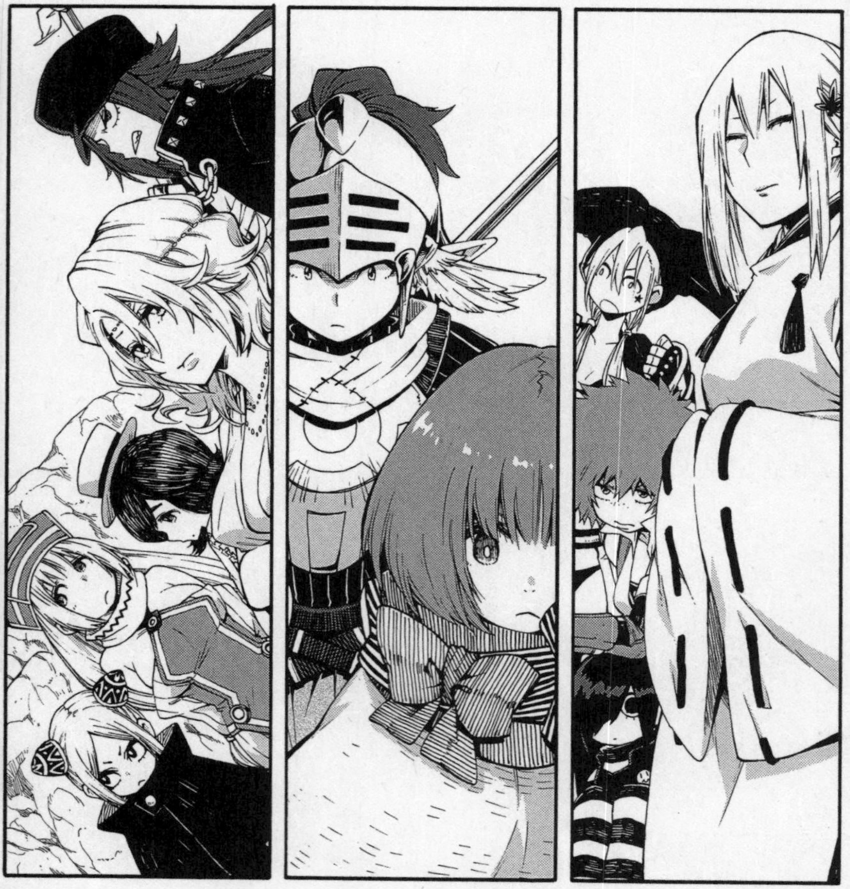

CHAPTER : 15 FRIENDS

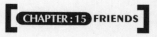

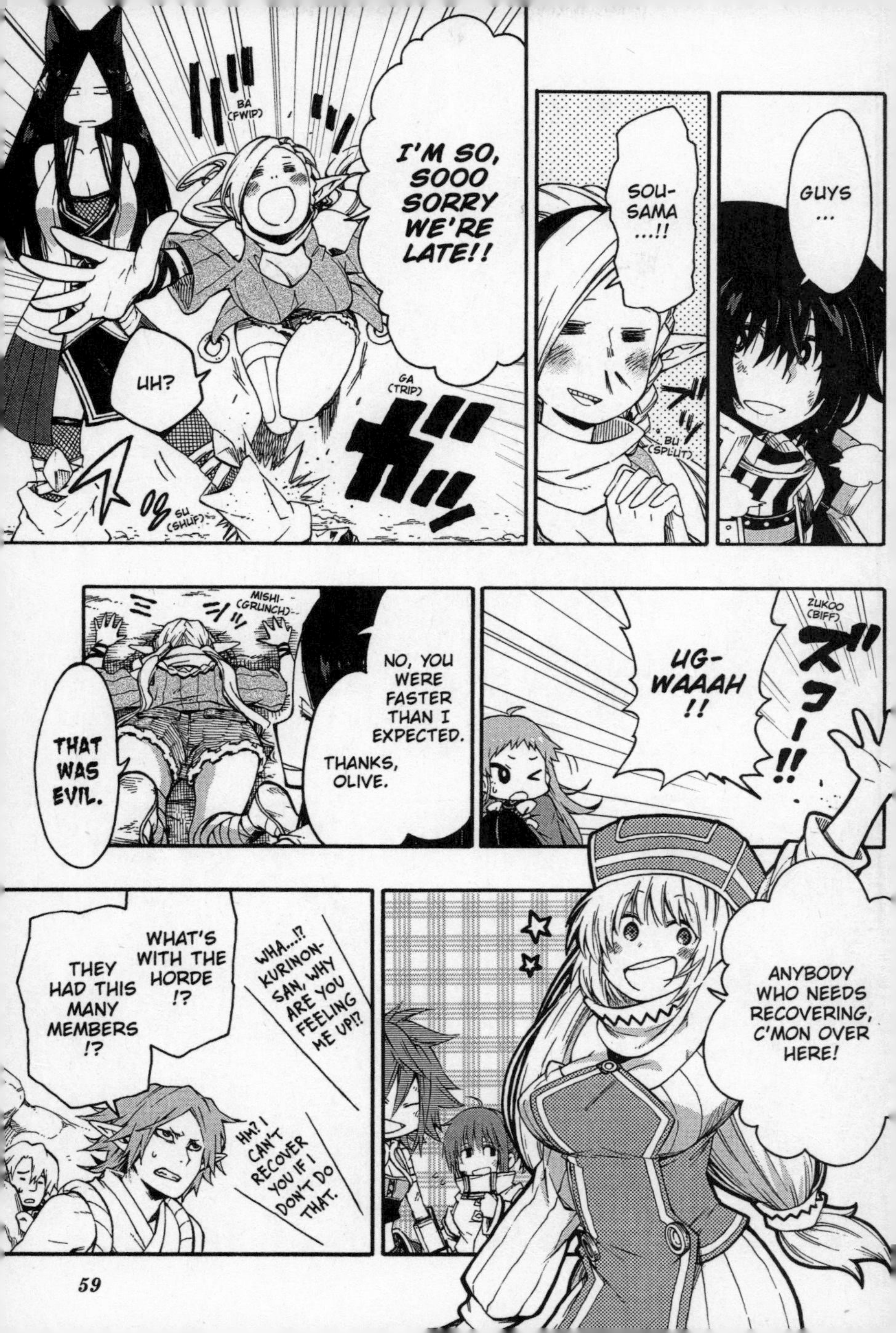
GUYS ...
SOU-SAMA ...!!
BU (SPLUT)
I'M SO, SOOO SORRY WE'RE LATE!!
BA (FWIP)
GA (TRIP)
UH?
SU (SHUF)
ZUKOO (BIFF)
UG-WAAAH!!
NO, YOU WERE FASTER THAN I EXPECTED.
THANKS, OLIVE.
MISHI- (GRUNCH)
THAT WAS EVIL.
ANYBODY WHO NEEDS RECOVERING, C'MON OVER HERE!
WHAT'S WITH THE HORDE!?
THEY HAD THIS MANY MEMBERS!?
WHA...!? KURINON-SAN, WHY ARE YOU FEELING ME UP!?
HM? I CAN'T RECOVER YOU IF I DON'T DO THAT.

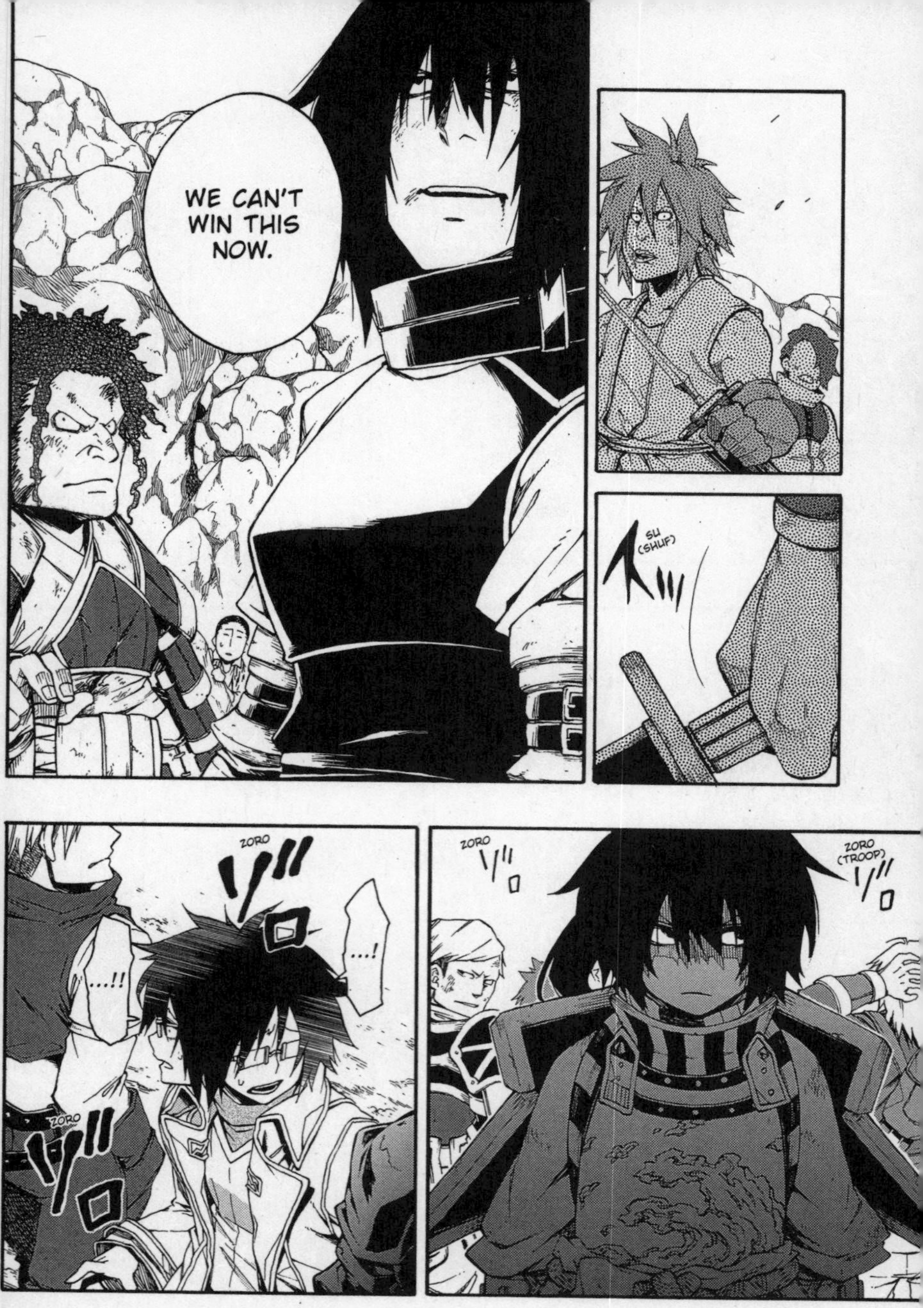
SU (SHUF)
WE CAN'T WIN THIS NOW.
ZORO (TROOP)
ZORO
ZORO
...!
...!!
ZORO

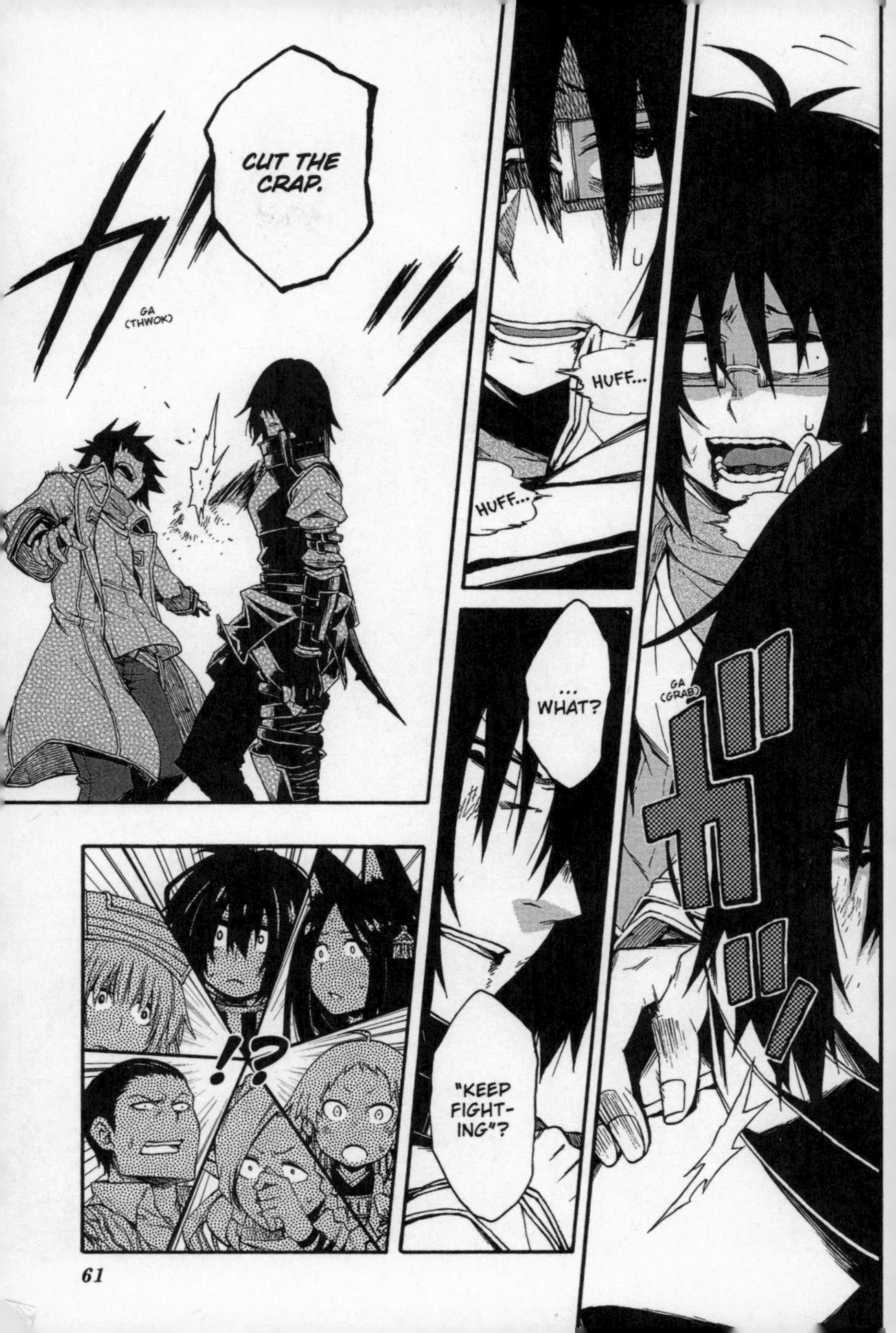
GA (GRAB)
HUFF...
HUFF...
... WHAT?
"KEEP FIGHT-ING"?
CUT THE CRAP.
GA (THWOK)
!?

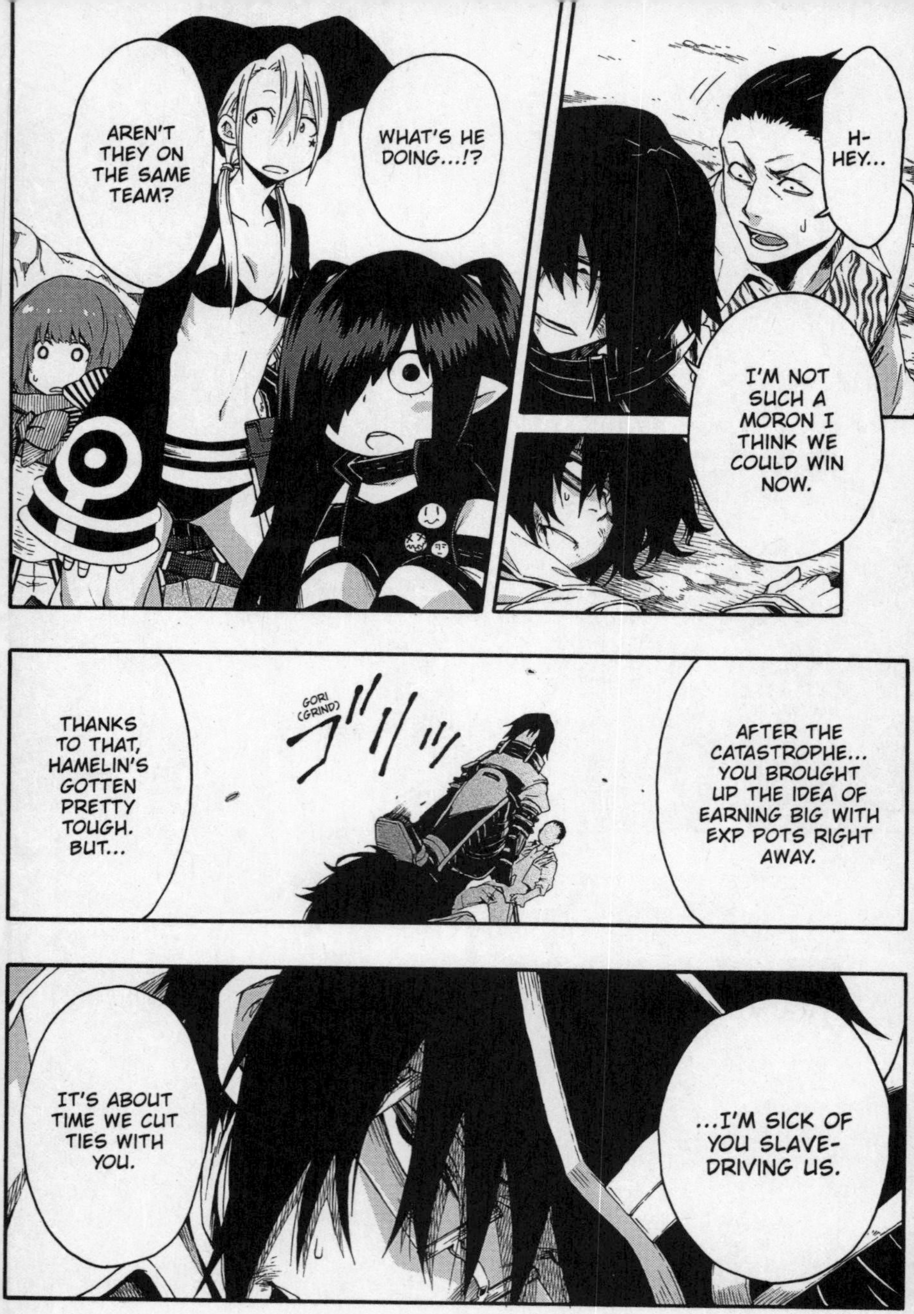
H- HEY...
I'M NOT SUCH A MORON I THINK WE COULD WIN NOW.
WHAT'S HE DOING...!?
AREN'T THEY ON THE SAME TEAM?
AFTER THE CATASTROPHE... YOU BROUGHT UP THE IDEA OF EARNING BIG WITH EXP POTS RIGHT AWAY.
GORI (GRIND)
THANKS TO THAT, HAMELIN'S GOTTEN PRETTY TOUGH. BUT...
...I'M SICK OF YOU SLAVE-DRIVING US.
IT'S ABOUT TIME WE CUT TIES WITH YOU.

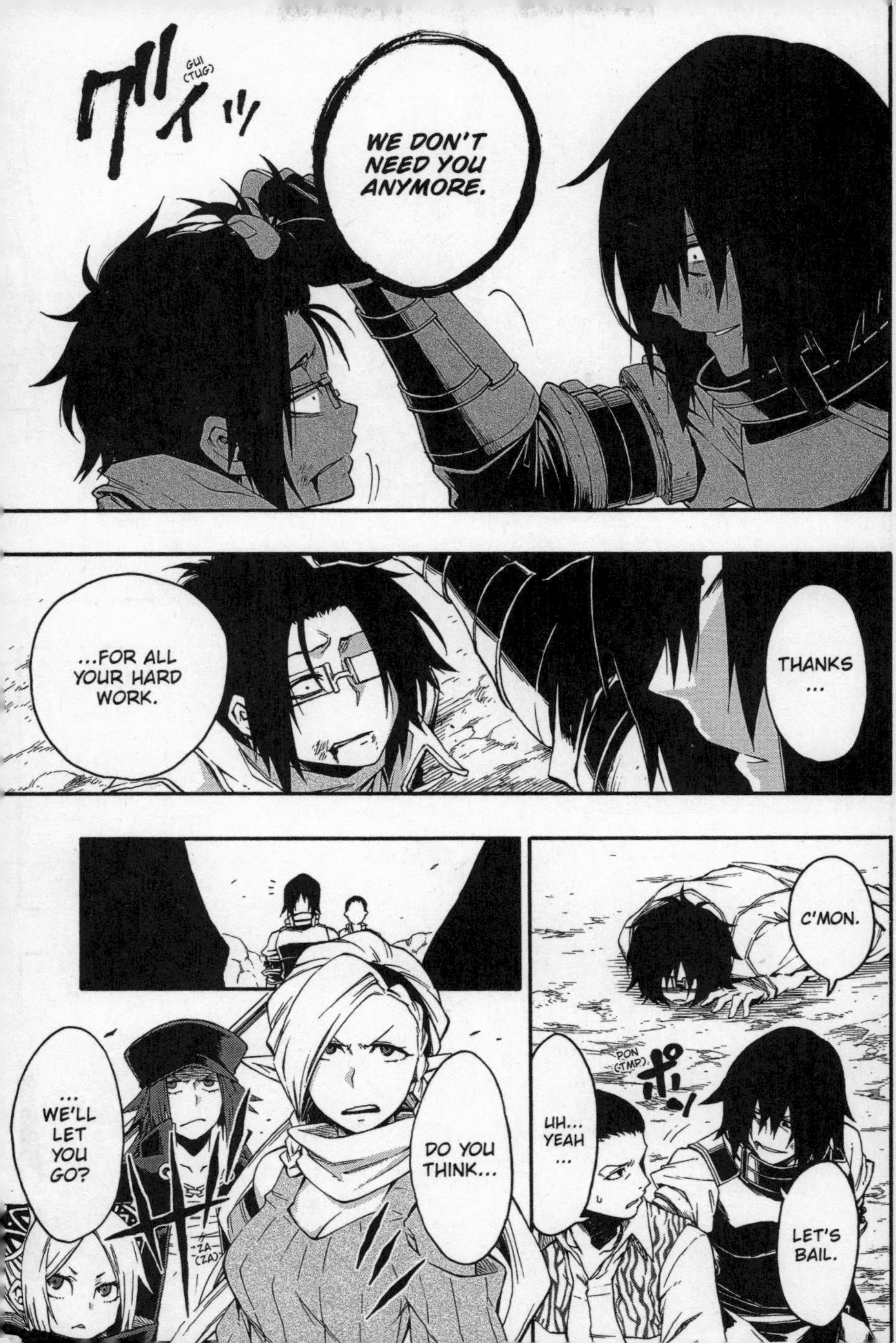
グイッ
GUI (TUG)
WE DON'T NEED YOU ANYMORE.
THANKS ...
...FOR ALL YOUR HARD WORK.
C'MON.
PON (TMP)
LET'S BAIL.
UH... YEAH ...
DO YOU THINK...
... WE'LL LET YOU GO?
ZA (ZA)

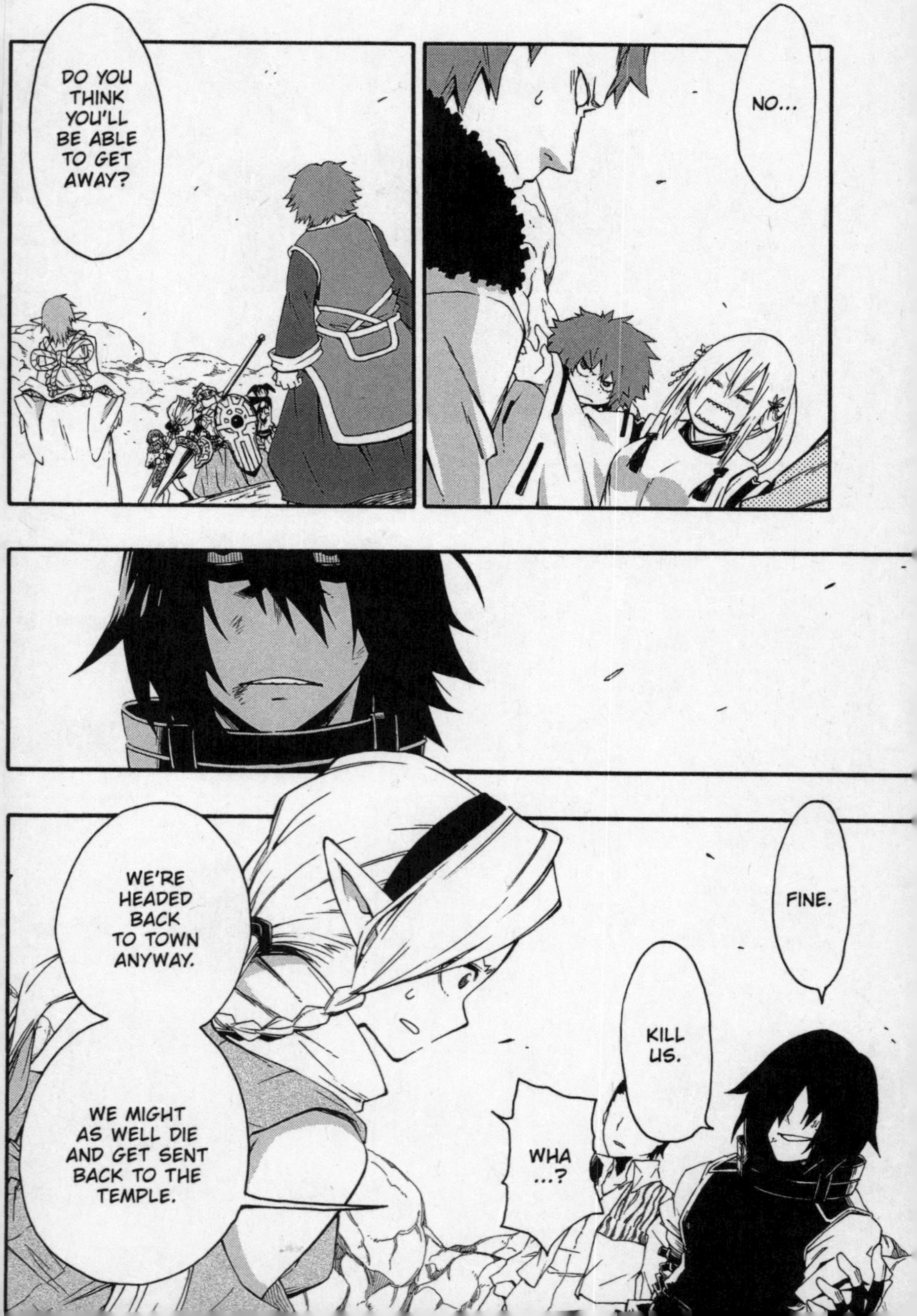
NO...
DO YOU THINK YOU'LL BE ABLE TO GET AWAY?
FINE.
KILL US.
WHA ...?
WE'RE HEADED BACK TO TOWN ANYWAY.
WE MIGHT AS WELL DIE AND GET SENT BACK TO THE TEMPLE.

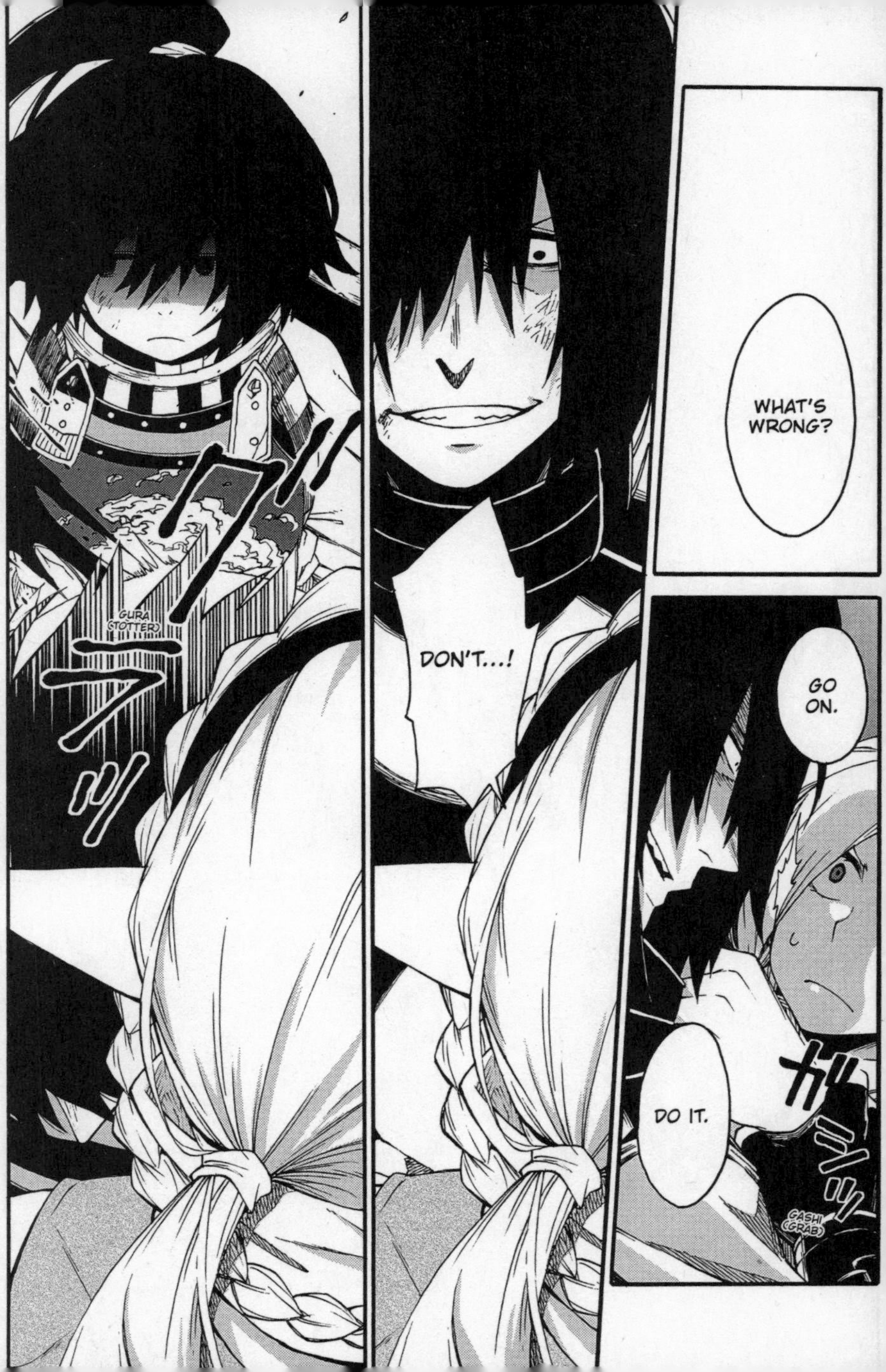
WHAT'S WRONG?
GO ON.
DO IT.
GASHI (GRAB)
DON'T...!
GURA (STOTTER)

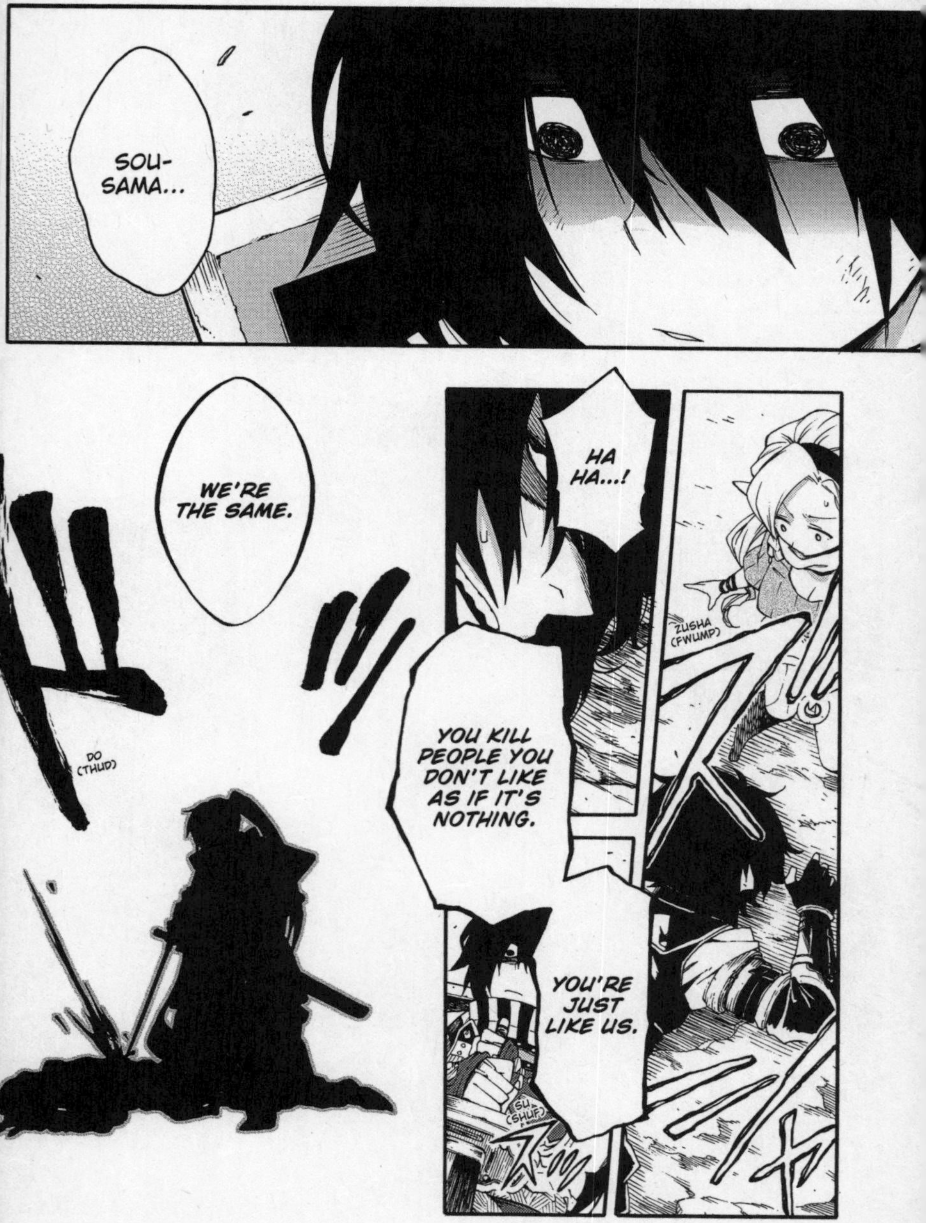
SOU-SAMA...
ZUSHA (FWUMP)
HA HA...!
YOU KILL PEOPLE YOU DON'T LIKE AS IF IT'S NOTHING.
YOU'RE JUST LIKE US.
SU (SHUF)
WE'RE THE SAME.
DO (THUD)

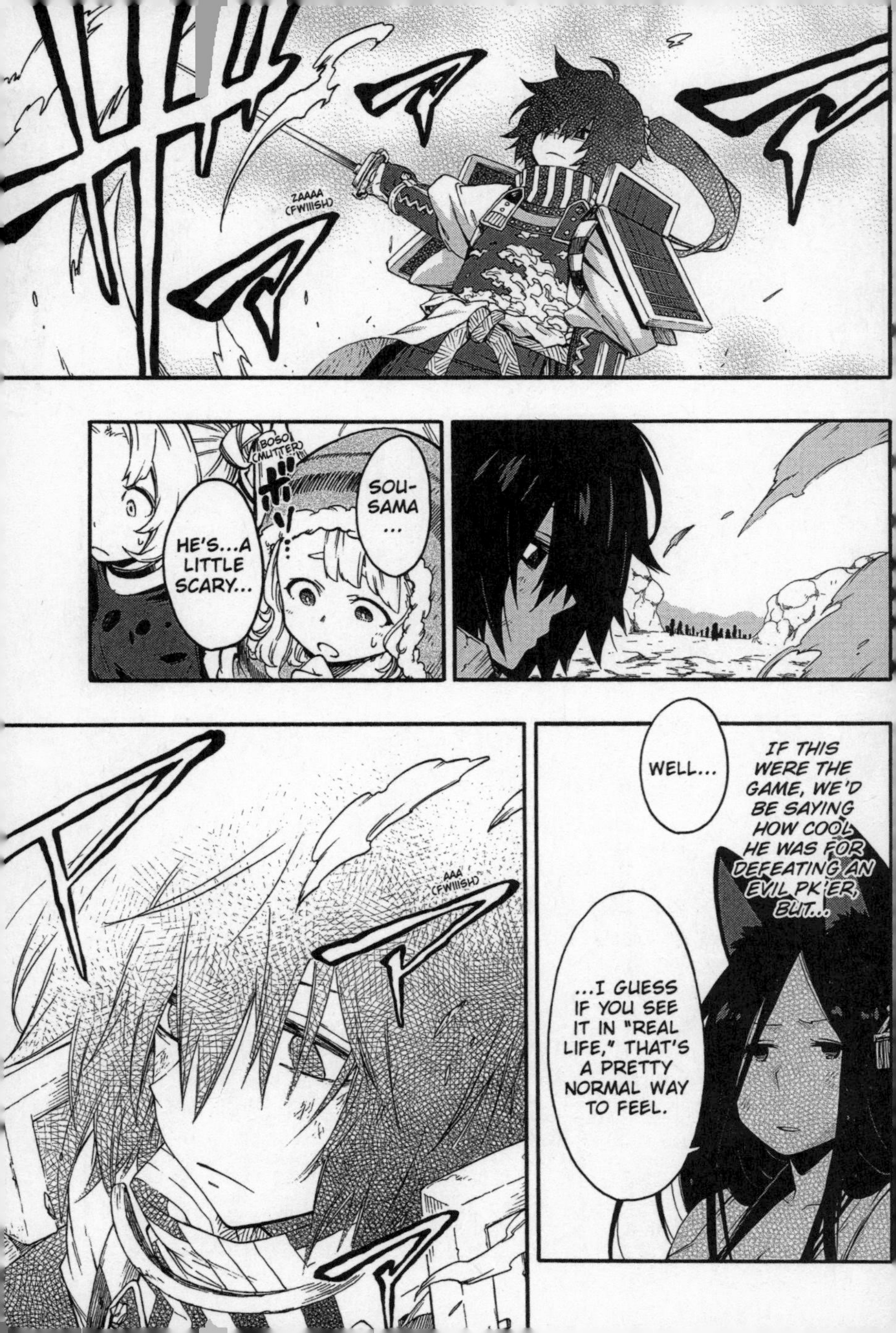
ZAAAA (FWIIISH)
SOU-SAMA...
BOSO (MUTTER)
HE'S...A LITTLE SCARY...
IF THIS WERE THE GAME, WE'D BE SAYING HOW COOL HE WAS FOR DEFEATING AN EVIL PK'ER, BUT...
WELL...
...I GUESS IF YOU SEE IT IN "REAL LIFE," THAT'S A PRETTY NORMAL WAY TO FEEL.
AAA (FWIIISH)

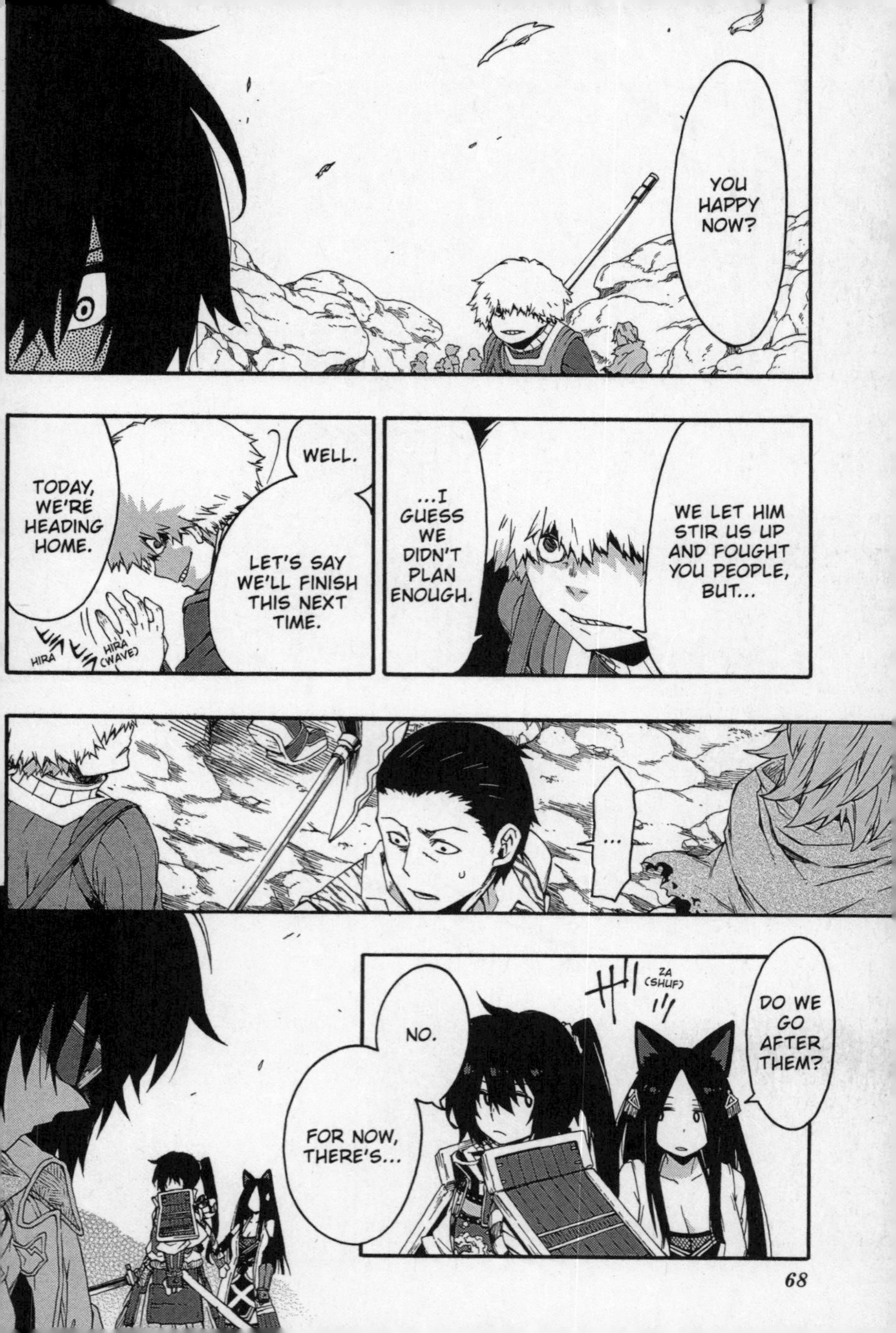
YOU HAPPY NOW?
WE LET HIM STIR US UP AND FOUGHT YOU PEOPLE, BUT...
...I GUESS WE DIDN'T PLAN ENOUGH.
WELL.
LET'S SAY WE'LL FINISH THIS NEXT TIME.
TODAY, WE'RE HEADING HOME.
HIRA HIRA (WAVE)
...
ZA (SHUF)
DO WE GO AFTER THEM?
NO.
FOR NOW, THERE'S...

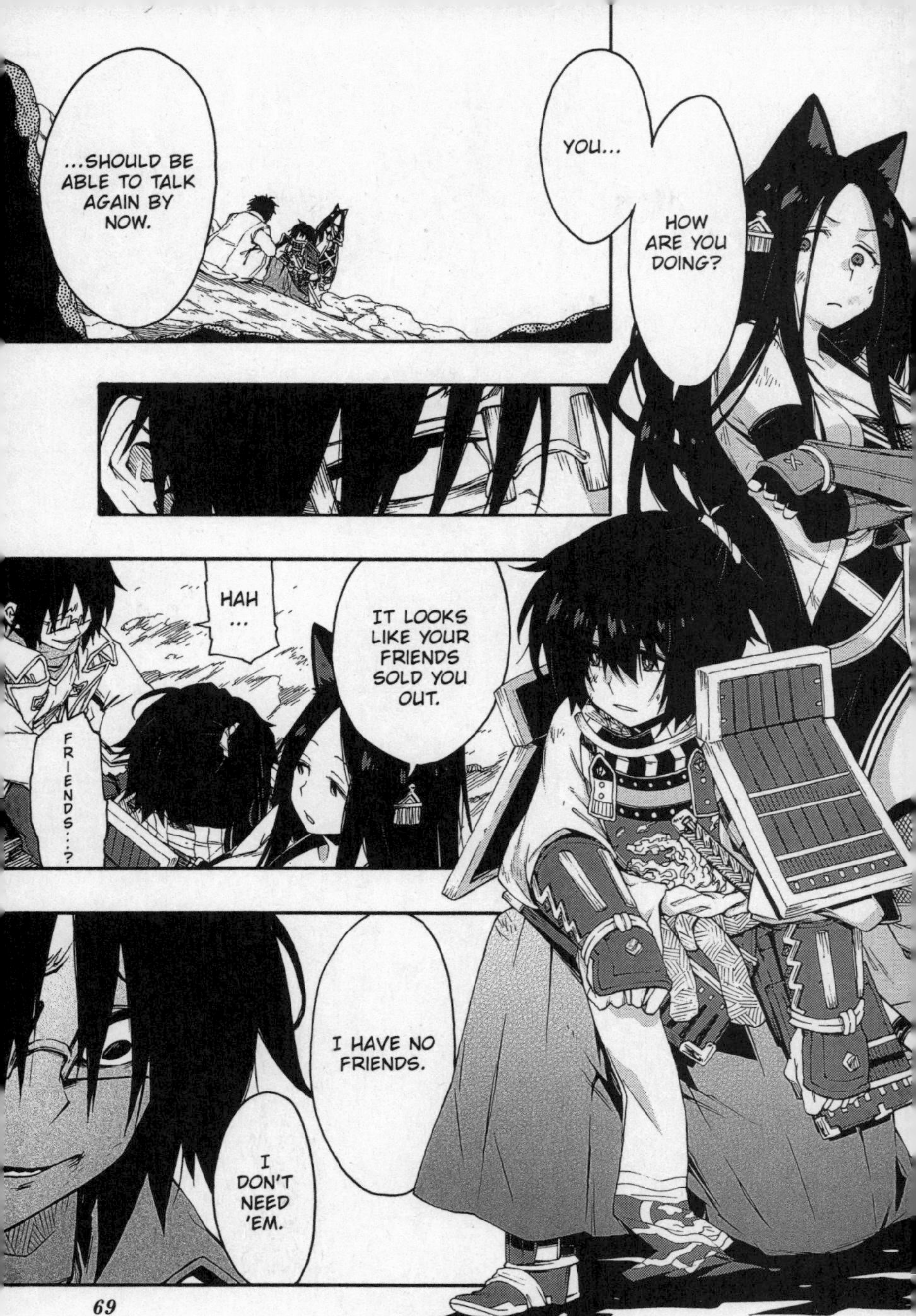
YOU...
HOW ARE YOU DOING?
...SHOULD BE ABLE TO TALK AGAIN BY NOW.
IT LOOKS LIKE YOUR FRIENDS SOLD YOU OUT.
HAH ...
FRIENDS...?
I HAVE NO FRIENDS.
I DON'T NEED 'EM.

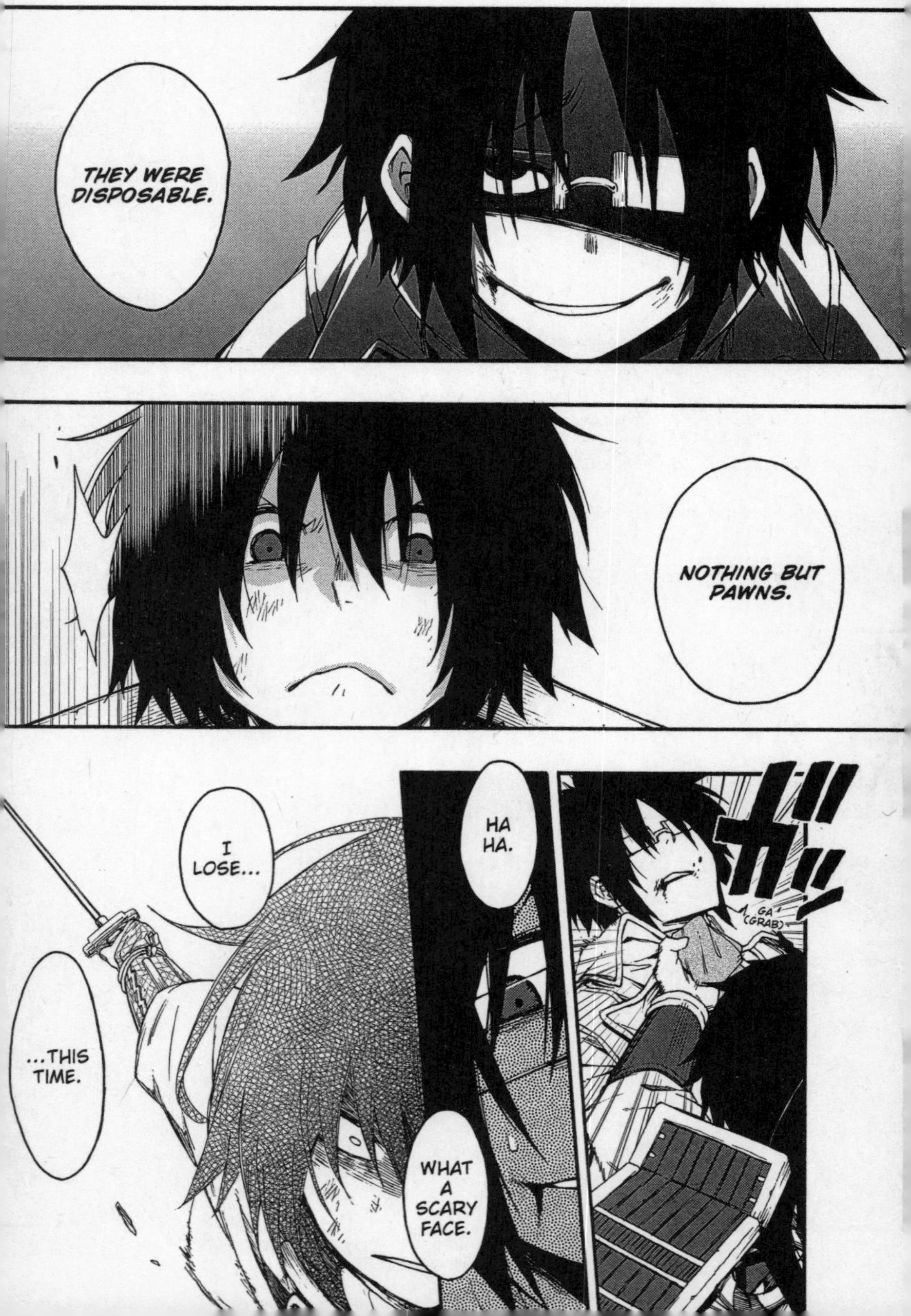
THEY WERE DISPOSABLE.
NOTHING BUT PAWNS.
HA HA.
ガッ
GA (GRAB)
WHAT A SCARY FACE.
I LOSE...
...THIS TIME.

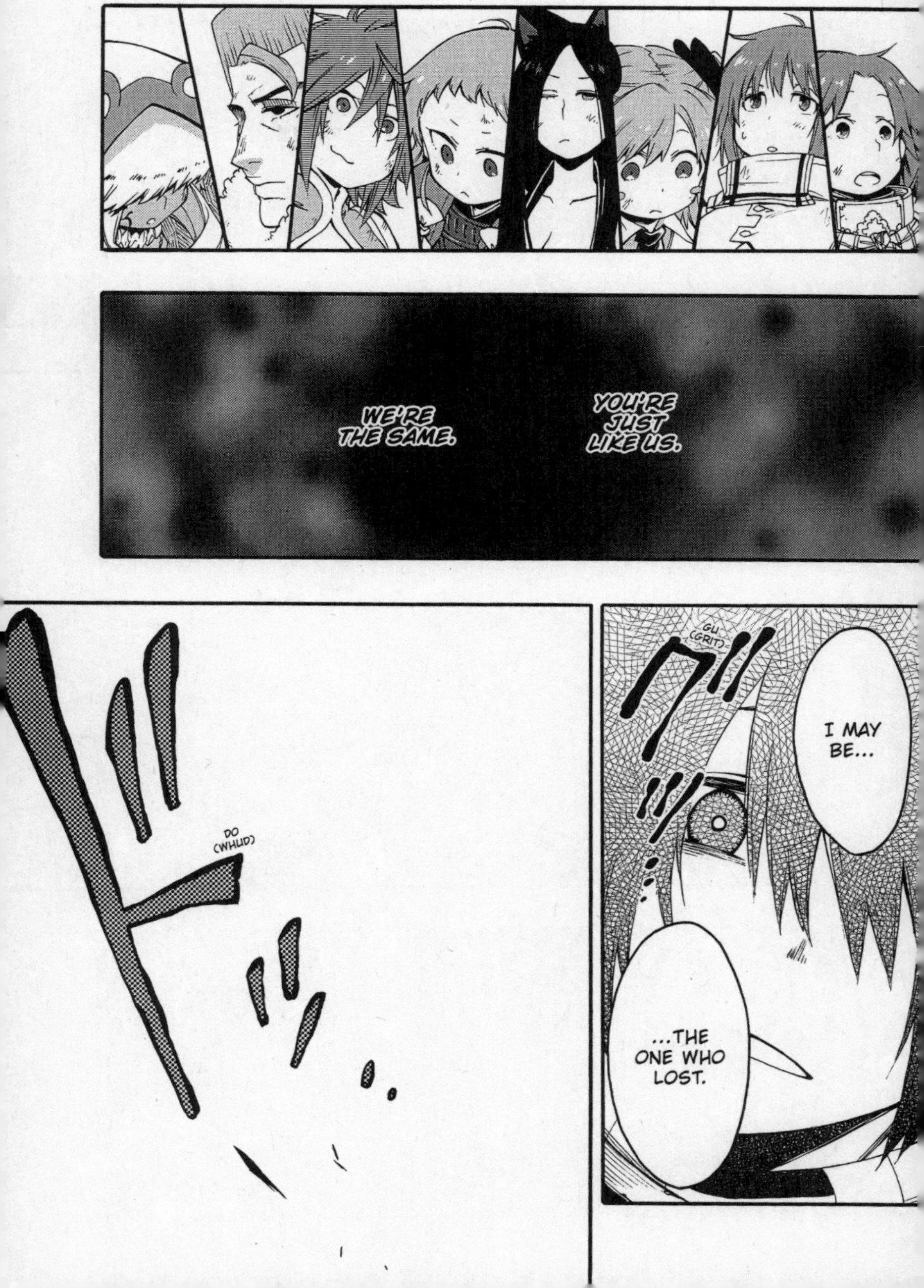
YOU'RE JUST LIKE US.
WE'RE THE SAME.
GU (GRIT)
I MAY BE...
...THE ONE WHO LOST.
DO (WHUD)

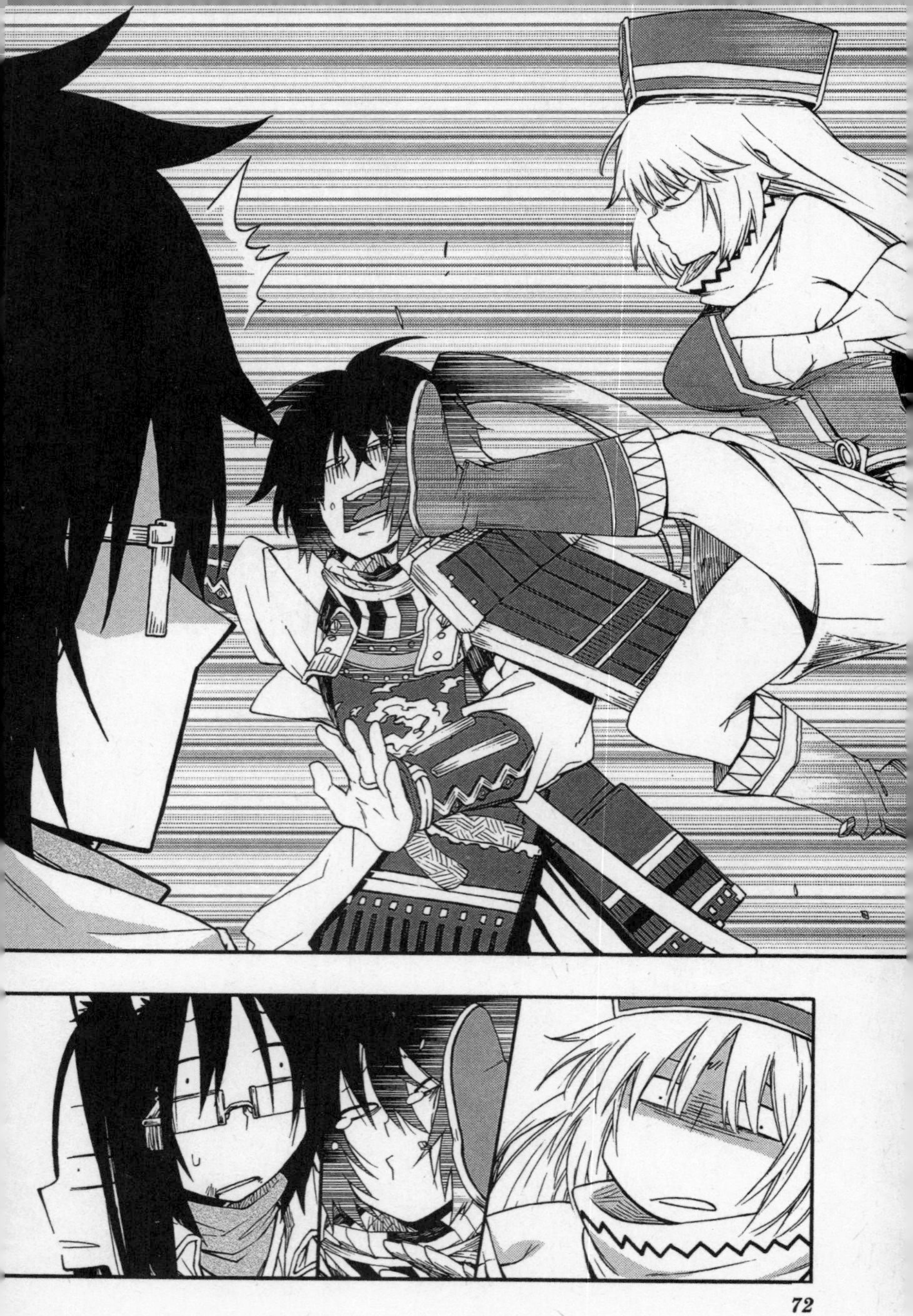

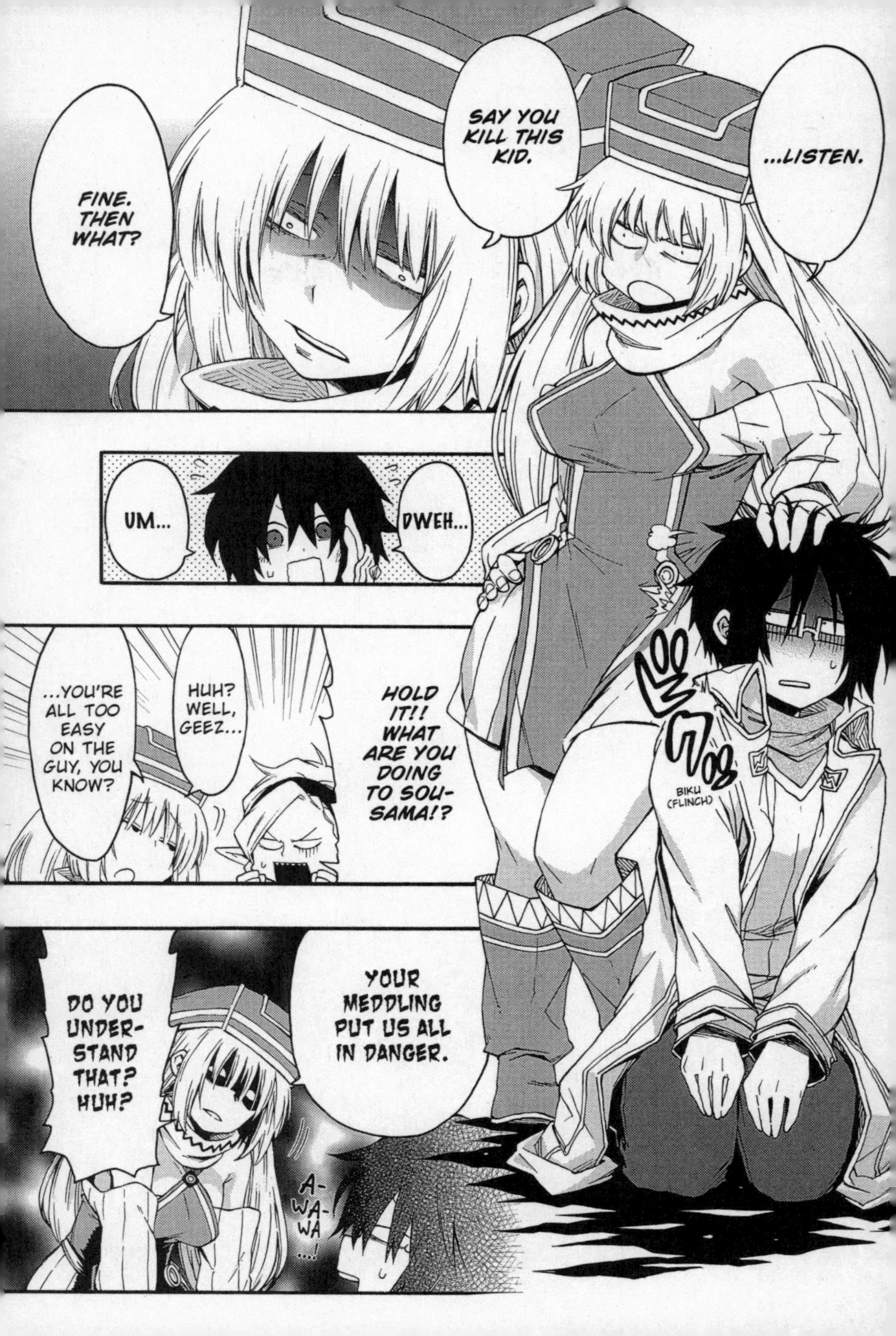
...LISTEN.
SAY YOU KILL THIS KID.
FINE. THEN WHAT?
BIKU (FLINCH)
DWEH...
UM...
HOLD IT!! WHAT ARE YOU DOING TO SOU-SAMA!?
HUH? WELL, GEEZ...
...YOU'RE ALL TOO EASY ON THE GUY, YOU KNOW?
YOUR MEDDLING PUT US ALL IN DANGER.
DO YOU UNDER-STAND THAT? HUH?
A-WA-WA...!

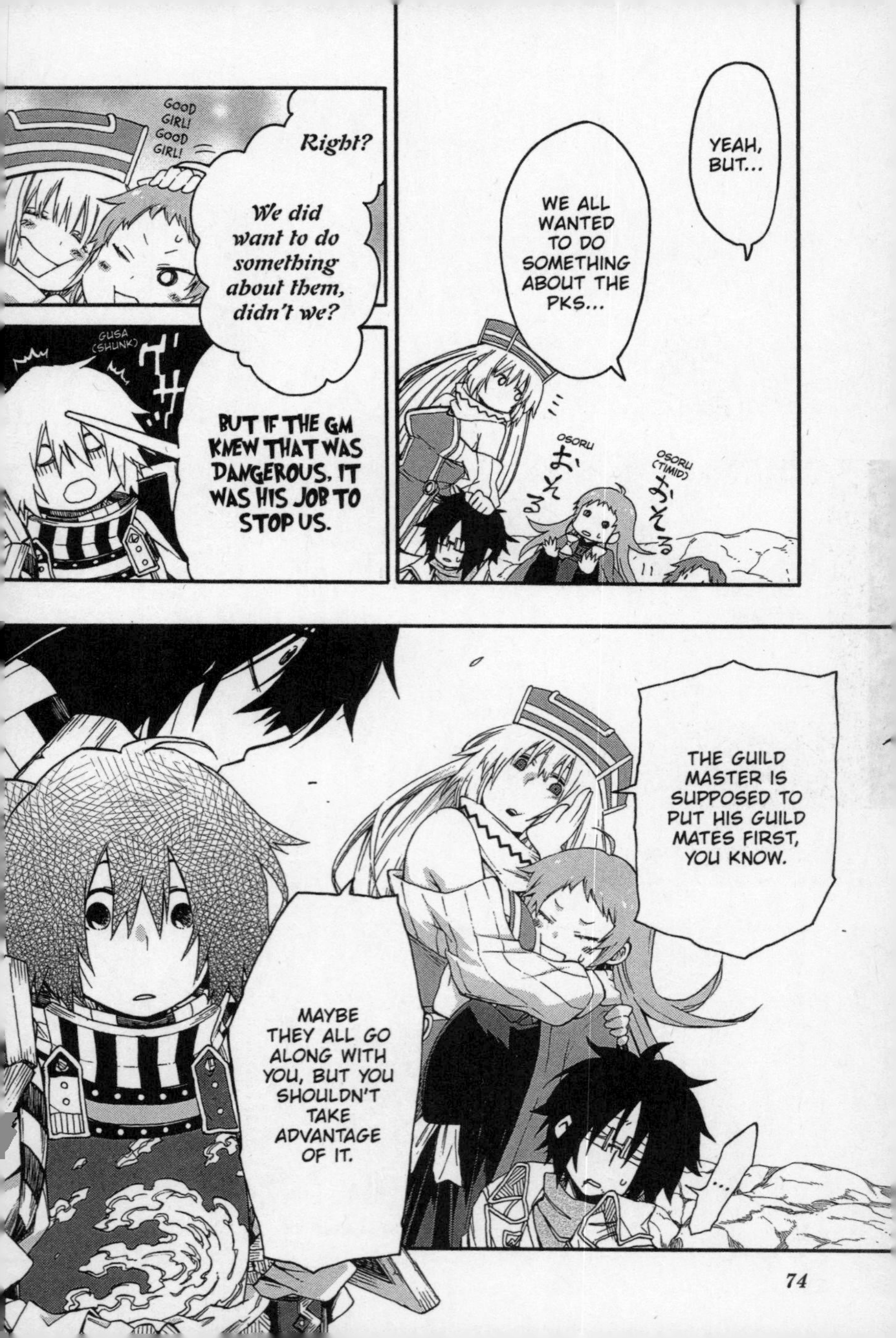
YEAH, BUT...
WE ALL WANTED TO DO SOMETHING ABOUT THE PKS...
OSORU おそる
OSORU (TIMID) おそる
GOOD GIRL! GOOD GIRL!
Right?
We did want to do something about them, didn't we?
GUSA (SHUNK)
BUT IF THE GM KNEW THAT WAS DANGEROUS, IT WAS HIS JOB TO STOP US.
THE GUILD MASTER IS SUPPOSED TO PUT HIS GUILD MATES FIRST, YOU KNOW.
MAYBE THEY ALL GO ALONG WITH YOU, BUT YOU SHOULDN'T TAKE ADVANTAGE OF IT.
...

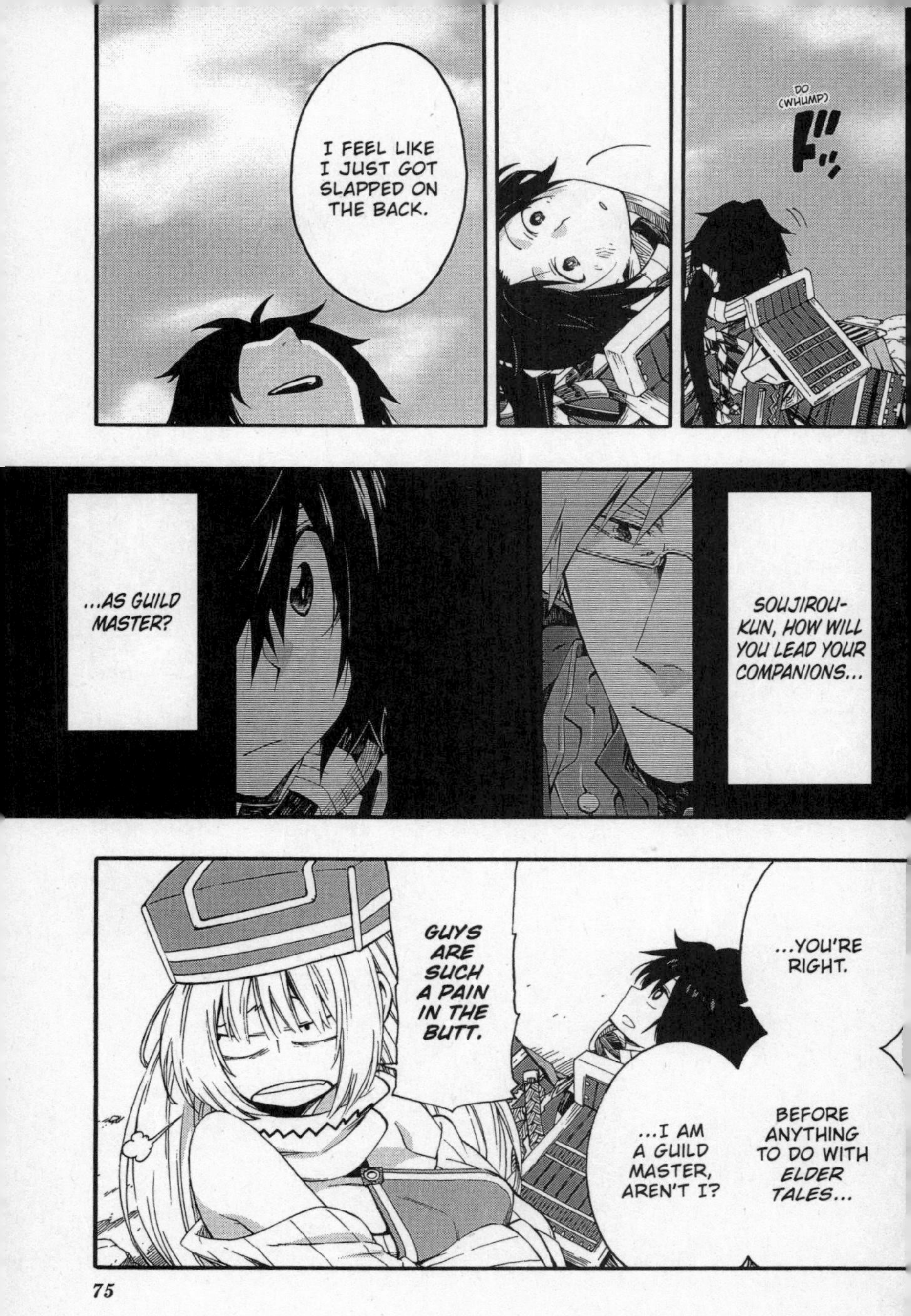
DO (WHUMP)
I FEEL LIKE I JUST GOT SLAPPED ON THE BACK.
SOUJIROU-KUN, HOW WILL YOU LEAD YOUR COMPANIONS...
...AS GUILD MASTER?
...YOU'RE RIGHT.
BEFORE ANYTHING TO DO WITH *ELDER TALES*...
...I AM A GUILD MASTER, AREN'T I?
GUYS ARE SUCH A PAIN IN THE BUTT.

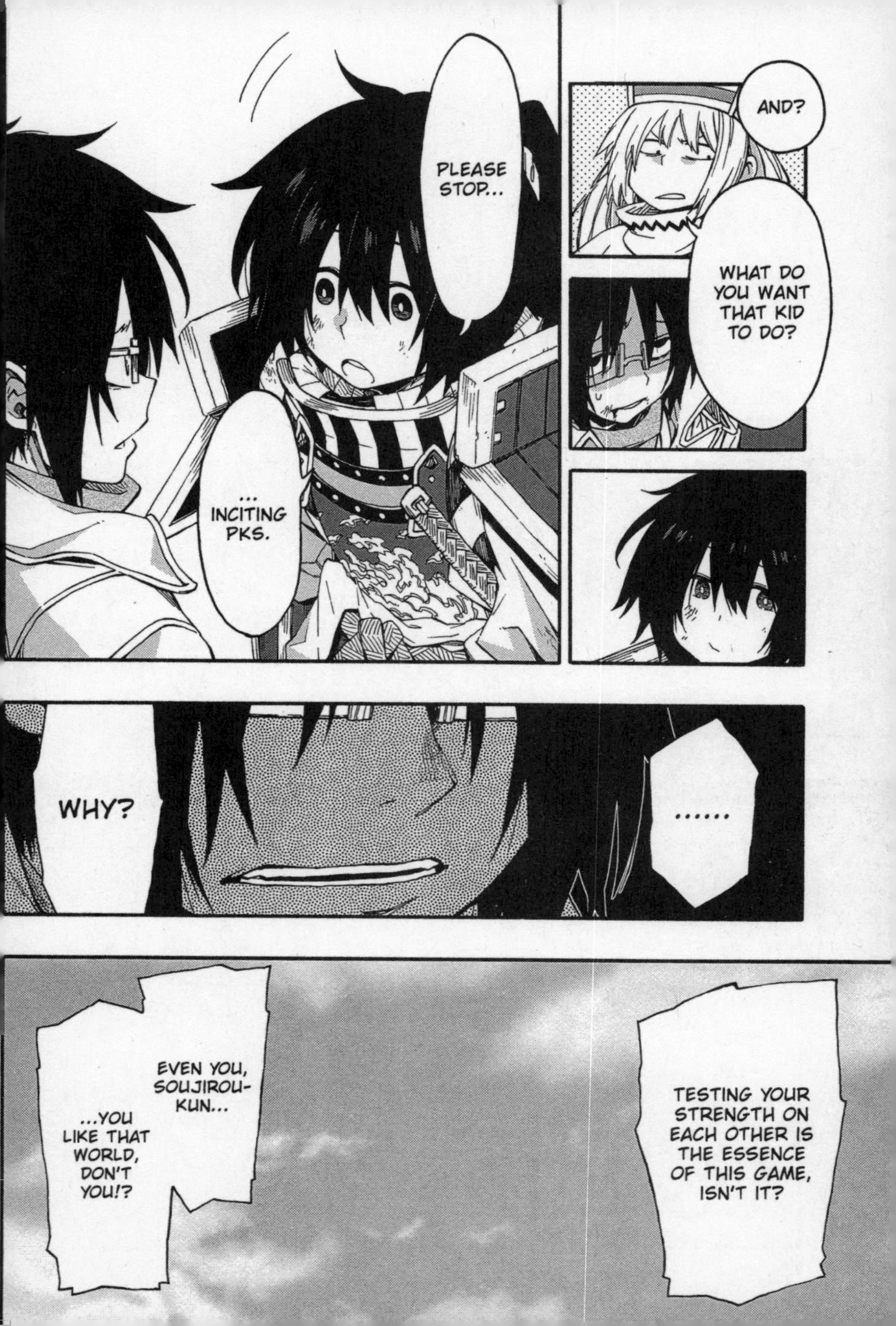
AND?
WHAT DO YOU WANT THAT KID TO DO?
PLEASE STOP...
...INCITING PKS.
......
WHY?
TESTING YOUR STRENGTH ON EACH OTHER IS THE ESSENCE OF THIS GAME, ISN'T IT?
EVEN YOU, SOUJIROU-KUN...
...YOU LIKE THAT WORLD, DON'T YOU!?

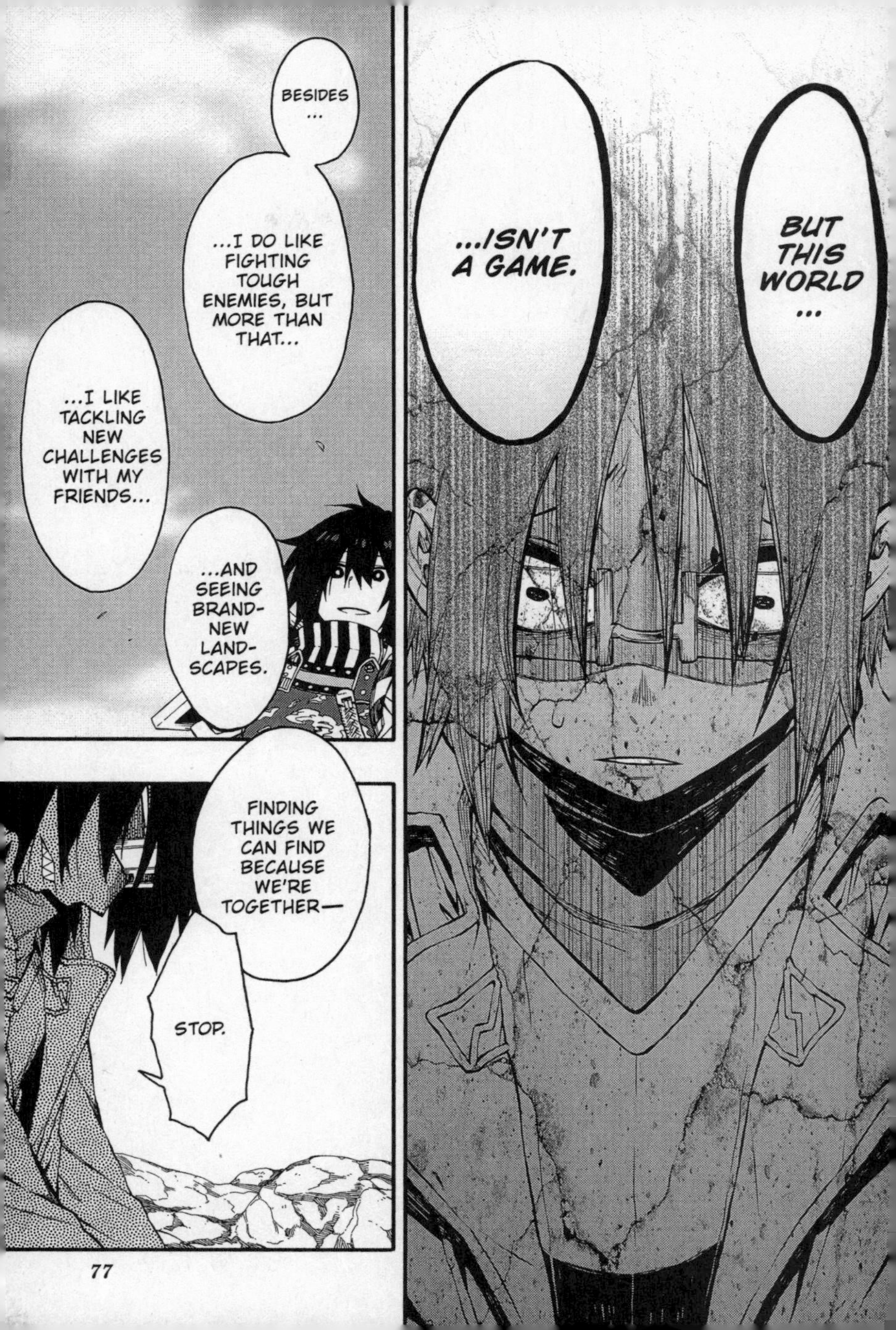
BUT THIS WORLD ...
...ISN'T A GAME.
BESIDES ...
...I DO LIKE FIGHTING TOUGH ENEMIES, BUT MORE THAN THAT...
...I LIKE TACKLING NEW CHALLENGES WITH MY FRIENDS...
...AND SEEING BRAND-NEW LAND-SCAPES.
FINDING THINGS WE CAN FIND BECAUSE WE'RE TOGETHER—
STOP.

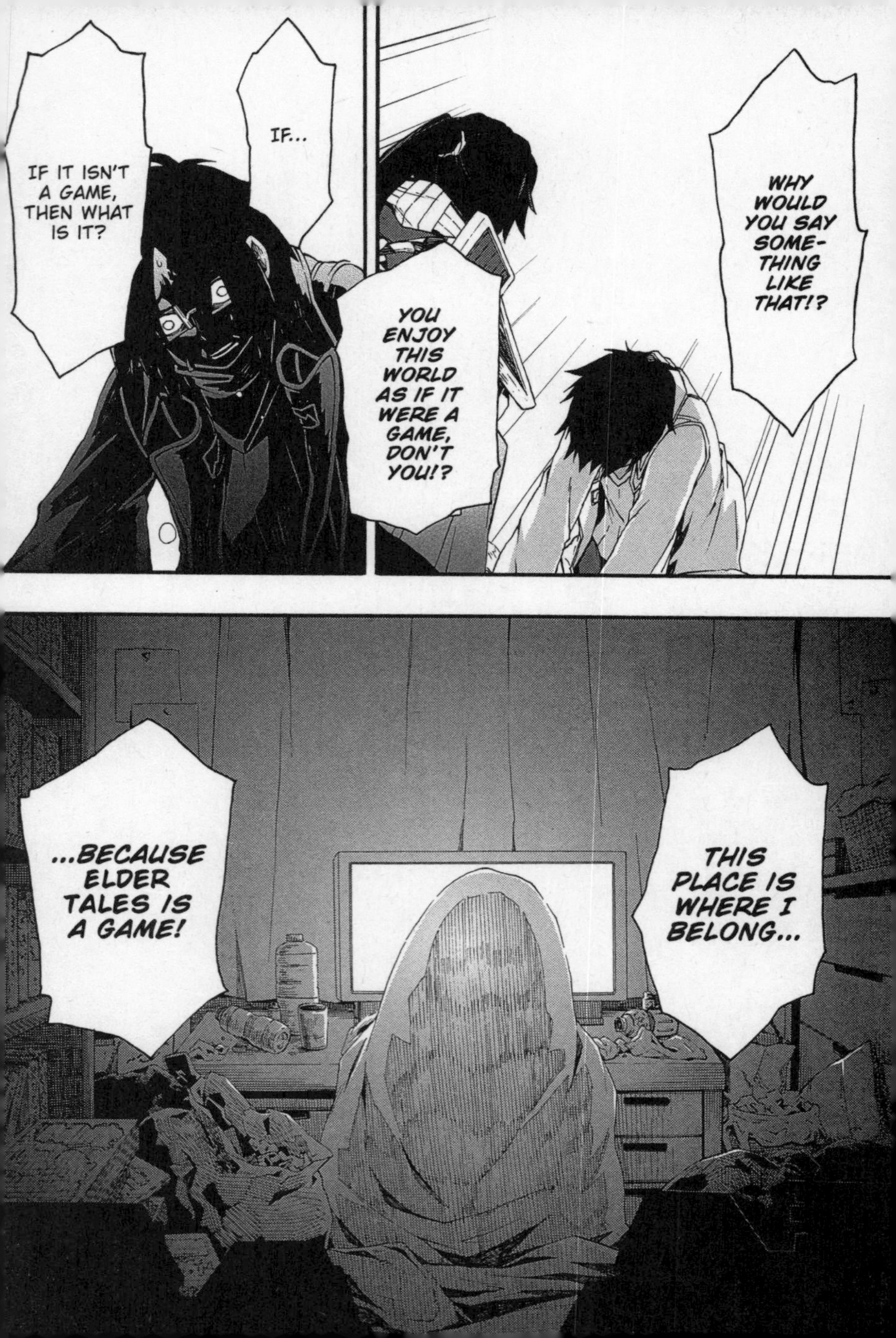
WHY WOULD YOU SAY SOMETHING LIKE THAT!?
YOU ENJOY THIS WORLD AS IF IT WERE A GAME, DON'T YOU!?
IF...
IF IT ISN'T A GAME, THEN WHAT IS IT?
THIS PLACE IS WHERE I BELONG...
...BECAUSE ELDER TALES IS A GAME!

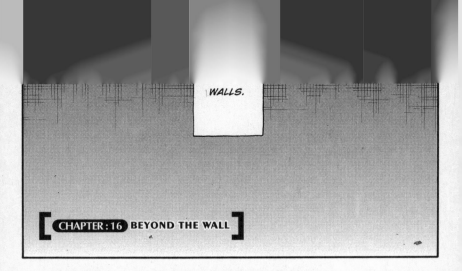

WALLS.
CHAPTER : 16 BEYOND THE WALL
WALLS.
WALLS.
WALLS.
WALLS.
THIS WORL...
...IS DIVIDED BY WALLS.
YOU CAN'T SEE ANYBODY ELSE, BUT...
...IN EX-CHANGE...
...NOBODY CAN SEE YOU HERE.
BUT...

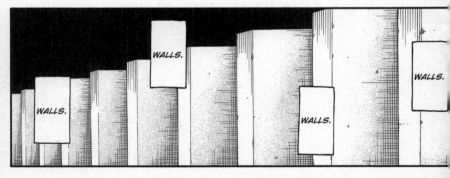

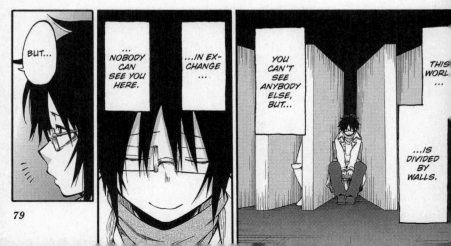

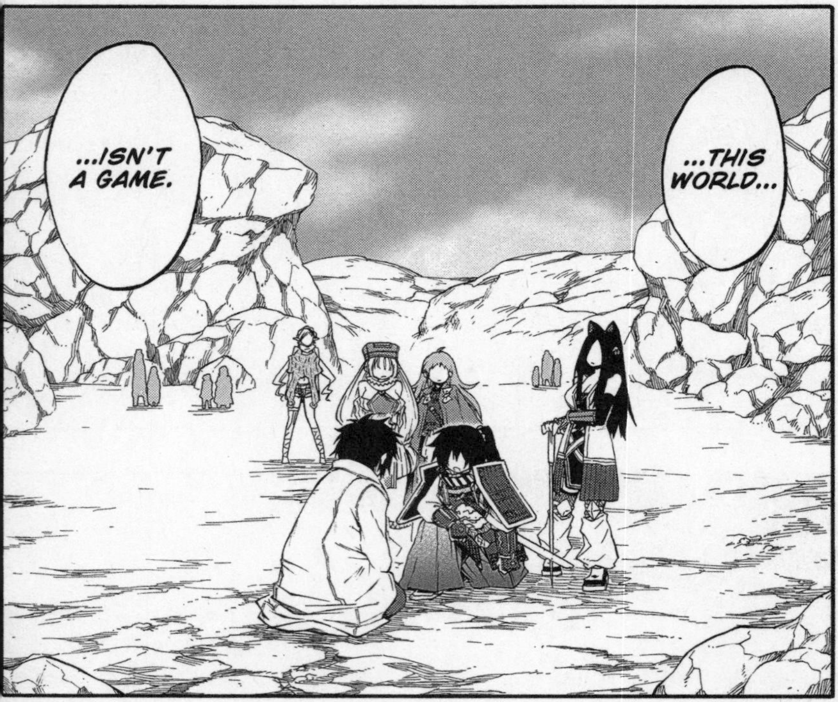
...THIS WORLD...
...ISN'T A GAME.

CHAPTER : 16 BEYOND THE WALL

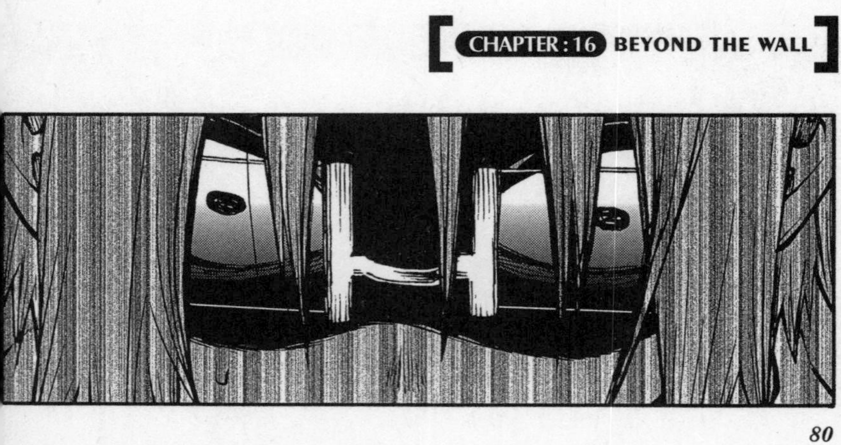

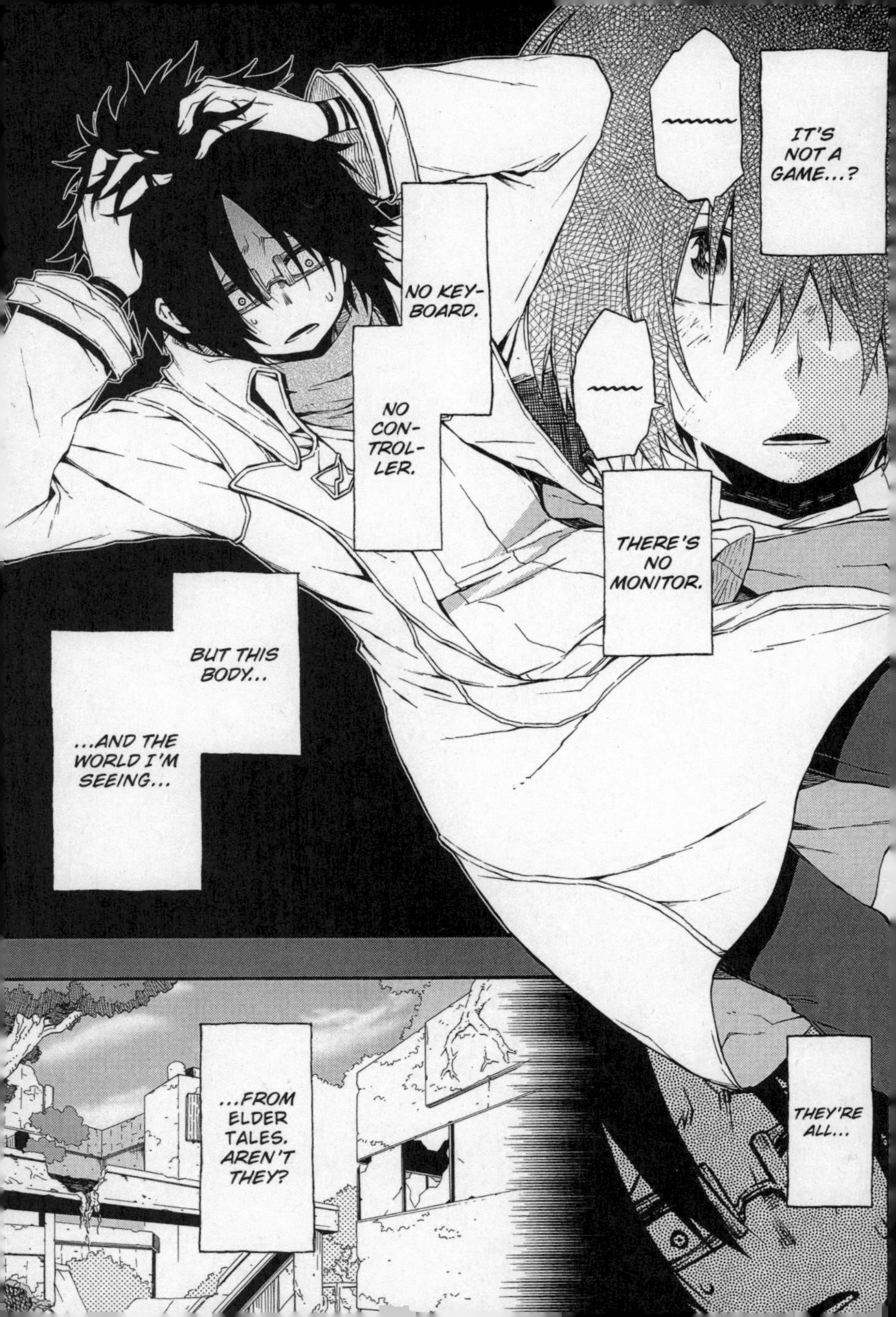
IT'S NOT A GAME...?
THERE'S NO MONITOR.
NO KEY-BOARD.
NO CON-TROL-LER.
BUT THIS BODY...
...AND THE WORLD I'M SEEING...
THEY'RE ALL...
...FROM ELDER TALES. AREN'T THEY?

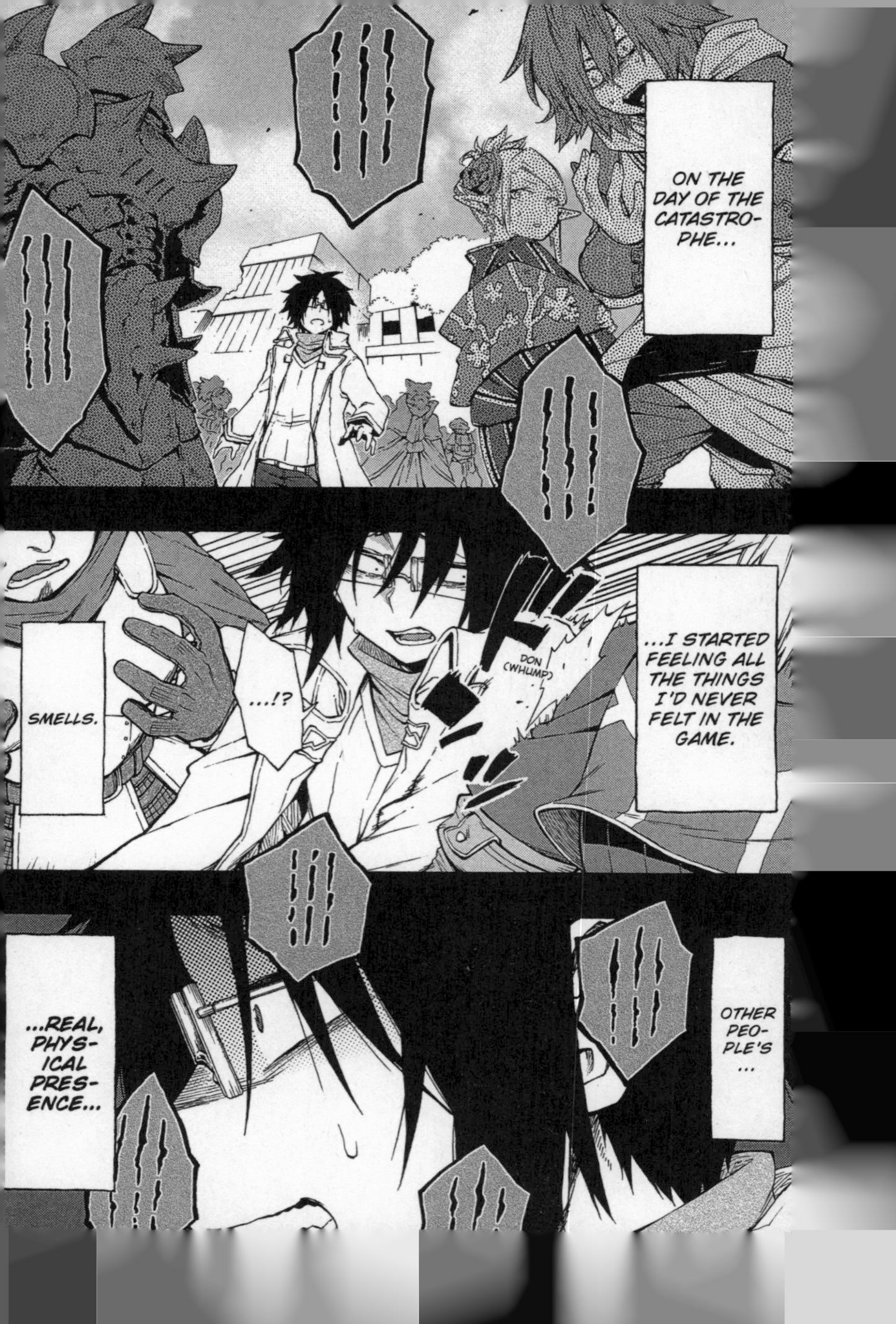
ON THE DAY OF THE CATASTRO-PHE...
...I STARTED FEELING ALL THE THINGS I'D NEVER FELT IN THE GAME.
DON (WHUMP)
...!?
SMELLS.
OTHER PEO-PLE'S...
...REAL, PHYS-ICAL PRES-ENCE...

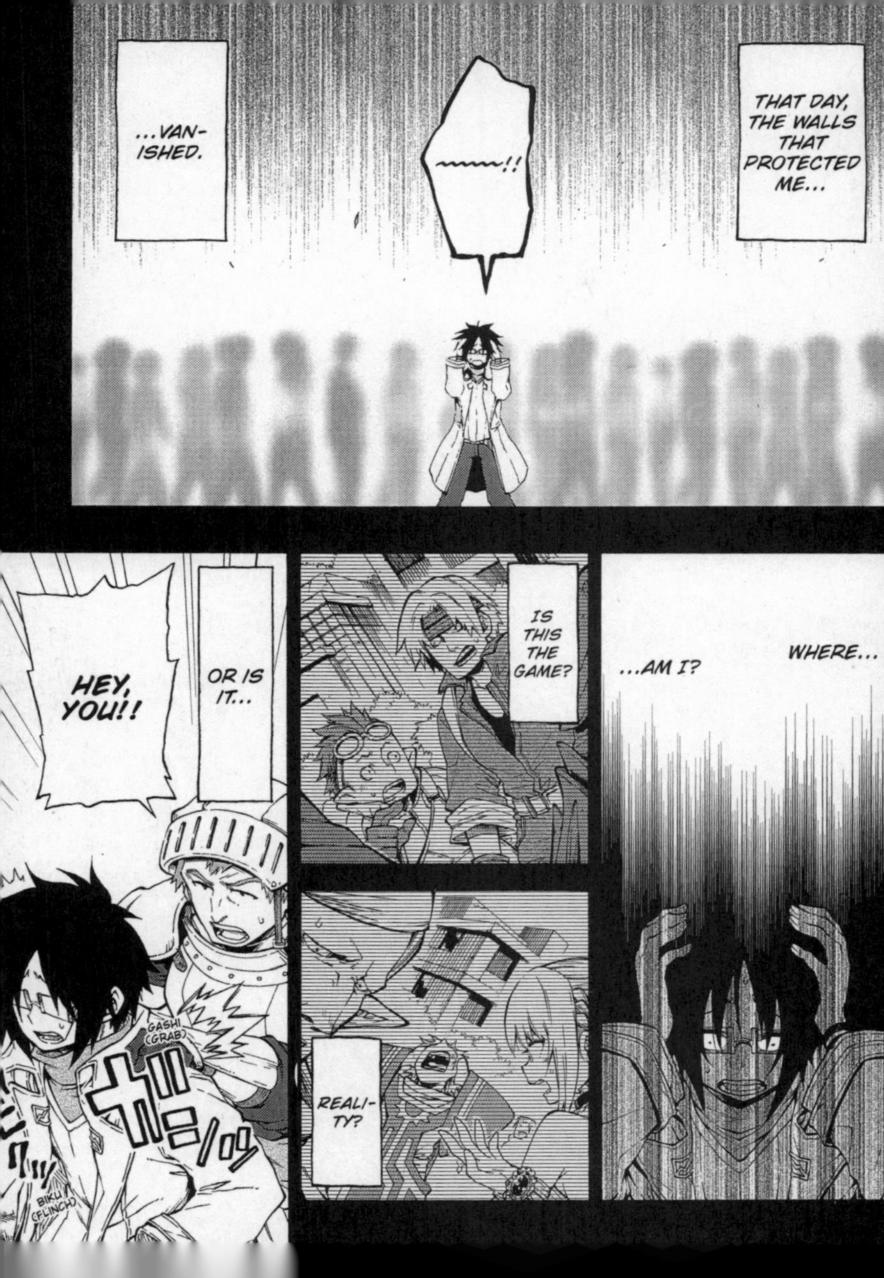
THAT DAY, THE WALLS THAT PROTECTED ME...
~~~!!
...VAN-ISHED.
WHERE...
...AM I?
IS THIS THE GAME?
REALI-TY?
OR IS IT...
HEY, YOU!!
GASHI (GRAB)
BIKU (FLINCH)
~~~

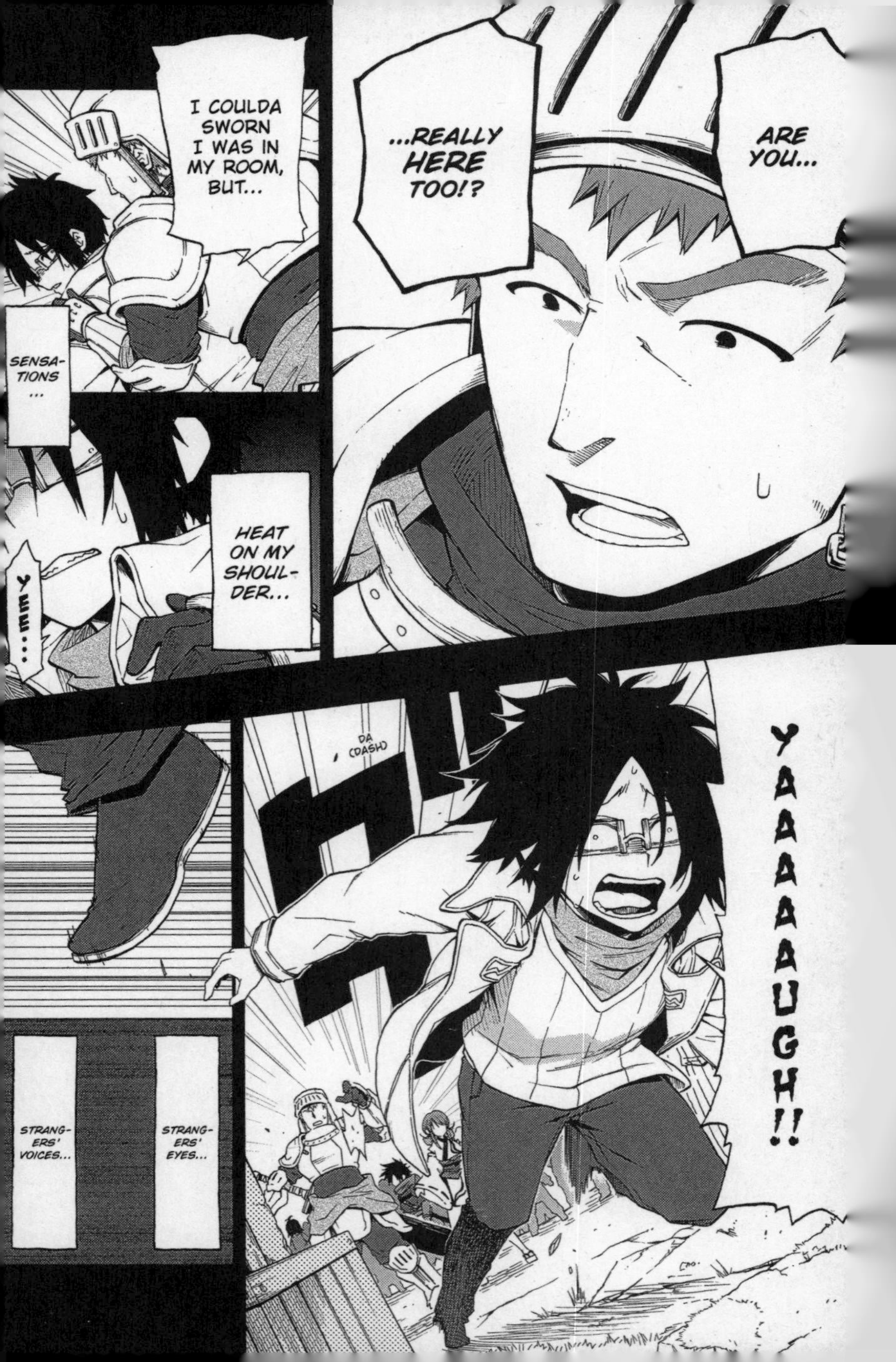
ARE YOU...
...REALLY HERE TOO!?
I COULDA SWORN I WAS IN MY ROOM, BUT...
SENSATIONS...
HEAT ON MY SHOULDER...
YEEE...
YAAAAAUGH!!
DA (DASH)
STRANGERS' EYES...
STRANGERS' VOICES...

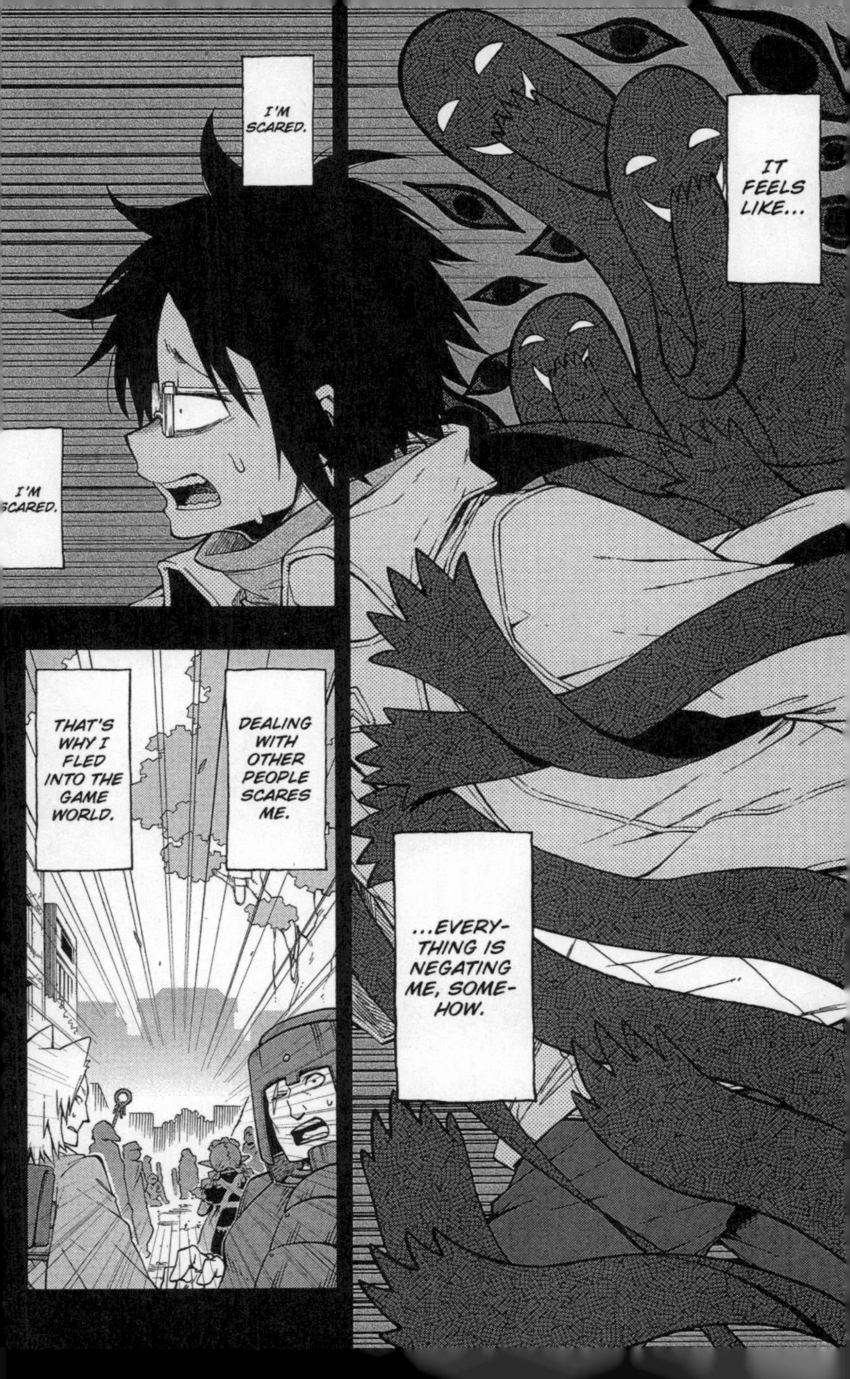
IT FEELS LIKE...
...EVERY-THING IS NEGATING ME, SOME-HOW.
I'M SCARED.
I'M SCARED.
DEALING WITH OTHER PEOPLE SCARES ME.
THAT'S WHY I FLED INTO THE GAME WORLD.

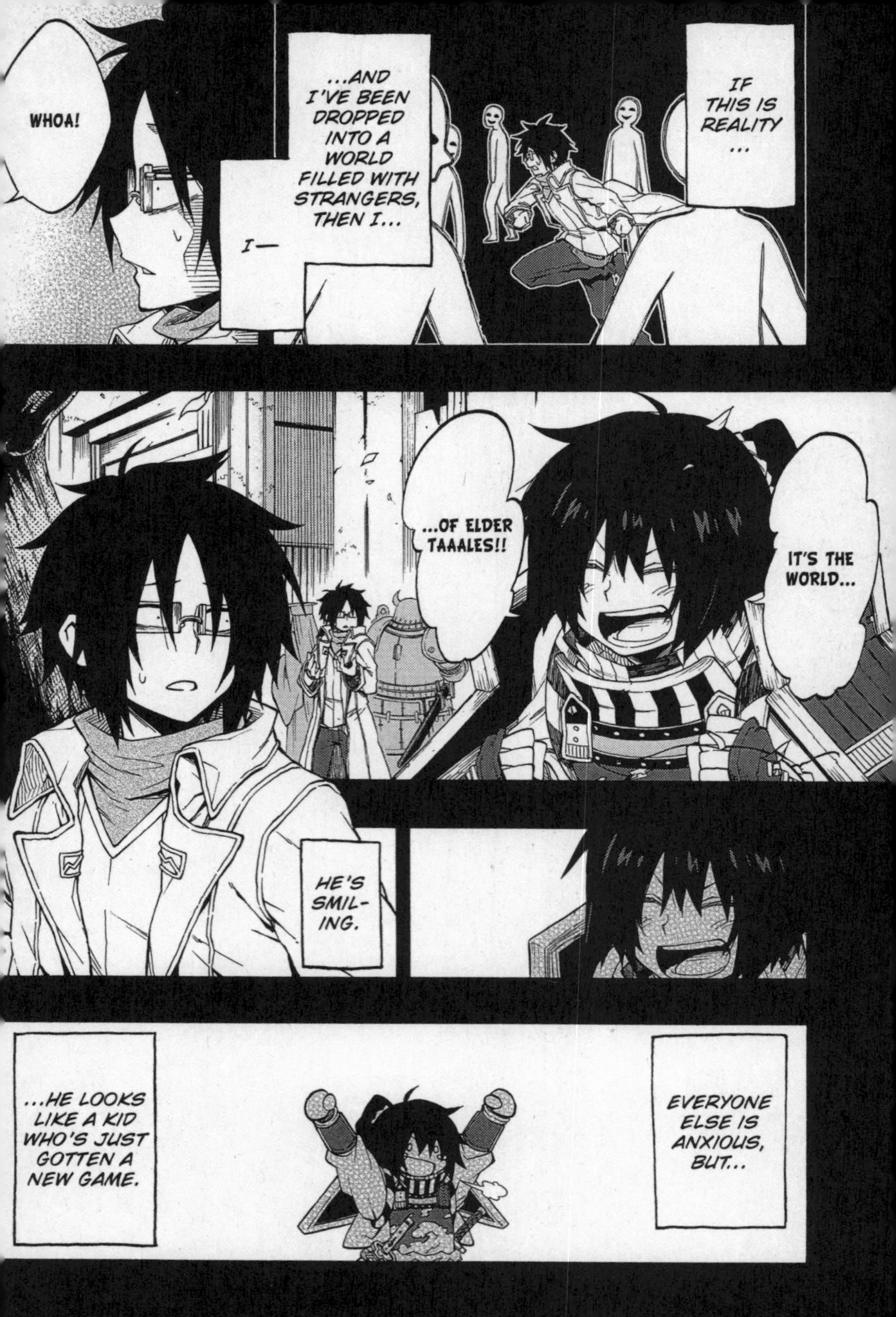
IF THIS IS REALITY ...
...AND I'VE BEEN DROPPED INTO A WORLD FILLED WITH STRANGERS, THEN I...
I—
WHOA!
IT'S THE WORLD...
...OF ELDER TAAALES!!
HE'S SMIL-ING.
EVERYONE ELSE IS ANXIOUS, BUT...
...HE LOOKS LIKE A KID WHO'S JUST GOTTEN A NEW GAME.

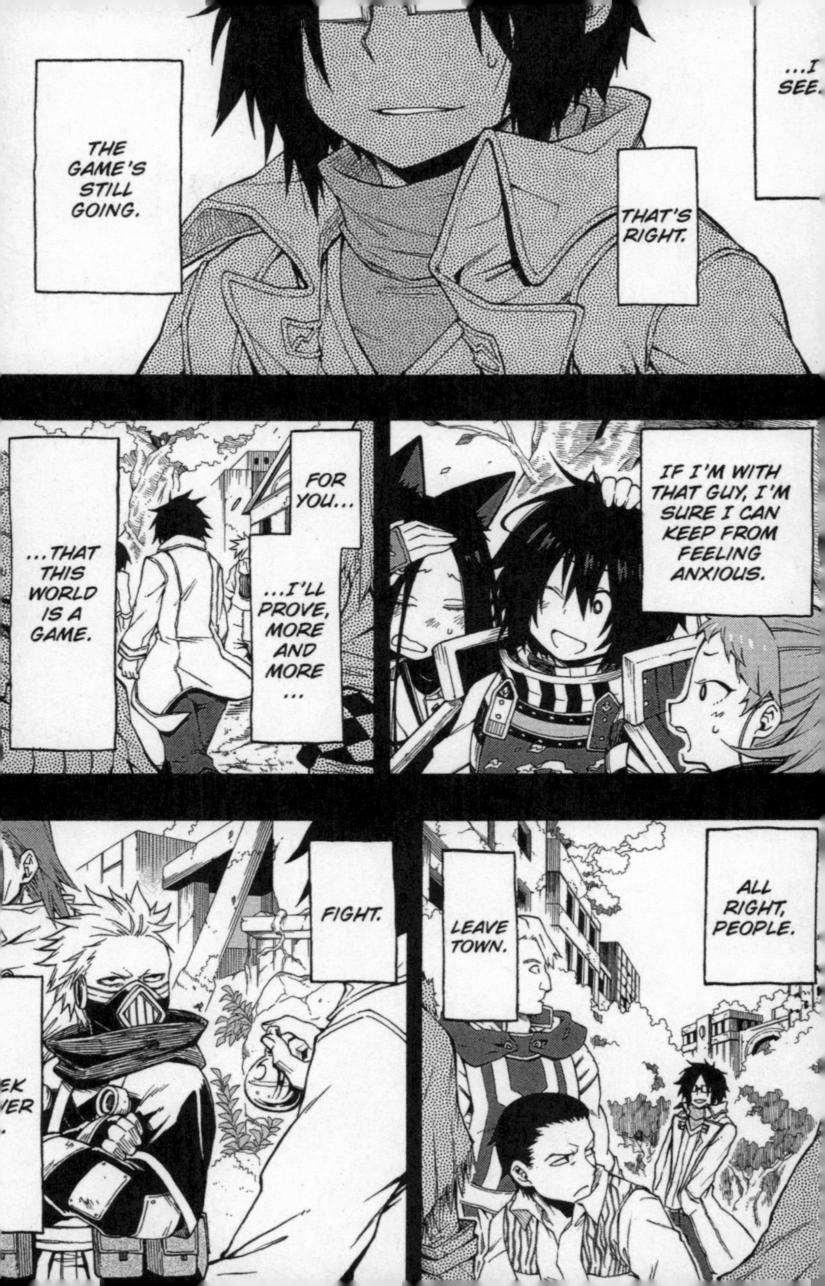
...I SEE.
THAT'S RIGHT.
THE GAME'S STILL GOING.
IF I'M WITH THAT GUY, I'M SURE I CAN KEEP FROM FEELING ANXIOUS.
FOR YOU...
...I'LL PROVE, MORE AND MORE ...
...THAT THIS WORLD IS A GAME.
ALL RIGHT, PEOPLE.
LEAVE TOWN.
FIGHT.

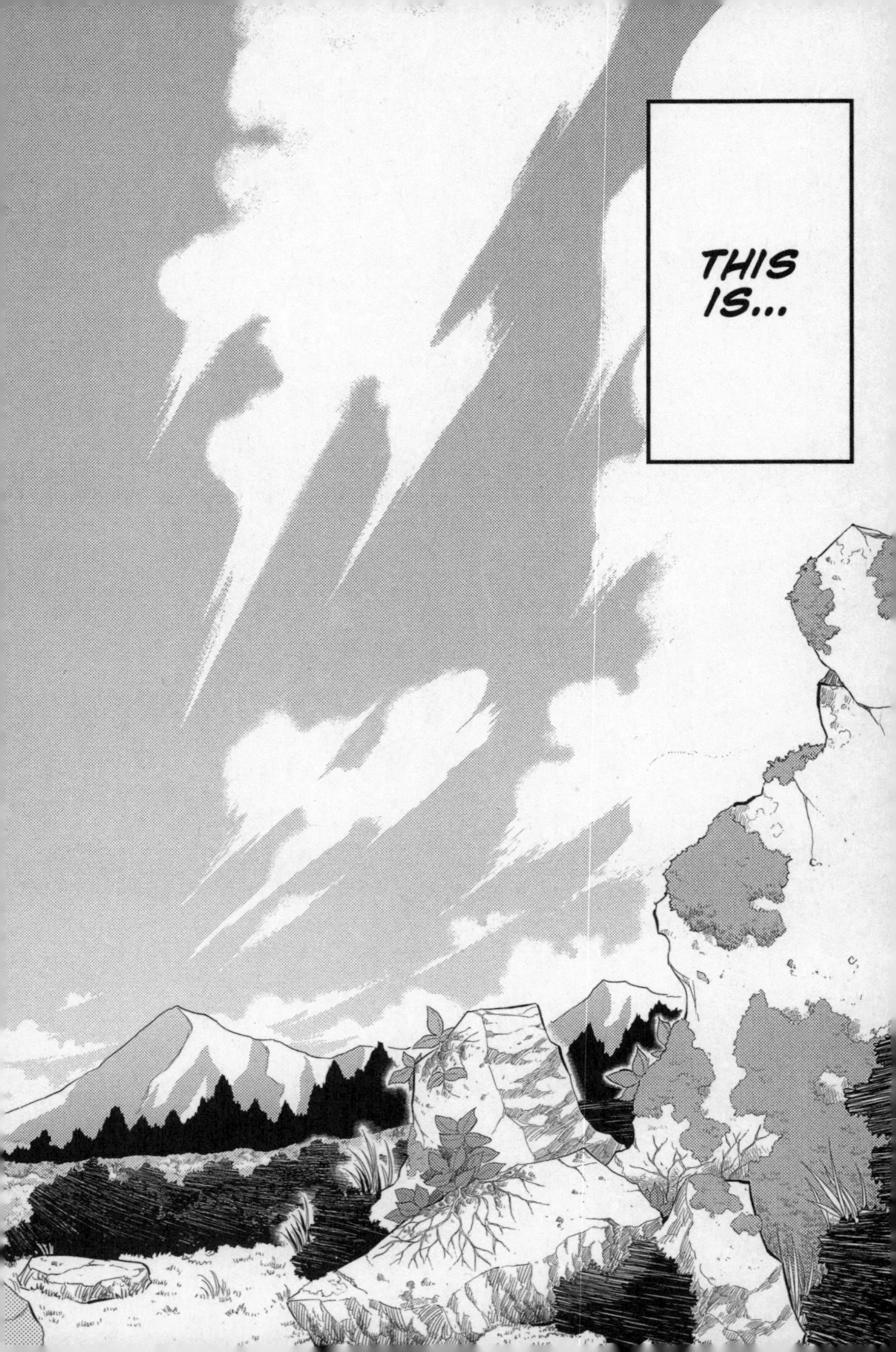
THIS IS...

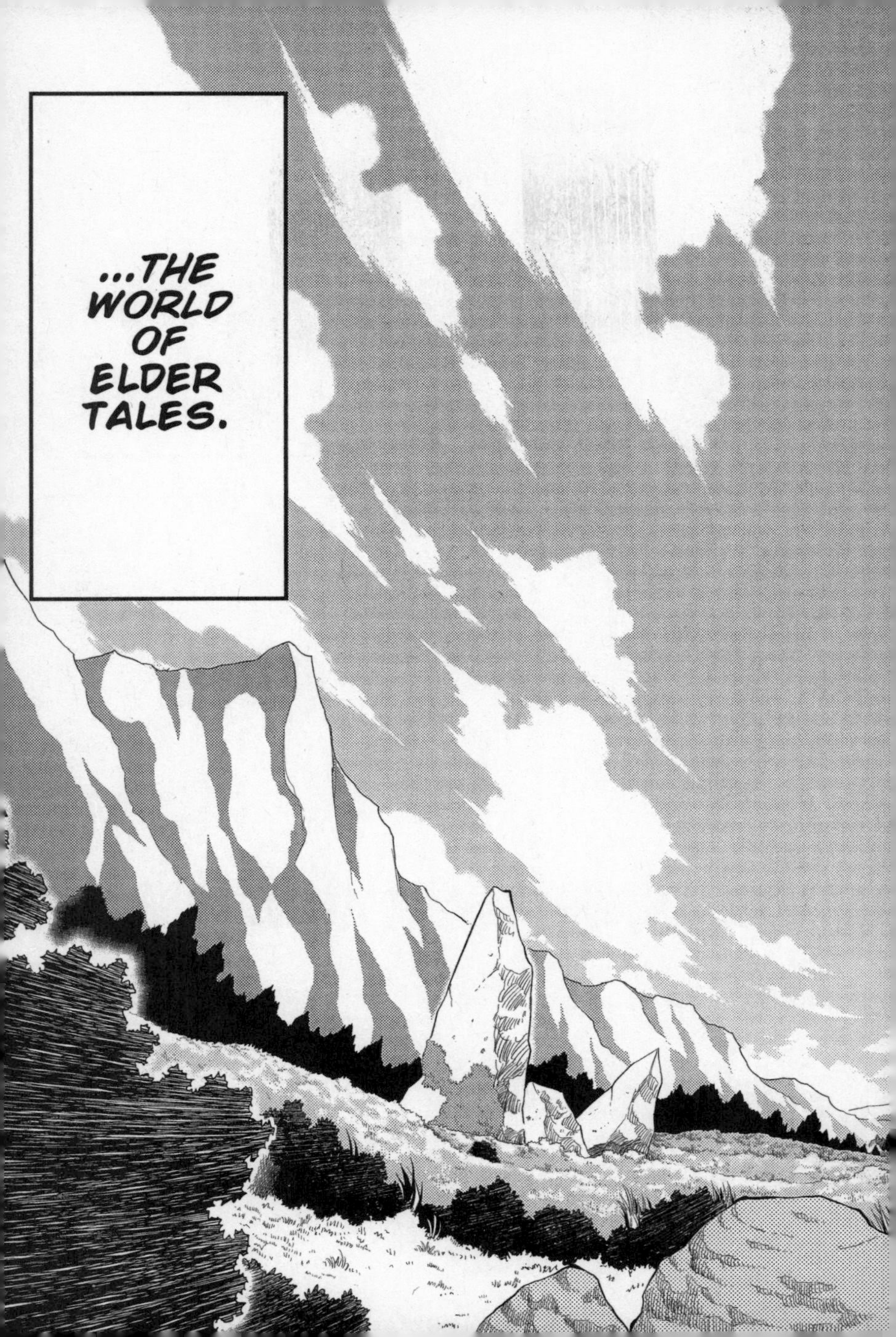
...THE WORLD OF ELDER TALES.

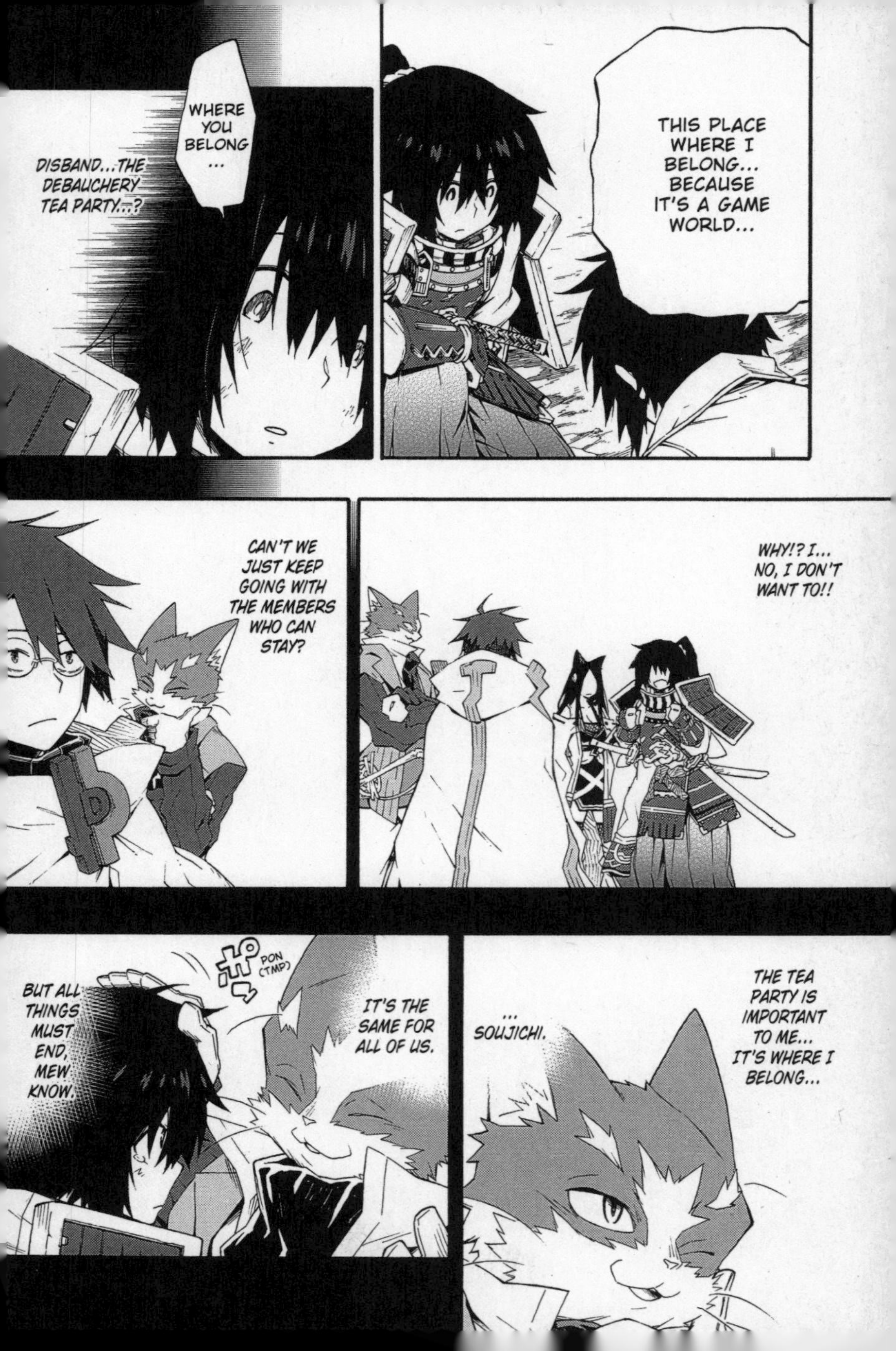
THIS PLACE WHERE I BELONG... BECAUSE IT'S A GAME WORLD...
WHERE YOU BELONG ...
DISBAND...THE DEBAUCHERY TEA PARTY...?
WHY!? I... NO, I DON'T WANT TO!!
CAN'T WE JUST KEEP GOING WITH THE MEMBERS WHO CAN STAY?
THE TEA PARTY IS IMPORTANT TO ME... IT'S WHERE I BELONG...
... SOUJICHI.
ポン
PON (TMP)
IT'S THE SAME FOR ALL OF US.
BUT ALL THINGS MUST END, MEW KNOW.

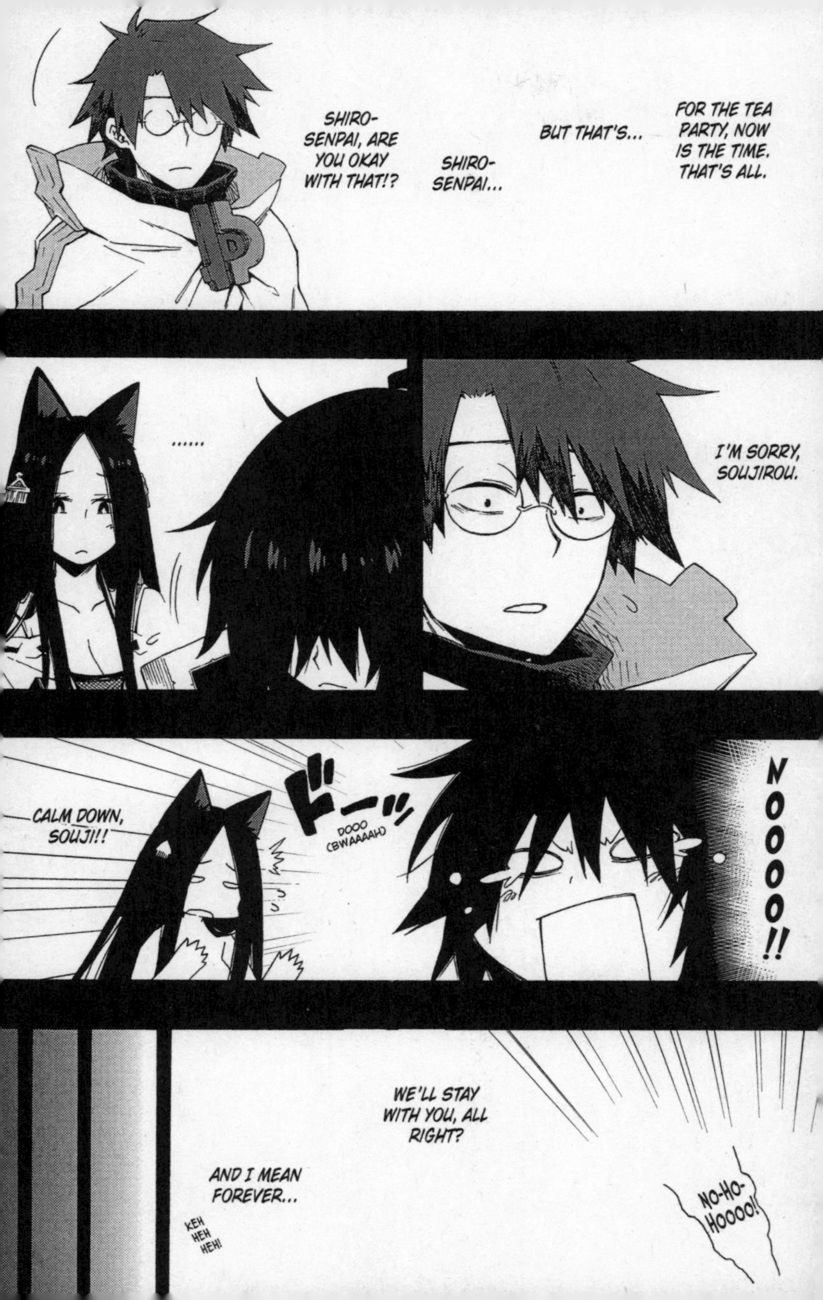
FOR THE TEA PARTY, NOW IS THE TIME. THAT'S ALL.
BUT THAT'S...
SHIRO-SENPAI...
SHIRO-SENPAI, ARE YOU OKAY WITH THAT!?
I'M SORRY, SOUJIROU.
......
NOOOOO!!
ドーッ
DOOO (BWAAAAH)
CALM DOWN, SOUJI!!
WE'LL STAY WITH YOU, ALL RIGHT?
NO-HO-HOOOO!
AND I MEAN FOREVER...
KEH HEH HEH!

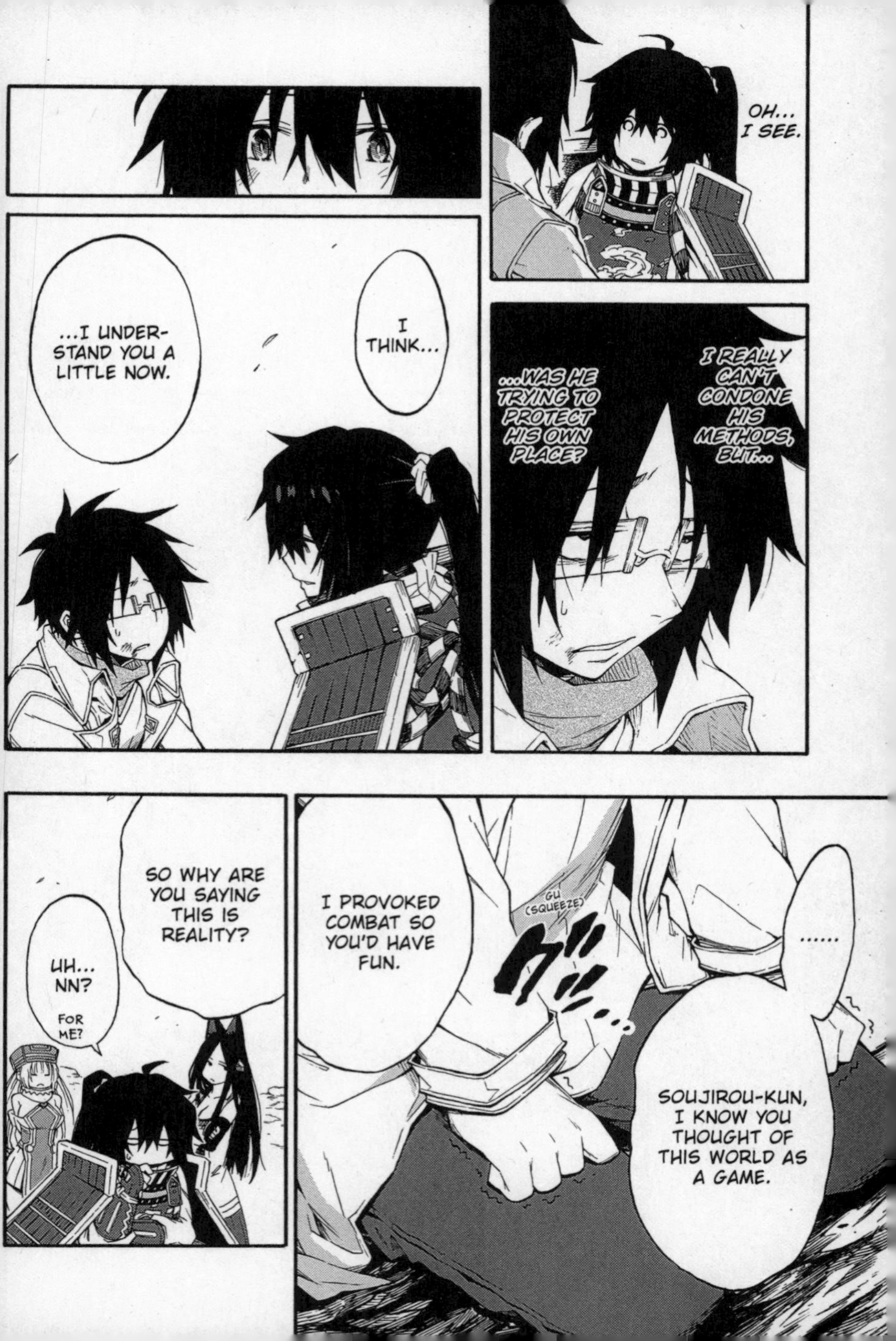
OH... I SEE.
I REALLY CAN'T CONDONE HIS METHODS, BUT...
...WAS HE TRYING TO PROTECT HIS OWN PLACE?
I THINK...
...I UNDER-STAND YOU A LITTLE NOW.
......
SOUJIROU-KUN, I KNOW YOU THOUGHT OF THIS WORLD AS A GAME.
GU (SQUEEZE)
I PROVOKED COMBAT SO YOU'D HAVE FUN.
SO WHY ARE YOU SAYING THIS IS REALITY?
UH... NN?
FOR ME?

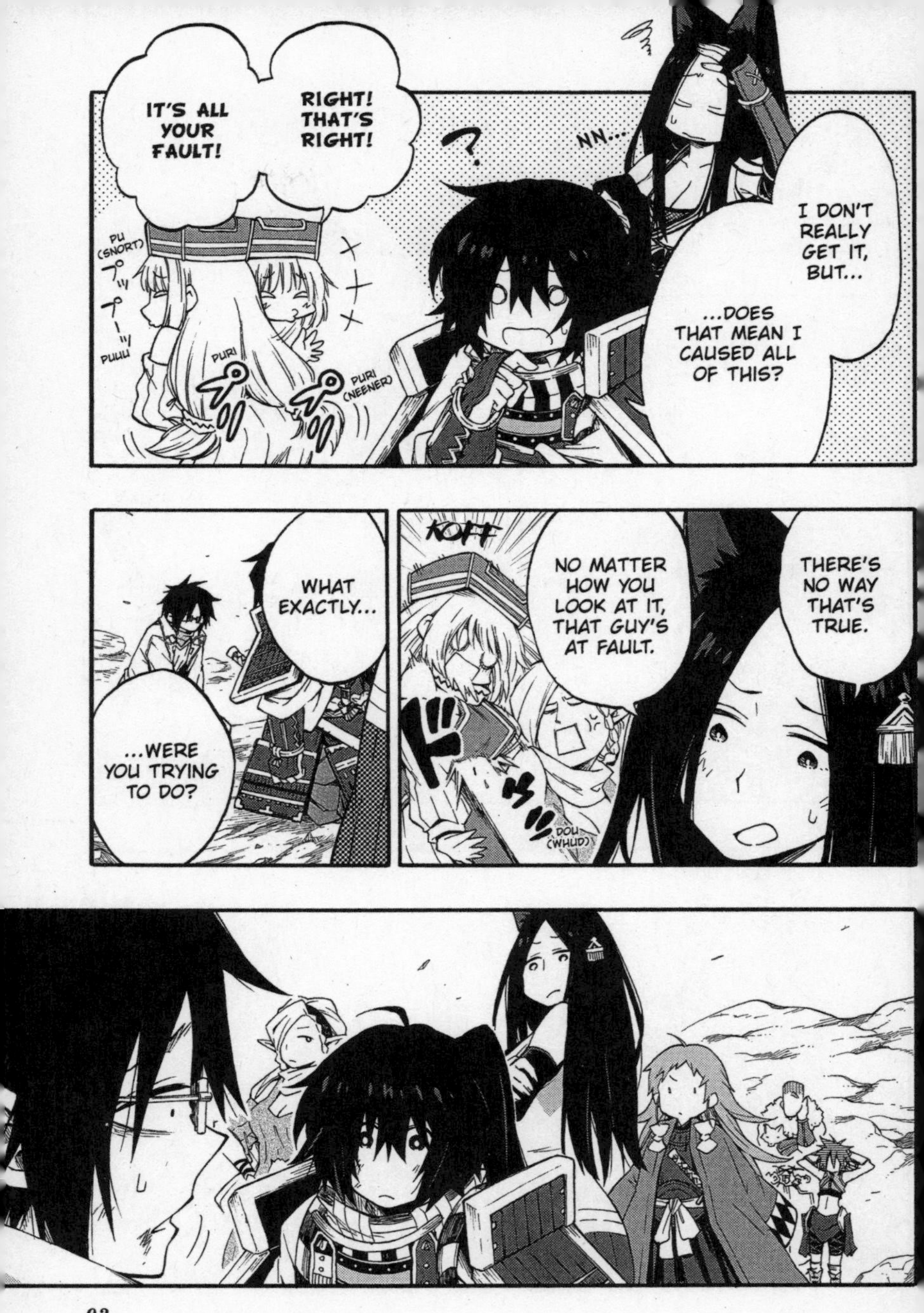
NN...
I DON'T REALLY GET IT, BUT...
...DOES THAT MEAN I CAUSED ALL OF THIS?
?
RIGHT! THAT'S RIGHT!
IT'S ALL YOUR FAULT!
PU (SNORT)
PUUU
PURI
PURI (NEENER)
THERE'S NO WAY THAT'S TRUE.
NO MATTER HOW YOU LOOK AT IT, THAT GUY'S AT FAULT.
KOFF
DOU (WHUD)
WHAT EXACTLY...
...WERE YOU TRYING TO DO?

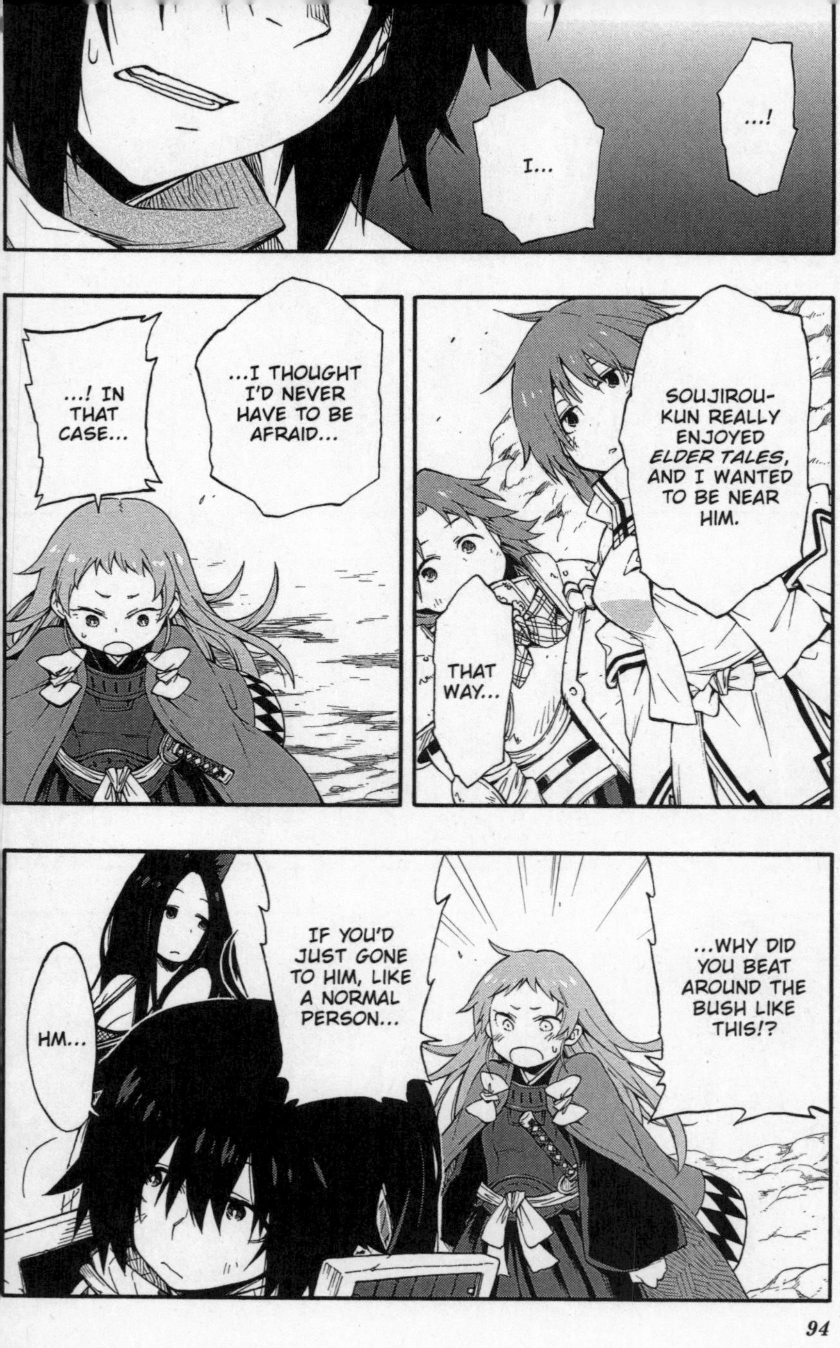

...!
I...
SOUJIROU-KUN REALLY ENJOYED *ELDER TALES*, AND I WANTED TO BE NEAR HIM.
THAT WAY...
...I THOUGHT I'D NEVER HAVE TO BE AFRAID...
...! IN THAT CASE...
...WHY DID YOU BEAT AROUND THE BUSH LIKE THIS!?
IF YOU'D JUST GONE TO HIM, LIKE A NORMAL PERSON...
HM...

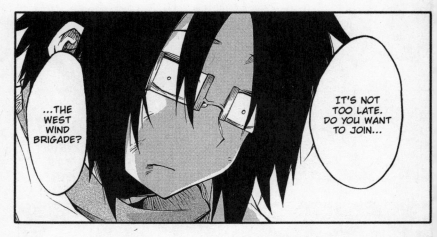

IT'S NOT TOO LATE. DO YOU WANT TO JOIN...
...THE WEST WIND BRIGADE?
HUH!? BOSS, WHAT ARE YOU SAYING!?
SHE'S RIGHT, SOU-SAMA! OBJECTION! OBJECTION!!
BUT...
...HE SAYS HE WANTS TO STAY NEAR ME.
WE'D FEEL BETTER IF WE WERE ABLE TO KEEP AN EYE ON HIM TOO, RIGHT?
UH... UMMM...

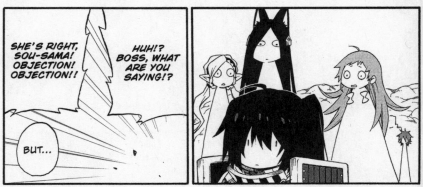

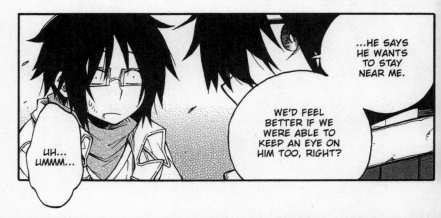

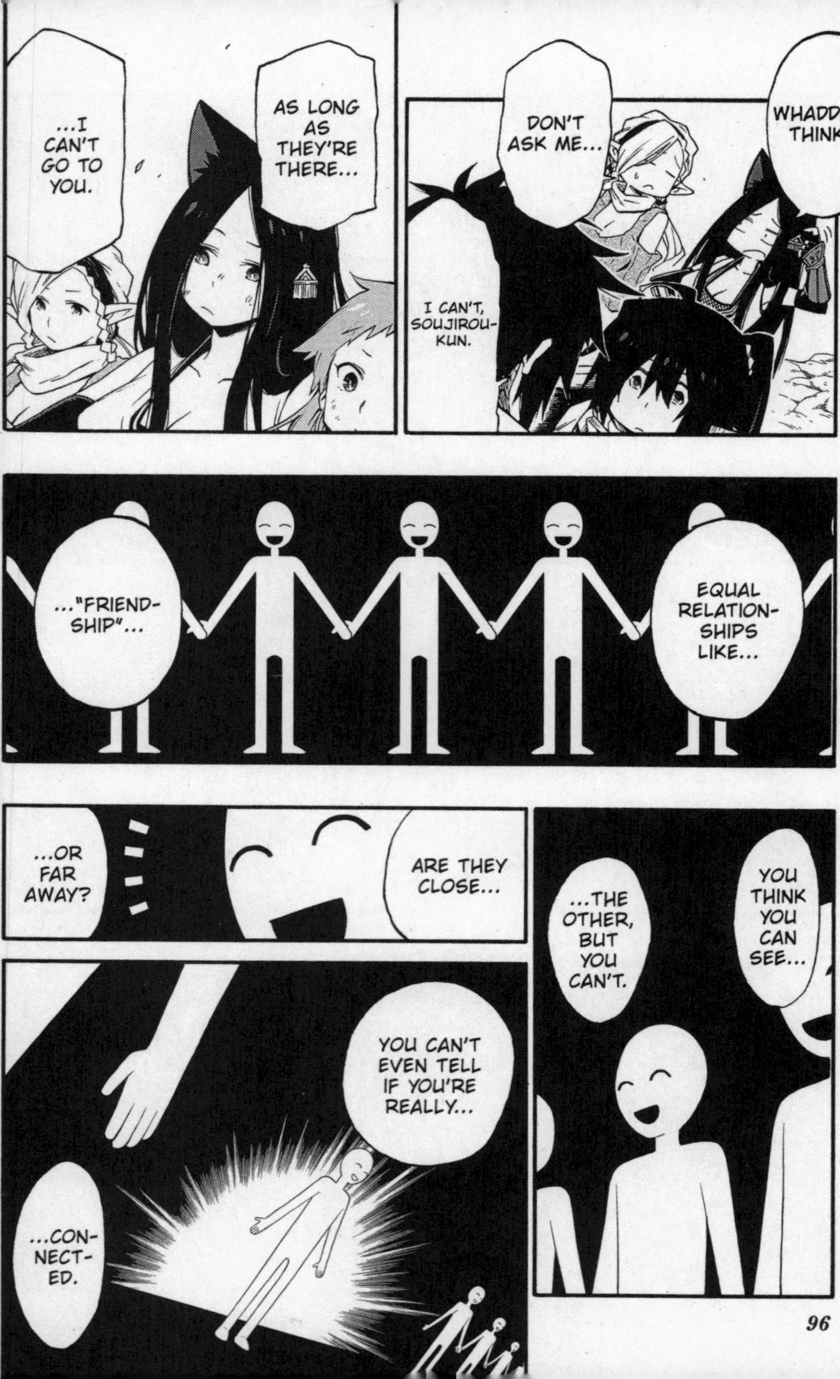
WHADDAYA THINK?
DON'T ASK ME...
I CAN'T, SOUJIROU-KUN.
AS LONG AS THEY'RE THERE...
...I CAN'T GO TO YOU.
EQUAL RELATION-SHIPS LIKE...
..."FRIEND-SHIP"...
YOU THINK YOU CAN SEE...
...THE OTHER, BUT YOU CAN'T.
ARE THEY CLOSE...
...OR FAR AWAY?
YOU CAN'T EVEN TELL IF YOU'RE REALLY...
...CON-NECT-ED.

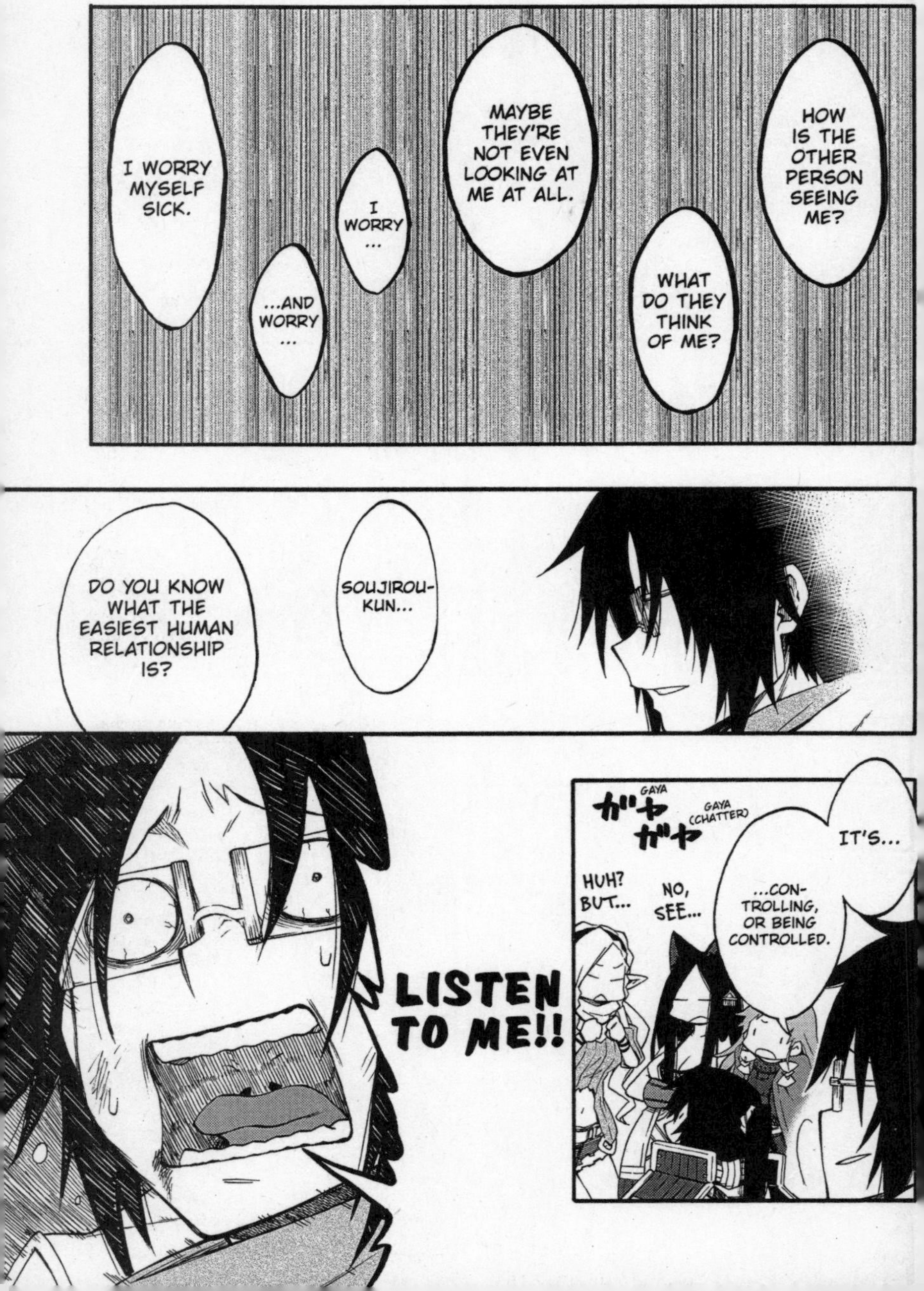
HOW IS THE OTHER PERSON SEEING ME?
WHAT DO THEY THINK OF ME?
MAYBE THEY'RE NOT EVEN LOOKING AT ME AT ALL.
I WORRY...
...AND WORRY...
I WORRY MYSELF SICK.
SOUJIROU-KUN...
DO YOU KNOW WHAT THE EASIEST HUMAN RELATIONSHIP IS?
IT'S...
...CON-TROLLING, OR BEING CONTROLLED.
ガヤ GAYA
ガヤ GAYA (CHATTER)
NO, SEE...
HUH? BUT...
LISTEN TO ME!!

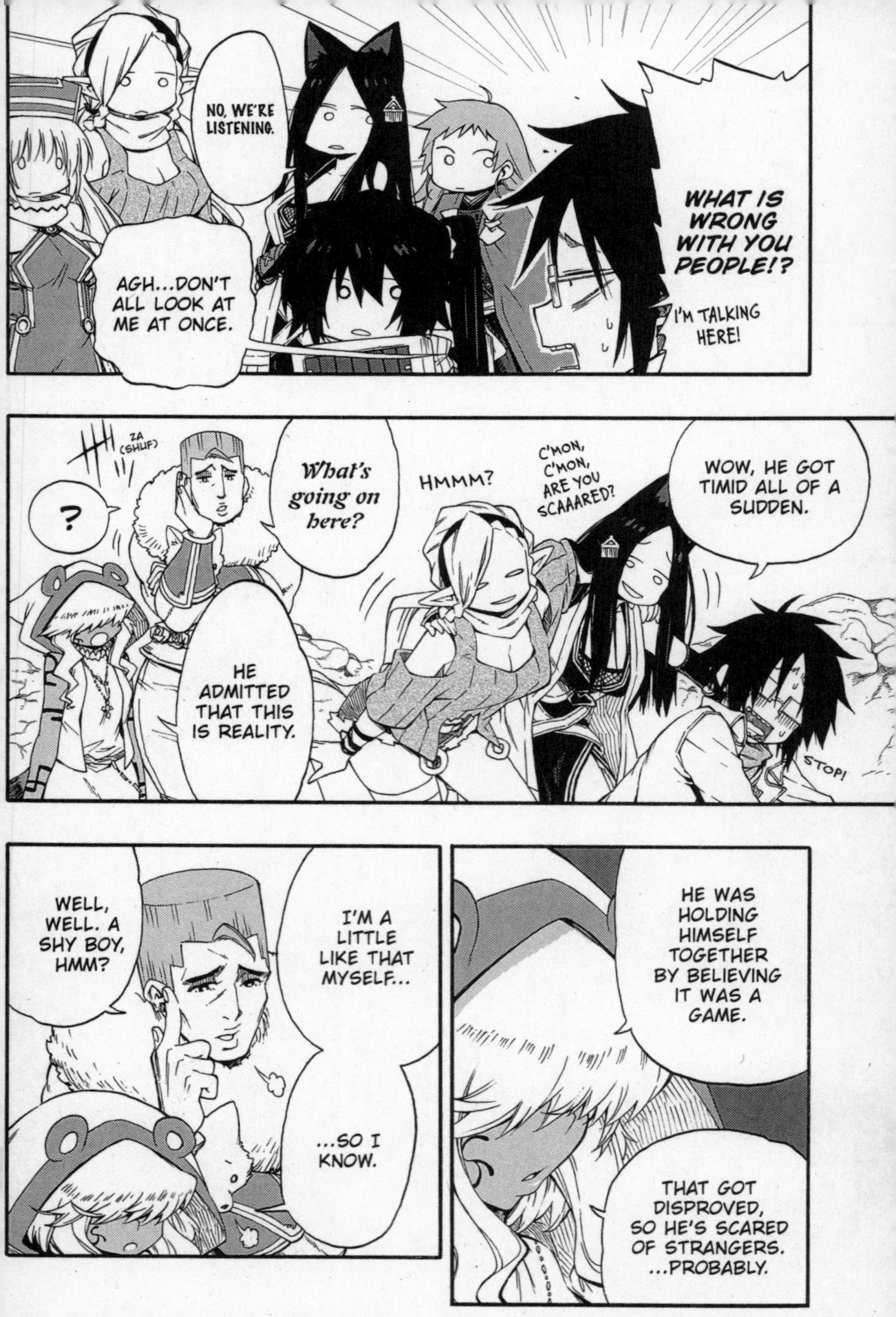
WHAT IS WRONG WITH YOU PEOPLE!?
I'M TALKING HERE!
NO, WE'RE LISTENING.
AGH...DON'T ALL LOOK AT ME AT ONCE.
WOW, HE GOT TIMID ALL OF A SUDDEN.
STOP!
C'MON, C'MON, ARE YOU SCAAARED?
HMMM?
What's going on here?
HE ADMITTED THAT THIS IS REALITY.
ZA (SHUF)
?
HE WAS HOLDING HIMSELF TOGETHER BY BELIEVING IT WAS A GAME.
THAT GOT DISPROVED, SO HE'S SCARED OF STRANGERS. ...PROBABLY.
I'M A LITTLE LIKE THAT MYSELF...
...SO I KNOW.
WELL, WELL. A SHY BOY, HMM?

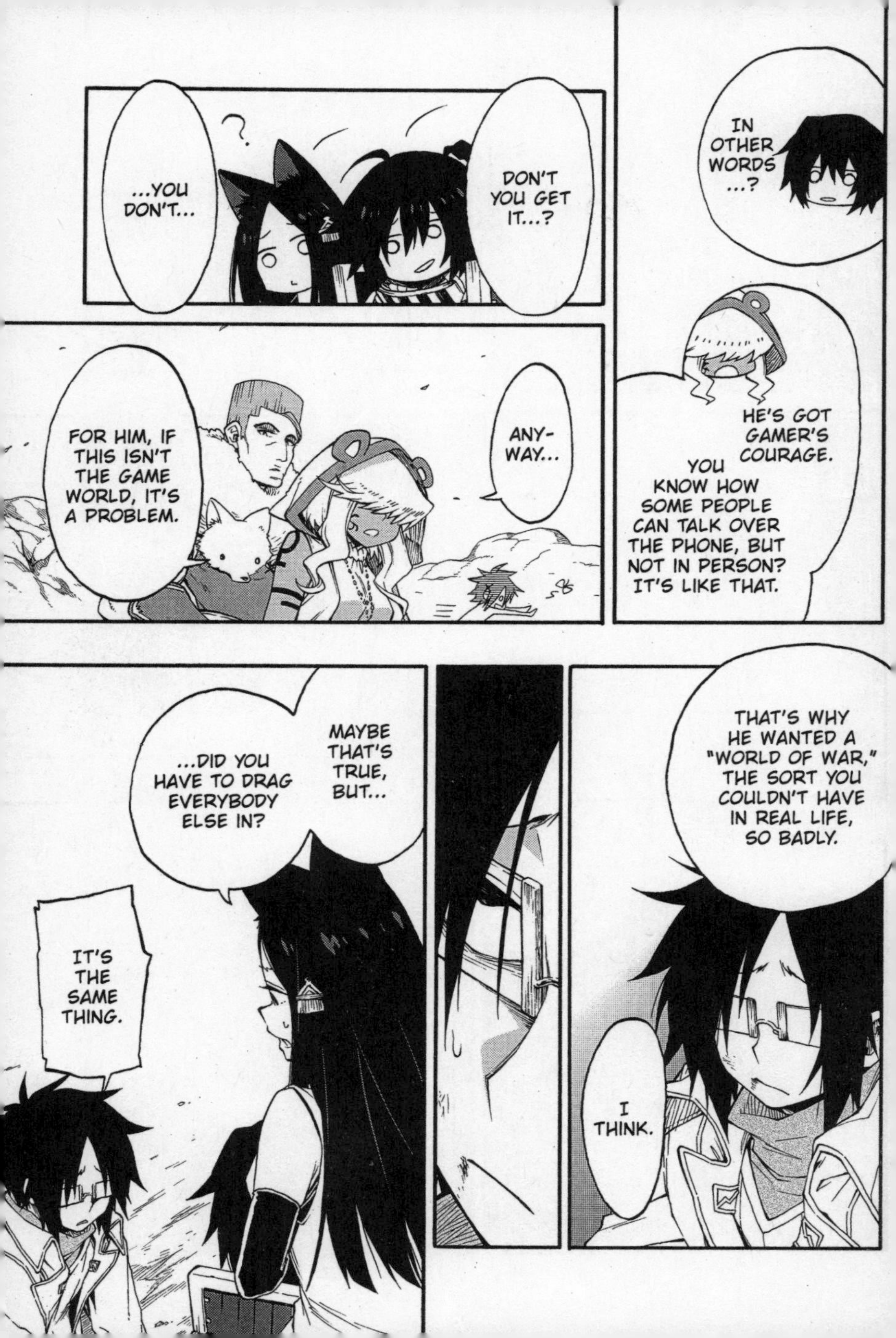
IN OTHER WORDS...?
HE'S GOT GAMER'S COURAGE.
YOU KNOW HOW SOME PEOPLE CAN TALK OVER THE PHONE, BUT NOT IN PERSON? IT'S LIKE THAT.
DON'T YOU GET IT...?
...YOU DON'T...
ANY-WAY...
FOR HIM, IF THIS ISN'T THE GAME WORLD, IT'S A PROBLEM.
THAT'S WHY HE WANTED A "WORLD OF WAR," THE SORT YOU COULDN'T HAVE IN REAL LIFE, SO BADLY.
I THINK.
MAYBE THAT'S TRUE, BUT...
...DID YOU HAVE TO DRAG EVERYBODY ELSE IN?
IT'S THE SAME THING.

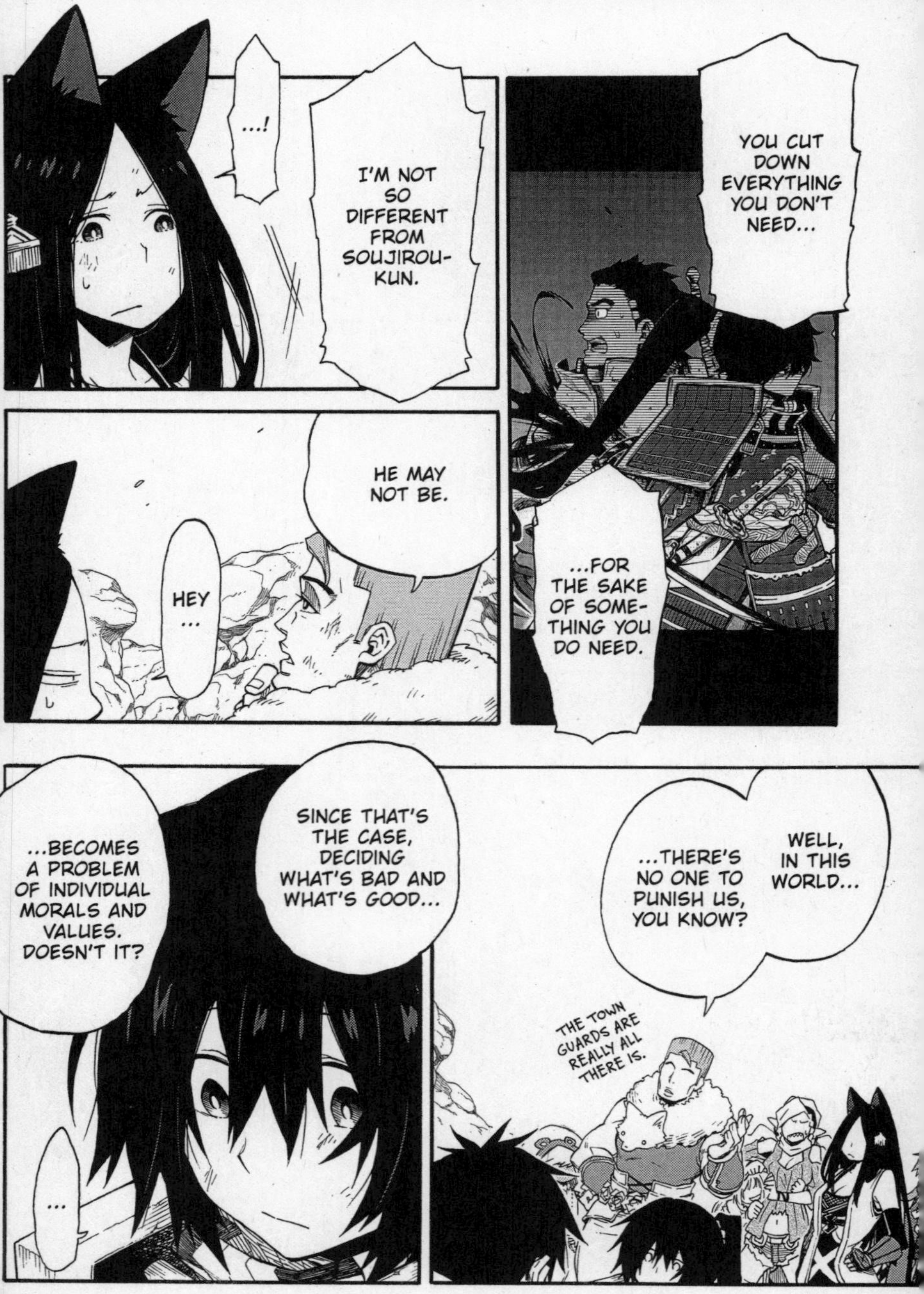
YOU CUT DOWN EVERYTHING YOU DON'T NEED...
...FOR THE SAKE OF SOMETHING YOU DO NEED.
I'M NOT SO DIFFERENT FROM SOUJIROU-KUN.
...!
HE MAY NOT BE.
HEY ...
WELL, IN THIS WORLD...
...THERE'S NO ONE TO PUNISH US, YOU KNOW?
THE TOWN GUARDS ARE REALLY ALL THERE IS.
SINCE THAT'S THE CASE, DECIDING WHAT'S BAD AND WHAT'S GOOD...
...BECOMES A PROBLEM OF INDIVIDUAL MORALS AND VALUES. DOESN'T IT?
...

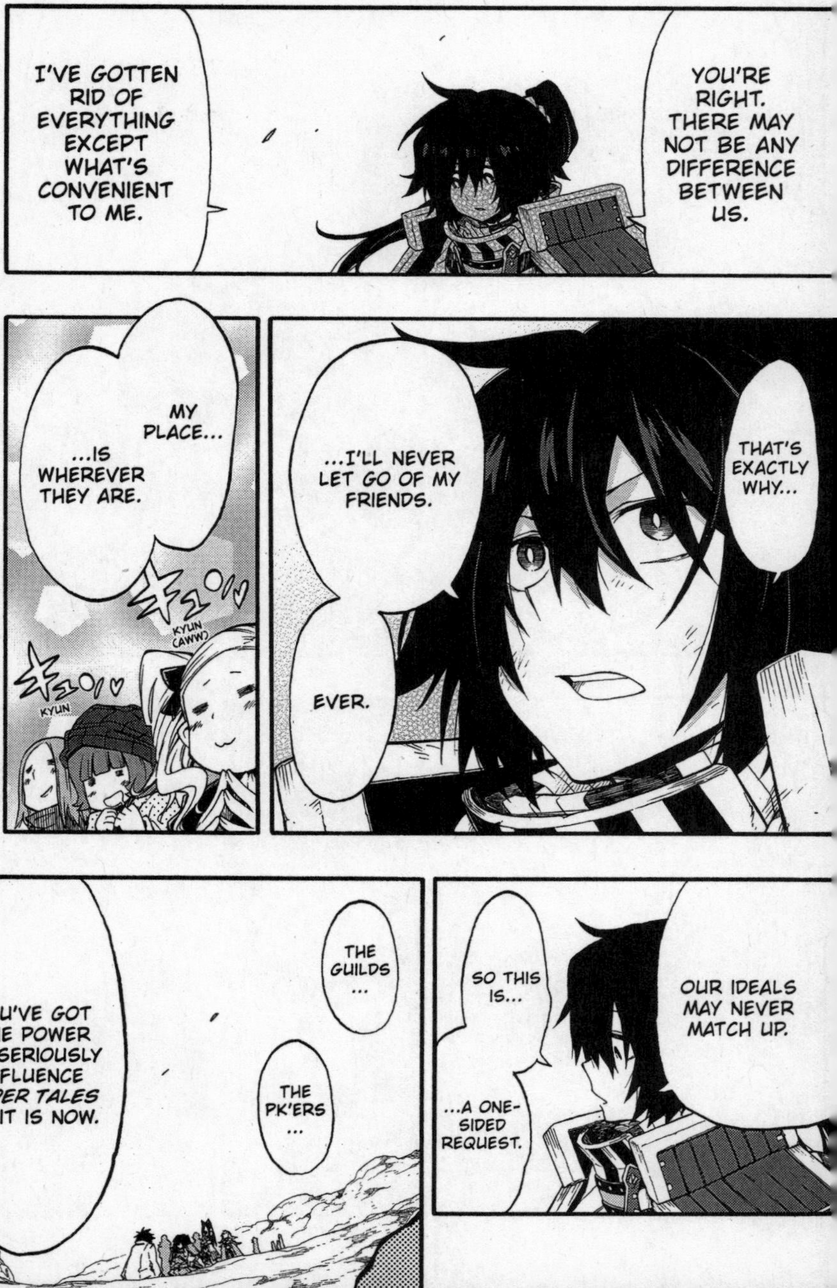
YOU'RE RIGHT. THERE MAY NOT BE ANY DIFFERENCE BETWEEN US.
I'VE GOTTEN RID OF EVERYTHING EXCEPT WHAT'S CONVENIENT TO ME.
THAT'S EXACTLY WHY...
...I'LL NEVER LET GO OF MY FRIENDS.
EVER.
MY PLACE...
...IS WHEREVER THEY ARE.
KYUN (AWW)
KYUN
OUR IDEALS MAY NEVER MATCH UP.
SO THIS IS...
...A ONE-SIDED REQUEST.
THE GUILDS ...
THE PK'ERS ...
YOU'VE GOT THE POWER TO SERIOUSLY INFLUENCE *ELDER TALES* AS IT IS NOW.

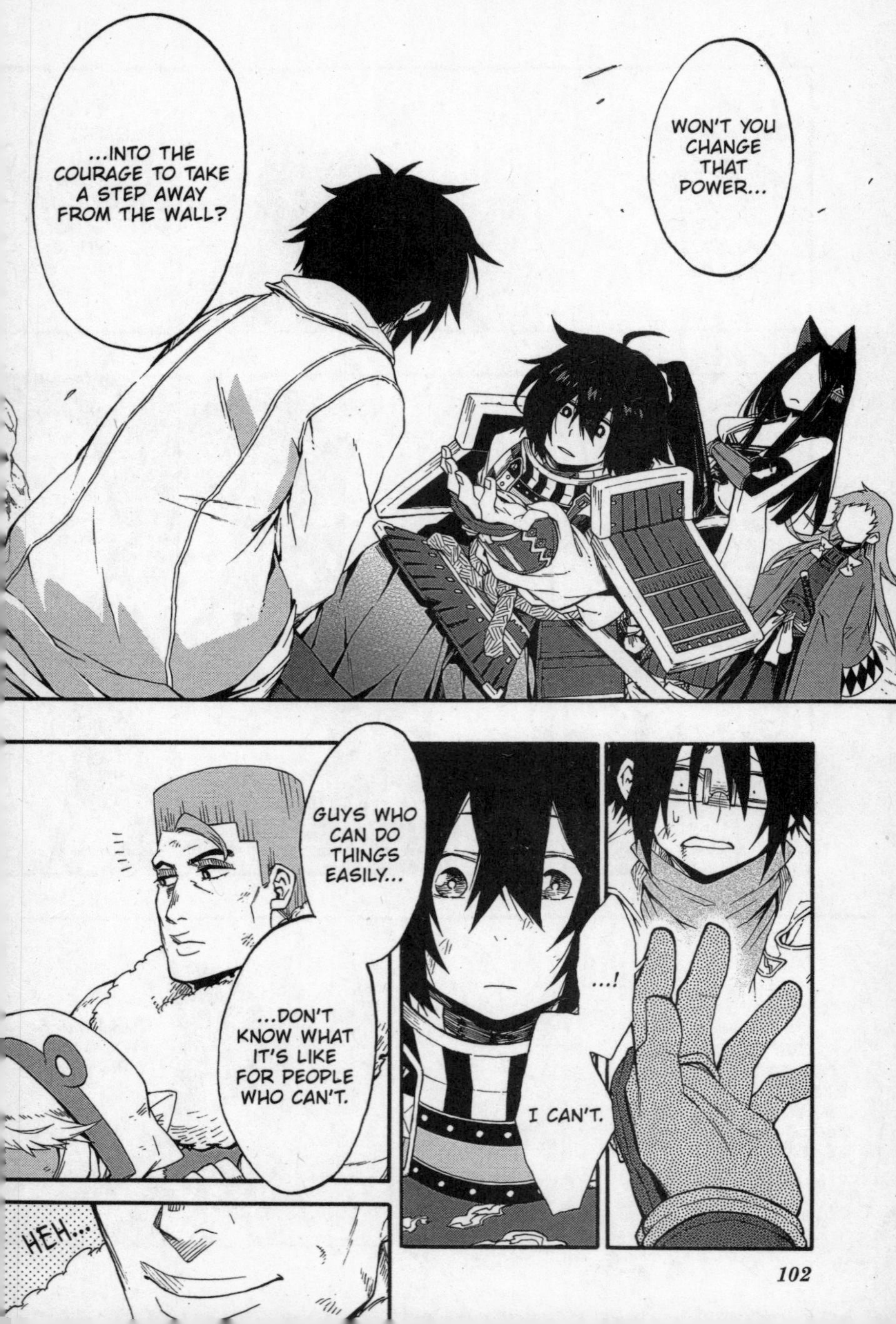
WON'T YOU CHANGE THAT POWER...
...INTO THE COURAGE TO TAKE A STEP AWAY FROM THE WALL?
...!
I CAN'T.
GUYS WHO CAN DO THINGS EASILY...
...DON'T KNOW WHAT IT'S LIKE FOR PEOPLE WHO CAN'T.
HEH...

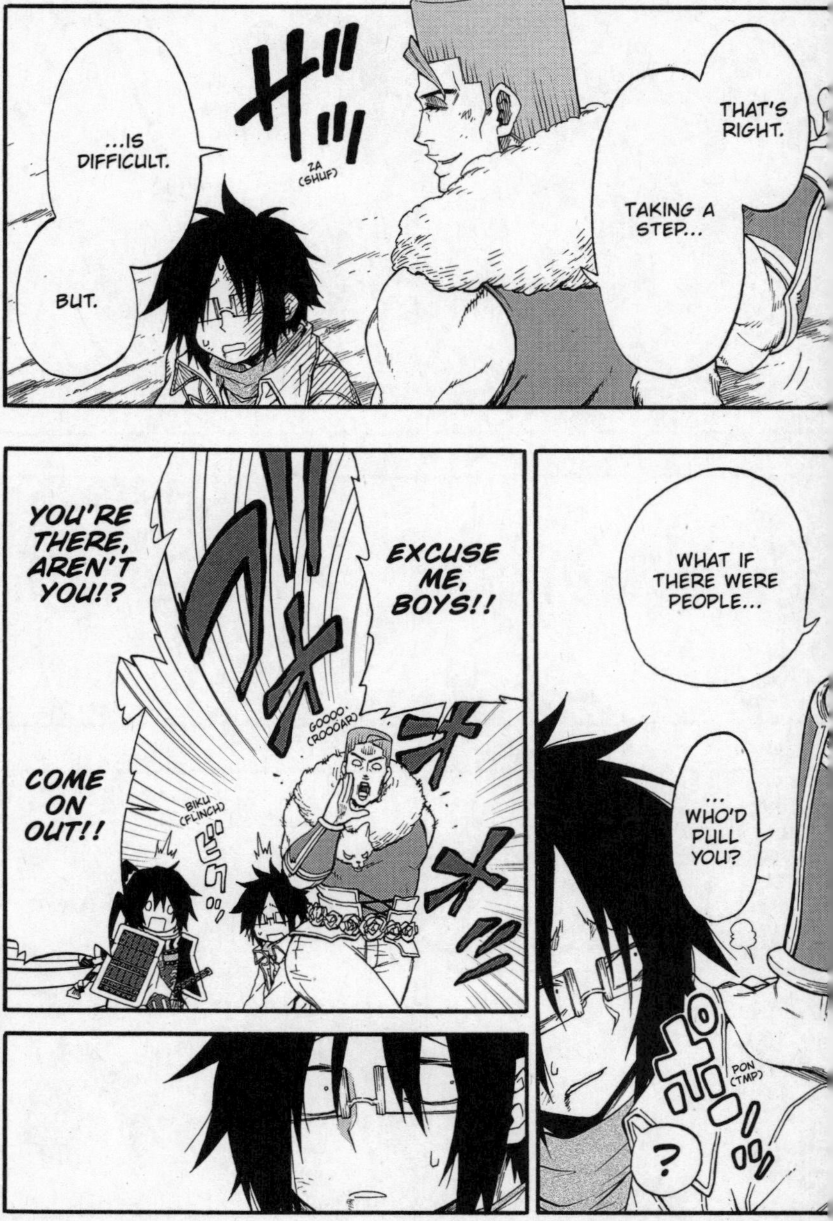
THAT'S RIGHT.
TAKING A STEP...
ZA (SHUF)
...IS DIFFICULT.
BUT.
WHAT IF THERE WERE PEOPLE...
...WHO'D PULL YOU?
PON (TMP)
?
EXCUSE ME, BOYS!!
YOU'RE THERE, AREN'T YOU!?
GOOOO. (ROOOAR)
COME ON OUT!!
BIKU (FLINCH)

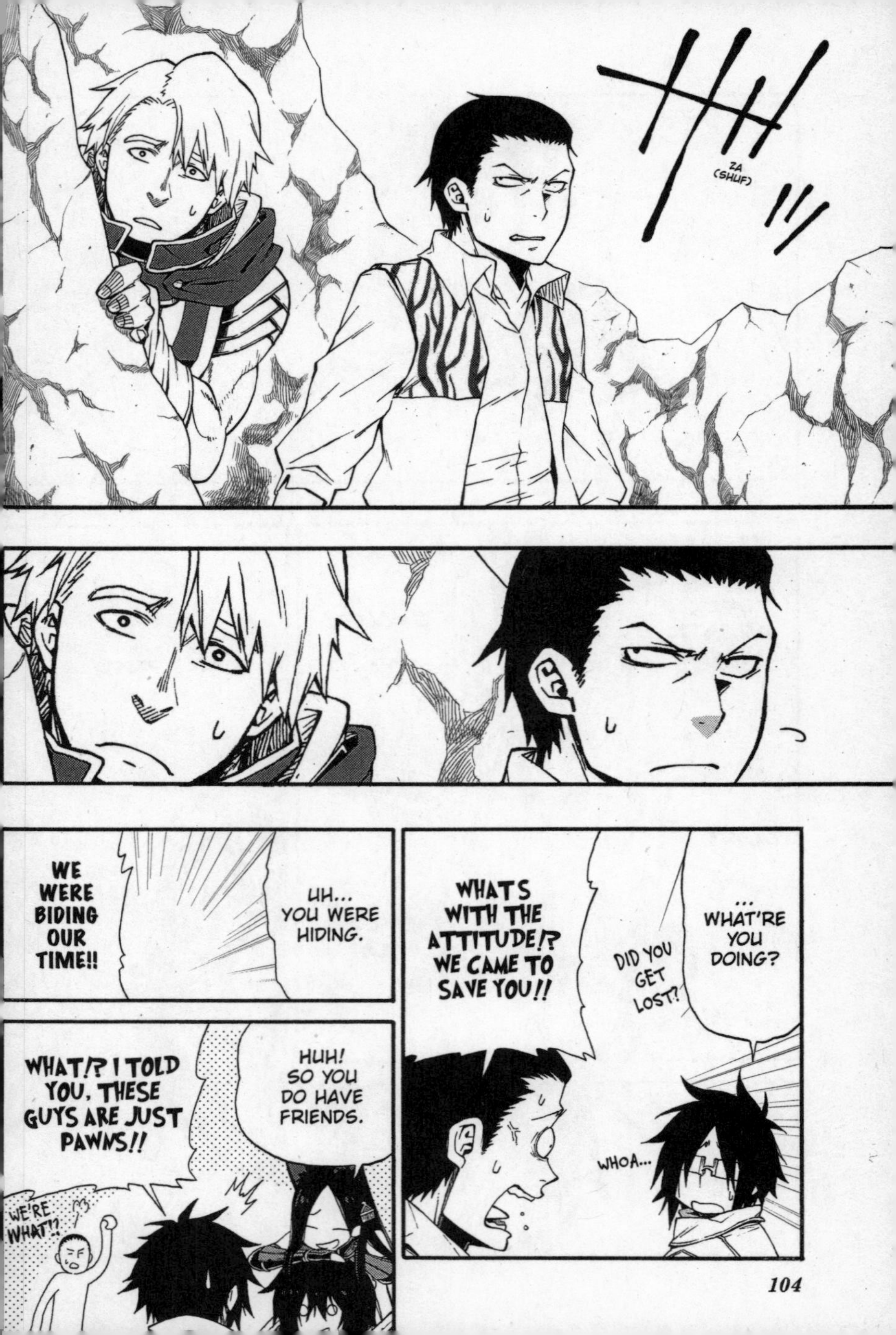
ZA
(SHUF)
... WHAT'RE YOU DOING?
DID YOU GET LOST?
WHATS WITH THE ATTITUDE!? WE CAME TO SAVE YOU!!
WHOA...
UH... YOU WERE HIDING.
WE WERE BIDING OUR TIME!!
HUH! SO YOU DO HAVE FRIENDS.
WHAT!? I TOLD YOU, THESE GUYS ARE JUST PAWNS!!
WE'RE WHAT!?

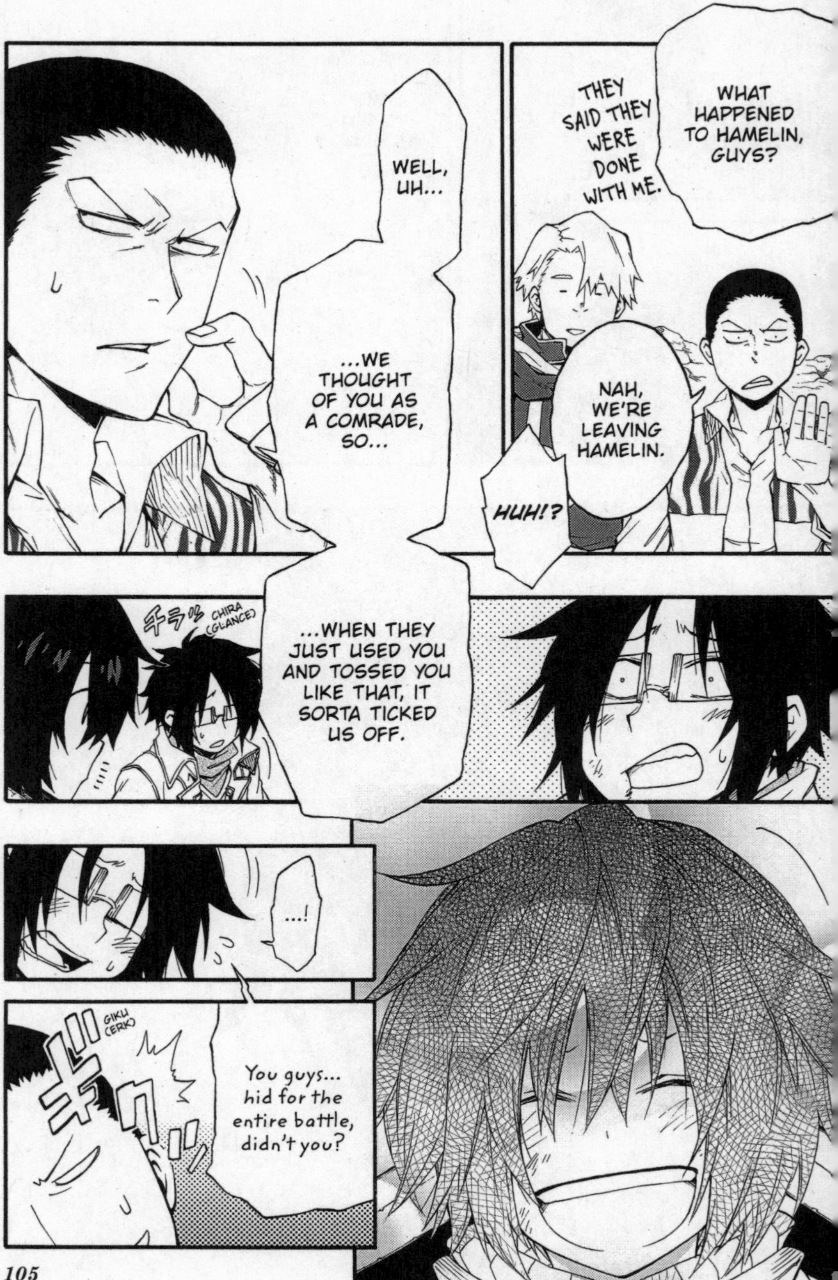
WHAT HAPPENED TO HAMELIN, GUYS?
THEY SAID THEY WERE DONE WITH ME.
NAH, WE'RE LEAVING HAMELIN.
HUH!?
WELL, UH...
...WE THOUGHT OF YOU AS A COMRADE, SO...
...WHEN THEY JUST USED YOU AND TOSSED YOU LIKE THAT, IT SORTA TICKED US OFF.
チラッ CHIRA (GLANCE)
...!
ギクッ GIKU (ERK)
You guys... hid for the entire battle, didn't you?

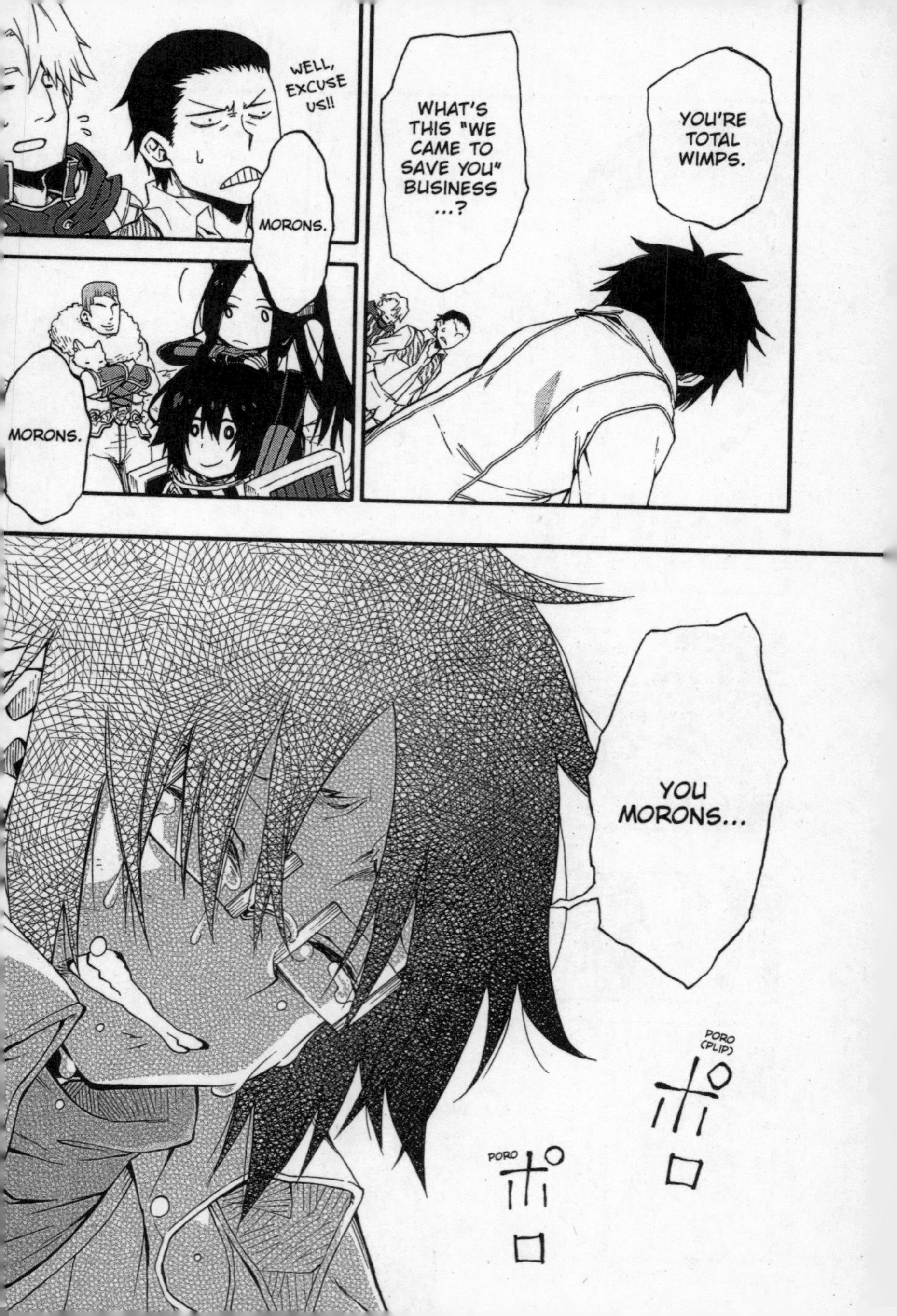
YOU'RE TOTAL WIMPS.
WHAT'S THIS "WE CAME TO SAVE YOU" BUSINESS ...?
MORONS.
WELL, EXCUSE US!!
MORONS.
YOU MORONS...
PORO (PLIP)
PORO

LOG HORIZON
THE WEST WIND BRIGADE

LOG HORIZON
THE WEST WIND BRIGADE

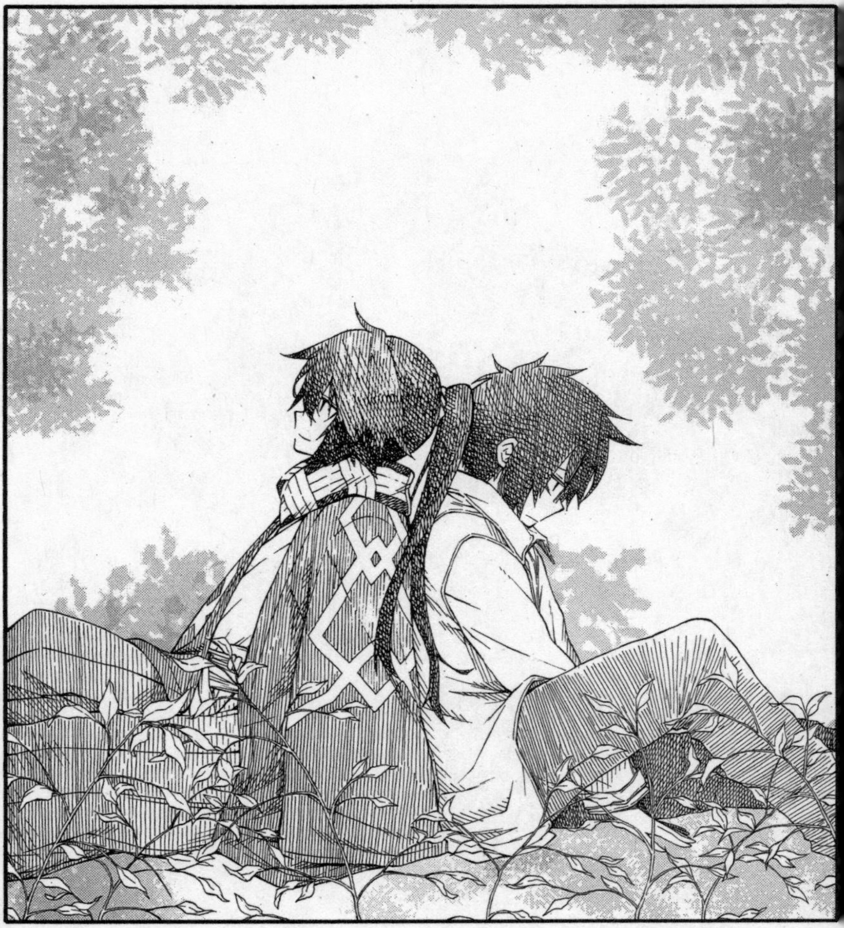

CHAPTER : 17 BYE-BYE, SEE YOU LATER

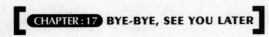

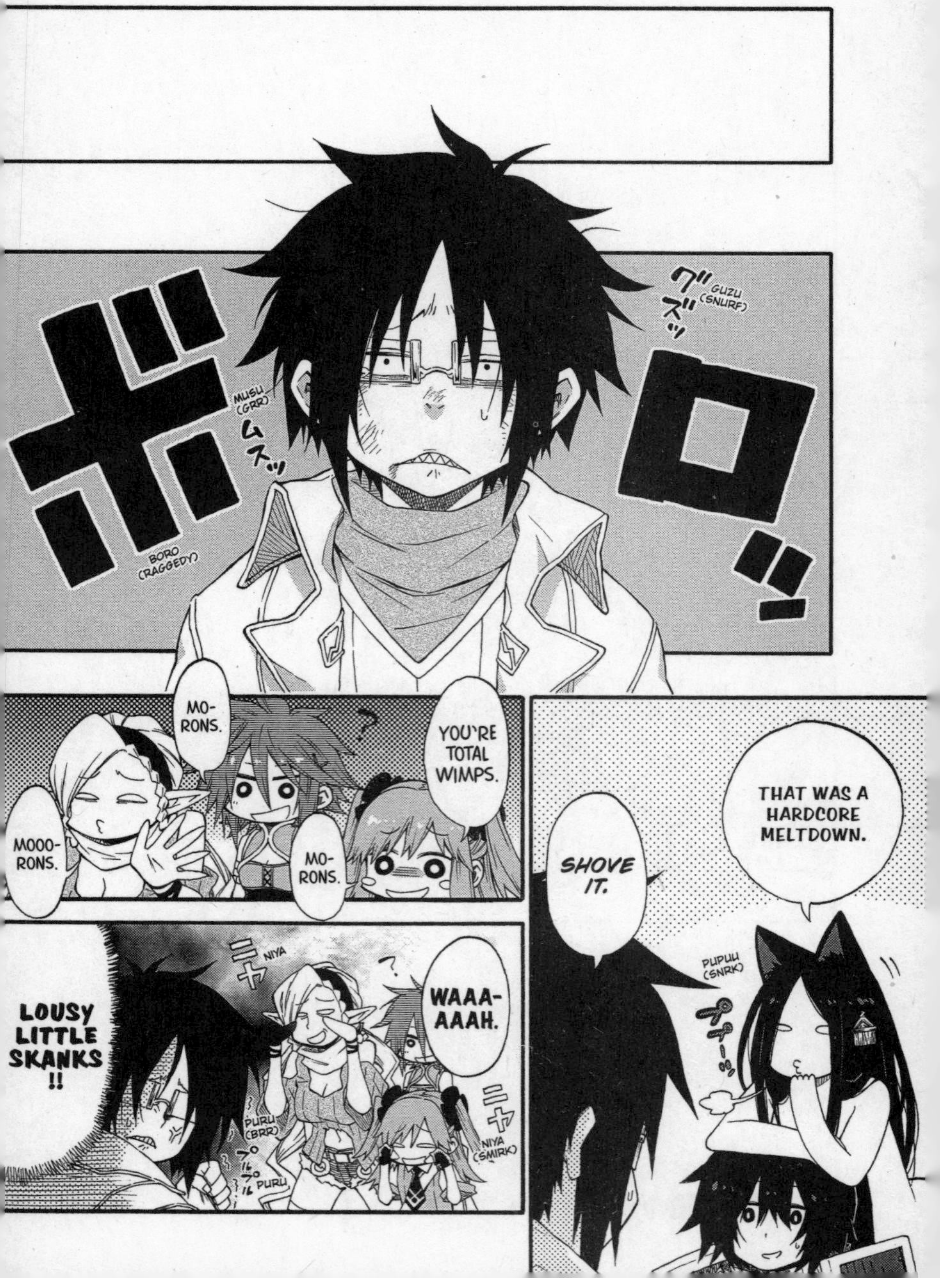

グズッ
GUZU (SNURF)
ボロッ
BORO (RAGGEDY)
ムスッ
MUSU (GRR)
THAT WAS A HARDCORE MELTDOWN.
SHOVE IT.
PUPUU (SNRK)
YOU'RE TOTAL WIMPS.
MO-RONS.
MO-RONS.
MOOO-RONS.
WAAAA-AAAH.
ニヤ
NIYA
ニヤ
NIYA (SMIRK)
PURU (BRR)
PURU
LOUSY LITTLE SKANKS!!

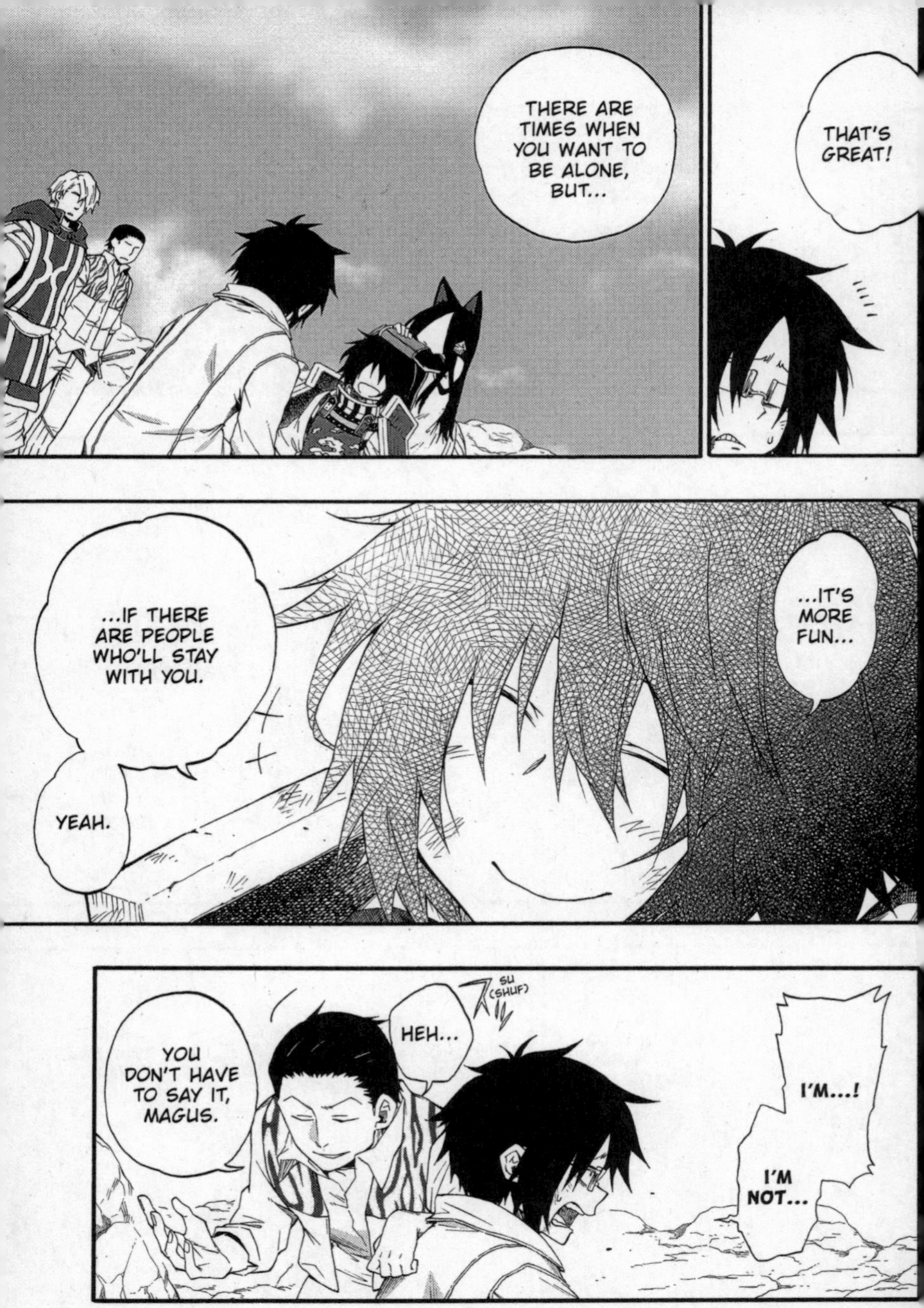
THAT'S GREAT!
THERE ARE TIMES WHEN YOU WANT TO BE ALONE, BUT...
...IT'S MORE FUN...
...IF THERE ARE PEOPLE WHO'LL STAY WITH YOU.
YEAH.
I'M...!
I'M NOT...
SU (SHUF)
HEH...
YOU DON'T HAVE TO SAY IT, MAGUS.

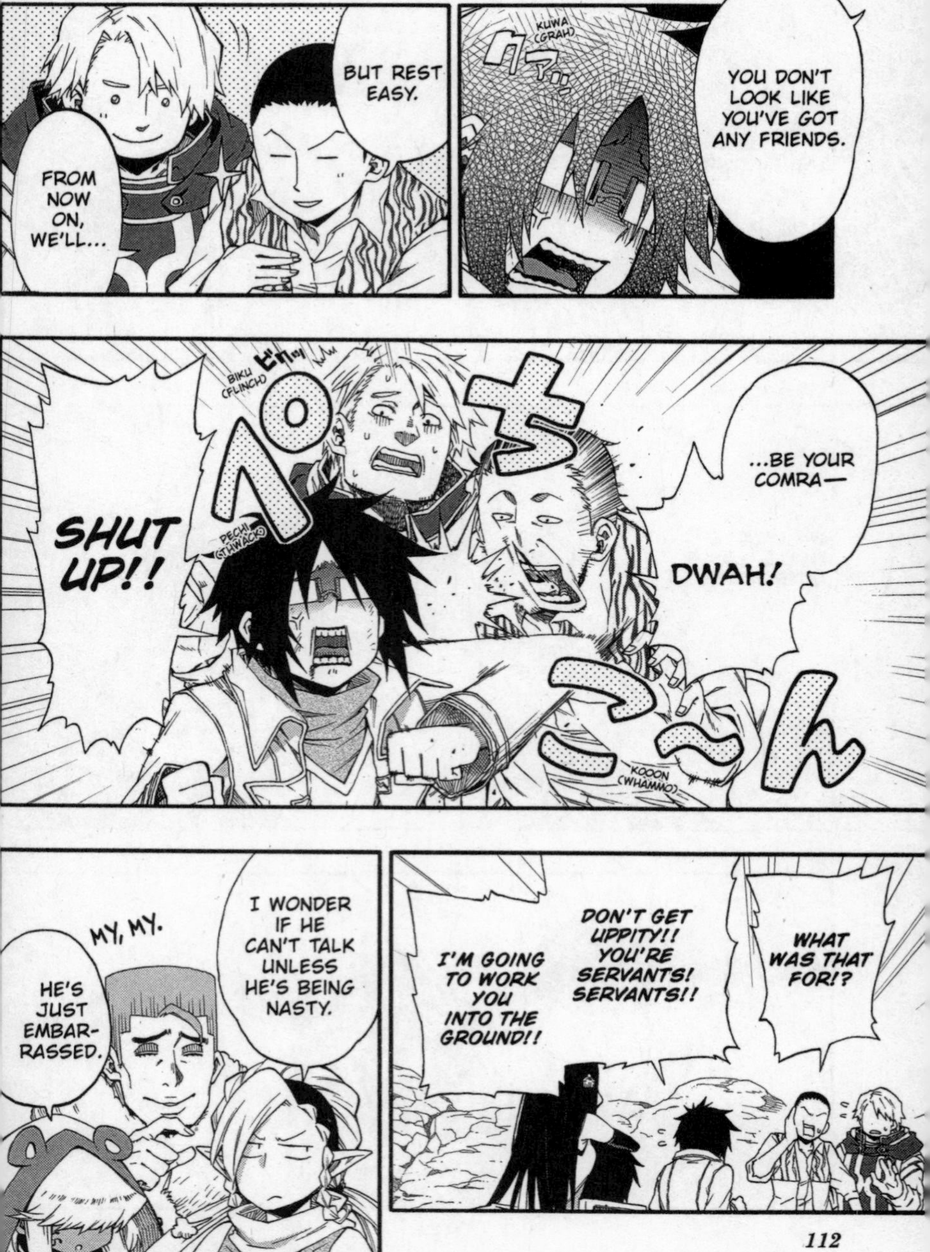
KUWA (GRAH)
YOU DON'T LOOK LIKE YOU'VE GOT ANY FRIENDS.
BUT REST EASY.
FROM NOW ON, WE'LL...
...BE YOUR COMRA—
BIKU (FLINCH)
DWAH!
SHUT UP!!
PECHI (THWACK)
KOOON (WHAMMO)
WHAT WAS THAT FOR!?
DON'T GET UPPITY!! YOU'RE SERVANTS! SERVANTS!!
I'M GOING TO WORK YOU INTO THE GROUND!!
I WONDER IF HE CAN'T TALK UNLESS HE'S BEING NASTY.
MY, MY.
HE'S JUST EMBARRASSED.

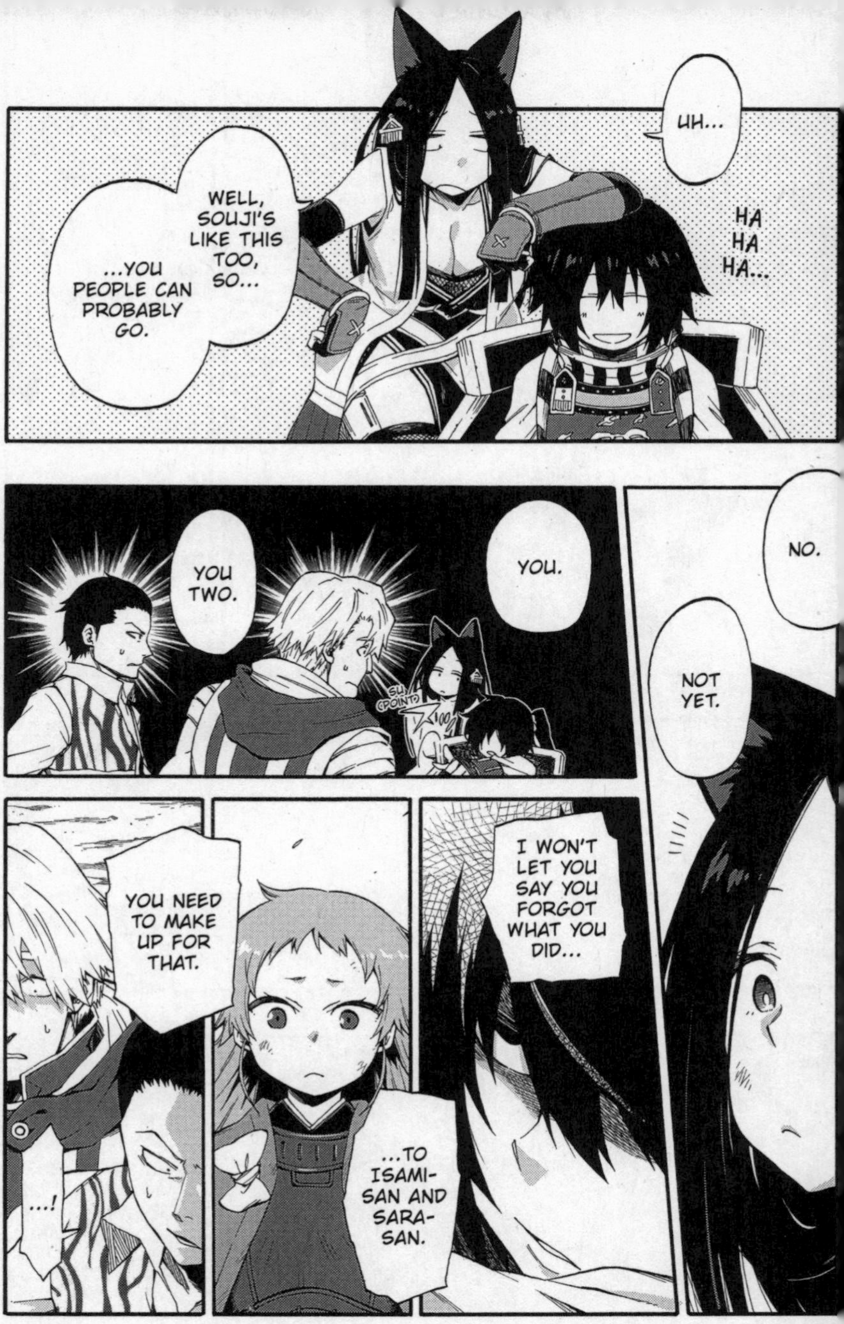
UH...
HA HA HA...
WELL, SOUJI'S LIKE THIS TOO, SO...
...YOU PEOPLE CAN PROBABLY GO.
NO.
NOT YET.
YOU.
YOU TWO.
SU (POINT)
I WON'T LET YOU SAY YOU FORGOT WHAT YOU DID...
YOU NEED TO MAKE UP FOR THAT.
...TO ISAMI-SAN AND SARA-SAN.
...!

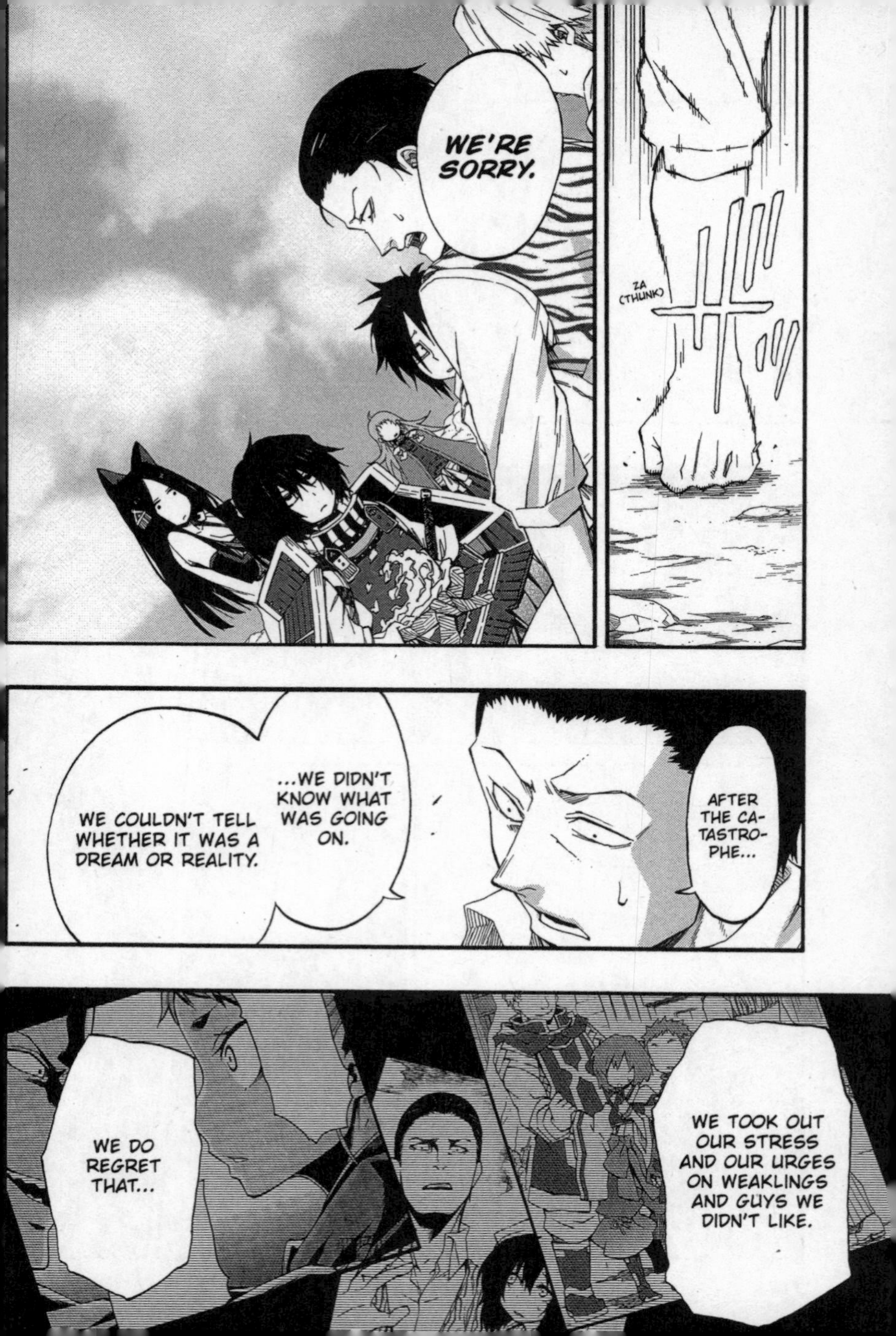
ZA (THUNK)
WE'RE SORRY.
AFTER THE CA-TASTRO-PHE...
...WE DIDN'T KNOW WHAT WAS GOING ON.
WE COULDN'T TELL WHETHER IT WAS A DREAM OR REALITY.
WE TOOK OUT OUR STRESS AND OUR URGES ON WEAKLINGS AND GUYS WE DIDN'T LIKE.
WE DO REGRET THAT...

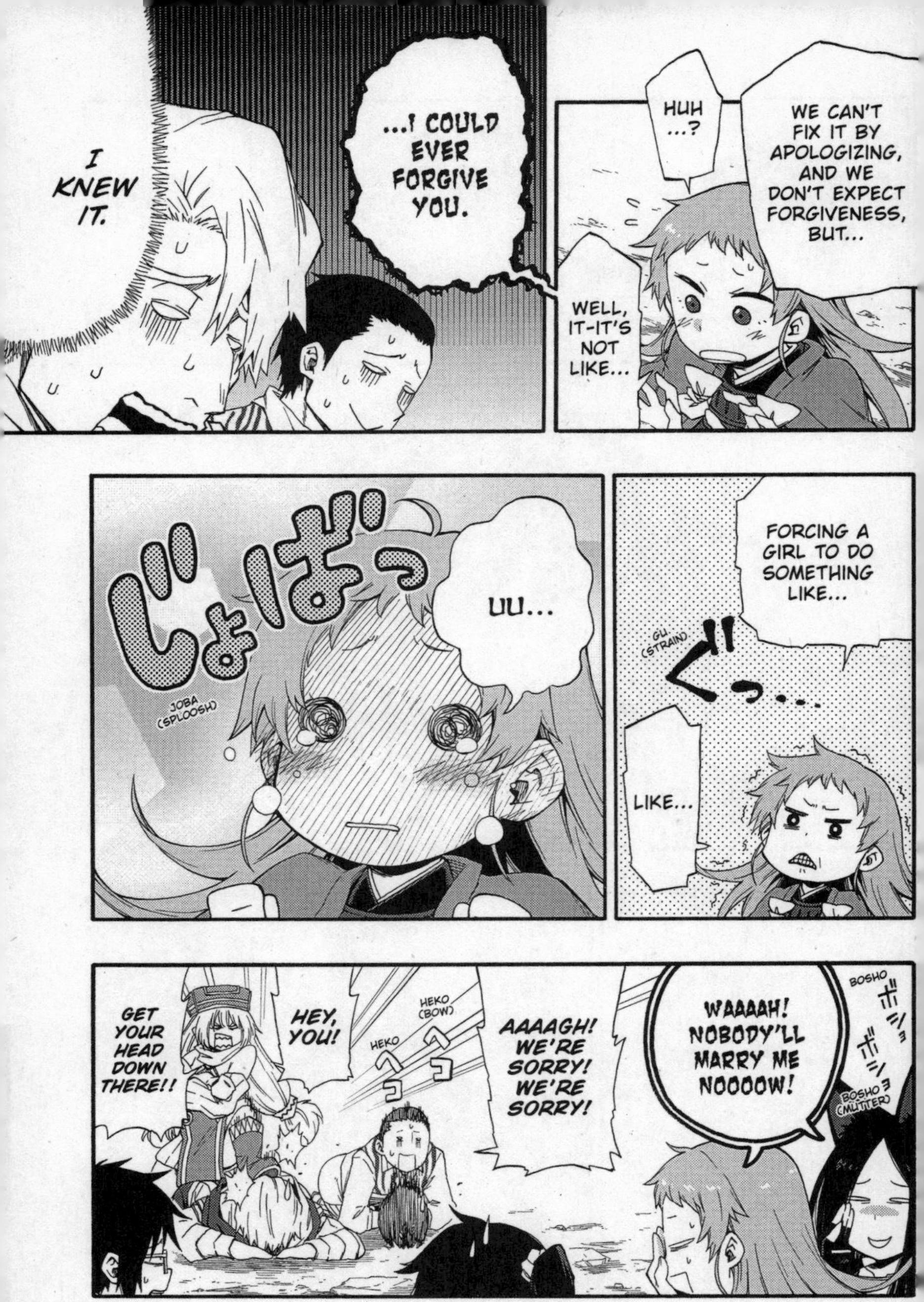
WE CAN'T FIX IT BY APOLOGIZING, AND WE DON'T EXPECT FORGIVENESS, BUT...
HUH ...?
WELL, IT-IT'S NOT LIKE...
...I COULD EVER FORGIVE YOU.
I KNEW IT.
FORCING A GIRL TO DO SOMETHING LIKE...
ぐっ...
GU (STRAIN)
LIKE...
UU...
じょばっ
JOBA (SPLOOSH)
BOSHO
ボショ
ボショ
BOSHO (MUTTER)
WAAAAH! NOBODY'LL MARRY ME NOOOOW!
AAAAGH! WE'RE SORRY! WE'RE SORRY!
HEKO (BOW)
へこ
HEKO
へこ
HEY, YOU!
GET YOUR HEAD DOWN THERE!!

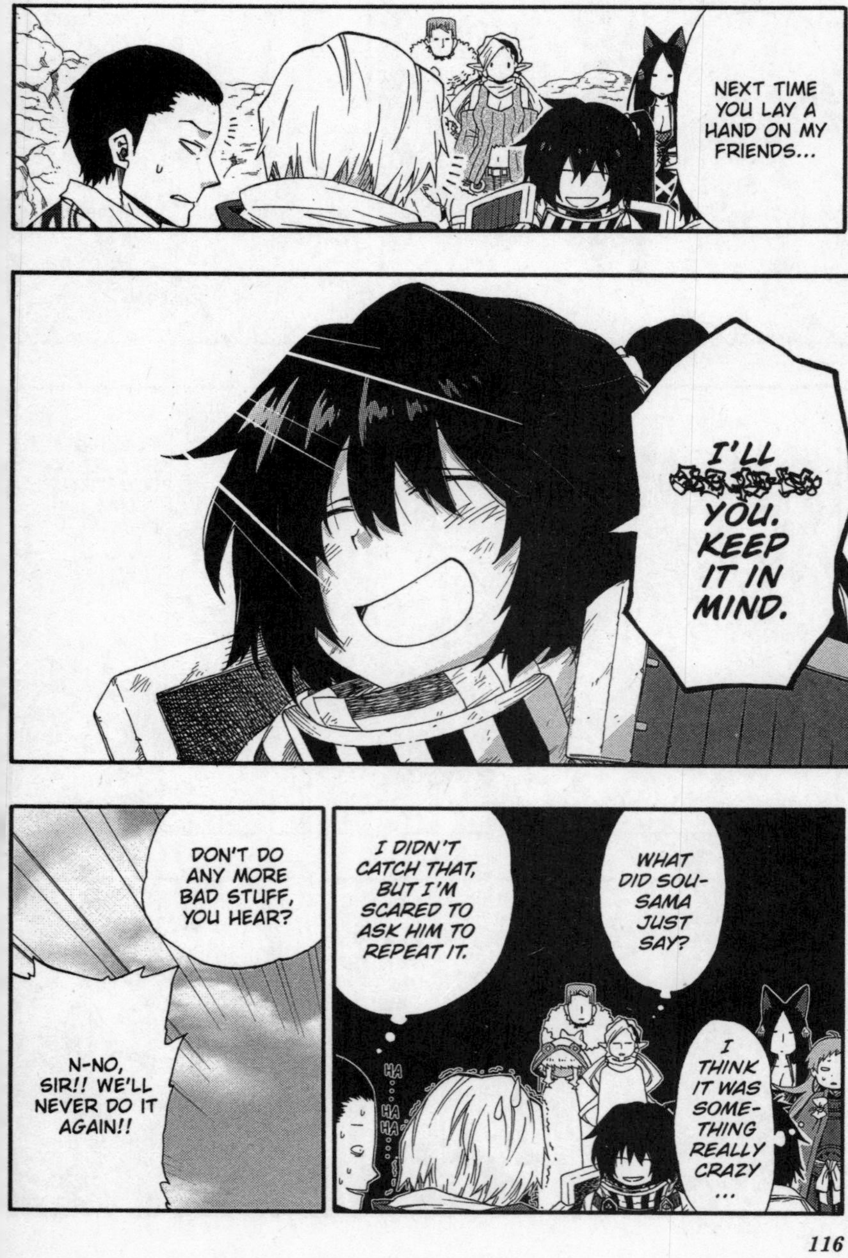
NEXT TIME YOU LAY A HAND ON MY FRIENDS...
I'LL
YOU. KEEP IT IN MIND.
WHAT DID SOU-SAMA JUST SAY?
I DIDN'T CATCH THAT, BUT I'M SCARED TO ASK HIM TO REPEAT IT.
I THINK IT WAS SOME-THING REALLY CRAZY...
HA... HA HA...
DON'T DO ANY MORE BAD STUFF, YOU HEAR?
N-NO, SIR!! WE'LL NEVER DO IT AGAIN!!

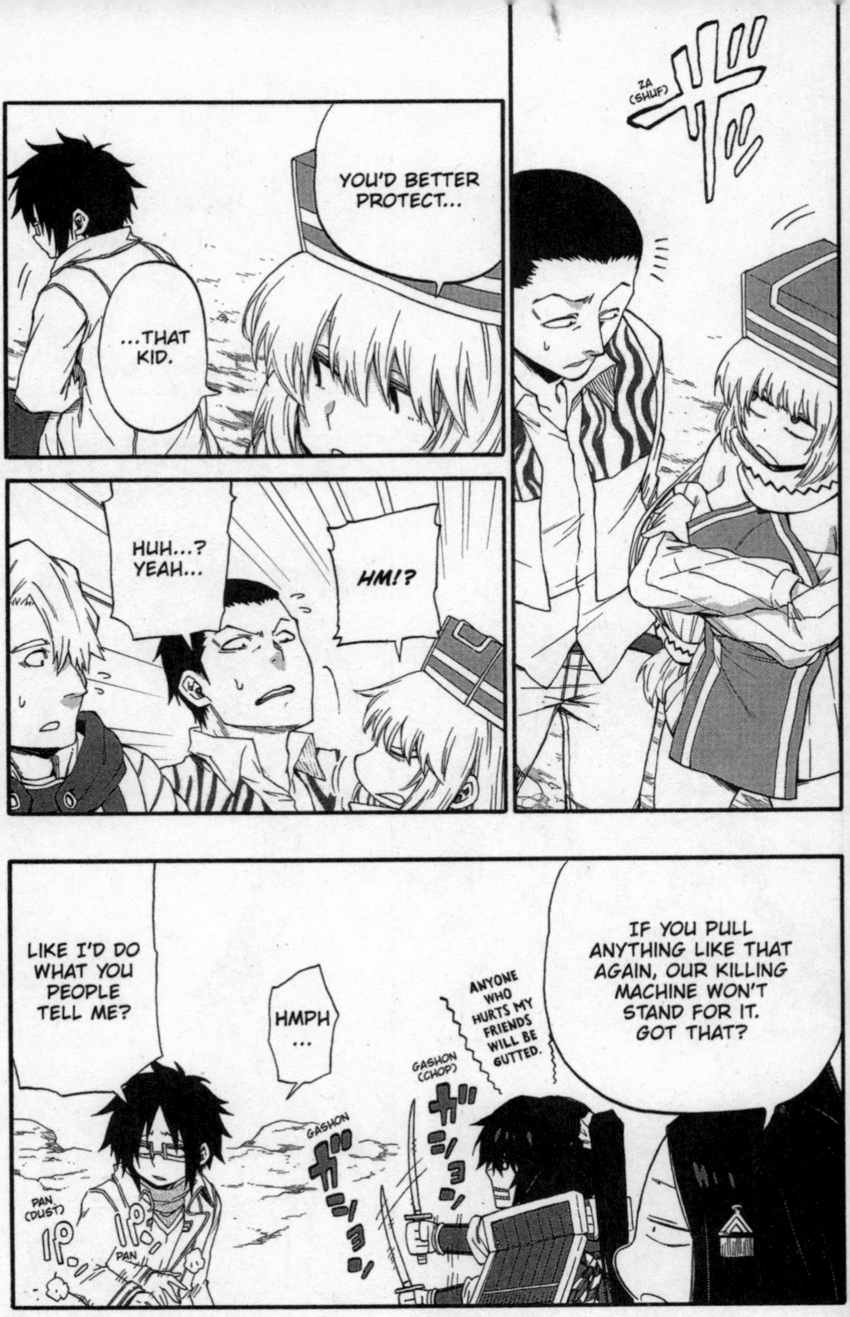
ZA (SHUF)
YOU'D BETTER PROTECT...
...THAT KID.
HM!?
HUH...? YEAH...
IF YOU PULL ANYTHING LIKE THAT AGAIN, OUR KILLING MACHINE WON'T STAND FOR IT. GOT THAT?
ANYONE WHO HURTS MY FRIENDS WILL BE GUTTED.
GASHON (CHOP)
GASHON
HMPH ...
LIKE I'D DO WHAT YOU PEOPLE TELL ME?
PAN (DUST)
PAN

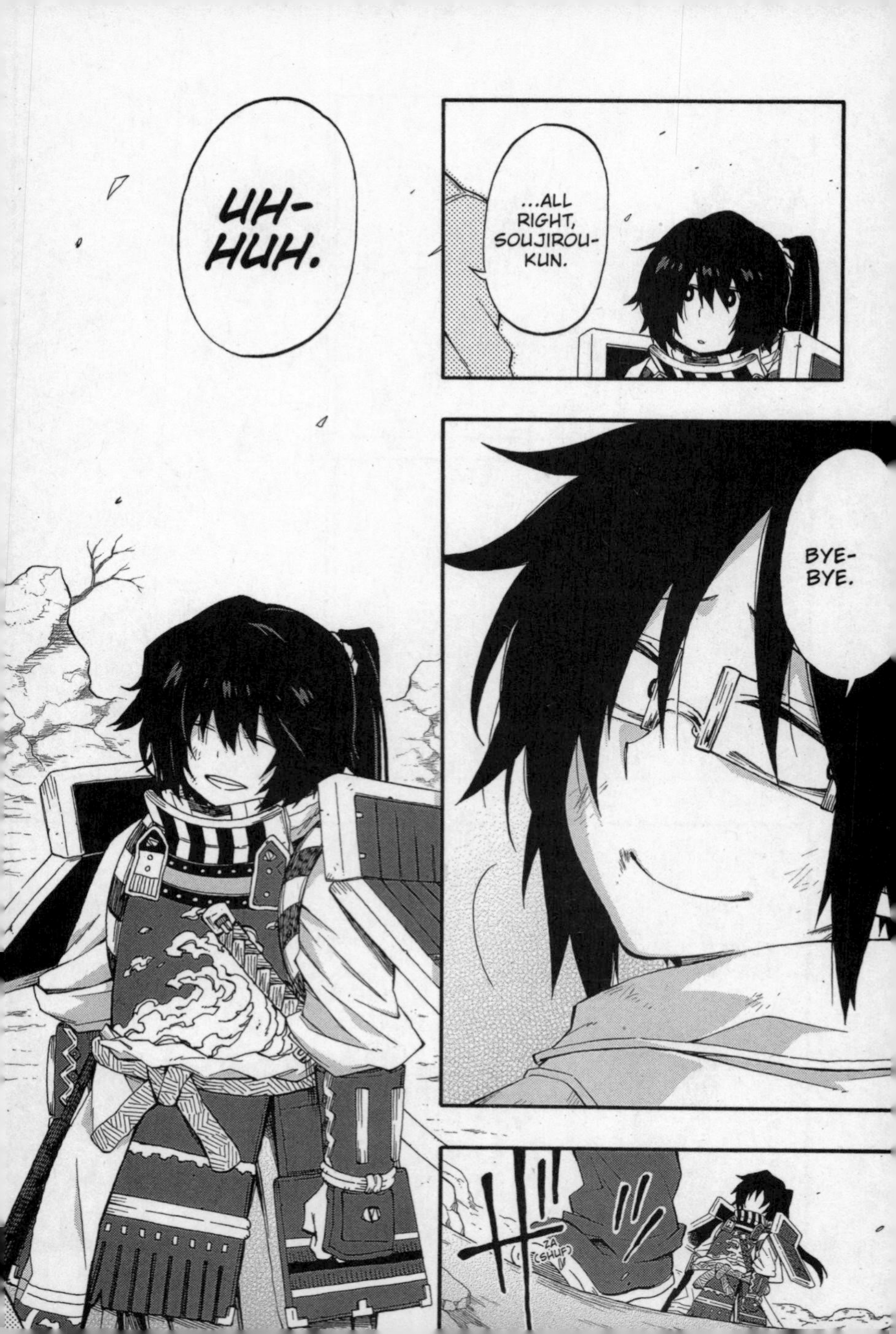
...ALL RIGHT, SOUJIROU-KUN.
BYE-BYE.
ZA
(SHUF)
UH-HUH.

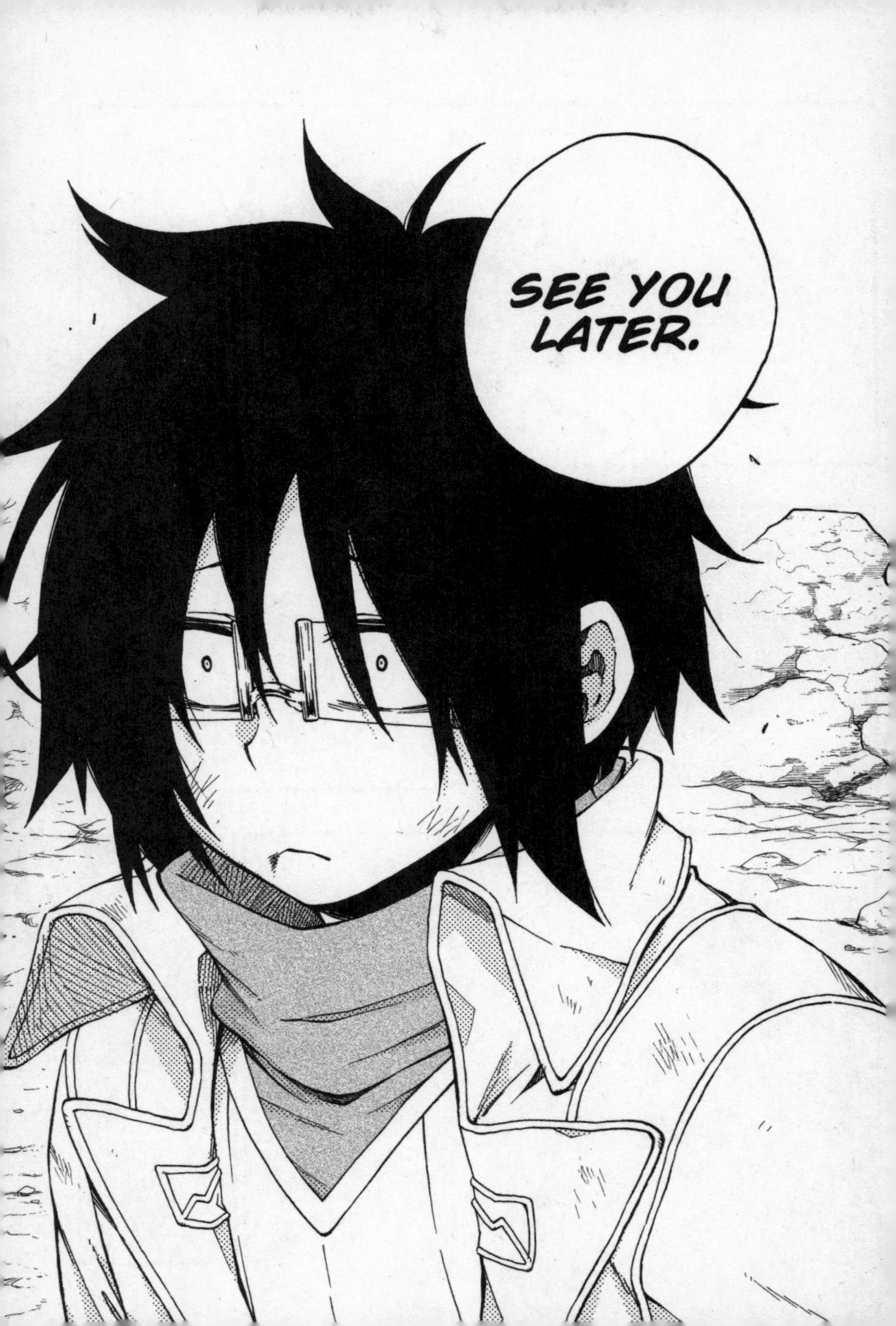
SEE YOU LATER.

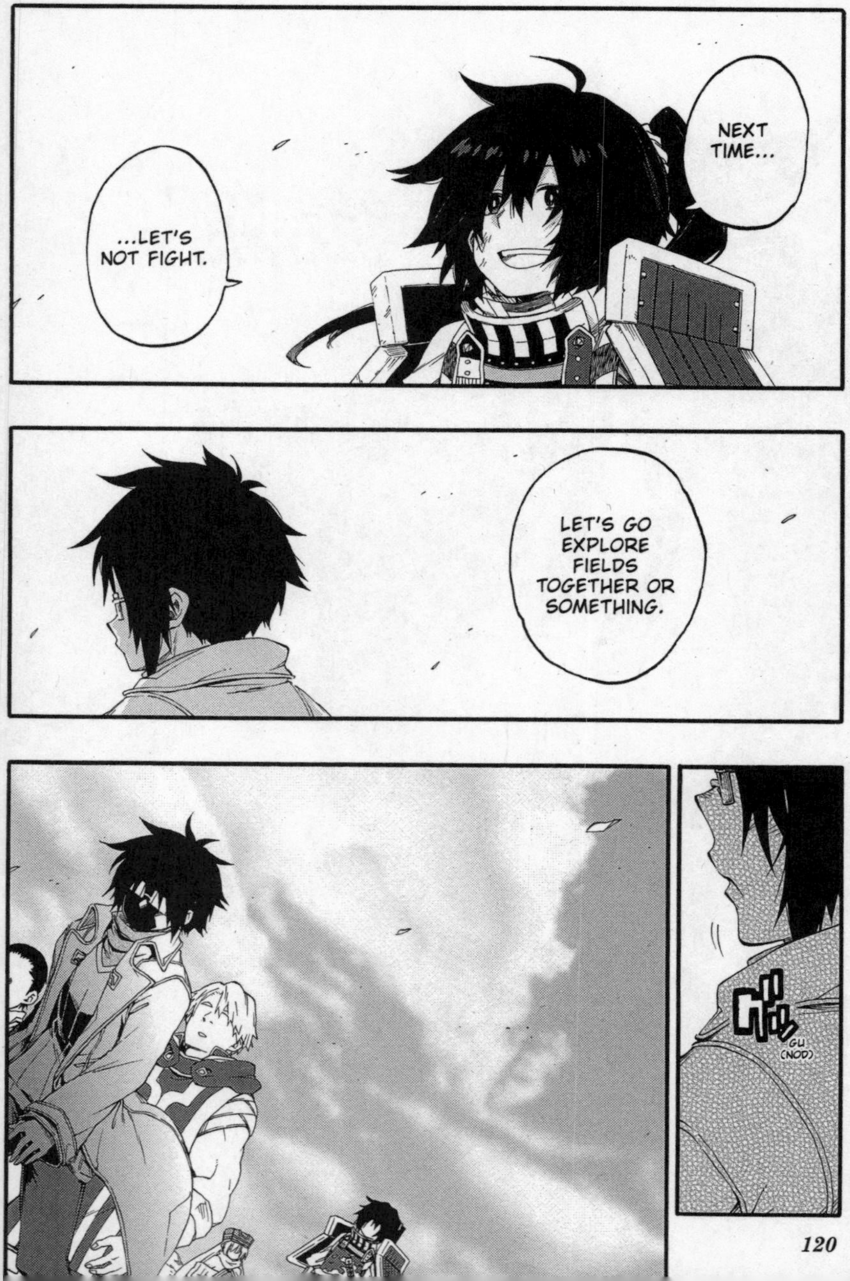
NEXT TIME...
...LET'S NOT FIGHT.
LET'S GO EXPLORE FIELDS TOGETHER OR SOMETHING.
GU (NOD)

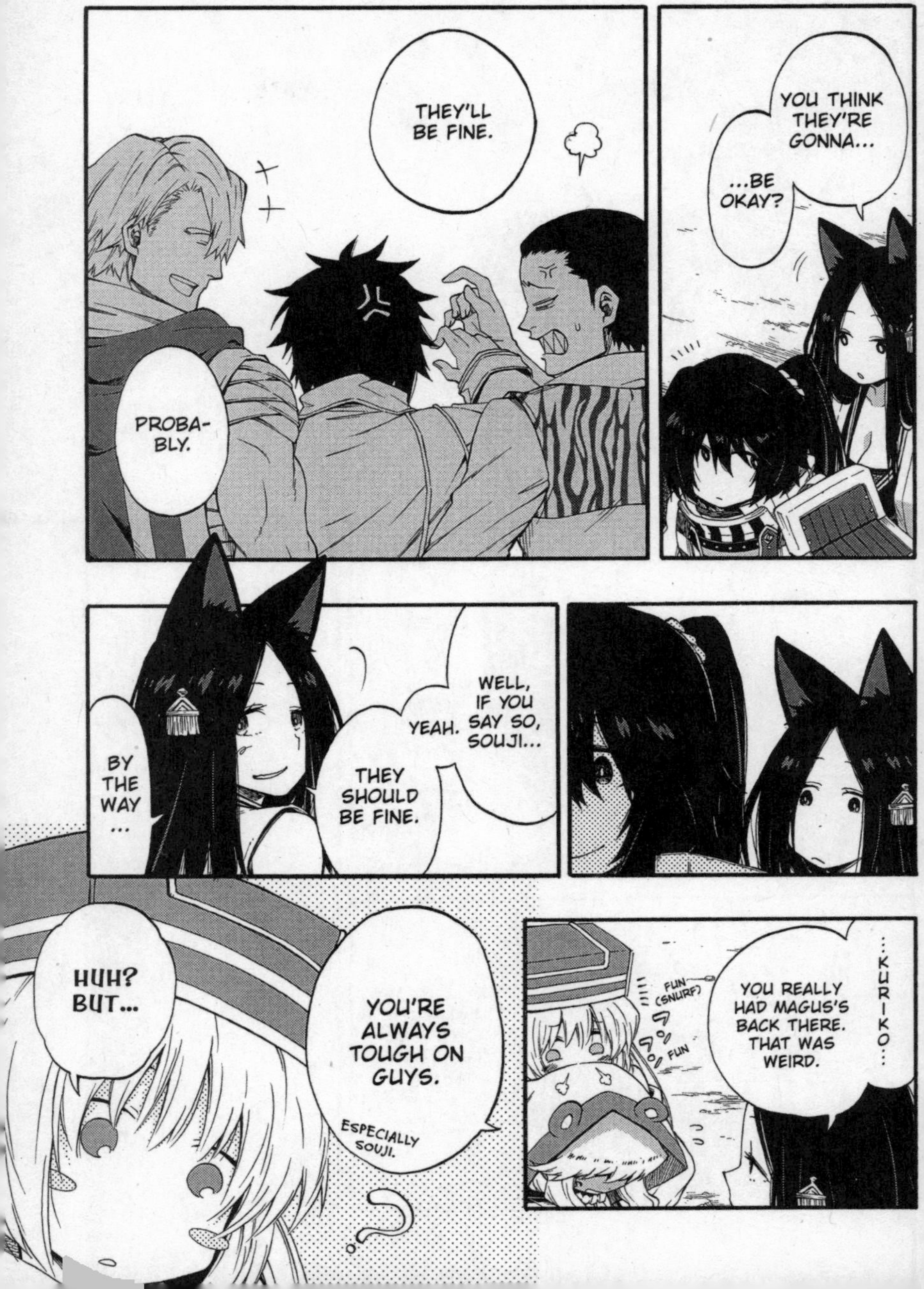
YOU THINK THEY'RE GONNA...
...BE OKAY?
THEY'LL BE FINE.
PROBA-BLY.
WELL, IF YOU SAY SO, SOUJI...
YEAH.
THEY SHOULD BE FINE.
BY THE WAY...
...KURIKO...
YOU REALLY HAD MAGUS'S BACK THERE. THAT WAS WEIRD.
FUN (SNURF)
FUN
HUH? BUT...
YOU'RE ALWAYS TOUGH ON GUYS.
ESPECIALLY SOUJI.

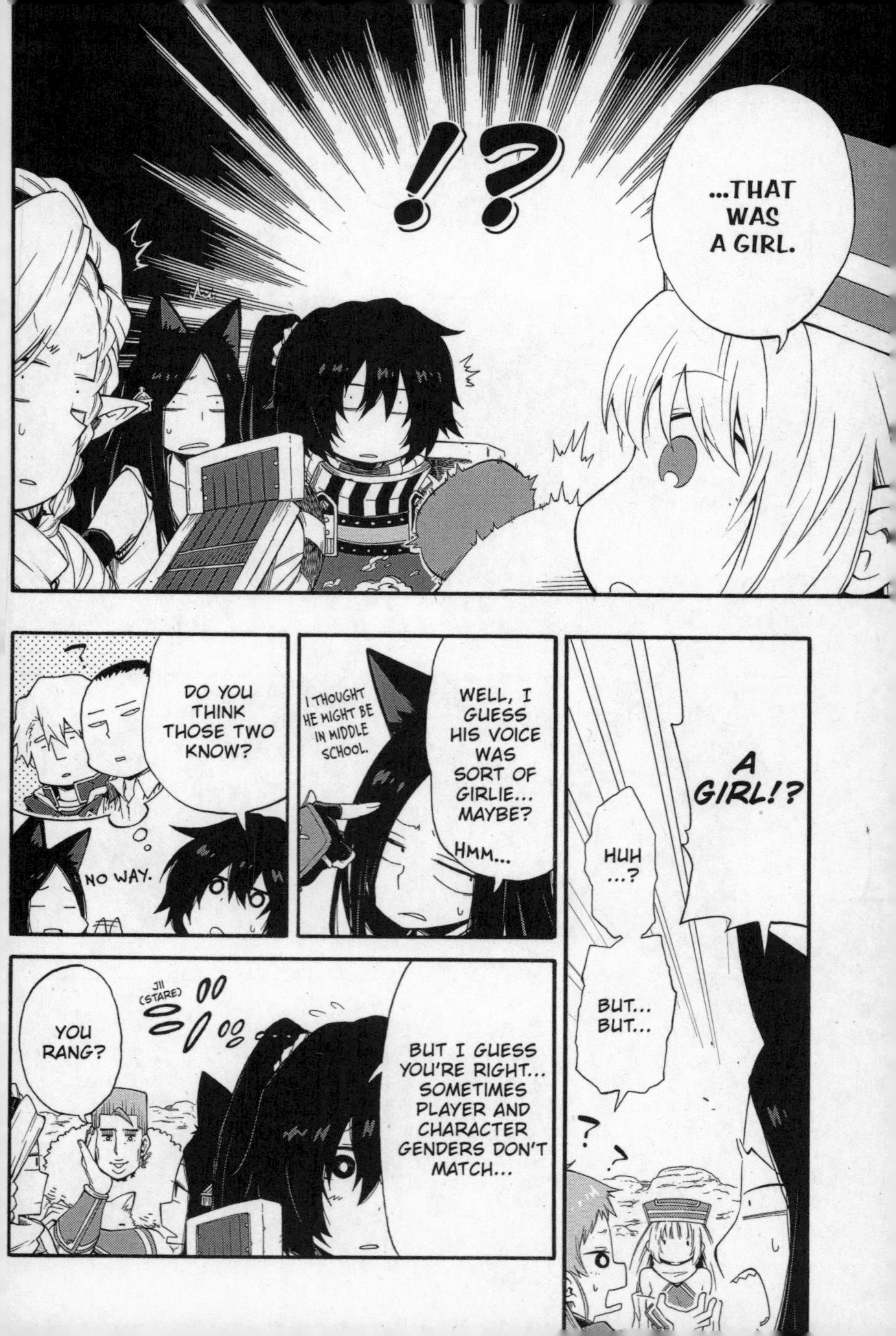
...THAT WAS A GIRL.
!?
A GIRL!?
HUH ...?
BUT... BUT...
WELL, I GUESS HIS VOICE WAS SORT OF GIRLIE... MAYBE?
I THOUGHT HE MIGHT BE IN MIDDLE SCHOOL.
HMM...
DO YOU THINK THOSE TWO KNOW?
NO WAY.
BUT I GUESS YOU'RE RIGHT... SOMETIMES PLAYER AND CHARACTER GENDERS DON'T MATCH...
JII (STARE)
YOU RANG?

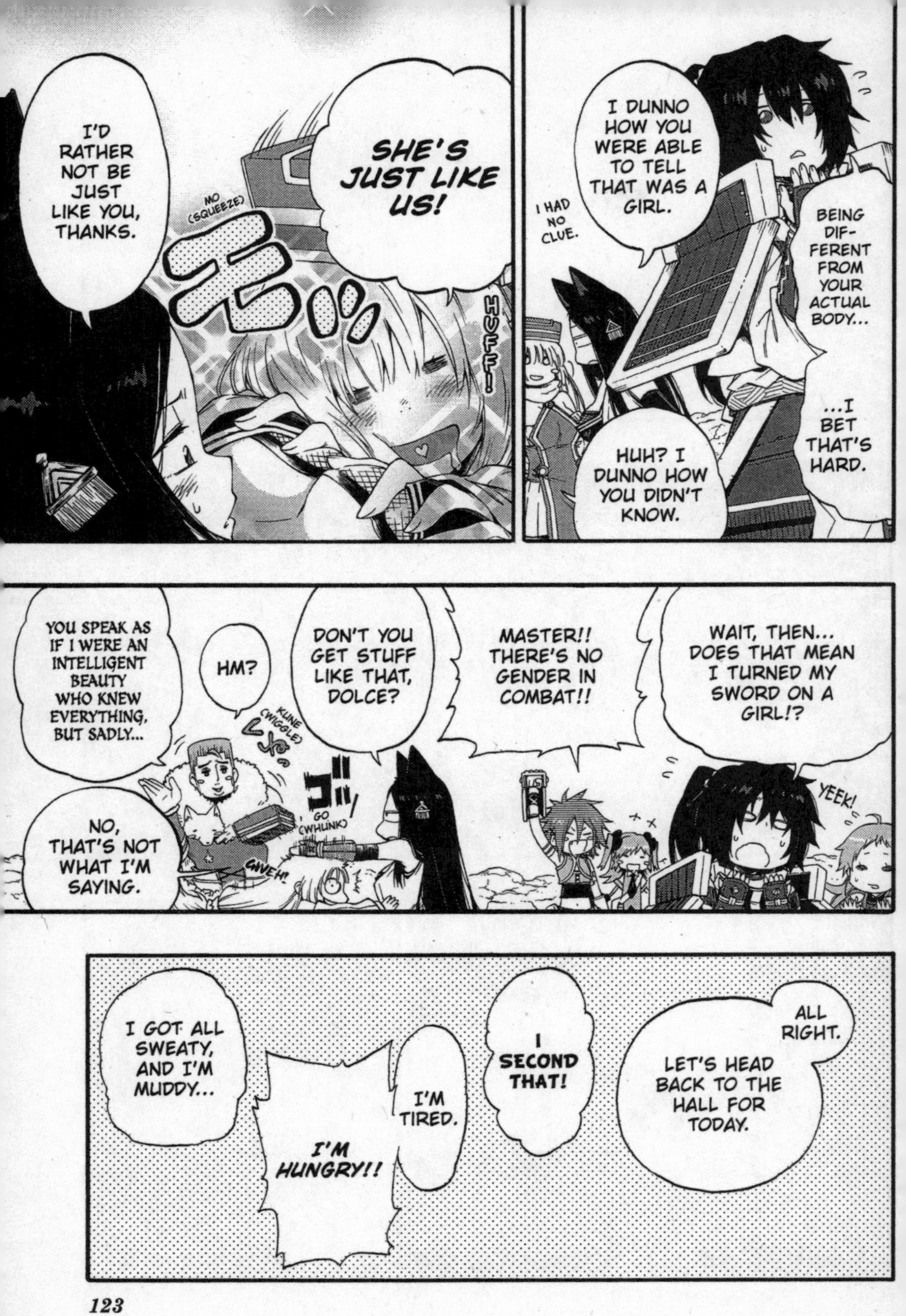
I DUNNO HOW YOU WERE ABLE TO TELL THAT WAS A GIRL.
BEING DIF-FERENT FROM YOUR ACTUAL BODY...
I HAD NO CLUE.
...I BET THAT'S HARD.
HUH? I DUNNO HOW YOU DIDN'T KNOW.
SHE'S JUST LIKE US!
MO (SQUEEZE)
HUFF!
I'D RATHER NOT BE JUST LIKE YOU, THANKS.
WAIT, THEN... DOES THAT MEAN I TURNED MY SWORD ON A GIRL!?
YEEK!
MASTER!! THERE'S NO GENDER IN COMBAT!!
DON'T YOU GET STUFF LIKE THAT, DOLCE?
GO (WHUNK)
KUNE (WIGGLE)
HM?
GNYEH!
YOU SPEAK AS IF I WERE AN INTELLIGENT BEAUTY WHO KNEW EVERYTHING, BUT SADLY...
NO, THAT'S NOT WHAT I'M SAYING.
ALL RIGHT.
LET'S HEAD BACK TO THE HALL FOR TODAY.
I SECOND THAT!
I'M TIRED.
I'M HUNGRY!!
I GOT ALL SWEATY, AND I'M MUDDY...

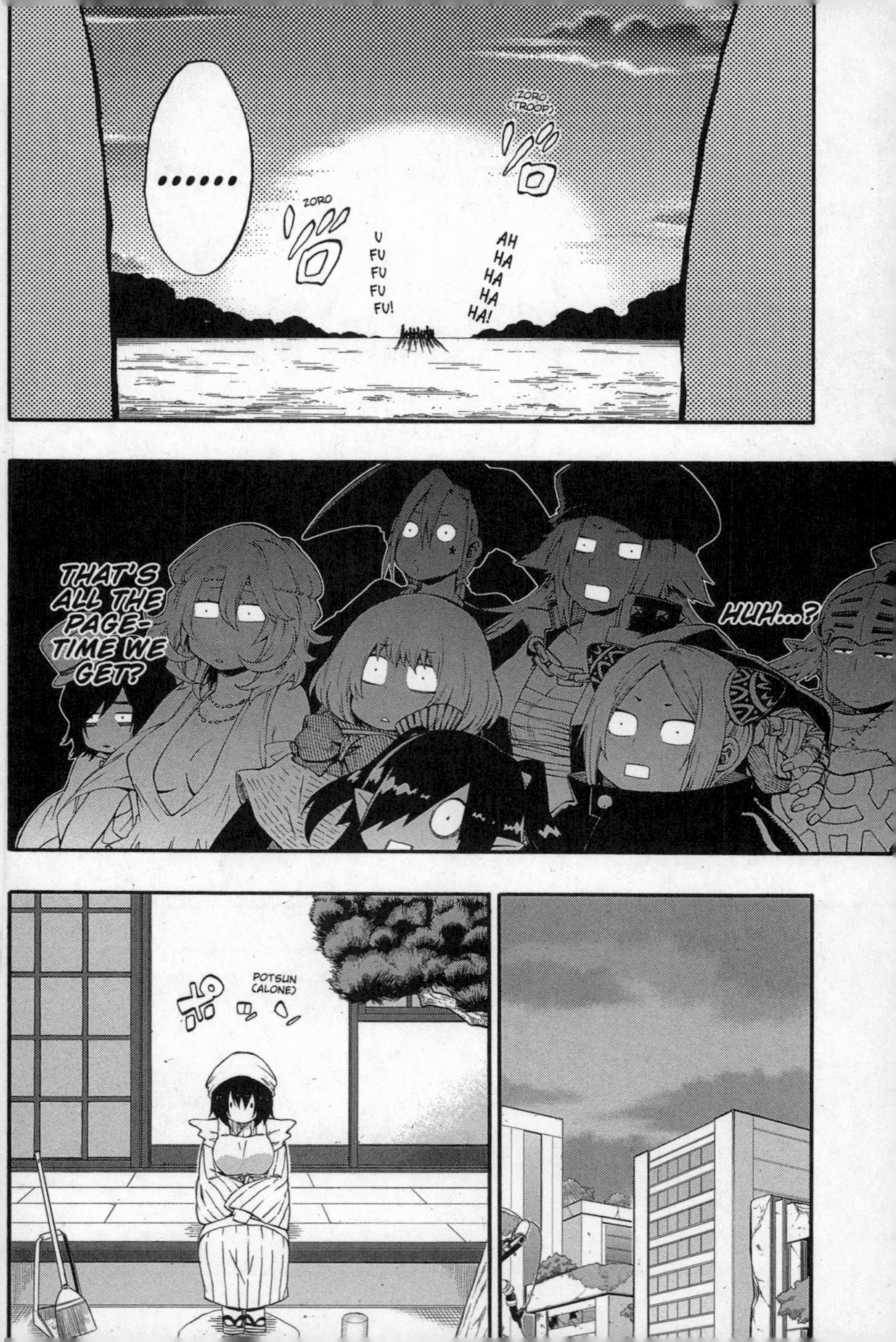
ZORO (TROOP)
AH HA HA HA HA!
U FU FU FU FU!
ZORO
......
HUH...?
THAT'S ALL THE PAGE-TIME WE GET?
POTSUN (ALONE)

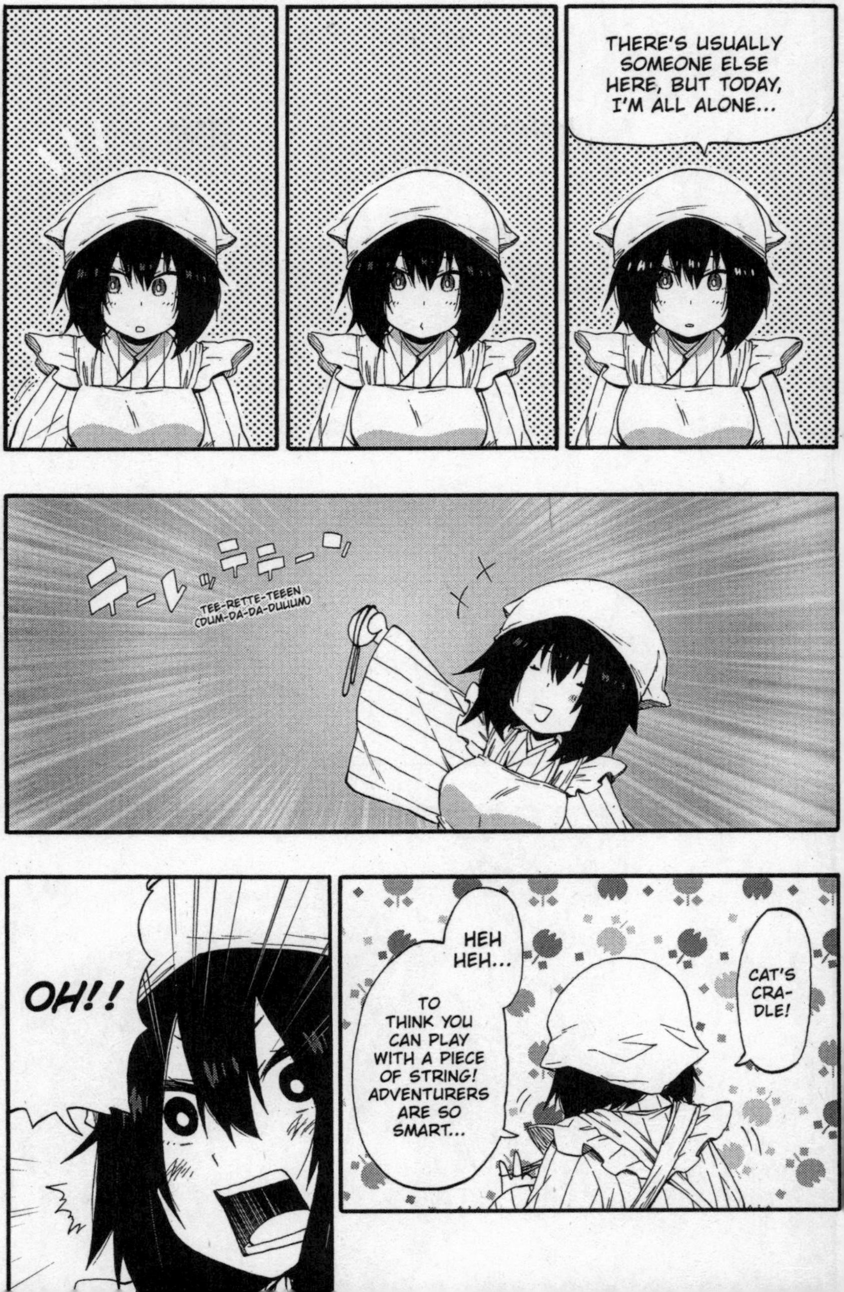
THERE'S USUALLY SOMEONE ELSE HERE, BUT TODAY, I'M ALL ALONE...
TEE-RETTE-TEEEN (DUM-DA-DA-DUUUM)
CAT'S CRA-DLE!
HEH HEH...
TO THINK YOU CAN PLAY WITH A PIECE OF STRING! ADVENTURERS ARE SO SMART...
OH!!

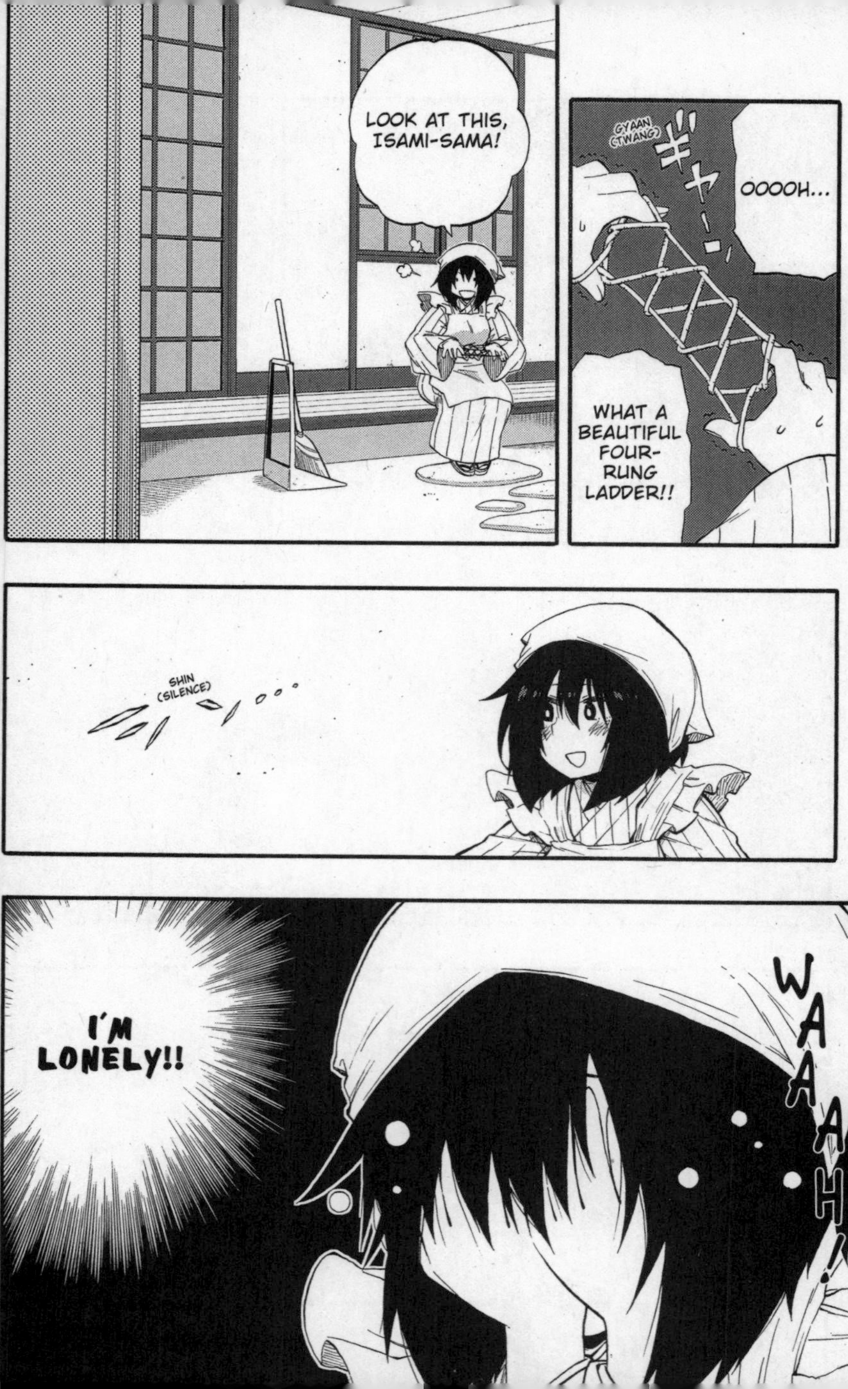
GYAAN (TWANG)
ギャーン
OOOOH...
WHAT A BEAUTIFUL FOUR-RUNG LADDER!!
LOOK AT THIS, ISAMI-SAMA!
SHIN (SILENCE)
WAAAAH!
I'M LONELY!!

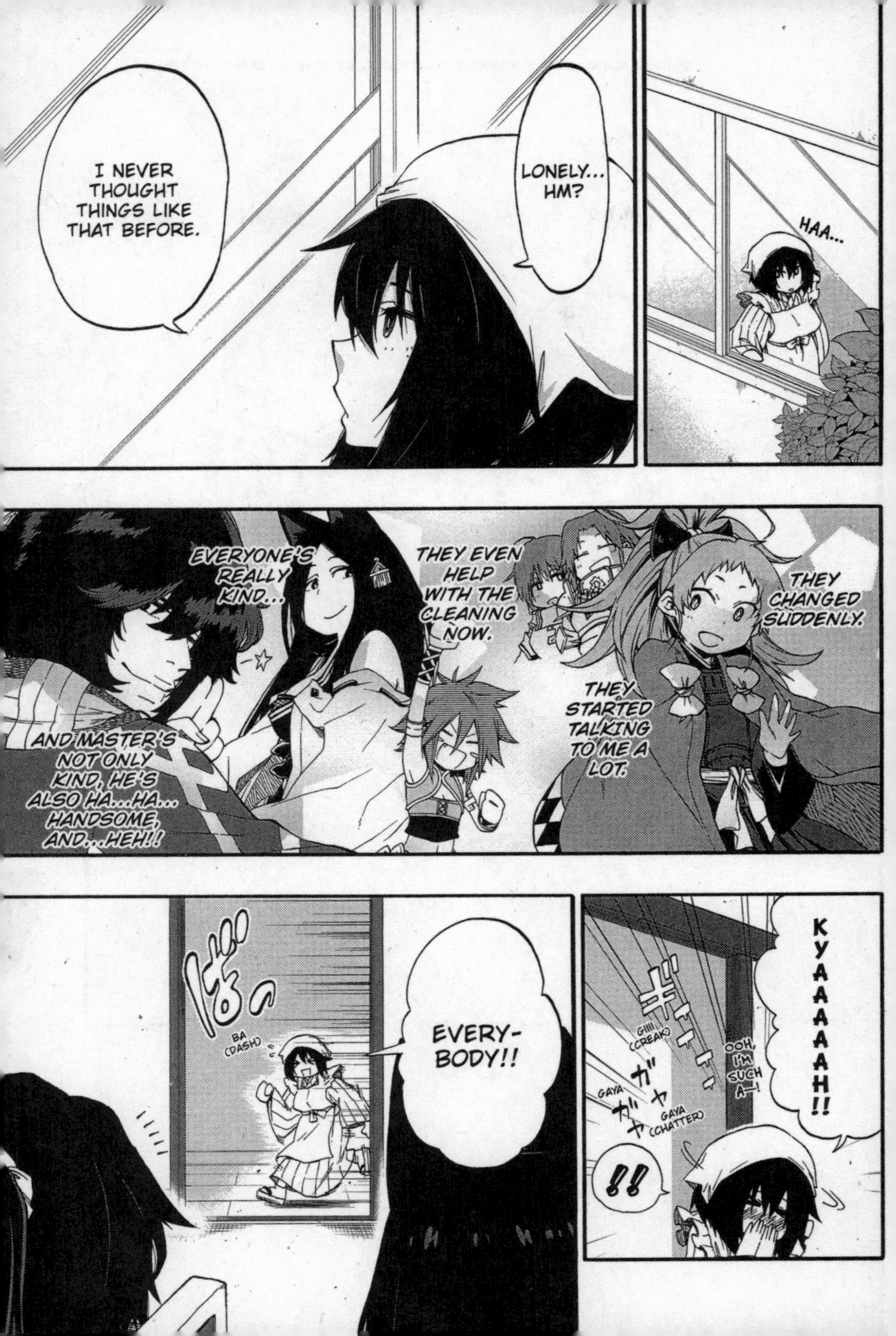
HAA...
LONELY... HM?
I NEVER THOUGHT THINGS LIKE THAT BEFORE.
THEY CHANGED SUDDENLY.
THEY STARTED TALKING TO ME A LOT.
THEY EVEN HELP WITH THE CLEANING NOW.
EVERYONE'S REALLY KIND...
AND MASTER'S NOT ONLY KIND, HE'S ALSO HA...HA... HANDSOME, AND...HEH!!
KYAAAAAAH!!
OOH, I'M SUCH A—!
GIII (CREAK)
GAYA GAYA (CHATTER)
!!
EVERY-BODY!!
BA (DASH)

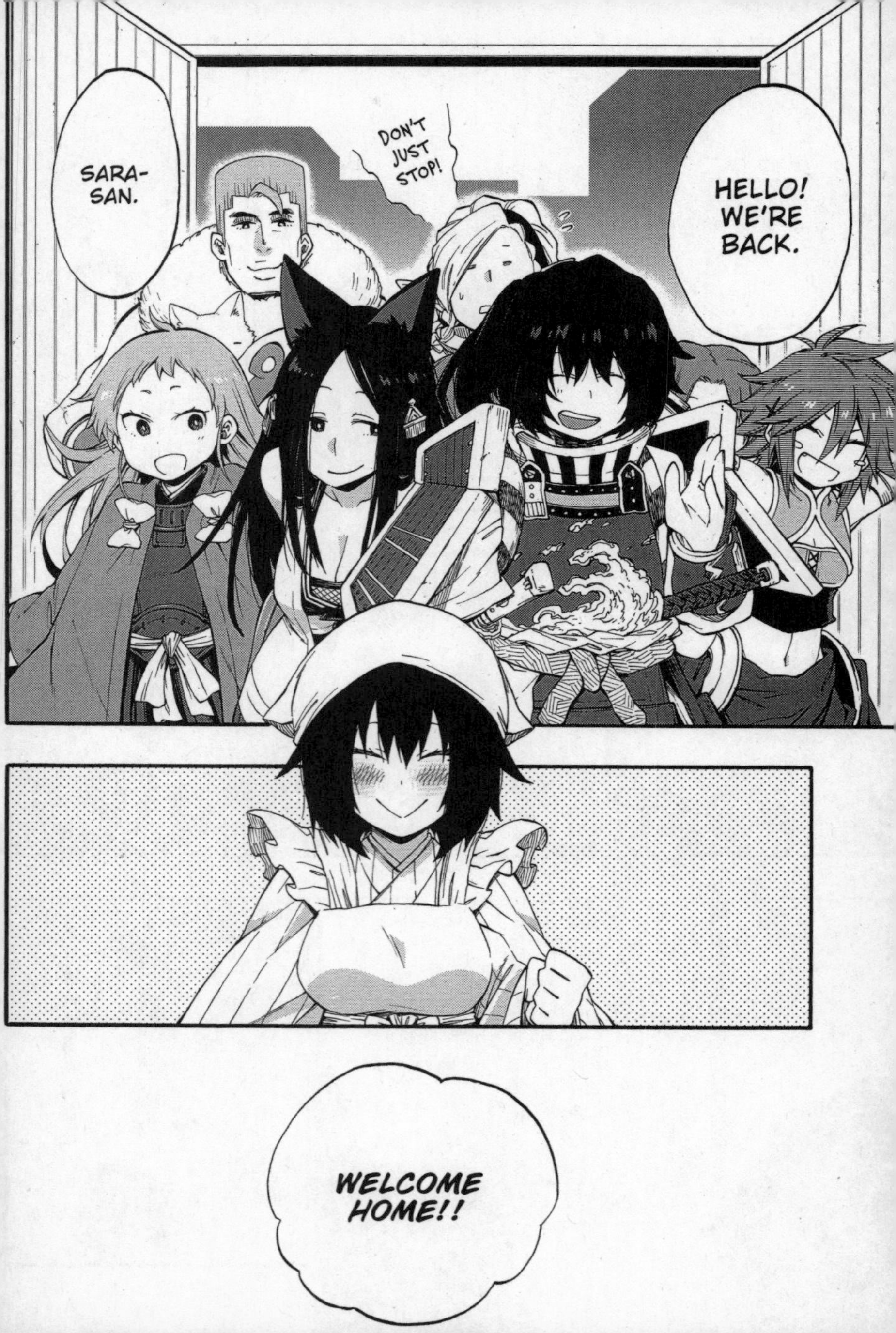
HELLO! WE'RE BACK.
DON'T JUST STOP!
SARA-SAN.
WELCOME HOME!!

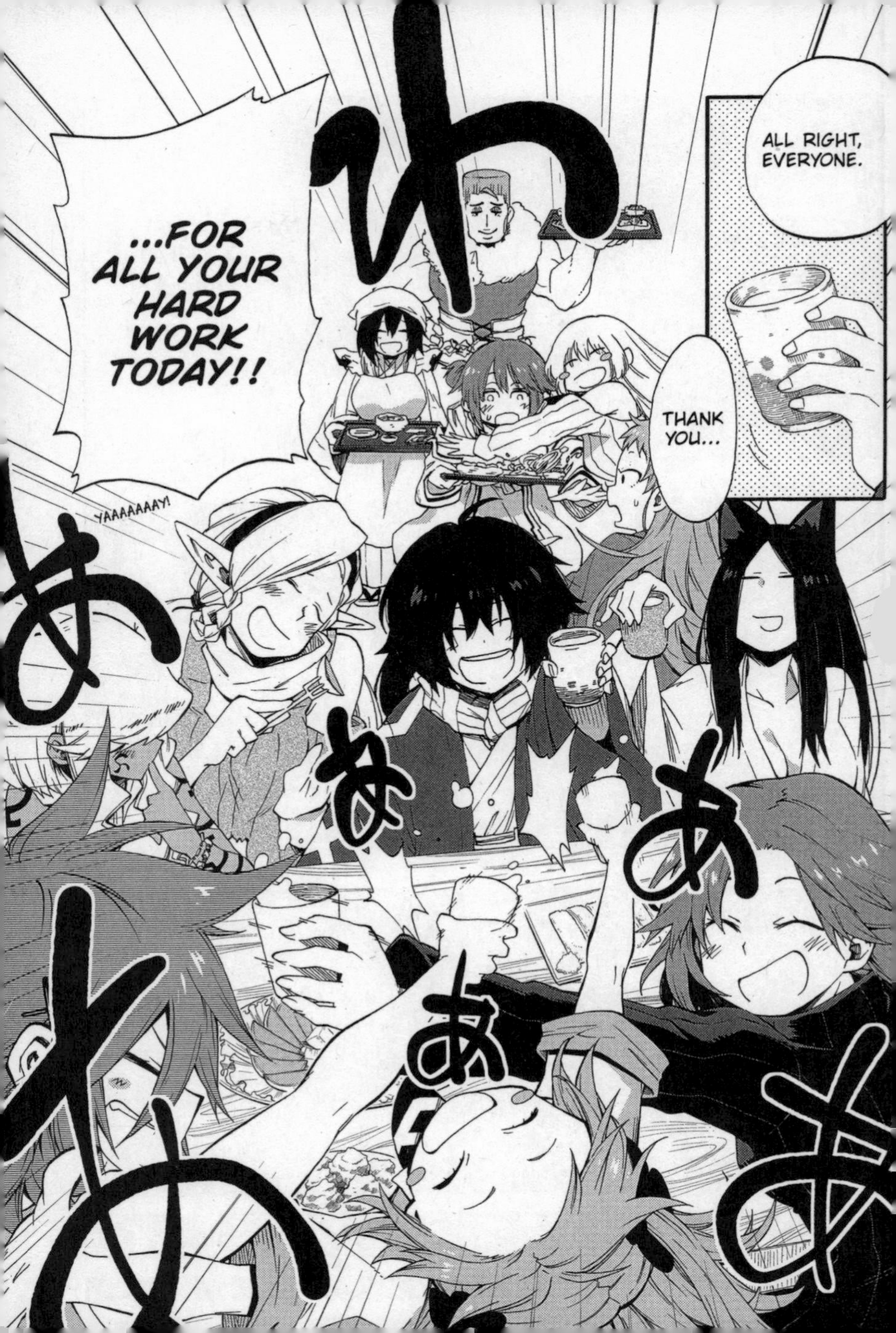
ALL RIGHT, EVERYONE.
THANK YOU...
...FOR ALL YOUR HARD WORK TODAY!!
YAAAAAAAY!
わあああああああ

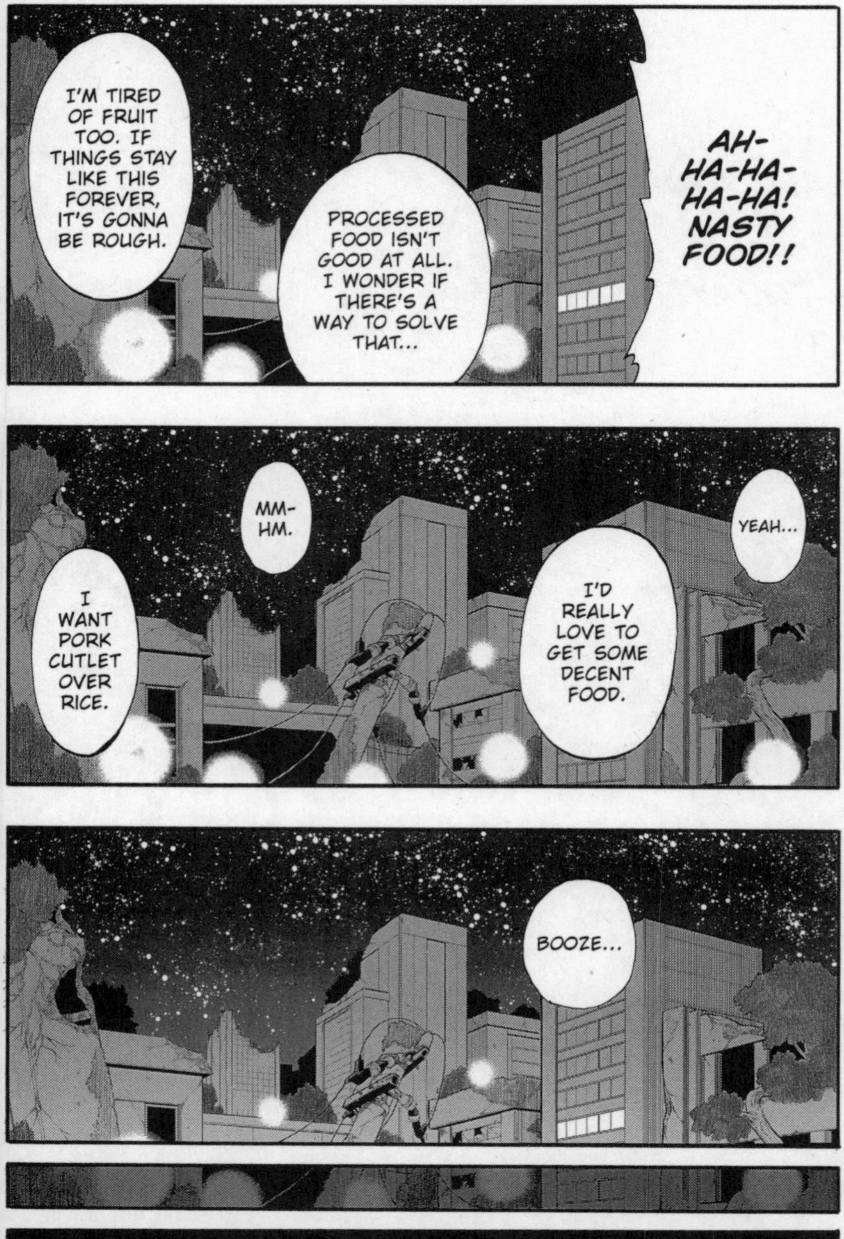
AH-HA-HA-HA-HA! NASTY FOOD!!
PROCESSED FOOD ISN'T GOOD AT ALL. I WONDER IF THERE'S A WAY TO SOLVE THAT...
I'M TIRED OF FRUIT TOO. IF THINGS STAY LIKE THIS FOREVER, IT'S GONNA BE ROUGH.
YEAH...
I'D REALLY LOVE TO GET SOME DECENT FOOD.
MM-HM.
I WANT PORK CUTLET OVER RICE.
BOOZE...

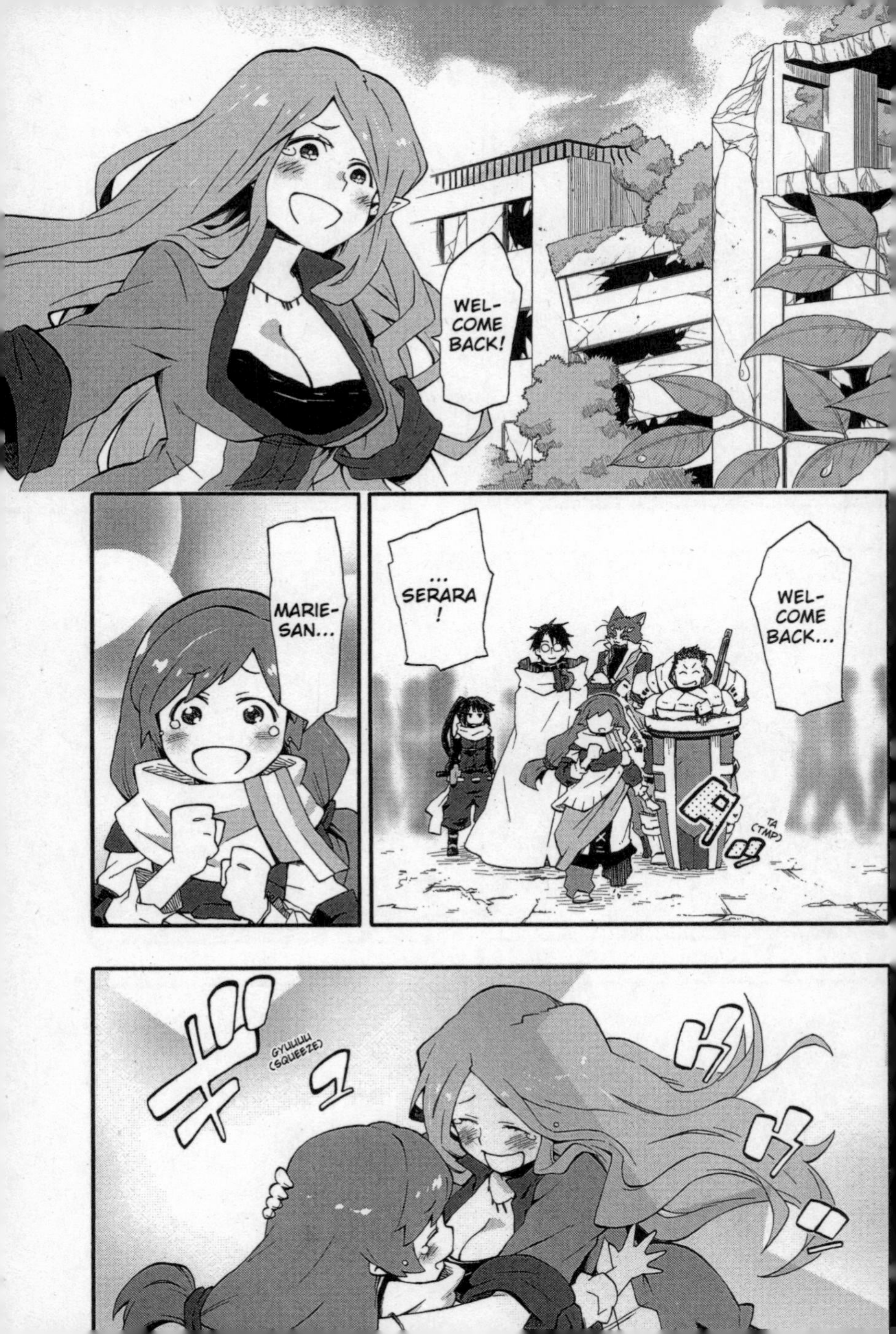
WEL-COME BACK!
WEL-COME BACK...
... SERARA!
TA (TMP)
MARIE-SAN...
GYUUUUU (SQUEEZE)

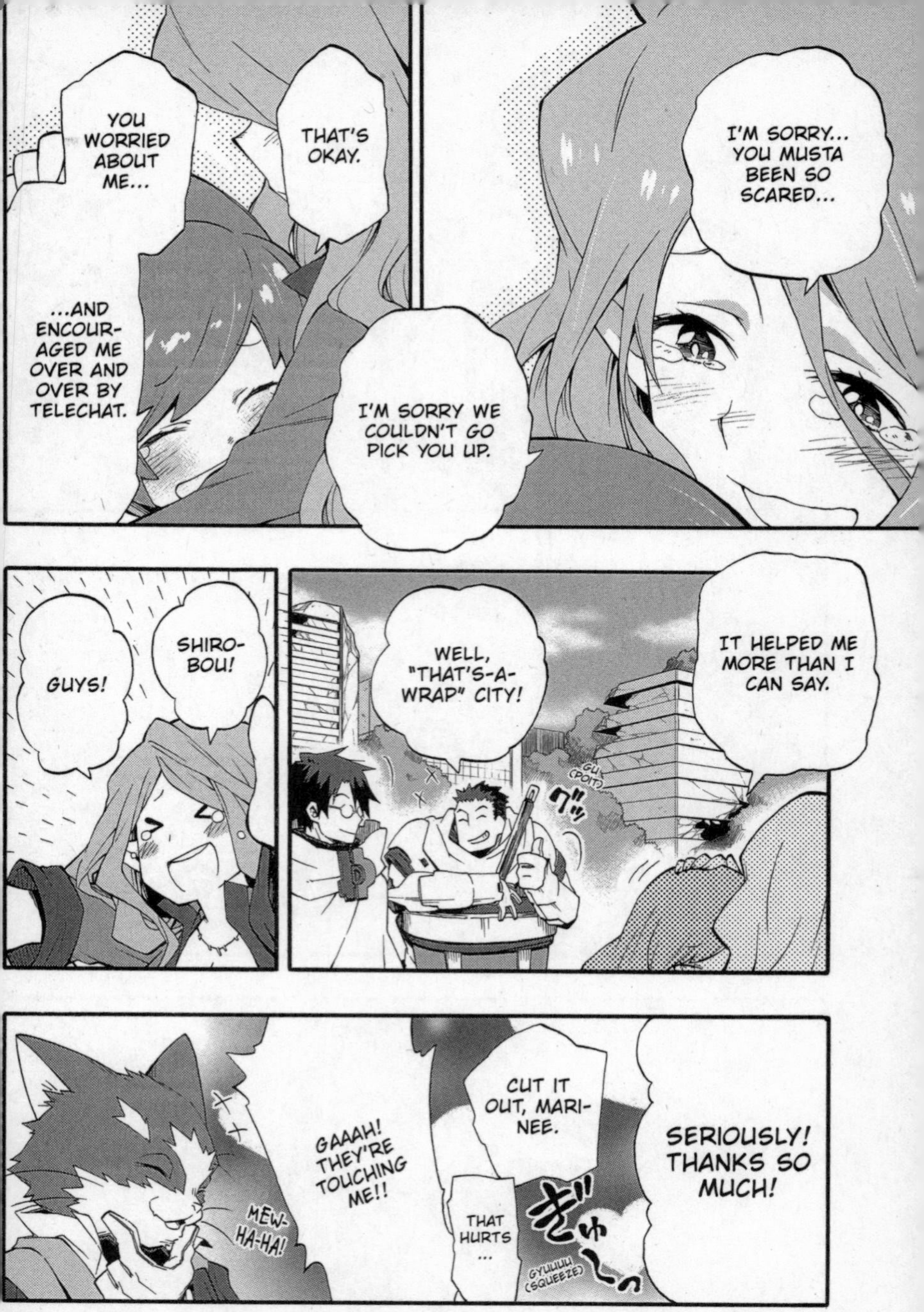
I'M SORRY... YOU MUSTA BEEN SO SCARED...
I'M SORRY WE COULDN'T GO PICK YOU UP.
THAT'S OKAY.
YOU WORRIED ABOUT ME...
...AND ENCOURAGED ME OVER AND OVER BY TELECHAT.
IT HELPED ME MORE THAN I CAN SAY.
WELL, "THAT'S-A-WRAP" CITY!
GU (POIT)
SHIRO-BOU!
GUYS!
SERIOUSLY! THANKS SO MUCH!
CUT IT OUT, MARI-NEE.
GYUUUU (SQUEEZE)
THAT HURTS ...
GAAAH! THEY'RE TOUCHING ME!!
MEW-HA-HA!

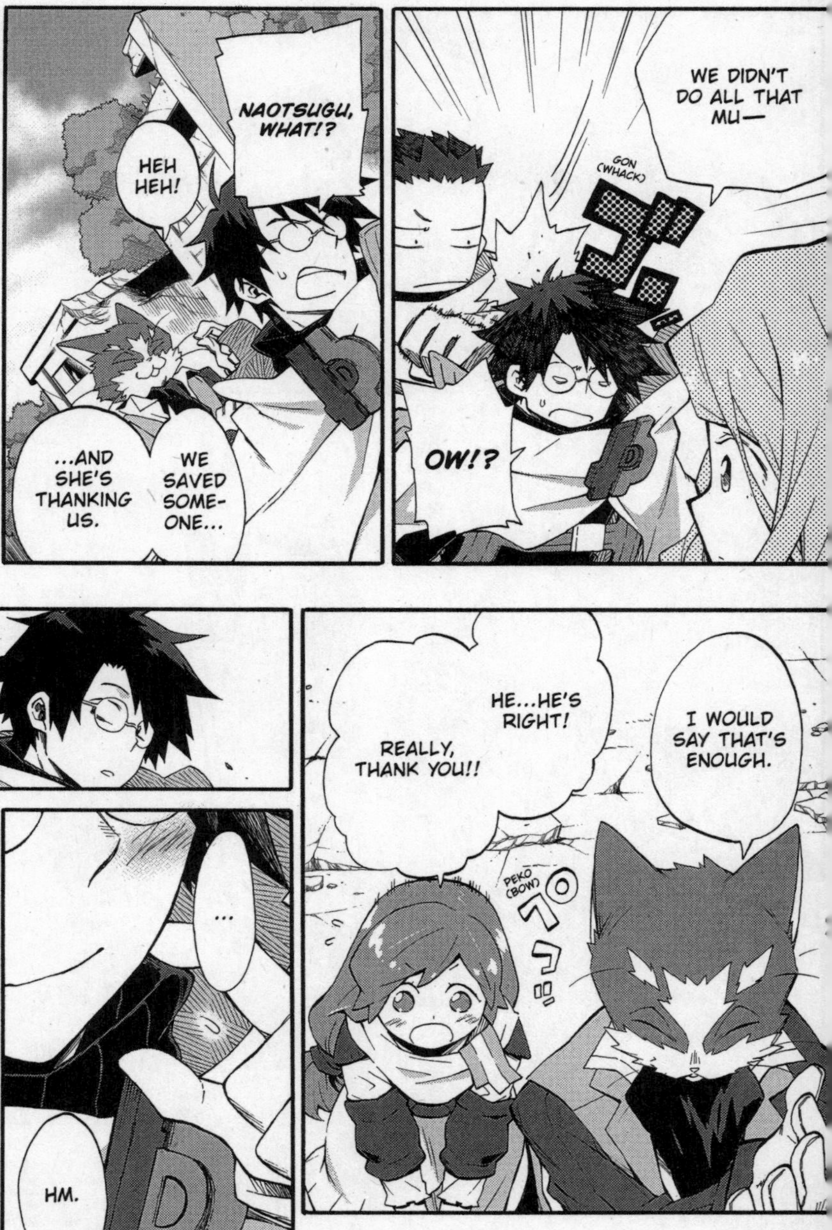
WE DIDN'T DO ALL THAT MU—
GON (WHACK)
OW!?
NAOTSUGU, WHAT!?
HEH HEH!
WE SAVED SOMEONE...
...AND SHE'S THANKING US.
I WOULD SAY THAT'S ENOUGH.
HE...HE'S RIGHT!
REALLY, THANK YOU!!
PEKO (BOW)
...
HM.

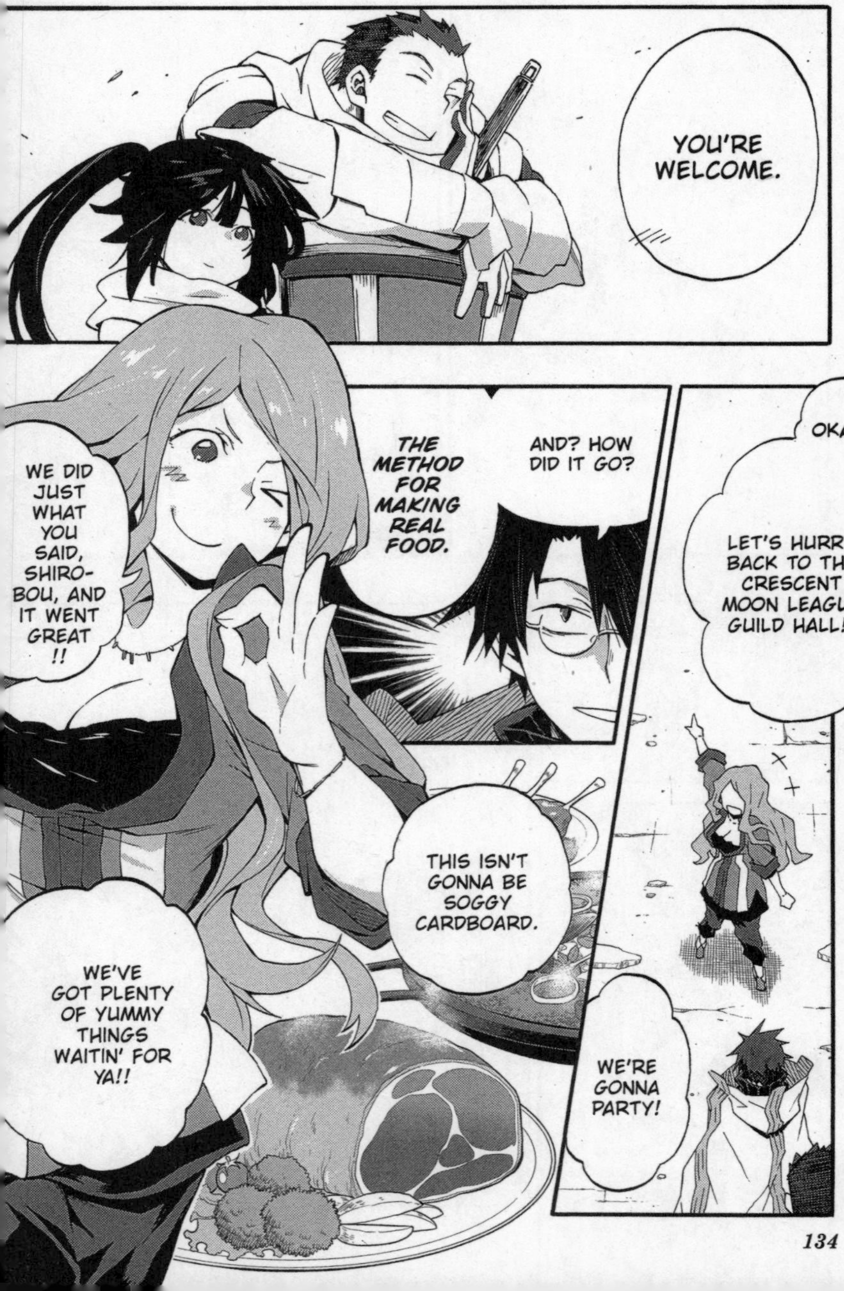
YOU'RE WELCOME.
OKAY!
LET'S HURRY BACK TO THE CRESCENT MOON LEAGUE GUILD HALL!!
WE'RE GONNA PARTY!
AND? HOW DID IT GO?
THE METHOD FOR MAKING REAL FOOD.
WE DID JUST WHAT YOU SAID, SHIRO-BOU, AND IT WENT GREAT!!
THIS ISN'T GONNA BE SOGGY CARDBOARD.
WE'VE GOT PLENTY OF YUMMY THINGS WAITIN' FOR YA!!

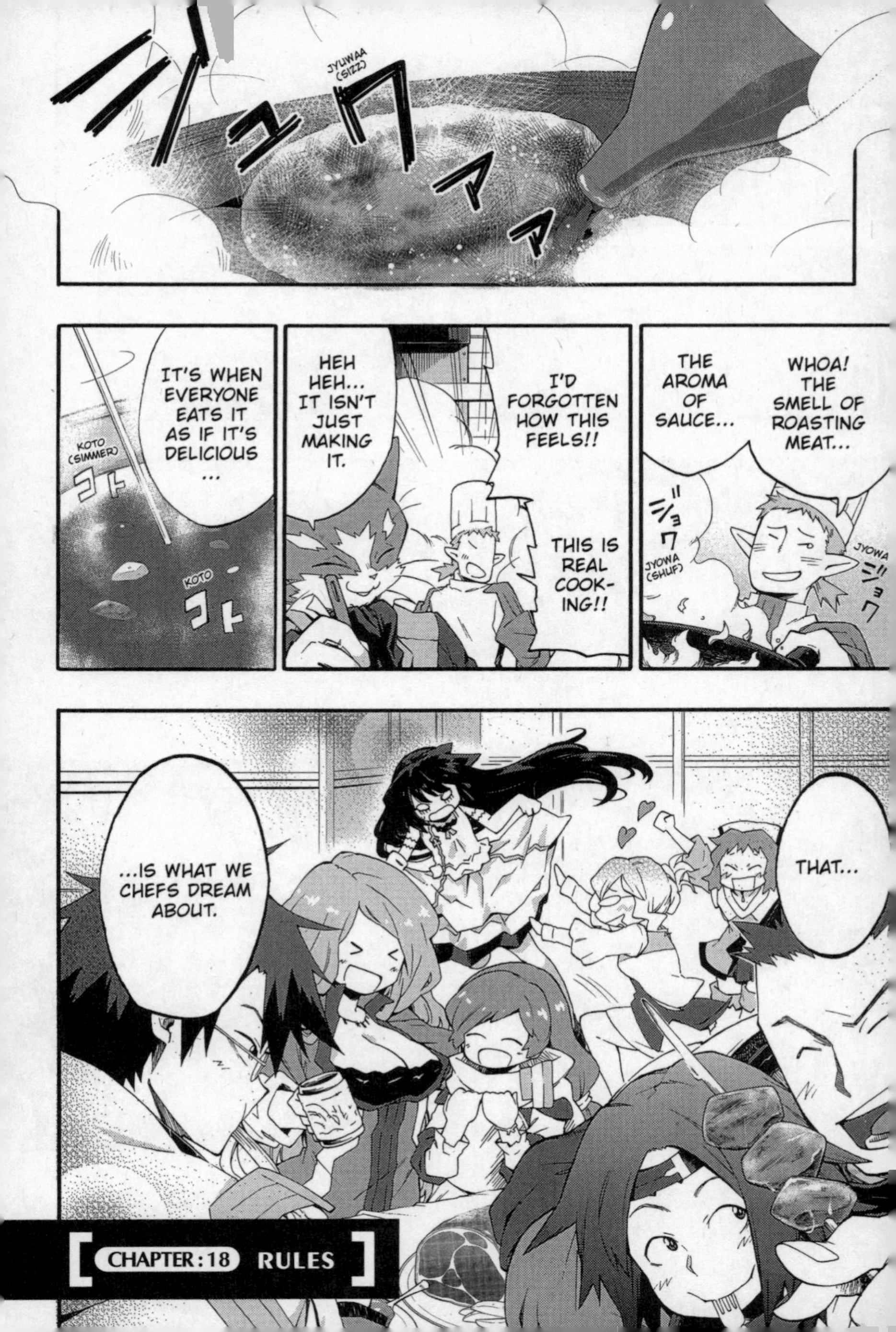
JYUWAA (SIZZ)
ジュワァァ
WHOA! THE SMELL OF ROASTING MEAT...
JYOWA
ジョワ
THE AROMA OF SAUCE...
ジョワ
JYOWA (SHUF)
I'D FORGOTTEN HOW THIS FEELS!!
THIS IS REAL COOKING!!
HEH HEH... IT ISN'T JUST MAKING IT.
IT'S WHEN EVERYONE EATS IT AS IF IT'S DELICIOUS...
KOTO (SIMMER)
コト
KOTO
コト
THAT...
...IS WHAT WE CHEFS DREAM ABOUT.

CHAPTER: 18 RULES

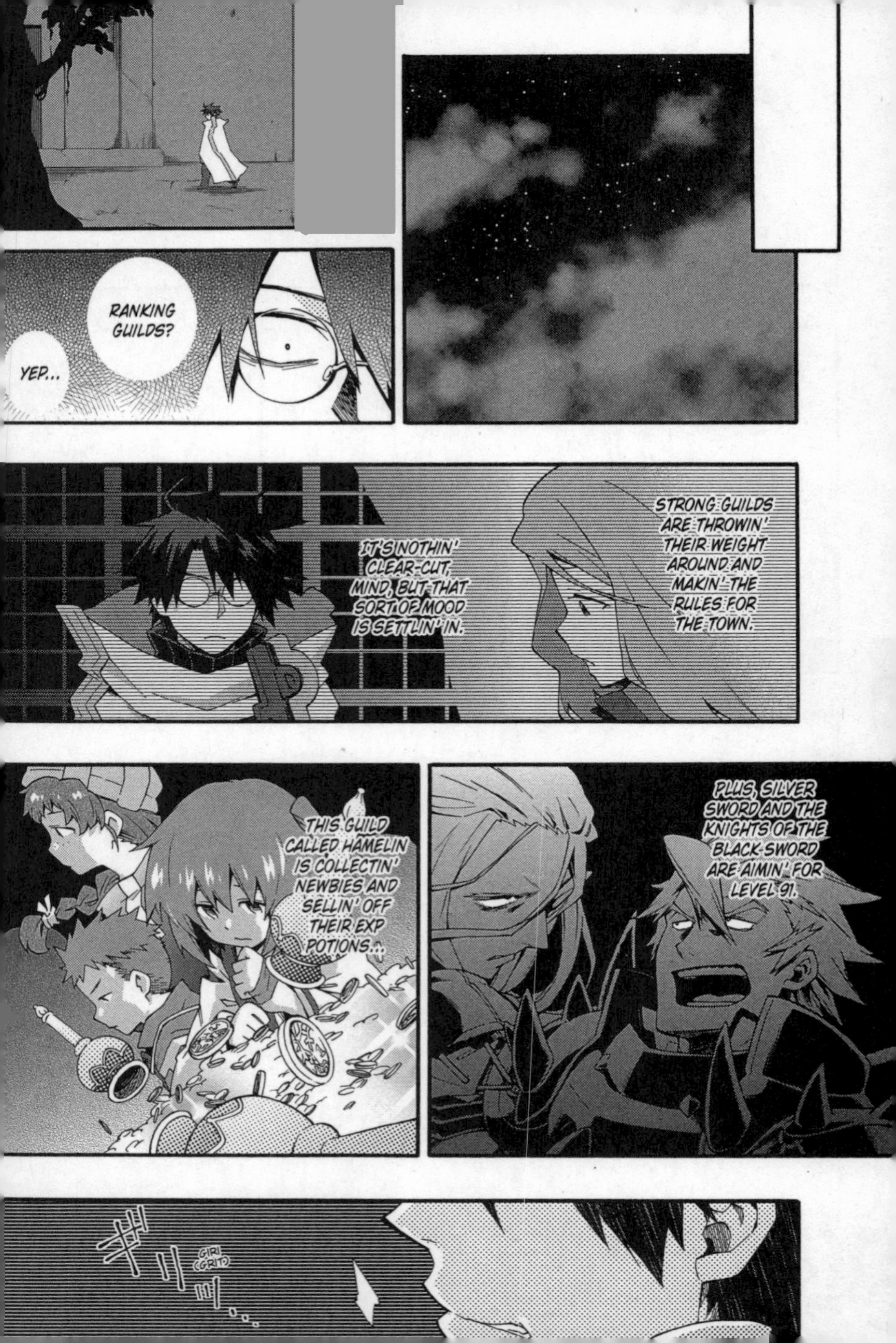
RANKING GUILDS?
YEP...
STRONG GUILDS ARE THROWIN' THEIR WEIGHT AROUND AND MAKIN' THE RULES FOR THE TOWN.
IT'S NOTHIN' CLEAR-CUT, MIND, BUT THAT SORT OF MOOD IS SETTLIN' IN.
PLUS, SILVER SWORD AND THE KNIGHTS OF THE BLACK SWORD ARE AIMIN' FOR LEVEL 91.
THIS GUILD CALLED HAMELIN IS COLLECTIN' NEWBIES AND SELLIN' OFF THEIR EXP POTIONS...
GIRI (GRIT)

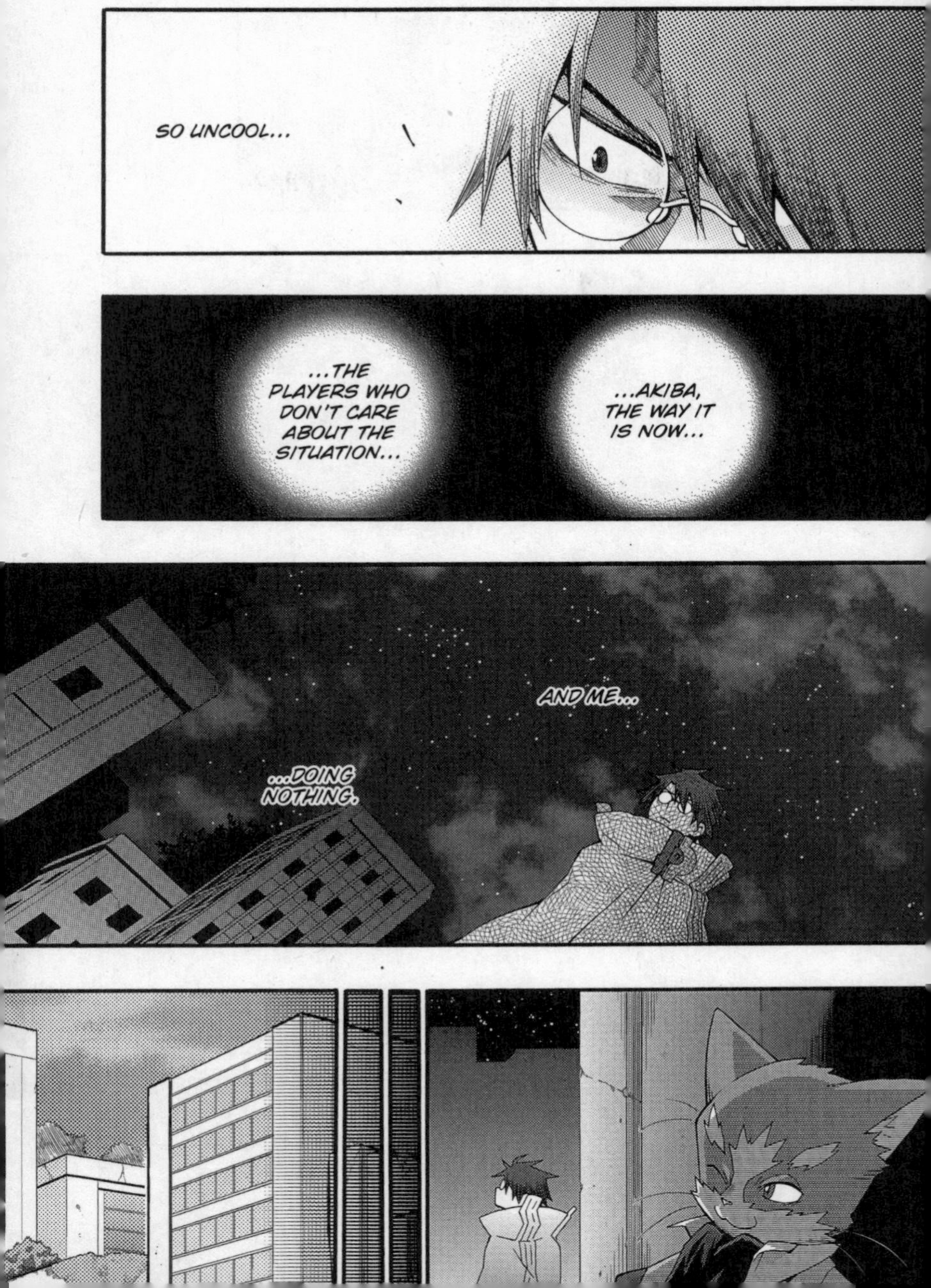
SO UNCOOL...
...AKIBA, THE WAY IT IS NOW...
...THE PLAYERS WHO DON'T CARE ABOUT THE SITUATION...
AND ME...
...DOING NOTHING.

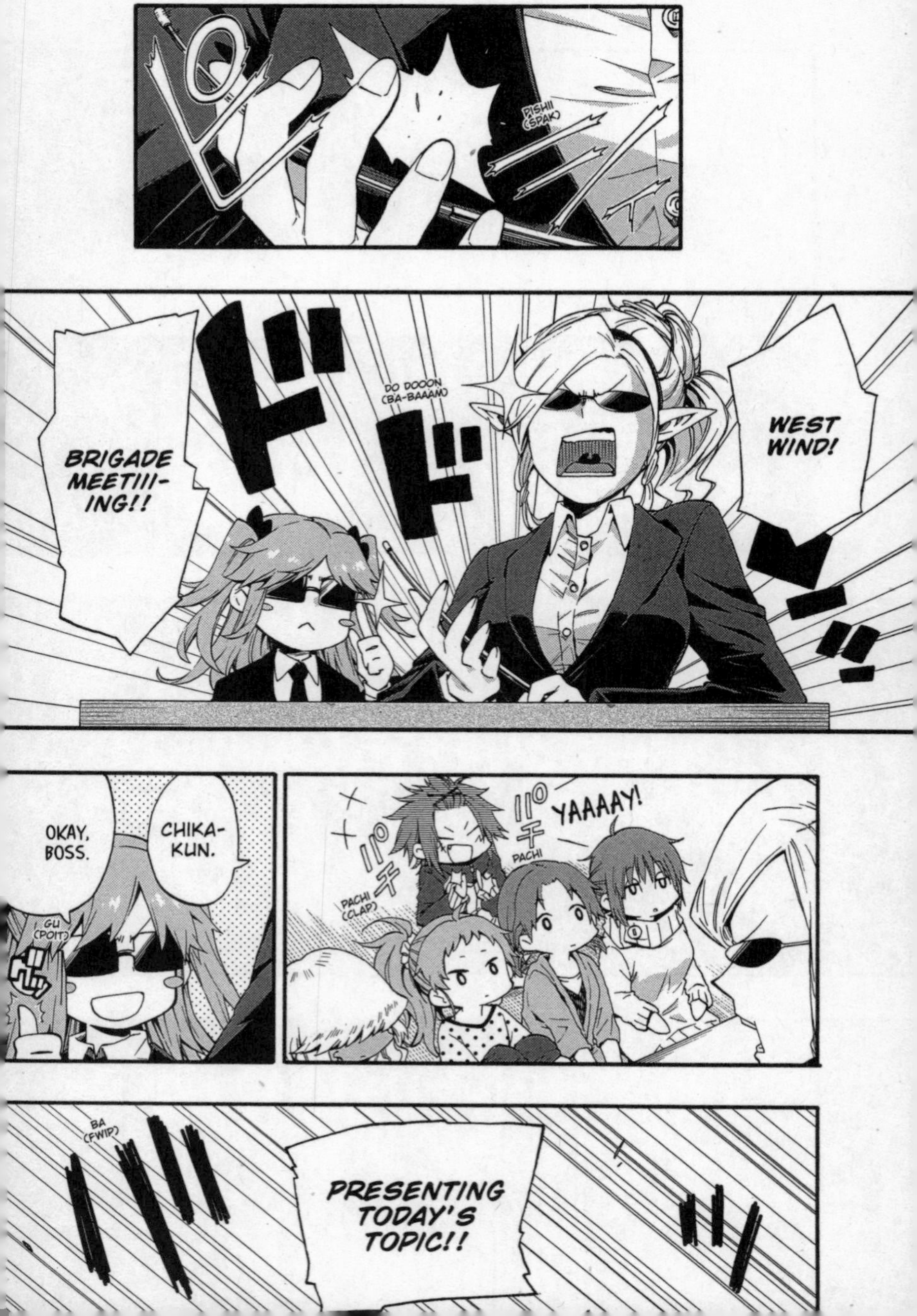
PISHII (SPAK)
WEST WIND!
DO DOOON (BA-BAAAM)
BRIGADE MEETIIII-ING!!
YAAAAY!
PACHI
PACHI (CLAP)
CHIKA-KUN.
OKAY, BOSS.
GU (POIT)
BA (FWIP)
PRESENTING TODAY'S TOPIC!!

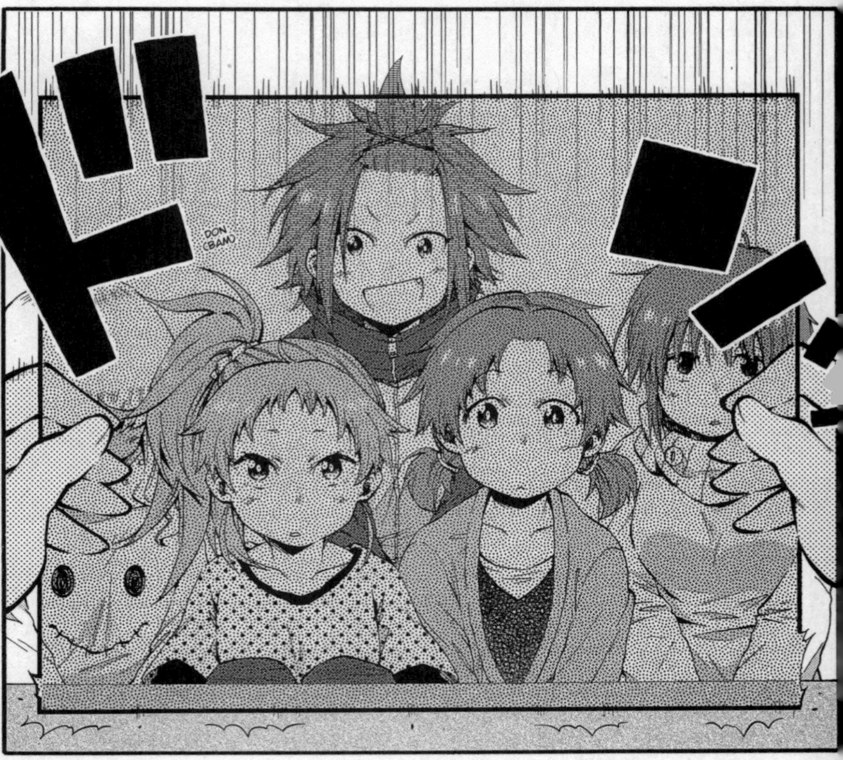
DON
(BAM)

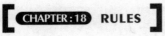

[CHAPTER : 18 RULES]

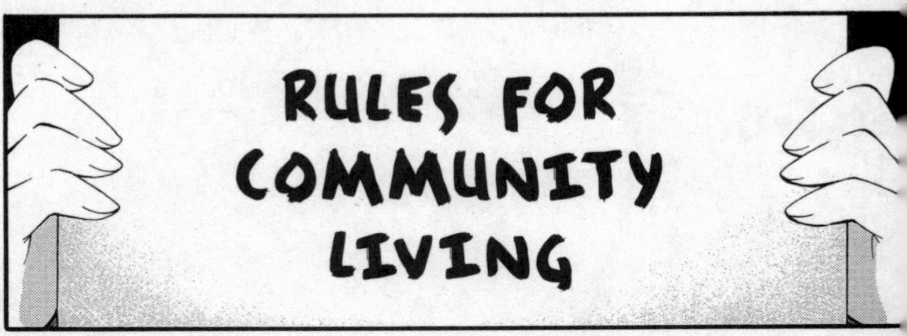
RULES FOR
COMMUNITY
LIVING

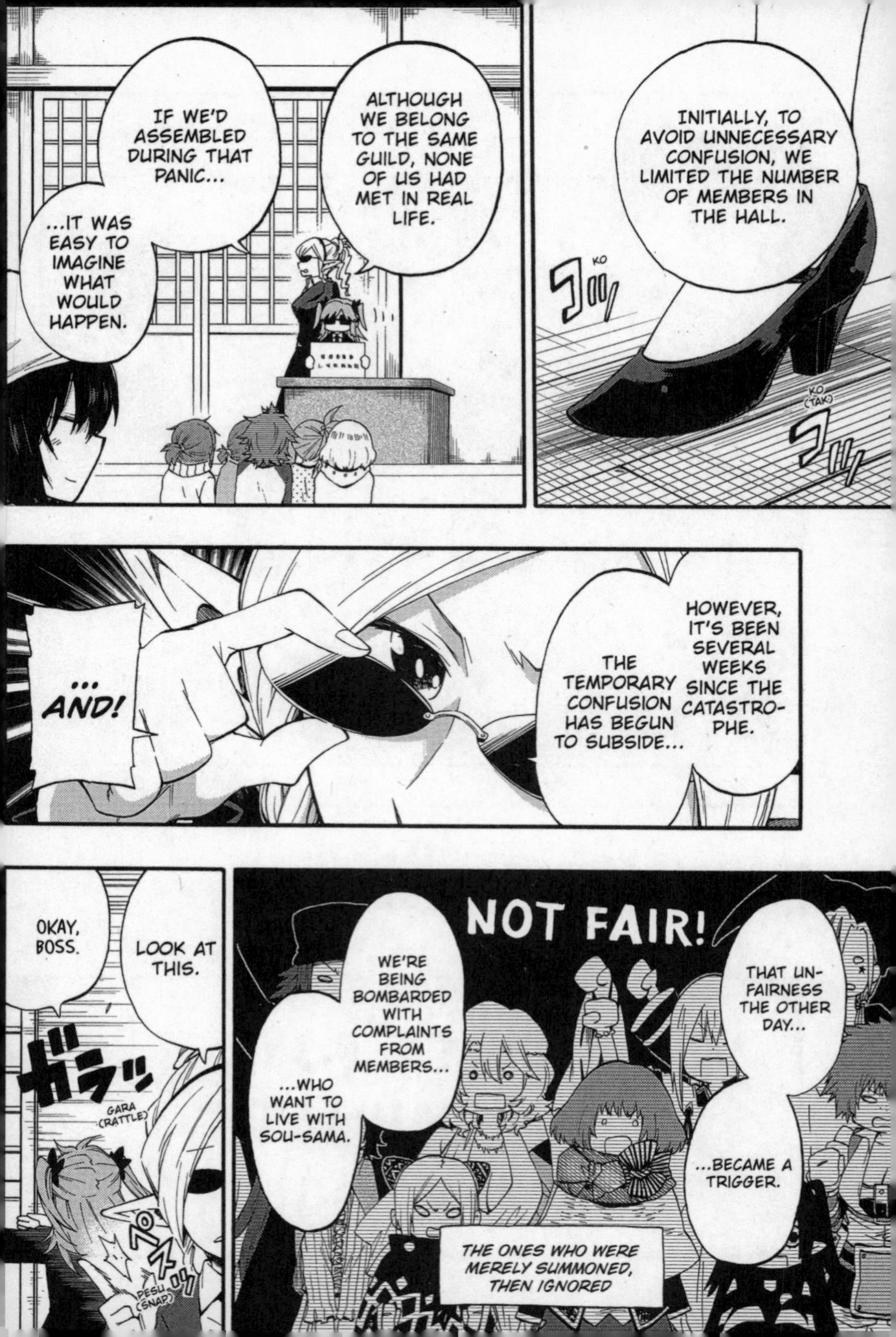
INITIALLY, TO AVOID UNNECESSARY CONFUSION, WE LIMITED THE NUMBER OF MEMBERS IN THE HALL.
KO
KO (TAK)
ALTHOUGH WE BELONG TO THE SAME GUILD, NONE OF US HAD MET IN REAL LIFE.
IF WE'D ASSEMBLED DURING THAT PANIC...
...IT WAS EASY TO IMAGINE WHAT WOULD HAPPEN.
HOWEVER, IT'S BEEN SEVERAL WEEKS SINCE THE CATASTRO-PHE.
THE TEMPORARY CONFUSION HAS BEGUN TO SUBSIDE...
...AND!
NOT FAIR!
THAT UN-FAIRNESS THE OTHER DAY...
...BECAME A TRIGGER.
WE'RE BEING BOMBARDED WITH COMPLAINTS FROM MEMBERS...
...WHO WANT TO LIVE WITH SOU-SAMA.
THE ONES WHO WERE MERELY SUMMONED, THEN IGNORED
LOOK AT THIS.
OKAY, BOSS.
GARA (RATTLE)
PESU (SNAP)

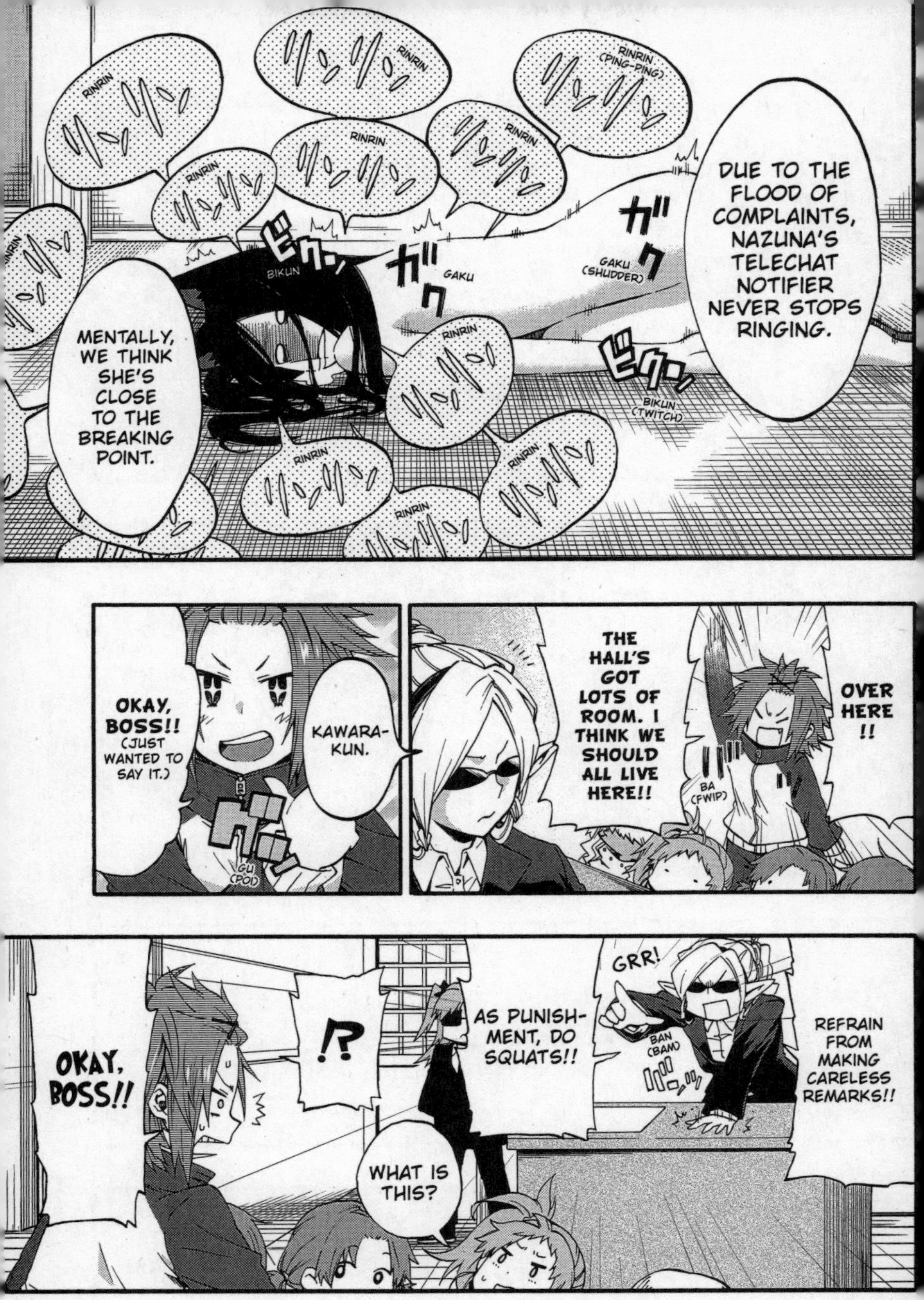
RINRIN (PING-PING)
DUE TO THE FLOOD OF COMPLAINTS, NAZUNA'S TELECHAT NOTIFIER NEVER STOPS RINGING.
GAKU (SHUDDER)
BIKUN (TWITCH)
RINRIN
RINRIN
RINRIN
RINRIN
RINRIN
GAKU
BIKUN
RINRIN
RINRIN
RINRIN
RINRIN
MENTALLY, WE THINK SHE'S CLOSE TO THE BREAKING POINT.
OVER HERE!!
BA (FWIP)
THE HALL'S GOT LOTS OF ROOM. I THINK WE SHOULD ALL LIVE HERE!!
KAWARA-KUN.
OKAY, BOSS!! (JUST WANTED TO SAY IT.)
GU (POI)
REFRAIN FROM MAKING CARELESS REMARKS!!
GRR!
BAN (BAM)
AS PUNISH-MENT, DO SQUATS!!
!?
OKAY, BOSS!!
WHAT IS THIS?

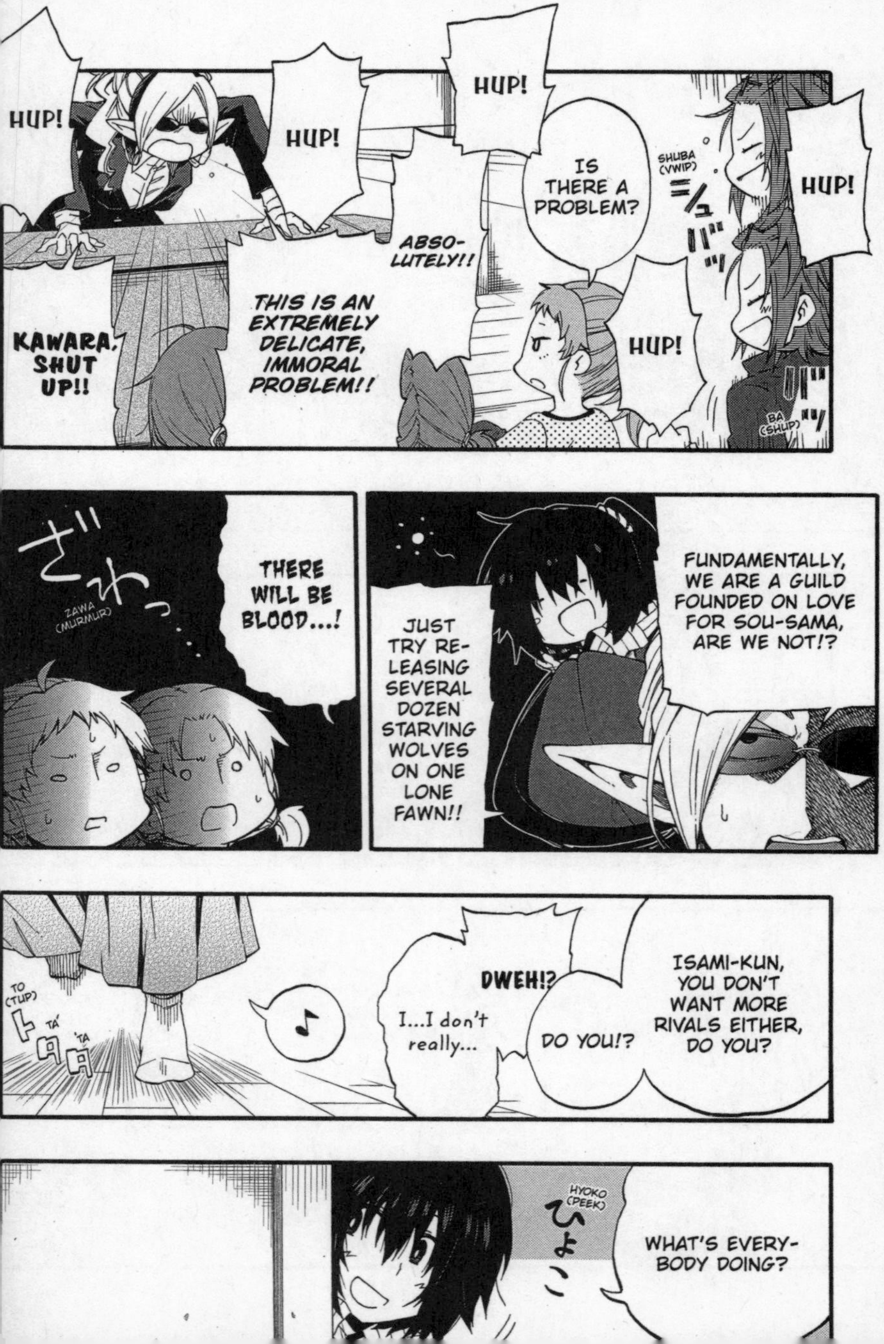
HUP!
HUP!
SHUBA (VWIP)
IS THERE A PROBLEM?
ABSO-LUTELY!!
HUP!
BA (SHUP)
HUP!
HUP!
THIS IS AN EXTREMELY DELICATE, IMMORAL PROBLEM!!
KAWARA, SHUT UP!!
FUNDAMENTALLY, WE ARE A GUILD FOUNDED ON LOVE FOR SOU-SAMA, ARE WE NOT!?
JUST TRY RE-LEASING SEVERAL DOZEN STARVING WOLVES ON ONE LONE FAWN!!
THERE WILL BE BLOOD...!
ZAWA (MURMUR)
ISAMI-KUN, YOU DON'T WANT MORE RIVALS EITHER, DO YOU?
DO YOU!?
DWEH!?
I...I don't really...
♪
TO (TUP)
TA
TA
WHAT'S EVERY-BODY DOING?
HYOKO (PEEK)

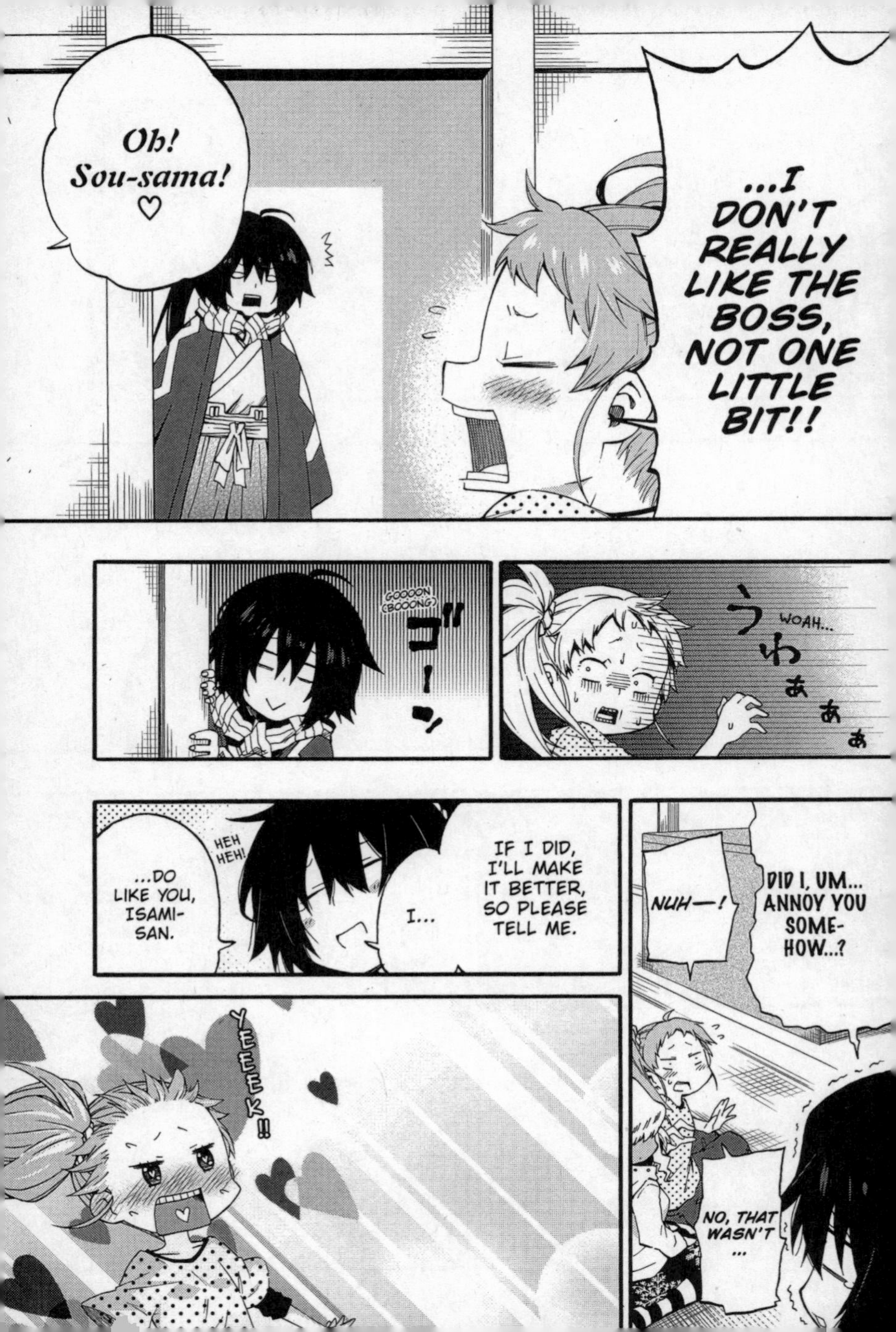
...I DON'T REALLY LIKE THE BOSS, NOT ONE LITTLE BIT!!
Oh! Sou-sama! ♡
うわあああ
WOAH...
ゴーン
GOOOON (BOOONG)
DID I, UM... ANNOY YOU SOME-HOW...?
NUH—!
NO, THAT WASN'T ...
IF I DID, I'LL MAKE IT BETTER, SO PLEASE TELL ME.
I...
HEH HEH!
...DO LIKE YOU, ISAMI-SAN.
YEEEEK!!

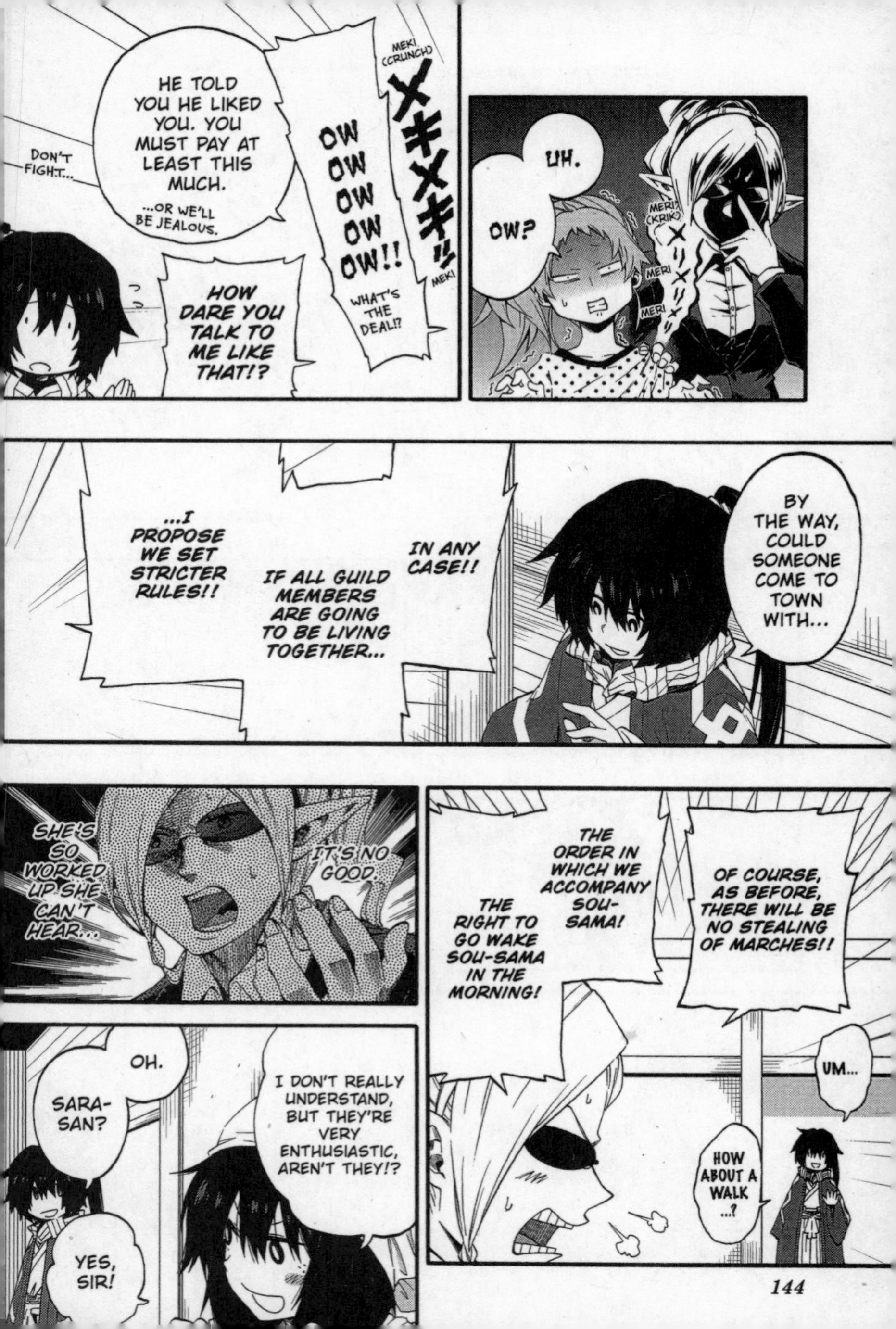
UH.
OW?
MERI! (KRIK)
MERI
MERI
MEKI (CRUNCH)
OW OW OW OW OW!!
MEKI
WHAT'S THE DEAL!?
HE TOLD YOU HE LIKED YOU. YOU MUST PAY AT LEAST THIS MUCH.
...OR WE'LL BE JEALOUS.
HOW DARE YOU TALK TO ME LIKE THAT!?
DON'T FIGHT...
BY THE WAY, COULD SOMEONE COME TO TOWN WITH...
IN ANY CASE!!
IF ALL GUILD MEMBERS ARE GOING TO BE LIVING TOGETHER...
...I PROPOSE WE SET STRICTER RULES!!
OF COURSE, AS BEFORE, THERE WILL BE NO STEALING OF MARCHES!!
THE ORDER IN WHICH WE ACCOMPANY SOU-SAMA!
THE RIGHT TO GO WAKE SOU-SAMA IN THE MORNING!
UM...
HOW ABOUT A WALK ...?
IT'S NO GOOD.
SHE'S SO WORKED UP SHE CAN'T HEAR...
I DON'T REALLY UNDERSTAND, BUT THEY'RE VERY ENTHUSIASTIC, AREN'T THEY!?
OH.
SARA-SAN?
YES, SIR!

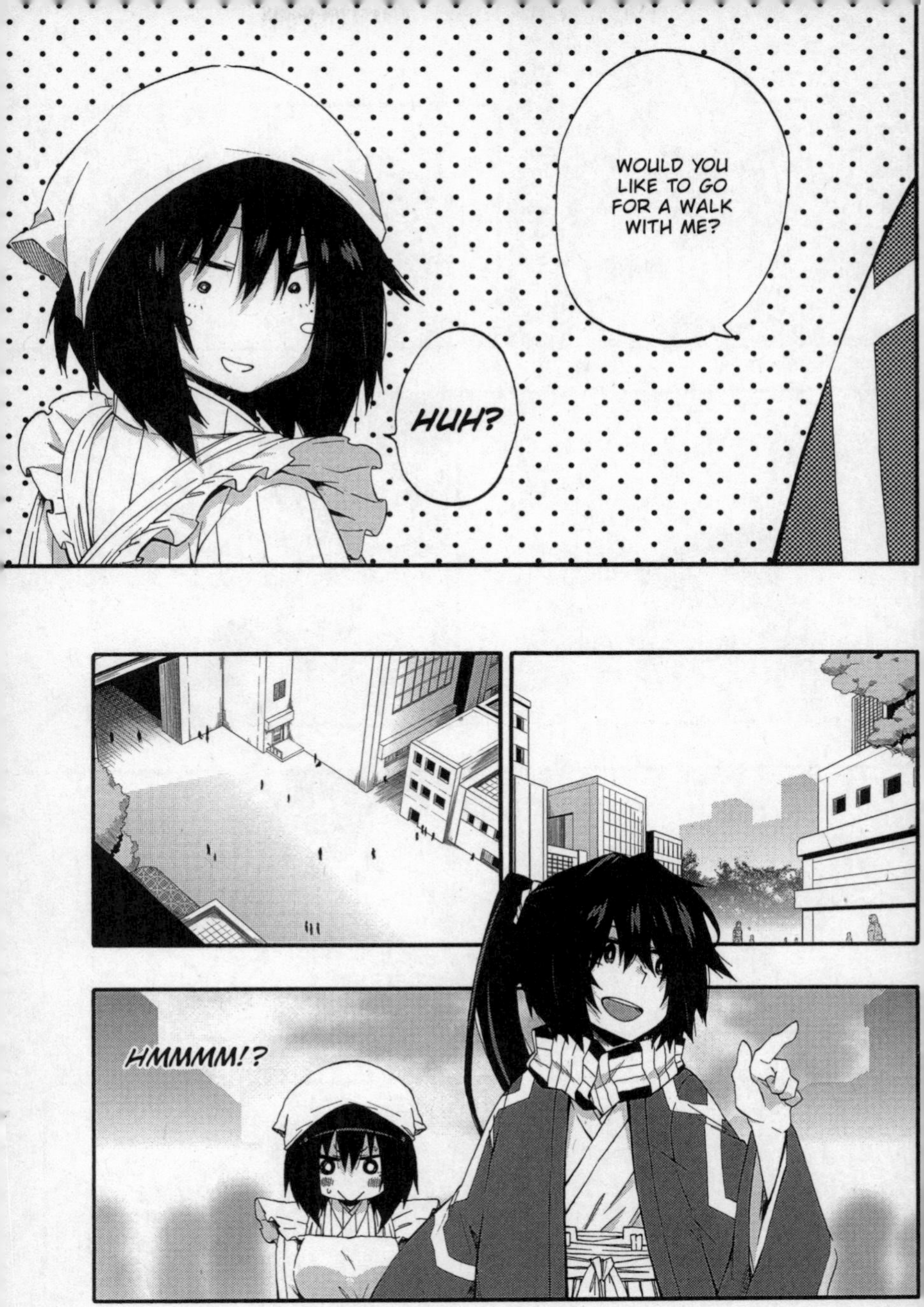
WOULD YOU LIKE TO GO FOR A WALK WITH ME?
HUH?
HMMMM!?

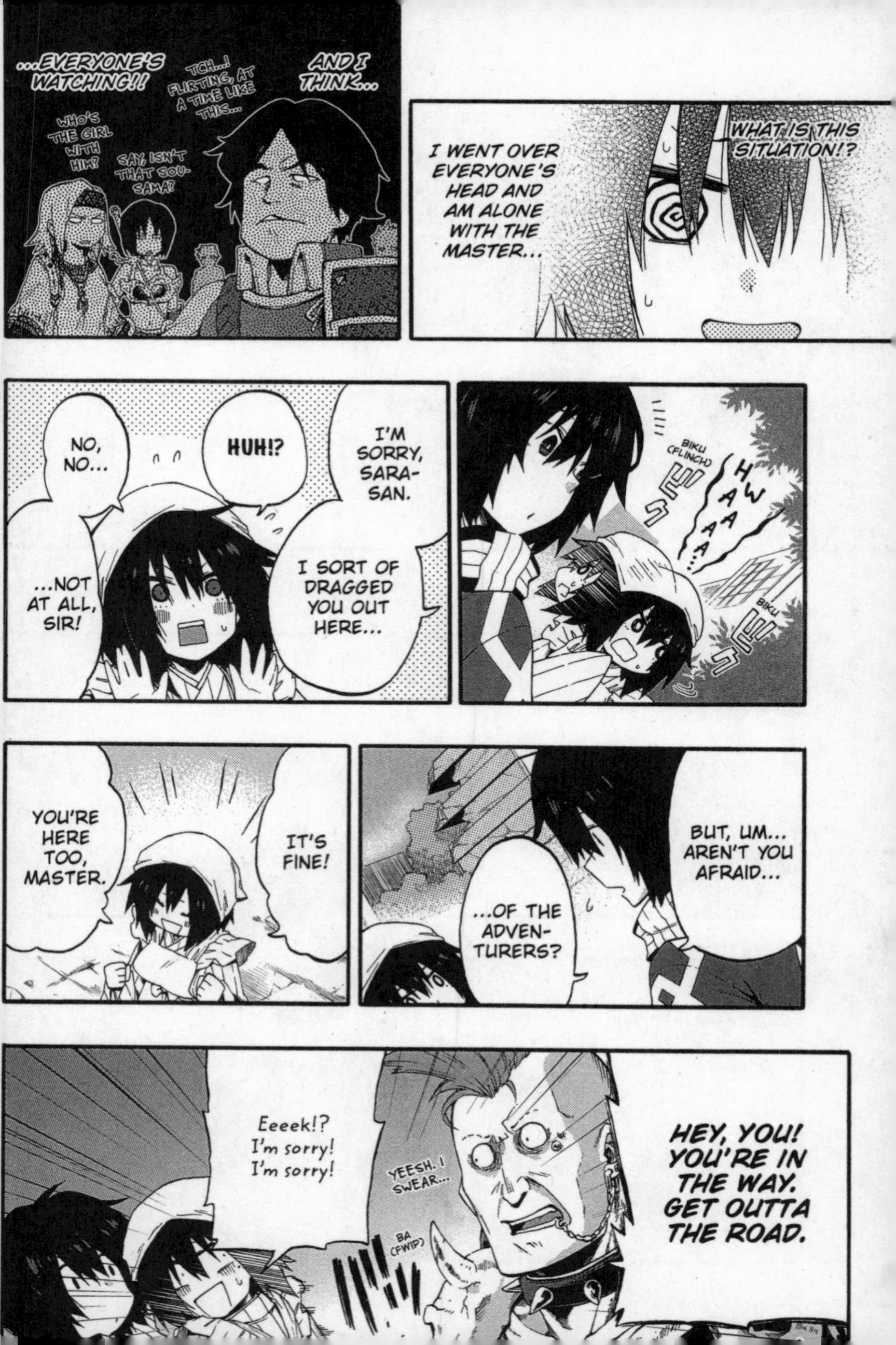

WHAT IS THIS SITUATION!?
I WENT OVER EVERYONE'S HEAD AND AM ALONE WITH THE MASTER...
AND I THINK...
TCH...! FLIRTING, AT A TIME LIKE THIS...
...EVERYONE'S WATCHING!!
WHO'S THE GIRL WITH HIM?
SAY, ISN'T THAT SOU-SAMA?
BIKU (FLINCH)
HWAAAA...
BIKU
I'M SORRY, SARA-SAN.
I SORT OF DRAGGED YOU OUT HERE...
HUH!?
NO, NO...
...NOT AT ALL, SIR!
BUT, UM... AREN'T YOU AFRAID...
...OF THE ADVEN-TURERS?
IT'S FINE!
YOU'RE HERE TOO, MASTER.
HEY, YOU! YOU'RE IN THE WAY. GET OUTTA THE ROAD.
YEESH. I SWEAR...
BA (FWIP)
Eeeek!? I'm sorry! I'm sorry!

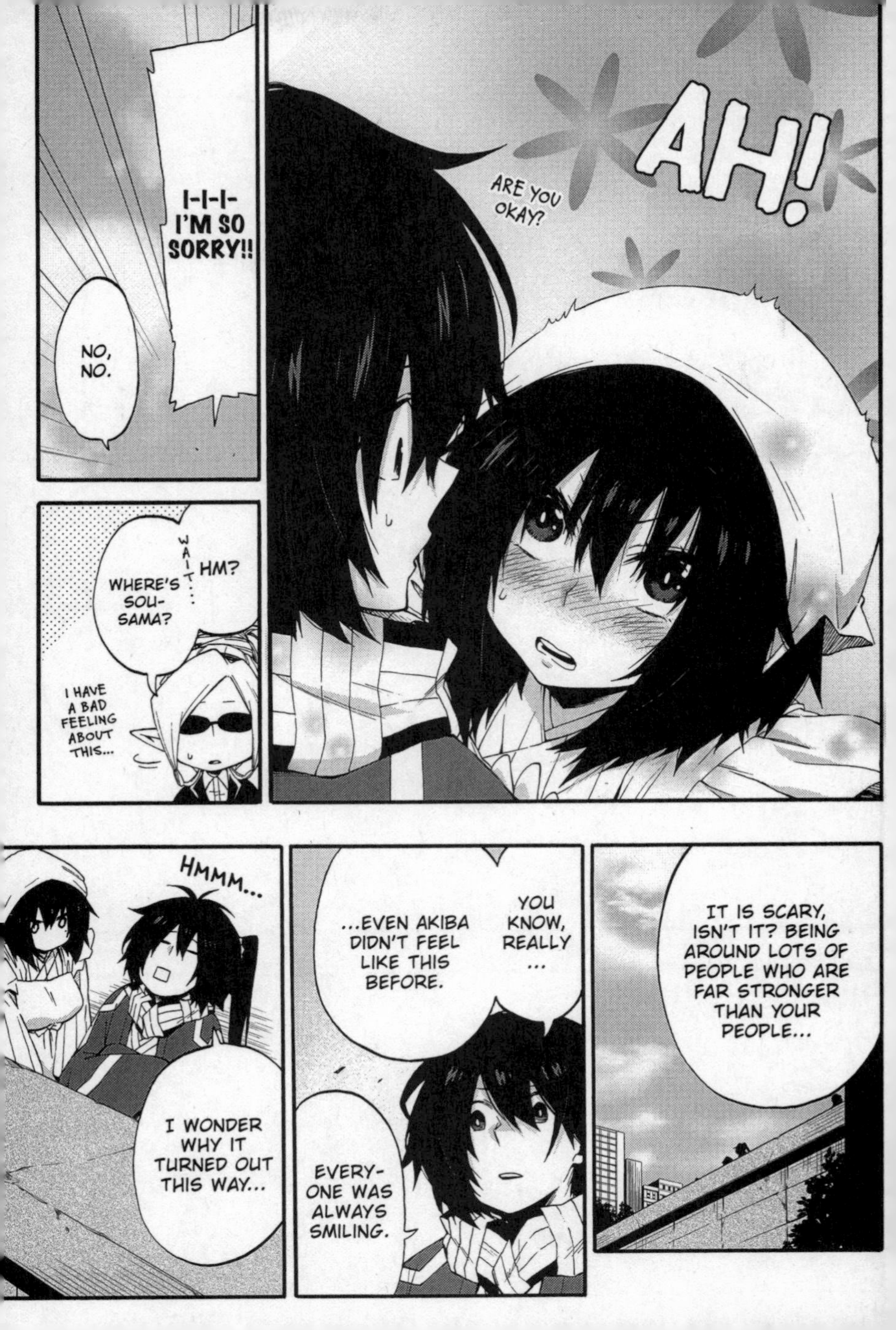
AH!
ARE YOU OKAY?
I-I-I- I'M SO SORRY!!
NO, NO.
HM?
WAIT...
WHERE'S SOU-SAMA?
I HAVE A BAD FEELING ABOUT THIS...
IT IS SCARY, ISN'T IT? BEING AROUND LOTS OF PEOPLE WHO ARE FAR STRONGER THAN YOUR PEOPLE...
YOU KNOW, REALLY...
...EVEN AKIBA DIDN'T FEEL LIKE THIS BEFORE.
EVERY-ONE WAS ALWAYS SMILING.
HMMM...
I WONDER WHY IT TURNED OUT THIS WAY...

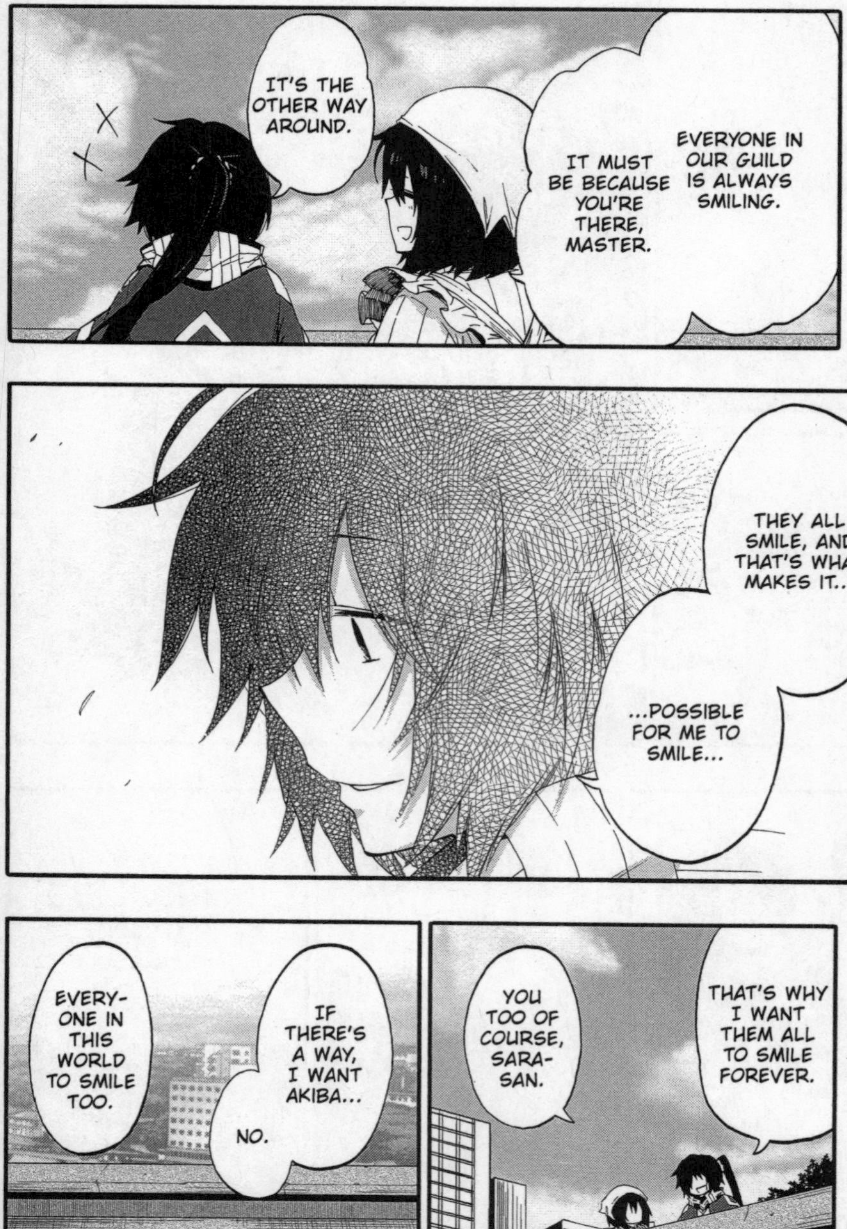
EVERYONE IN OUR GUILD IS ALWAYS SMILING.
IT MUST BE BECAUSE YOU'RE THERE, MASTER.
IT'S THE OTHER WAY AROUND.
THEY ALL SMILE, AND THAT'S WHAT MAKES IT...
...POSSIBLE FOR ME TO SMILE...
THAT'S WHY I WANT THEM ALL TO SMILE FOREVER.
YOU TOO OF COURSE, SARA-SAN.
IF THERE'S A WAY, I WANT AKIBA...
NO.
EVERY-ONE IN THIS WORLD TO SMILE TOO.

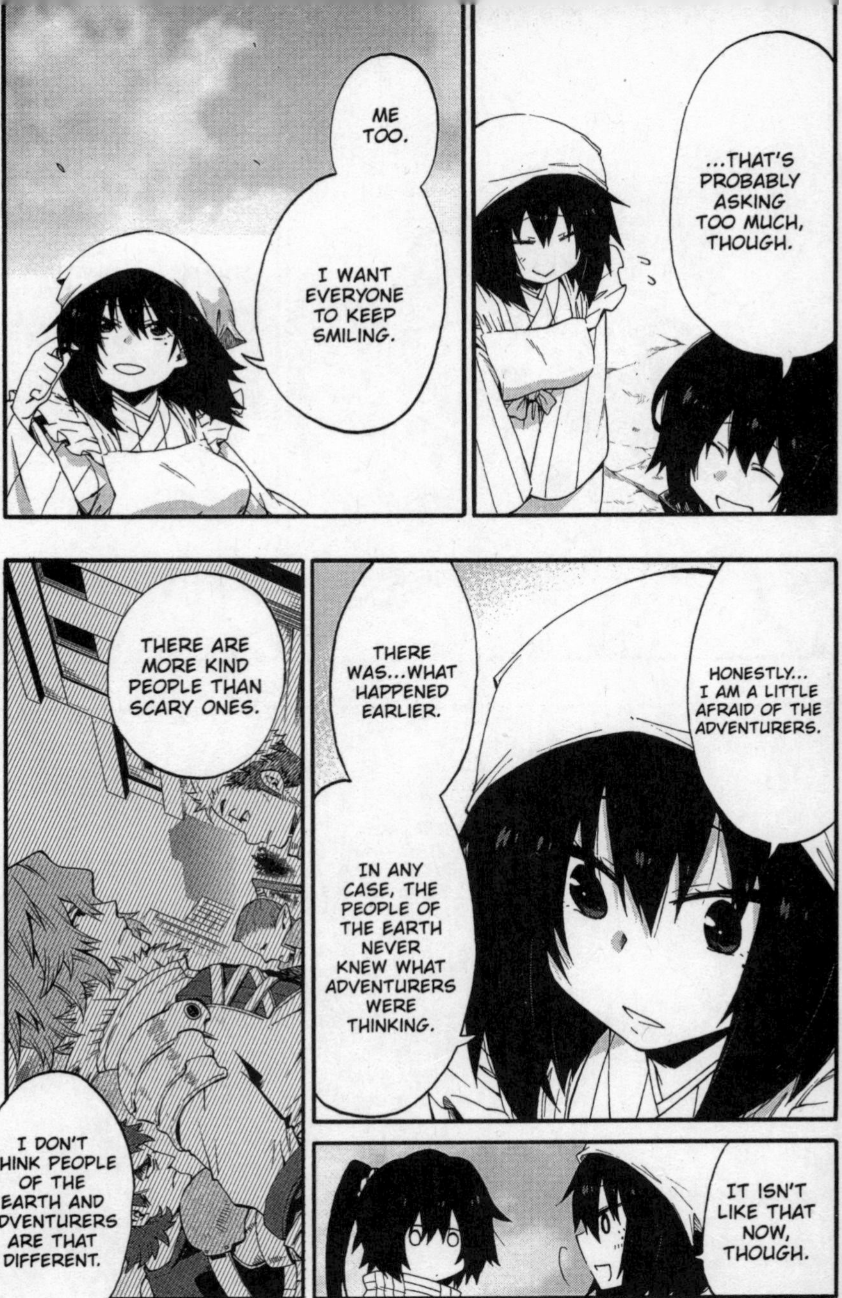
...THAT'S PROBABLY ASKING TOO MUCH, THOUGH.
ME TOO.
I WANT EVERYONE TO KEEP SMILING.
HONESTLY... I AM A LITTLE AFRAID OF THE ADVENTURERS.
THERE WAS...WHAT HAPPENED EARLIER.
IN ANY CASE, THE PEOPLE OF THE EARTH NEVER KNEW WHAT ADVENTURERS WERE THINKING.
IT ISN'T LIKE THAT NOW, THOUGH.
THERE ARE MORE KIND PEOPLE THAN SCARY ONES.
I DON'T THINK PEOPLE OF THE EARTH AND ADVENTURERS ARE THAT DIFFERENT.

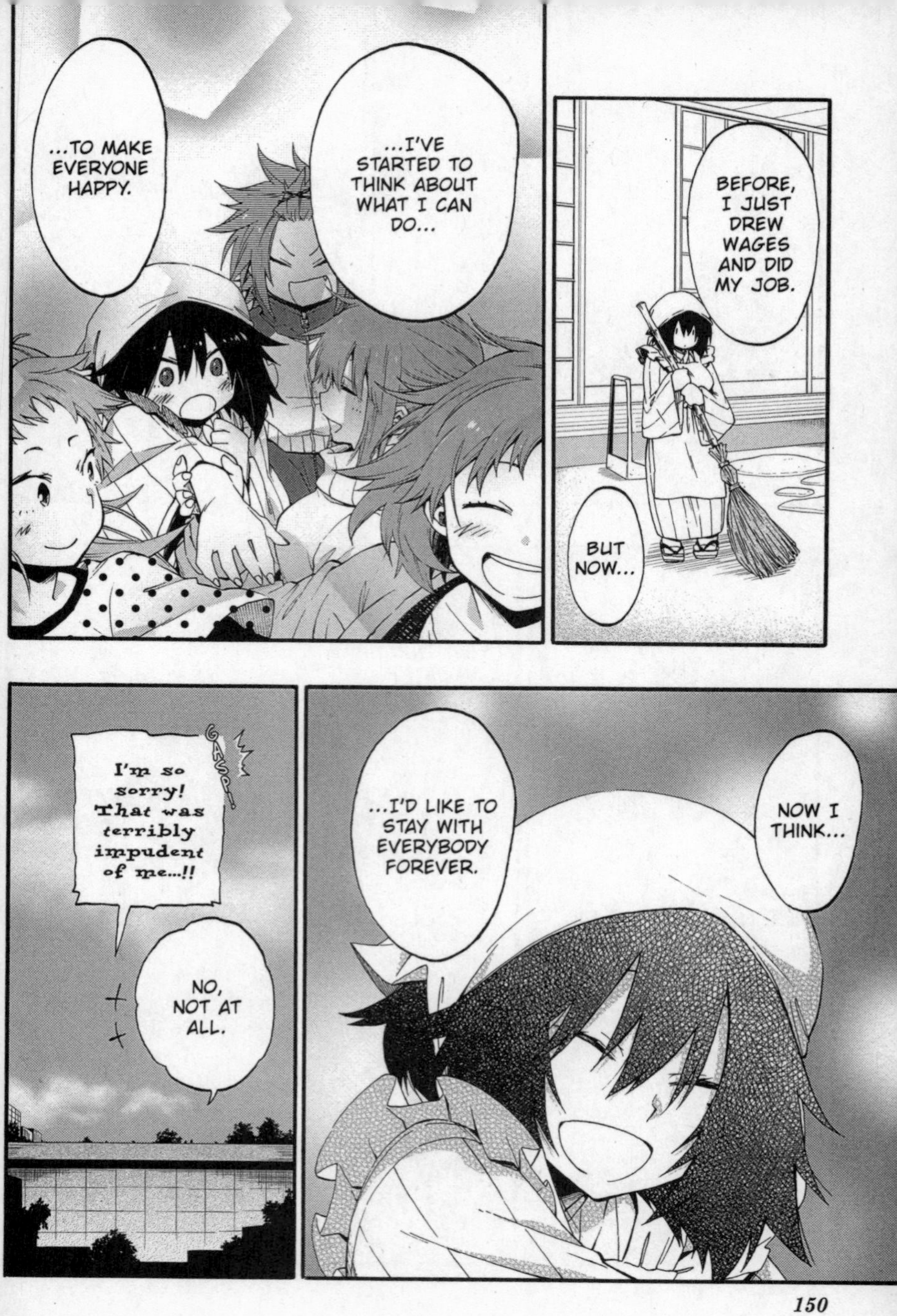
BEFORE, I JUST DREW WAGES AND DID MY JOB.
BUT NOW...
...I'VE STARTED TO THINK ABOUT WHAT I CAN DO...
...TO MAKE EVERYONE HAPPY.
NOW I THINK...
...I'D LIKE TO STAY WITH EVERYBODY FOREVER.
GASP!
I'm so sorry! That was terribly impudent of me...!!
NO, NOT AT ALL.

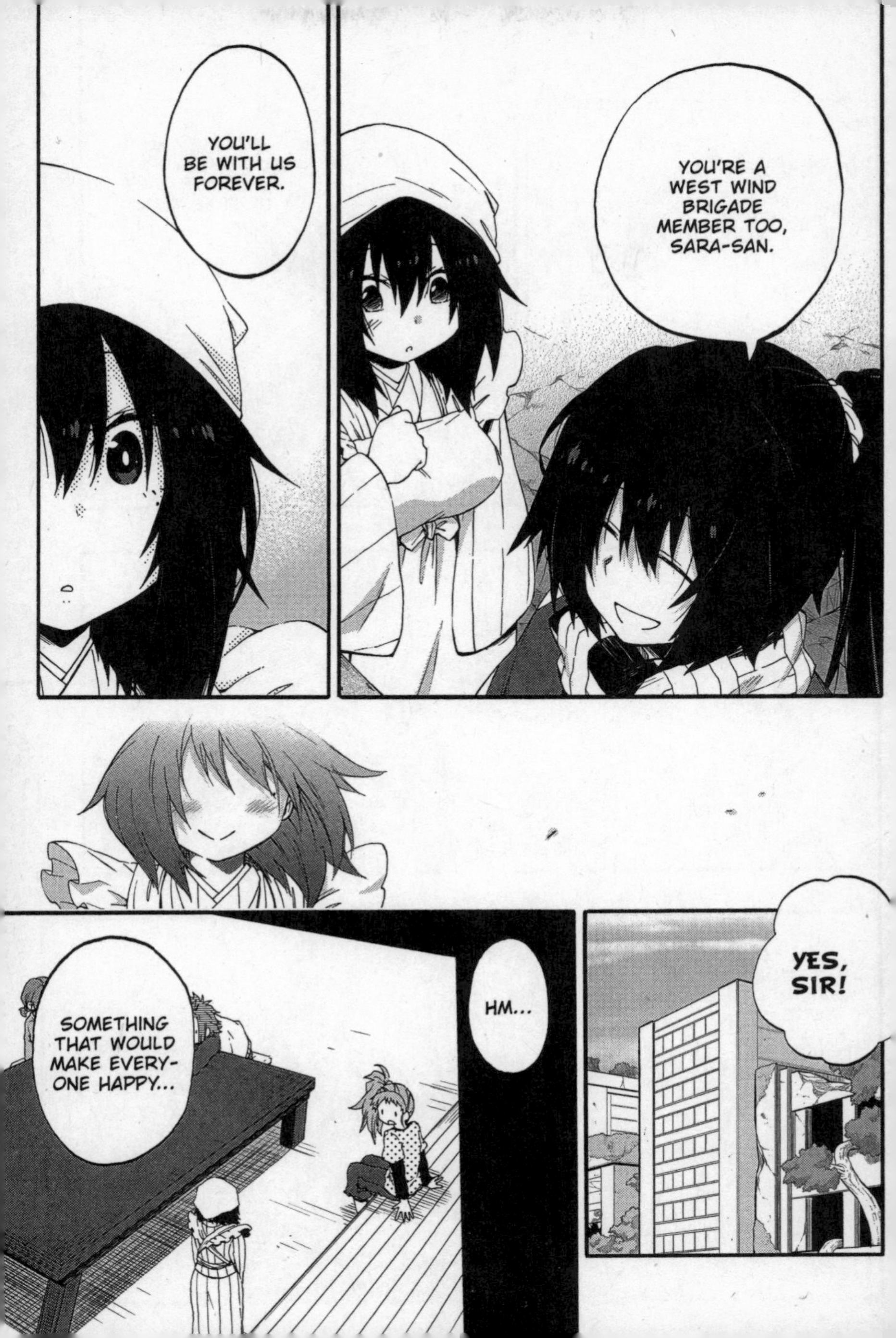
YOU'RE A WEST WIND BRIGADE MEMBER TOO, SARA-SAN.
YOU'LL BE WITH US FOREVER.
YES, SIR!
HM...
SOMETHING THAT WOULD MAKE EVERY-ONE HAPPY...

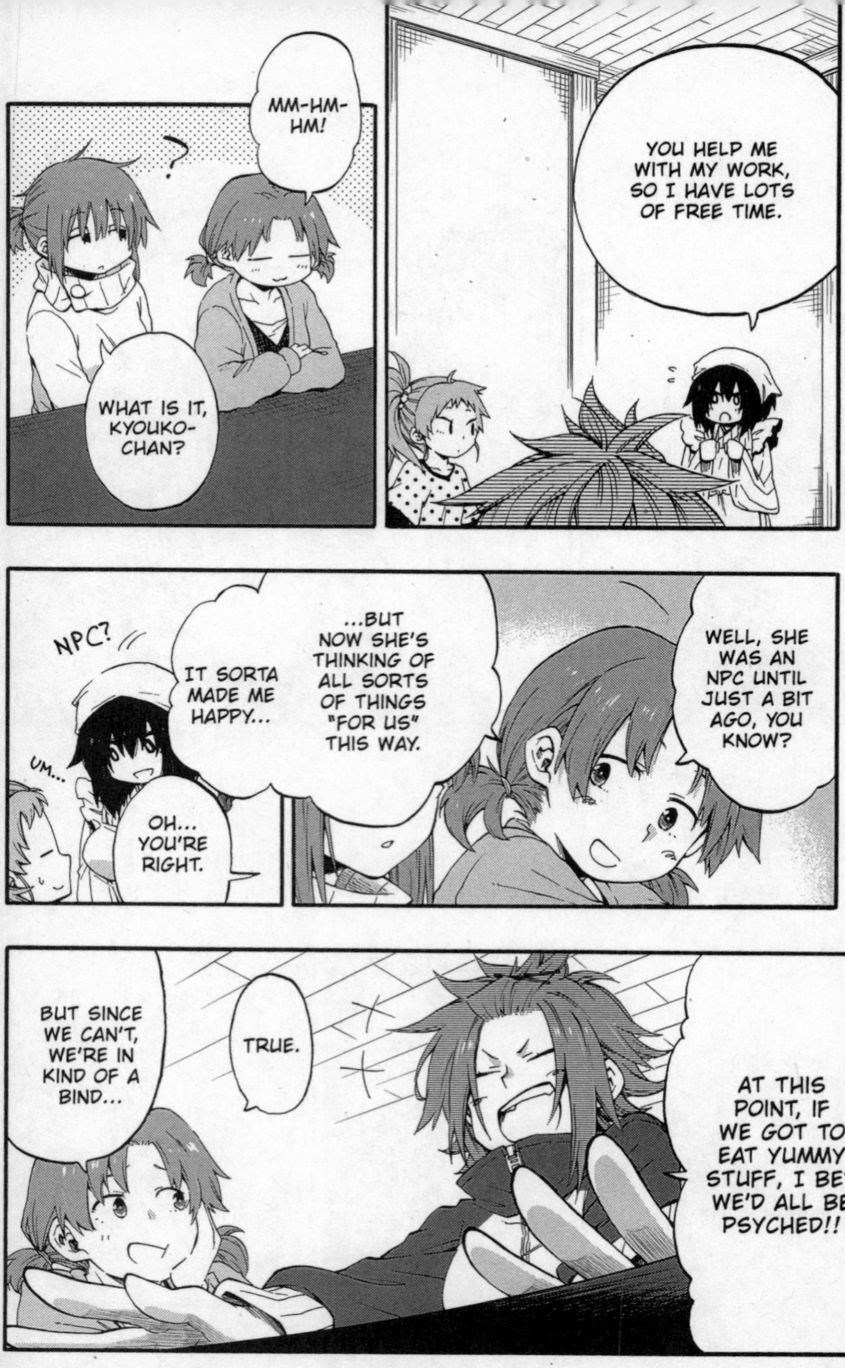
YOU HELP ME WITH MY WORK, SO I HAVE LOTS OF FREE TIME.
MM-HM-HM!
?
WHAT IS IT, KYOUKO-CHAN?
WELL, SHE WAS AN NPC UNTIL JUST A BIT AGO, YOU KNOW?
...BUT NOW SHE'S THINKING OF ALL SORTS OF THINGS "FOR US" THIS WAY.
IT SORTA MADE ME HAPPY...
NPC?
UM...
OH... YOU'RE RIGHT.
AT THIS POINT, IF WE GOT TO EAT YUMMY STUFF, I BET WE'D ALL BE PSYCHED!!
TRUE.
BUT SINCE WE CAN'T, WE'RE IN KIND OF A BIND...

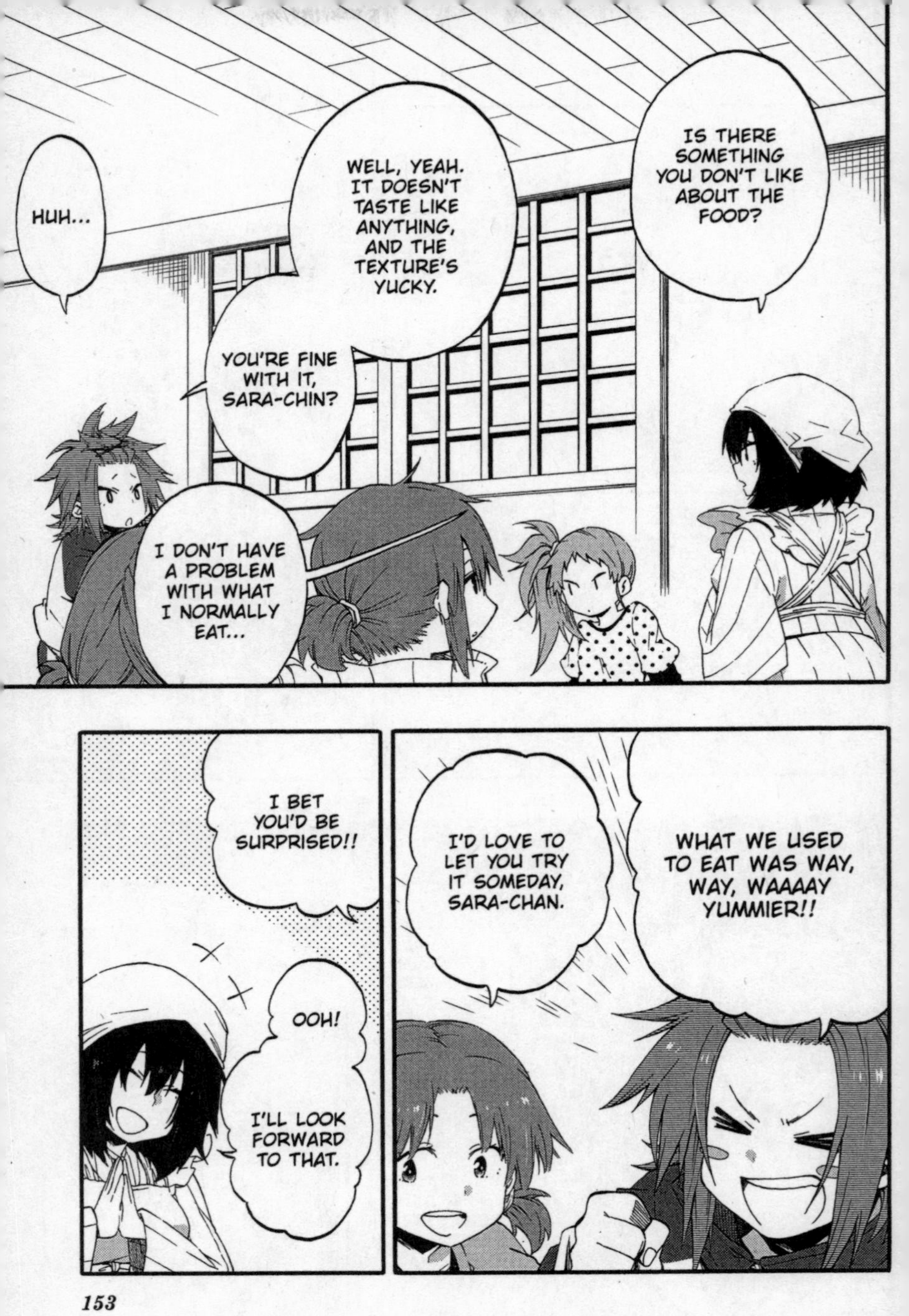
IS THERE SOMETHING YOU DON'T LIKE ABOUT THE FOOD?
WELL, YEAH. IT DOESN'T TASTE LIKE ANYTHING, AND THE TEXTURE'S YUCKY.
HUH...
YOU'RE FINE WITH IT, SARA-CHIN?
I DON'T HAVE A PROBLEM WITH WHAT I NORMALLY EAT...
WHAT WE USED TO EAT WAS WAY, WAY, WAAAAY YUMMIER!!
I'D LOVE TO LET YOU TRY IT SOMEDAY, SARA-CHAN.
I BET YOU'D BE SURPRISED!!
OOH!
I'LL LOOK FORWARD TO THAT.

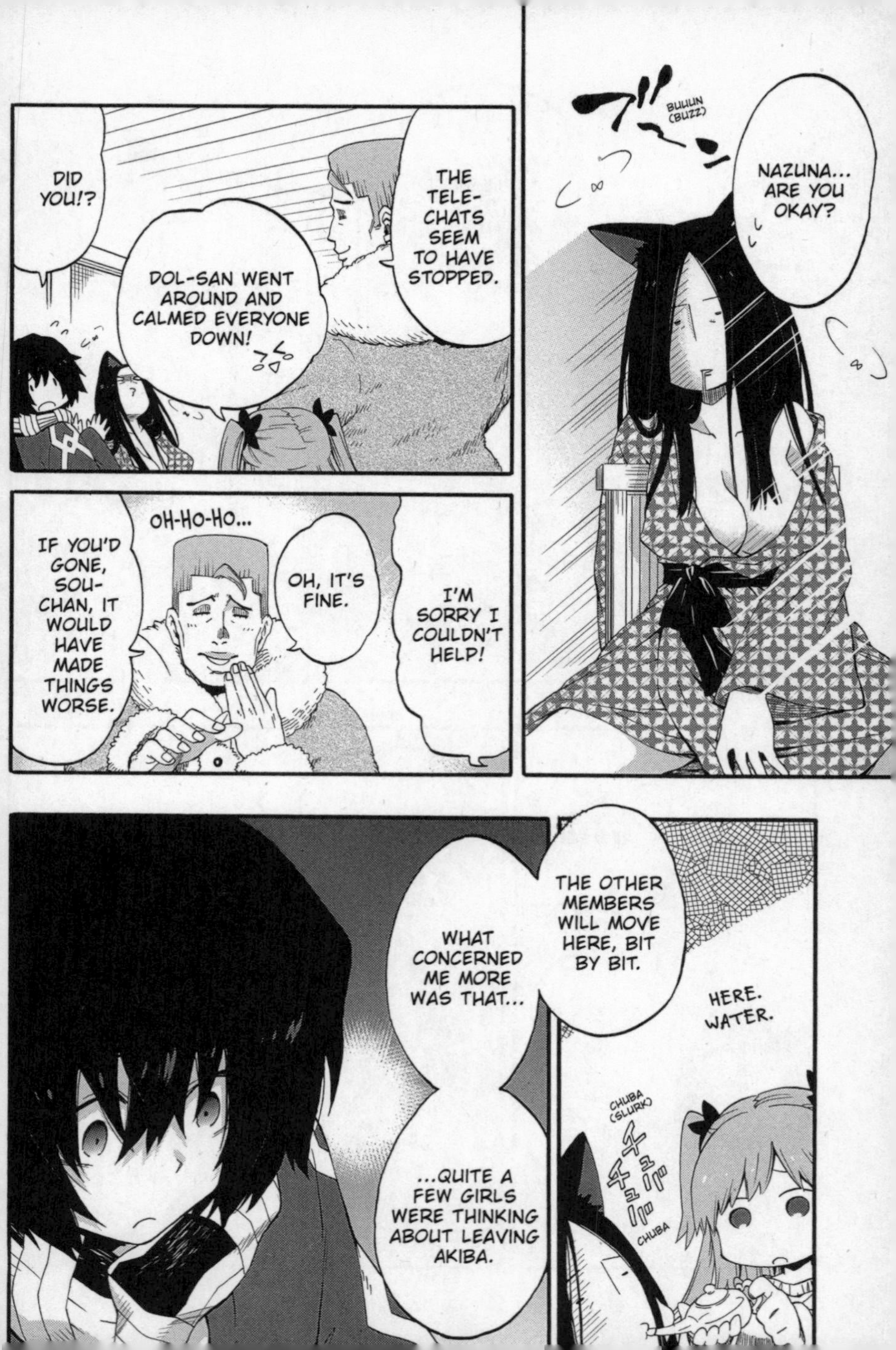
BUUUN (BUZZ)
NAZUNA... ARE YOU OKAY?
THE TELE-CHATS SEEM TO HAVE STOPPED.
DOL-SAN WENT AROUND AND CALMED EVERYONE DOWN!
DID YOU!?
I'M SORRY I COULDN'T HELP!
OH, IT'S FINE.
OH-HO-HO...
IF YOU'D GONE, SOU-CHAN, IT WOULD HAVE MADE THINGS WORSE.
THE OTHER MEMBERS WILL MOVE HERE, BIT BY BIT.
HERE. WATER.
CHUBA (SLURK)
CHUBA
WHAT CONCERNED ME MORE WAS THAT...
...QUITE A FEW GIRLS WERE THINKING ABOUT LEAVING AKIBA.

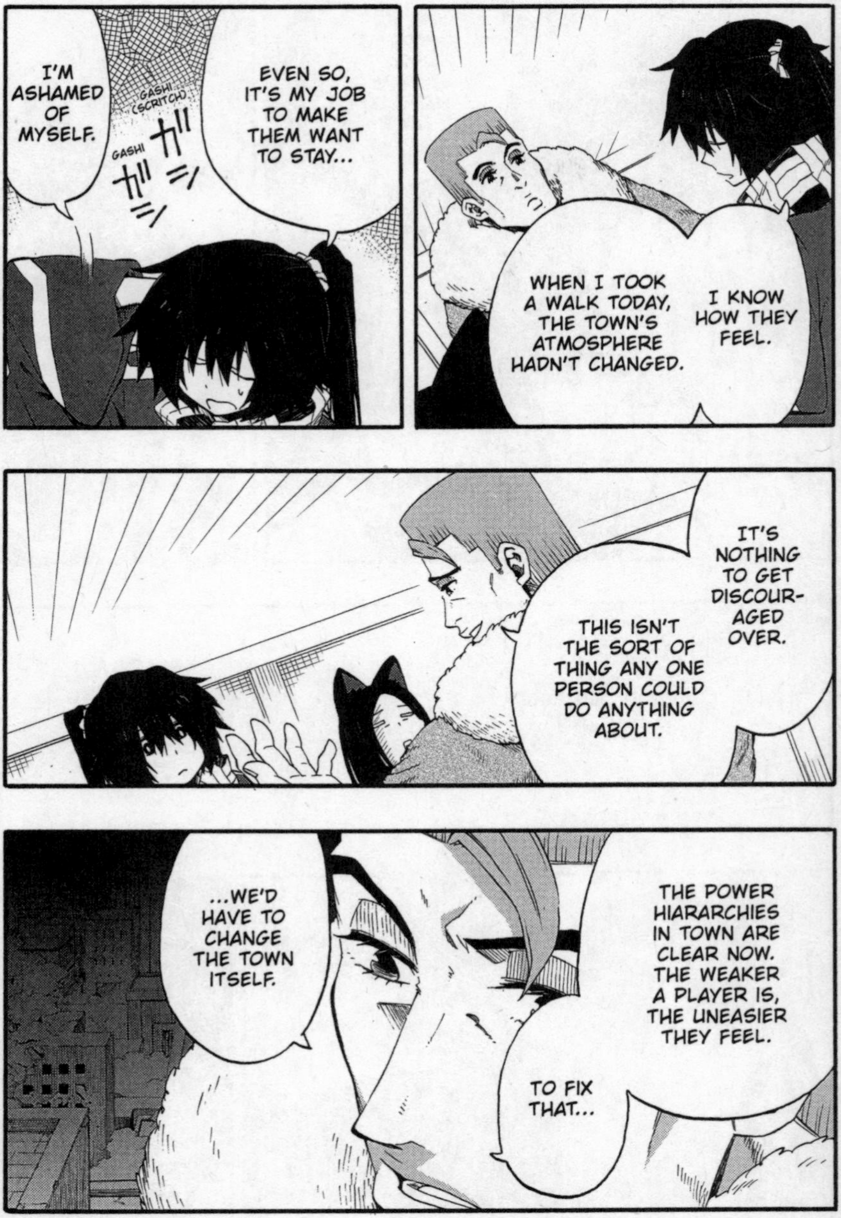
I KNOW HOW THEY FEEL.
WHEN I TOOK A WALK TODAY, THE TOWN'S ATMOSPHERE HADN'T CHANGED.
EVEN SO, IT'S MY JOB TO MAKE THEM WANT TO STAY...
GASHI (SCRITCH)
GASHI
I'M ASHAMED OF MYSELF.
IT'S NOTHING TO GET DISCOUR-AGED OVER.
THIS ISN'T THE SORT OF THING ANY ONE PERSON COULD DO ANYTHING ABOUT.
THE POWER HIARARCHIES IN TOWN ARE CLEAR NOW. THE WEAKER A PLAYER IS, THE UNEASIER THEY FEEL.
TO FIX THAT...
...WE'D HAVE TO CHANGE THE TOWN ITSELF.

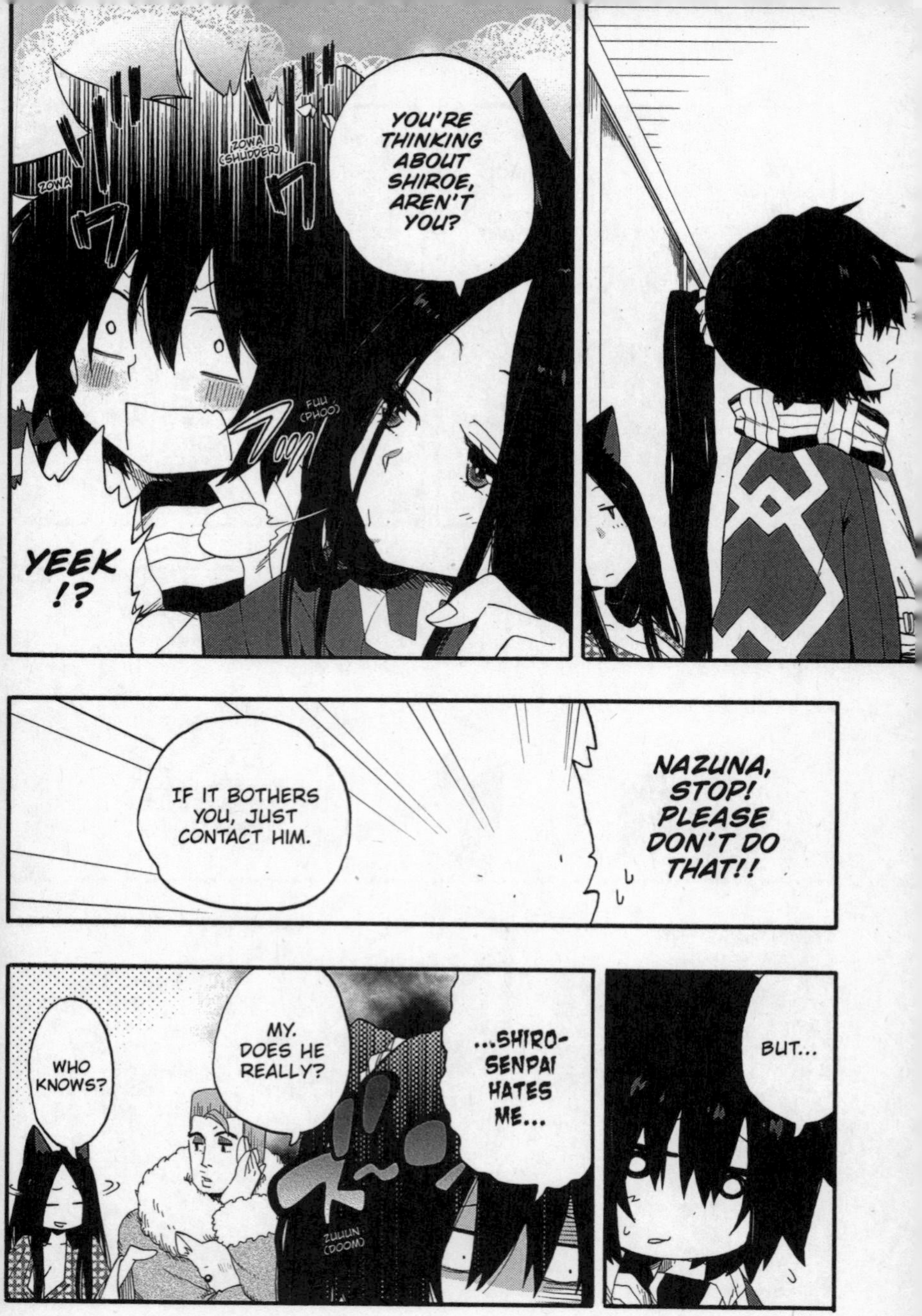
YOU'RE THINKING ABOUT SHIROE, AREN'T YOU?
ZOWA (SHUDDER)
ZOWA
FUU (PHOO)
YEEK!?
NAZUNA, STOP! PLEASE DON'T DO THAT!!
IF IT BOTHERS YOU, JUST CONTACT HIM.
BUT...
...SHIRO-SENPAI HATES ME...
MY. DOES HE REALLY?
WHO KNOWS?
ZUUUN (DOOM)

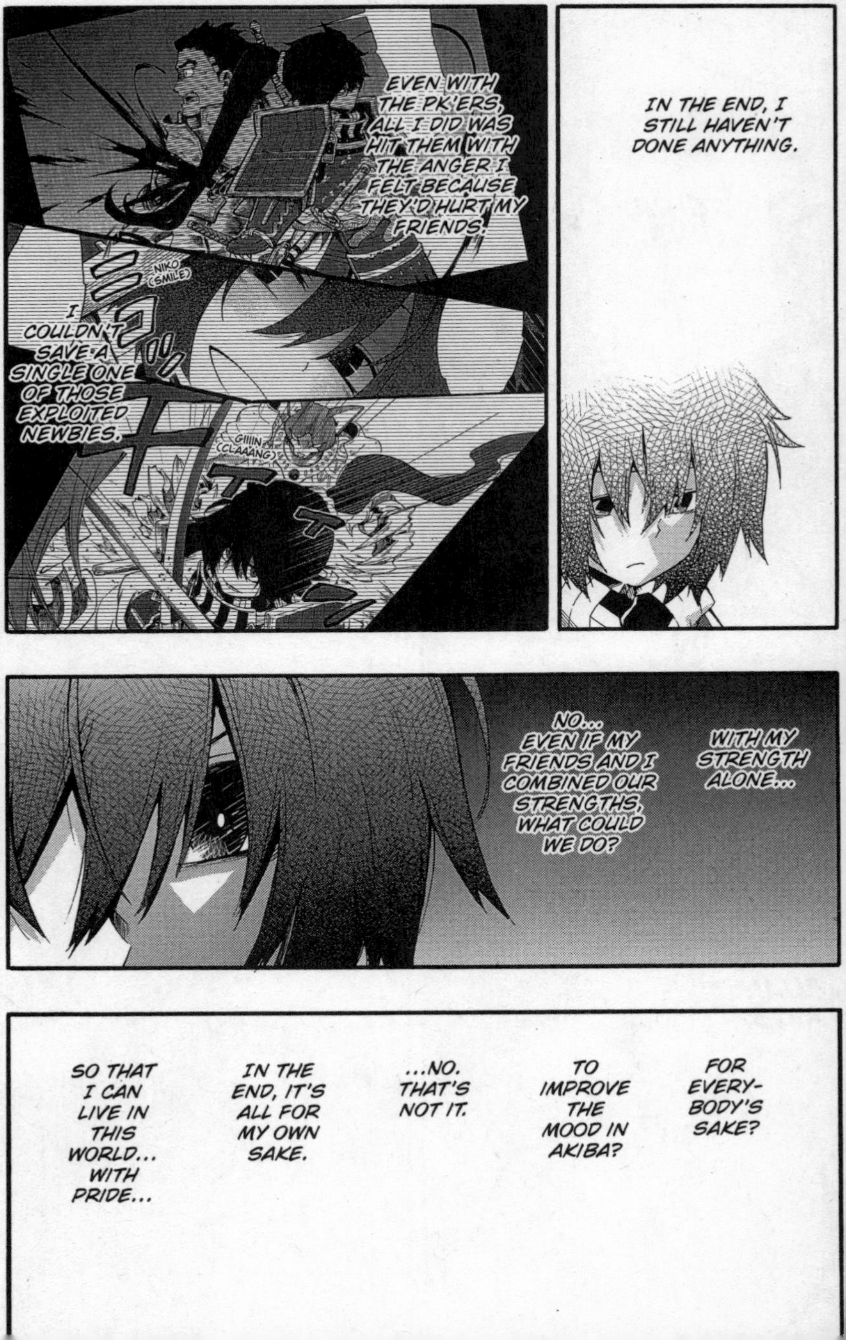
IN THE END, I STILL HAVEN'T DONE ANYTHING.
EVEN WITH THE PK'ERS, ALL I DID WAS HIT THEM WITH THE ANGER I FELT BECAUSE THEY'D HURT MY FRIENDS.
NIKO (SMILE)
I COULDN'T SAVE A SINGLE ONE OF THOSE EXPLOITED NEWBIES.
GIIIN (CLAAANG)
WITH MY STRENGTH ALONE...
NO... EVEN IF MY FRIENDS AND I COMBINED OUR STRENGTHS, WHAT COULD WE DO?
FOR EVERY-BODY'S SAKE?
TO IMPROVE THE MOOD IN AKIBA?
...NO. THAT'S NOT IT.
IN THE END, IT'S ALL FOR MY OWN SAKE.
SO THAT I CAN LIVE IN THIS WORLD... WITH PRIDE...

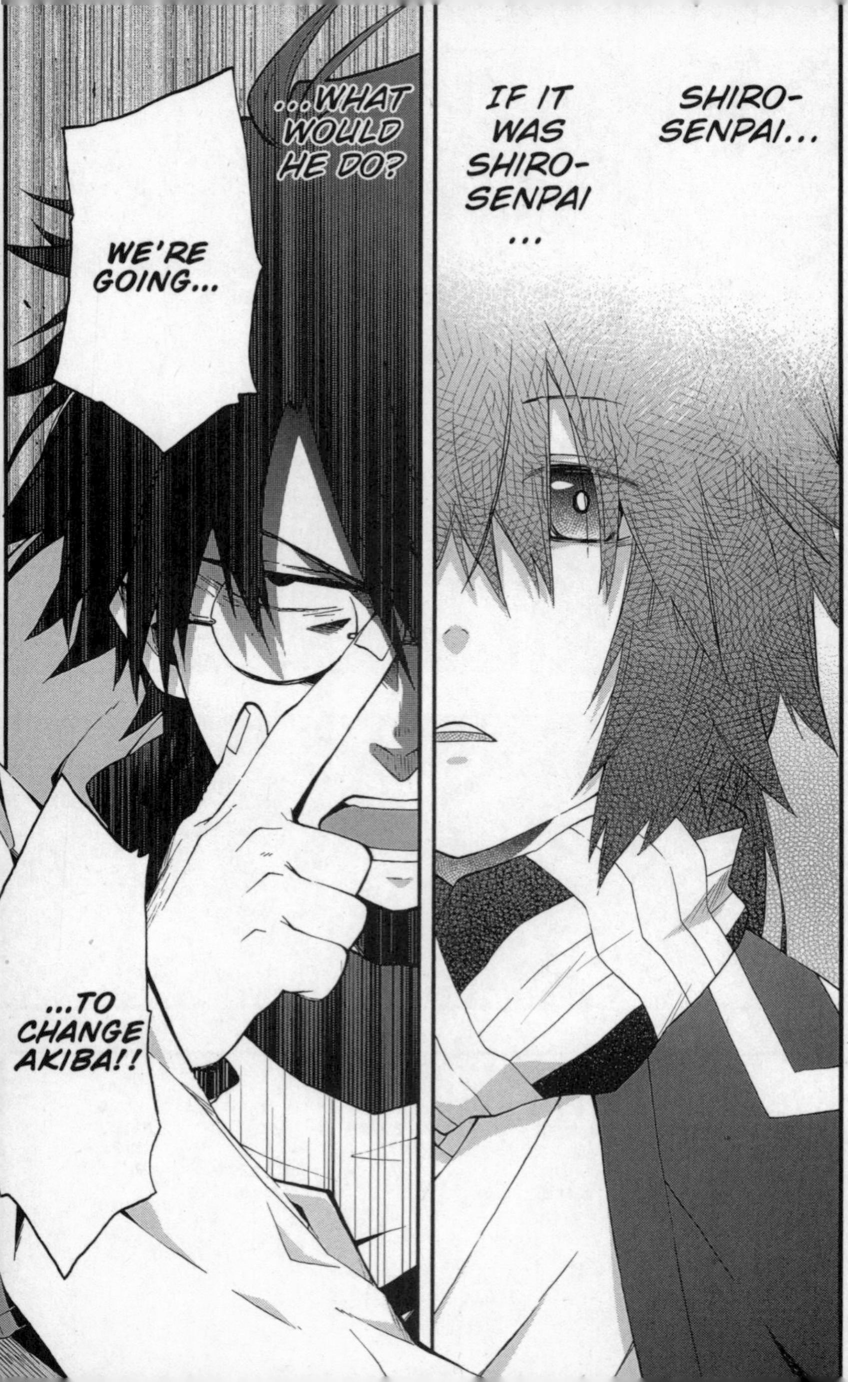
SHIRO-SENPAI...
IF IT WAS SHIRO-SENPAI...
...WHAT WOULD HE DO?
WE'RE GOING...
...TO CHANGE AKIBA!!

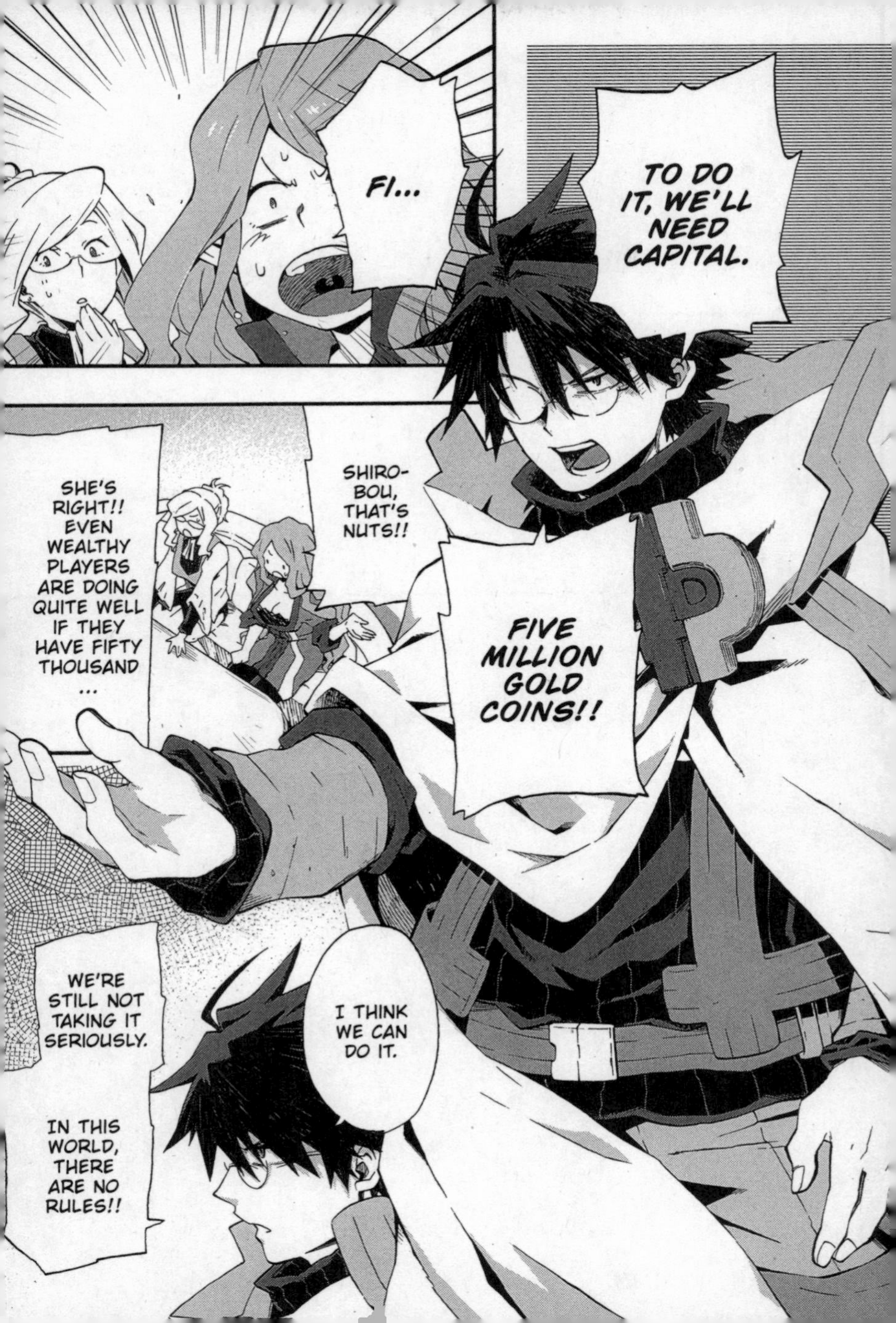
TO DO IT, WE'LL NEED CAPITAL.
FI...
FIVE MILLION GOLD COINS!!
SHIRO-BOU, THAT'S NUTS!!
SHE'S RIGHT!! EVEN WEALTHY PLAYERS ARE DOING QUITE WELL IF THEY HAVE FIFTY THOUSAND ...
I THINK WE CAN DO IT.
WE'RE STILL NOT TAKING IT SERIOUSLY.
IN THIS WORLD, THERE ARE NO RULES!!

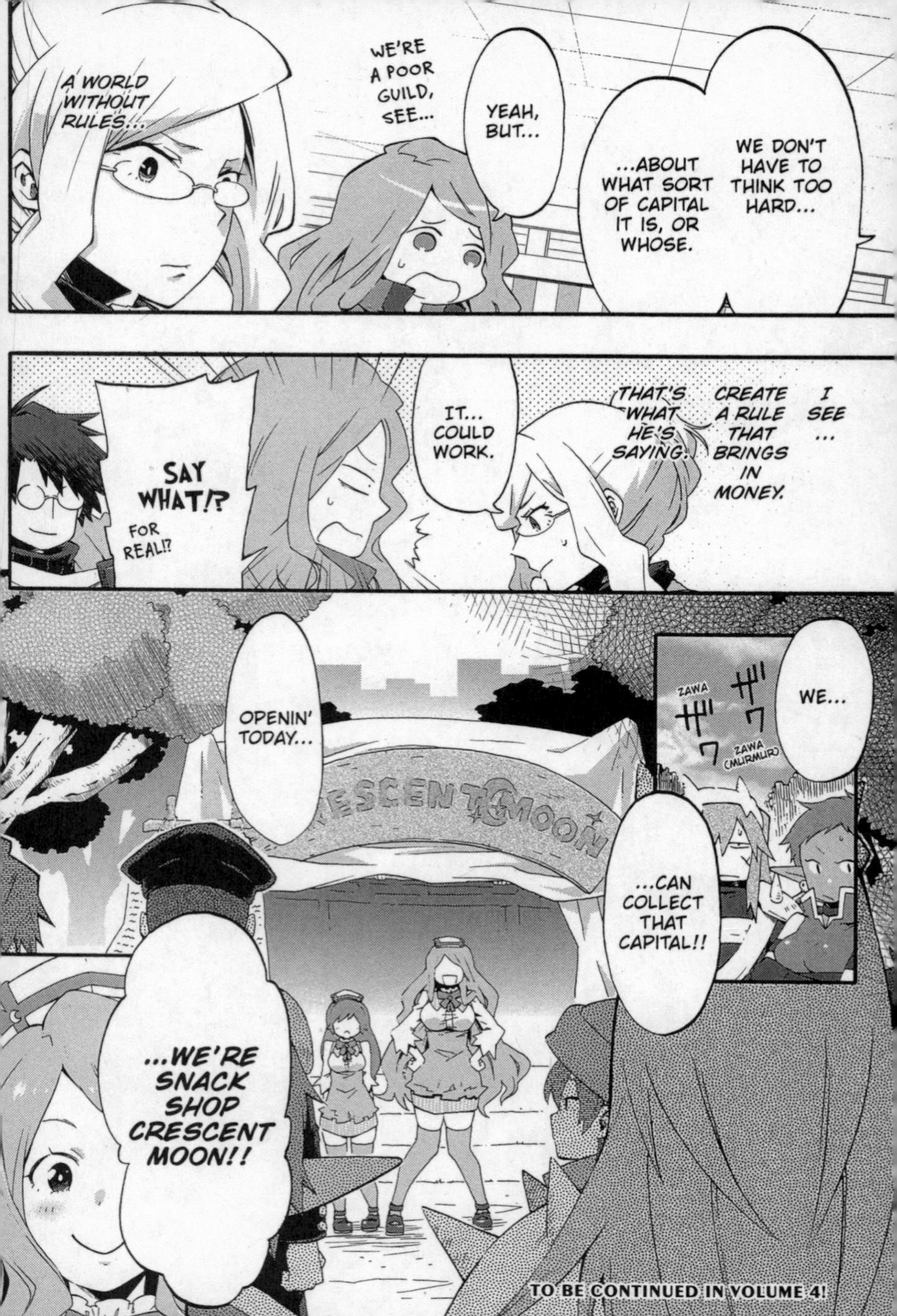
WE DON'T HAVE TO THINK TOO HARD...
...ABOUT WHAT SORT OF CAPITAL IT IS, OR WHOSE.
YEAH, BUT...
WE'RE A POOR GUILD, SEE...
A WORLD WITHOUT RULES...
I SEE...
CREATE A RULE THAT BRINGS IN MONEY.
THAT'S WHAT HE'S SAYING.
IT... COULD WORK.
SAY WHAT!?
FOR REAL!?
WE...
ザワ
ZAWA
ザワ
ZAWA (MURMUR)
...CAN COLLECT THAT CAPITAL!!
OPENIN' TODAY...
ESCENT MOON
...WE'RE SNACK SHOP CRESCENT MOON!!
TO BE CONTINUED IN VOLUME 4!

L✪G HORIZON
THE WEST WIND BRIGADE

EXTRA BONUS MANGA

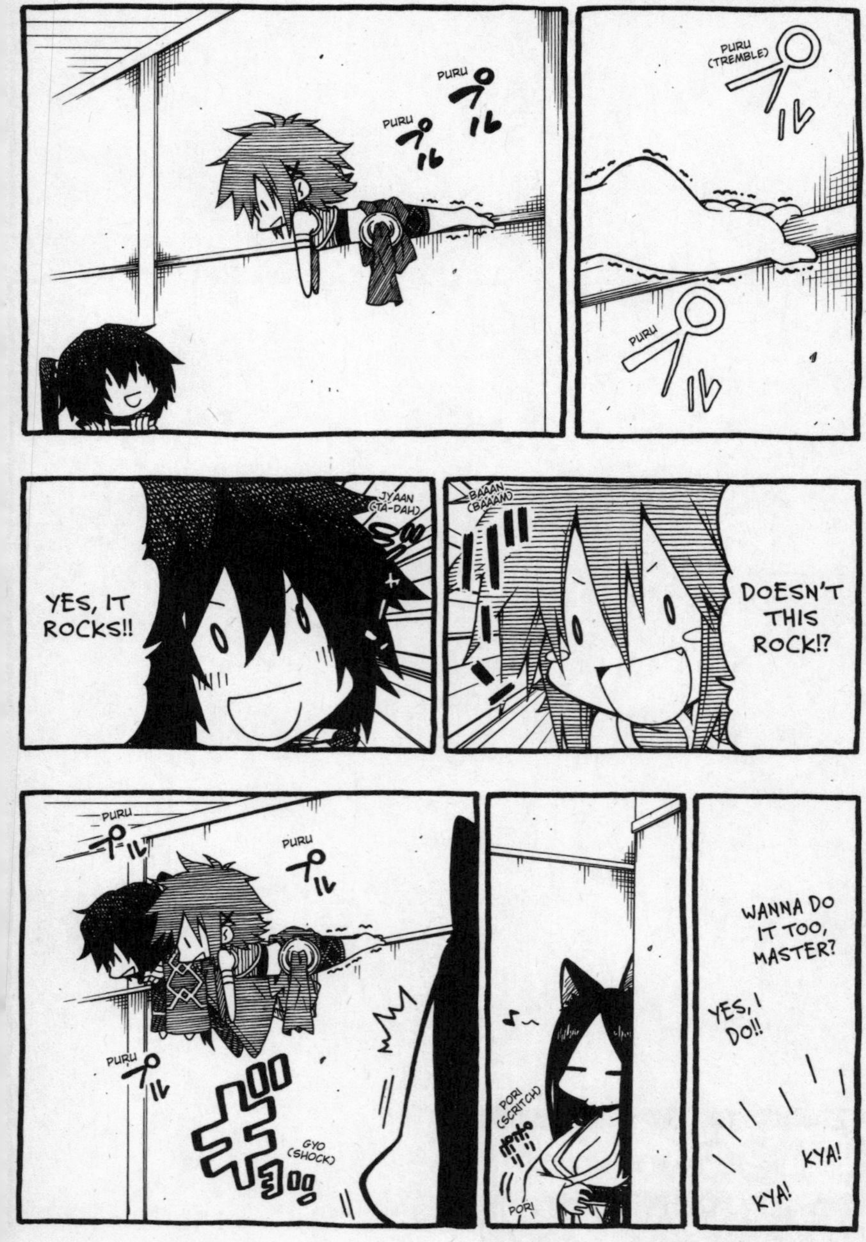
PURU (TREMBLE)
PURU
PURU
PURU
...
BAAAN (BAAAM)
DOESN'T THIS ROCK!?
JYAAN (TA-DAH)
YES, IT ROCKS!!
WANNA DO IT TOO, MASTER?
YES, I DO!!
KYA!
KYA!
PORI (SCRITCH)
PORI
PURU
PURU
PURU
GYO (SHOCK)